About the Author

B.V. Mays' stories are based on twenty years of experience in Eastern Europe. Living there at a time of economic and political transition, he was a senior executive for several multi-nationals and did contract work out of the US Embassy in Warsaw, Poland. He lives and works in Spokane, Washington, USA.

Contractor

B. V. Mays

Contractor

Olympia Publishers
London

www.olympiapublishers.com
OLYMPIA PAPERBACK EDITION

A CIP catalogue record for this title is
available from the British Library.

ISBN: 978-1-80074-010-5

This is a work of fiction.
Names, characters, places and incidents originate from the writer's imagination.
Any resemblance to actual persons, living or dead, is purely coincidental.

First Published in 2021

Olympia Publishers
Tallis House
2 Tallis Street
London
EC4Y 0AB

Printed in Great Britain

Acknowledgements

I would like to thank John Meyer at Cape Fear Publishing for his invaluable editorial assistance and advice.

CONTRACTOR

Andrew Gold is a contractor for the CIA operating out of the United States Embassy in Warsaw, Poland. The Berlin Wall has fallen and the Cold War is over but the world still faces an enormous threat from the specter of nuclear weapons and radioactive material being sold or stolen from hundreds of existing military and industrial sites all over the former Soviet-Bloc. Managing an official job and keeping a family life intact is as much a challenge for Andy as successfully carrying out the dangerous missions he is assigned.

Natalya

I shouldn't have worried about the time. It was only a few minutes after midnight when the knock at the door finally came. Without hesitation I welcomed my guests in but, from the anguished look on Natalya's face and the speed at which the three women slipped by me into the room, I knew I had other worries to deal with.

Two steps behind the last woman, was a man, wearing a black leather jacket and an overzealous smile. He clearly expected to be welcomed into my room with the others. I quickly shook my head and said in the best Russian I could to signal he wasn't welcome, *"Ya proshu proshcheniya. Tebe zdes' ne rady."*

He ignored me and reached forward to either shake my hand or keep the door open. My reaction surprised him... and me... as well. He walked into the fastest and hardest jab to the center of his chest that I could muster as I stood facing him. Unaccustomed to fighting but well aware that it was best to take care of matters quickly and decisively, it was over in a second. Tonight's disinformation run was not starting off well.

Knocking the wind out of him, I nearly broke my knuckle. He took the blow and then turned away, falling to his knees and trying to get his breath. Natalya barked out to him in Russian, "Leave us alone!" The man, still on his knees, waved us away with one hand and held his other hand to his chest. I waited until he stood and retreated back down the hallway. Not expecting that shot of adrenaline, I took a few deep breaths, stepped in, and closed the door. My guests were waiting for me.

They all wore furs, Natalya's the longest. She was still holding her hands near her face as she apologized. "He followed us, saying he wanted to make sure we were going to be safe. I couldn't convince him to stay away."

"Is he someone's pimp?" I asked without any hint of sympathy.

Natalya looked at the other women and replied, "He is a kind of agent for my colleagues here."

"He's not coming back, is he?" I asked the other two women. They were standing, beginning to act disinterested and staring at the snack trays and champagne I'd arranged on the table.

Natalya answered for them. "No. We are alone now. We apologize for being late."

With the level of tension falling quickly, they all took off their coats and began scanning the room. Natalya, whom I'd met in the lobby a couple of hours earlier, had changed since then, now wearing a short, tight, black sleeveless dress. It was cut quite low in the most fashionable European style. She wore conservative silver earrings and a small diamond-studded silver necklace. I handed her an envelope with nine hundred dollars for their "services."

Natalya slipped it into the pocket of her mink, smiled at me, and said, in Polish, "*Porzadku*." OK. Introducing Danuta and Ela, both smiling broadly, Natalya reached for one of the champagne bottles, which I had just uncorked. "May I pour?"

"Please do!" In my role as naïve American businessman, it was in character for me to defer to her. It usually worked better that way and made the package drop easier if all went well.

Natalya was taking charge. That seemed appropriate. I was coming to view her more as a madam for her girls than as their peer.

"Andy, Ela, and Danuta must drink *bruderschafts*," she playfully suggested, setting three glasses in front of us. She took one step away and scanned the room as we three began the *get to know you,* ritual, interlocking our arms to drink. I couldn't tell if she had seen the envelope I had stashed in the glass-fronted cabinet. I had hoped I could dictate when the three would spot the treasure and begin their maneuvering to steal it. Ela, a sandy blonde, and Danuta, a redhead, were quite beautiful and similarly dressed in tight-fitting dresses: gray and yellow. Slim but curvy. If I didn't know their actual profession, I would have said three Russian gymnasts had just joined me.

Ela and Danuta pulled me to the sofa and sat down on either side of me. Natalya stayed at the bar alternately sipping water and champagne. The other two women moved snacks onto their little plates but didn't eat. Instead, they constantly chewed mints as if to fend off a nicotine fit. I remembered I'd told Natalya when we met in the bar that I didn't smoke and preferred that they wouldn't either.

Much sooner than I had expected, Danuta and Ela began trying to work my clothes off. The anxiety from my surprise at the front door, though, had not yet worn off. The last thing on my mind was a threesome. I successfully kept my shirt on my back and stood to pour everyone another round of champagne. I wasn't putting up that much of a fight and kept my attention focused on the package — and on Natalya's wandering about. That took some work, as the temperature in the room was rising and I was finding it hard to concentrate.

While I could count on one hand, the number of times I'd let these kinds of things get out of hand, tonight's guests' predatory skills were making it very difficult. The last thing I wanted now was to wallow in waves of distracting and conflicted guilt over another extraordinary instance of infidelity to my wife. The desk chief's advice had been, "Be creative. Get the job done. Most importantly, don't allow the details of your job to follow you home." Renata's extreme fears and jealousy about my work on the road meant I could expect at least an hour of accusations whenever I came home from a trip. Knowing that had never helped me leave my job at work. Not at NatEx, and not for the CIA.

Natalya slowly paced the room, examining the furnishings and sometimes muttering to herself, "Nice drapes," "Real silver," "Fucking good olives." That was the only thing she ate from the snack trays. If I hadn't known she was searching for the envelope, I would have assumed she was doing her best to keep herself busy so she wouldn't have to see what she thought was happening on the sofa. Employing my best musical chairs moves, I left Danuta and Ela side by side; I was now on the opposite end of the sofa. Their look of exasperation reminded me of a Peter Sellers movie I couldn't quite remember the name of.

"Maybe you like a show?" Ela asked me sensing I was playing hard to get. She climbed into Danuta's lap and the two began kissing. Natalya stood and watched for a while then walked over to the bar and stared at me. I excused myself to the bathroom, leaving my two friends as they untangled themselves on the sofa. Along the way, I reached into the glass cabinet to make a show of touching the envelope. I didn't look at Natalya but I knew she had seen me do it. When I returned from the bathroom, it was already gone. Ela, the girl who had been working the hardest to promote a threesome, was gone, as well. Natalya was talking to Danuta in Russian, giving her instructions, I guessed. Natalya seemed more relaxed than before but turned her back as Danuta began asking me about my business. Did I know other American businessmen in Moscow very well? Was I very active in the American Chamber of Commerce? These were standard questions for escorts properly doing their job for the Russian intelligence services. When Natalya turned to face me again, I saw that she'd opened my mini-bar. She poured a bit of orange juice into my champagne glass. "Drink up, Andy." I looked at Natalya as she was pouring the juice. I'd expected the evening to be winding down now but her face said, "Let me stay a little longer."

I rambled on to Danuta about the AMCHAM guys. I knew her question had been bait for Foreign Intelligence efforts to get news about anything interesting involving American investments. Oil and gas ventures and permit applications were probably the most interesting, but any big project that might yield a huge bribe for the intelligence officers directly or for more senior officials was also of great interest. These conversations were the meat of the work I was doing and risking my life for. Risking my marriage, too. Whether it was for the money that kept Renata and our children living a far better life than average in Krakow or the satisfaction of working to dismantle Russian threats to Europe and the US, I felt some satisfaction that this mission, despite the clumsy beginnings, was going well. I knew the package was now in our adversaries' possession. It had something to do with aviation or avionics. I'd gone against my instructions and sneaked a peek at what I was delivering. I mentioned that American systems integrators were all excited about former Soviet Bloc countries getting a chance to buy F-16s and other Western weapons.

"Which ones?" Danuta wanted to know.

"The usual." I replied. Nothing more.

Natalya looked up. She had been reading from one of the old NatEx brochures I'd left on the bar. She said she needed to make a call — and for me to wait for her. I wasn't sure what that meant. I pointed to the phone in the bedroom. "Help yourself."

As Natalya spoke quietly in my bedroom, Danuta resumed efforts to remove my shirt. Thinking of Natalya's instructions to wait for her, once again, I put up enough resistance to keep from losing control of the situation. Danuta's skillful advances were breaking my defenses when Natalya appeared in the room. She stepped up to us, Danuta on top of me on the couch, and announced, "Goodbye, Danuta! Could you please leave me with Andy now?"

Danuta quickly removed herself from me and then kissed me full on the mouth. She gave me the Polish goodbye, "*Do widzenia.*"

Natalia and I stood together as Danuta gathered her things and left. Before closing the door, I glanced up and down the hallway, worried our earlier uninvited visitor might still be around.

When I returned, Natalya's expression had changed. She was staring at me as if trying to read what I was thinking. She was holding the envelope with the $900 I had given her earlier. "Do you want any of this back?" she asked. Her smile was much friendlier now, reminding me of our moments earlier in the evening.

I wasn't sure what to say but uttered, "No. You should keep it all, Natalya."

She came straight up to me and kissed me as she had in the lobby bar. She wrapped her arms around me and held me in a way that yearned to be held similarly. In that embrace, we stood in the middle of my room scarcely moving until I felt her heart beating against my chest and her soft breath on the side of my face. After several minutes, she finally pulled away in slow motion. Continuing the stare that she'd greeted me with earlier and placing her hand flat on my chest, she asked, "Do you have more Moscow visits lined up for selling *your* services, Andy?"

"Yes, Natalya," I told her, my heart aching to ask her to stay. I added, "Russia will probably be the main place where I work."

She nodded. "I hope I see you again." And then disappeared into the bathroom. I waited at the door for her to finish. She paused on her way out and I took her hand.

"Next time," Natalya suggested, "just tell Alyona if you want to see me again." As she strode toward the elevators, I scanned the hallway for anyone lurking about. Nothing. I closed the door. Natalya's scent lingered for the rest of the night.

US Embassy 'Marine Bar' — Warsaw, Poland

As many times as I had taken the walk from my apartment in Warsaw's city center to the US Embassy to pick up my assignments, I still got a sick feeling in my stomach crossing Marszalkowska Street. I wondered if I was being followed. It probably made no sense to worry about it anymore. Clint, head of the CIA Desk, assured me it was no longer necessary to hop three separate trams and a bus in opposite directions to shake my Russian 'tail.' Poles were now officially friends with the United States. This had always been true in the minds of most Poles but denied by the Soviet Union. As a good grad student, I understood the complexities of these relationships and the historical context of Poland's situation now. My wife, Renata, made sure I spoke the language well; drilled me into speaking almost without accent; and made sure I was well versed for every social event. All so as not to embarrass her with her friends, the elite of Krakow's Polish intelligentsia. In my world, as well, times were changing, along with the economic and political upheavals throughout Eastern Europe. Perhaps most important for me, though, there was still a steady stream of jobs to do. I was paid, in cash, without question. That had been the agreement. We stay together and I stay in Poland if I can keep the new way of life going. I'd heard the term '"trophy wife.' Renata's friends used the term 'trophy husband.' Disparagingly.

As usual, I could never make things just right for her. In order to guarantee that income, it made perfect sense to keep my flat in Warsaw, despite my employer's corporate failure in Europe and my departure from the company. That is, it made sense so long as Clint was keeping me on his cash payroll. Renata had no idea about the other life I was living.

The Soviet Union's fall caught a lot of people by surprise. In the lingering power vacuum, old alliances were being challenged. The CIA was busy monitoring those changing relationships, which included the status of Americans in the former Soviet empire. That included me. Clint had told me three times in the past two years that my name had shown up as a 'person of interest' in recorded Soviet — now just Russian — conversations. He told me I shouldn't take it personally. He maintained that the Russians, at least, suspected virtually all Americans living permanently in Warsaw of being spies.

"You've got a Russian tail on you about fifty percent of the time here in Warsaw. But he's a lazy sonofabitch. He strays after a while and gets drunk at the Metropol Hotel Bar." Clint would try to reassure me, saying, "You're clean. Once you got married and had a kid, they stopped thinking about you as much. We'll let you know when it's time to worry." But sometimes, even without Clint's permission, I found myself at least ill at ease.

This journey across town, three days before my encounter with Natalya in Moscow, felt different. I was walking to get instructions at the Embassy. I'd gotten a call from Jane, my contact with the U.S. Information Agency, who had helped me get jobs teaching English in Poland. She let me know there was a 'non-teaching gig' waiting for me, adding, "I hope you will finally refuse this one!" before she hung up the phone. Jane wasn't the biggest supporter of the work I was doing for Clint. She felt responsible for getting me hooked into the contractor jobs I was doing. Now she saw that Clint had been ramping up the risk level with each mission. That worried her.

In the early eighties, as a foreign exchange student at the Main School for Planning and Statistics in Warsaw, Communism 'raged' just outside the gates of the U.S. Embassy. Writing reports for Radio Free Europe and teaching English for the U.S. Information Agency kept this budding Soviet Studies expert more than financially solvent. Problem was, there were few places to spend it. The Marine Bar, inside the embassy, was a place you could spend a little to feel American again. It was a small unadorned café and pub whose regulars included lots of American students and businesspeople. If it made you feel better, you could grab a Budweiser and a pack of Doritos after the tedium of life outside. Even foreigners in Warsaw would wait in lines, sometimes for four hours, to buy a kilogram of meat and five rolls of toilet paper. In those days, buying anything you might want was controlled by ration cards that limited everything from sugar to pantyhose.

Martial law imposed in 1981 and the difficult times that followed had been forced upon Poland by the Soviet Union. It vowed to crush the Solidarity movement if the puppet government led by Wojciech Jaruzelski didn't. If Poland hadn't cracked down on the 'outrageous' dissidents led by Lech Walesa, a Soviet invasion was a real possibility. It had happened before: In Prague in the sixties, Budapest in the fifties. All that had made Poland an unpleasant place to live for the past ten years.

Back in Poland now, after an eighteen-month marital disaster in San Francisco, it was evident that things were starting to get better. Clint welcomed me back as a contractor and, as before, I went to the Marine Bar to get my assignments. But now, I no longer needed to visit the bar to feel American anymore. America had invaded Poland with a vengeance while we were gone. Doritos and Budweiser in the embassy's hole-in-the-wall bar had been replaced by McDonalds, Pizza Hut, and KFC on every corner in town. And for the burger and brew crowd, The Hard Rock Café had its sites planned in every major city in the country.

Blake, still the bartender at the Marine Bar, only once let on that he knew the notes he handed me came from the CIA desk. And on that one occasion, he made sure no one had heard him or seen that he'd handed me the note. Jane had always told me when I should approach Blake and discreetly ask if he had anything for me. For six years, the routine had remained the same. As the years went by, my tasks had gotten more complex, since I hadn't ever screwed up too badly in carrying out these little missions. This time, he leaned over to whisper to me: this note was not to leave the bar area. As always, Blake was my 'Mercury;' a messenger, he was delivering a 'task' for me to accept or refuse. These days, this was the only reason I ever went to the embassy bar.

For all those years, Blake's unwavering nonchalance had become unnerving. The complexity of my tasks expanded and the danger associated with them grew, but his cool demeanor never changed. As I'd gotten more anxious about each successive job, it had seemed only fair that Blake should somehow share in that nervous excitement. But... he'd never shown an iota of giving a rat's ass about anything I was doing.

Jane, on the other hand, was always upset that I would take every job I was offered. A lifetime Department of State employee, she never really understood that I needed the contractor cash to keep my marriage gig going — and had long ago started living off an adrenaline rush. That came every time I completed a mission behind the lines fighting a Cold

18

War, and now its aftermath in the post-Soviet era.

She'd started to distance herself from me. She had warned me, "If you get caught doing anything for these guys, the embassy will disavow any knowledge of your activities. You are alone in this. You are just a *contractor*." She got madder when I laughed and reminded her that the "disavow any knowledge" bit was a line out of the *Mission Impossible* TV series from the 1960s. She liked to remind me, "You teach English for the USIA American Language and Culture Program. I direct that program. That is all you and I have in common." But that wasn't true, either. It had been her stories about doing exactly what I was doing now that had inspired me to take on this work.

No tape recording ever self-destructed after my meetings with Blake at the Marine Bar. But then again, the rules we operated by said I couldn't take the note out of the bar. Blake was built like an NFL linebacker. Or maybe a tall version of a Navy SEAL. I had no intention of walking out of the U.S. Embassy with evidence that I was doing anything for the CIA. Officially, I wasn't. So on this unusual occasion, Blake did something else that was out of character. He came over to my table as I was weighing the advantages and disadvantages of accepting a mission in Moscow. He seemed worried that I might be copying the note onto a different piece of paper. It was clear that he didn't want me leaving with a pirated version any more than with the original. In fact, I had two lists on my paper: a plus column and a minus column.

My notes read:

Pluses	Minuses
*$2,500 plus expenses for less than one week (more than enough to calm the wife and pay a few months' rent in Warsaw)	*explain the trip to my wife (another strange disappearance)
*nothing classified delivered	*every prostitute in Moscow is working for spies
*meeting prostitutes (kindhearted — mostly — and not killers like the cabbies in Moscow)	*every real spy is a potential killer
*not likely to be recognized by anyone	*bullshit... they know me in Moscow

As much as I hated to admit it, I accepted many of these missions out of a loathing for the anger that hung over me every weekend when I returned to Krakow after working at NatEx in Warsaw.

Looming over me, Blake calmly took all papers I had spread out on the table. Sternly, he told me, "Follow the rules."

Someone sitting in CIA headquarters in Langley, Virginia must have been bored when they came up with those rules. The rules Blake was enforcing were what contractors like myself had to follow when getting our assignments. Because we were 'nobodies' who could disappear without anyone at the CIA even taking note of the fact, we weren't supposed to have any relationship with the head of the desk at the embassy. Before I got my first-ever assignment, Jane had explained how to behave and what to do. She had said that if I followed the rules every time, I would be fine, "as silly as they may seem," she added.

Simply stated, the rules boiled down to this: I was to come up to the bar and ask Blake, "Do you have anything for me today?" I wouldn't have a reason to go in if he didn't, so he would always respond by handing me a small envelope. In that envelope would be a proposed assignment. If I accepted the assignment, I was to order a beer. If I did not accept, I was to order wine. If I was uncertain about things and needed more time, I was to order a straight vodka or whiskey and then go sit down. That gave me another fifteen minutes to make a final decision. Who knows what would have happened if I had taken twenty minutes to decide? How would it have worked if I'd needed more time, maybe because I didn't like what they had me doing? Or if I felt unprepared or too inexperienced to safely carry out the mission? Blake seemed the type to manage his bar very well. And so, most of the time, I tried to follow the rules.

On this unusual occasion, as it turned out, the note Blake handed me read:

Take a package of documents to Moscow. Check in to the Leningradskaya Hotel on the 20th of March and show up at the Lobby Bar between 9 and 10 pm. Do not take the package to the bar. There will be one tall long-haired brunette, Natalya, waiting for you. Invite her to your room for the usual. She will suggest having two female guests join you, as well. You should accept. The package needs to be 'stolen' by your guests so that they think they have done so without your knowledge. We will be watching.

$2,500 plus expenses for one week.

As Blake collected my papers, he took an annoyed look at my pluses and minuses but then seemed relieved that my scribbling was not a copy of the note. Without asking, he turned back to the bar and returned with beer. Before he put it down, he hesitated. "You've never refused before."

"Thanks, Blake. I'll take the beer," I told him.

"Good luck," he responded. "And *do svidanya!*" he added.

"*Do svidanya,*" he says! He *does* read the messages and he does know what I'm doing. I should have guessed.

I rarely stuck around for any of the tiring talk in the bar. That was typically from Americans new to Poland. Figuring out how to extend your Polish visa? Or looking for advice on avoiding getting ripped off by taxi drivers? The way I figured it, those were things anyone who had chosen to come to Poland in the first place needed to figure out on their own. One thing I did enjoy about my visits to the Marine Bar was picking up the latest *International Herald Tribune*. The *Herald Tribune* is the European short version of *The New York Times* and it was one of those rags you could trust back in those days.

One headline in the newspaper caught my eye before I headed out of the embassy:

Former Soviet KGB Officer Arrested in Theft and Sale of 57 KGs of Plutonium to North Korea

I ripped out the article. I reminded myself to ask Clint about this sort of activity when I got back from Moscow. Radioactive materials were things I knew something about. My father had been a nuclear engineer who worked on fabricating nuclear fuels. It sounded like bad stuff was happening in Russia.

***

My encounter with Blake wasn't the only unusual break in standard operating procedures. Instead of me picking up the package I was to deliver from the embassy library the next morning, Jane showed up that evening at my flat in Warsaw. She'd never done that before. She had my package with her and asked if she could come in for a minute. Of course, I agreed and shut the door behind her.

She must have felt as awkward as I did. She hesitated a moment before speaking. "I have your package for Moscow. Clint threw it over the partition to me. I wanted to give you a last chance to back out of this one."

As surprised as I'd been to see her at my door, I was even more surprised by her statement — and her offer. I asked, "I'm a little confused, Jane. Can you tell me why making this particular delivery bothers you?"

"Getting involved in disinformation to Russian agents is about as close as you can get to being a full-fledged player. We still use contractors for this stuff but you have a family in Krakow." I winced as she again used my family to leverage my decision. "We worry you may have agreed to this too quickly. Without thinking about it. It puts you on lists that can turn black at any time."

That got my attention. "Turning black," was not good.

"Right now, Moscow is in one of those periods where the CIA desk is playing some higher-stakes games," Jane went on. "As the power structure in Russia gets more and more uncertain, we're finding that our hopes for better relations are being dashed. A couple of our people are missing." Jane's warnings brought to mind my cab ride from Hell in Moscow. I could easily imagine the truth to what she was saying. "The Warsaw guys are worried about it. They wanted me to remind you that this is a slightly different game you'll be playing, with a wholly different set of players on their side. And on our side, too."

This didn't quite add up for me. I had made three similar drops in Moscow under near identical circumstances. Wasn't it time to acknowledge that I could take care of myself and was learning the ropes pretty well? "Luck or not, Jane, I've been batting a thousand in this work. I've done this exact job before. Same hotel and same 'thieves.' What's different?"

"You ex-jocks are all the same. You think you're indestructible. This is a different type of information, and it's a higher-caliber recipient. And a greater chance of the recipient doing unexpected things. Andy, I know you take this seriously, but don't forget that I can have you safely teaching almost full-time — if you're up to it. You don't have to do this." This was the first time Jane had ever offered me more USIA work to offset the CIA stuff. She added, "As the State Department takes over the

USIA's responsibilities here, I can make sure you have a role in the new organization."

Instead of trying to figure this all out on the spot, I said what I thought Jane wanted to hear. "I really appreciate the personal attention tonight, Jane. Let's see how this goes. Based on what you've just revealed to me, this may be my last job."

She smiled at this and handed over the package. It was a normal-looking thick brown envelope with a string tie top. Something like a corporate internal mail pouch for memos or budgets or personnel files. It wasn't sealed.

As Jane stepped toward the elevator, she stretched a hand back toward me. "I suggest you not open it or look at what's inside."

I lied. "I never look at the stuff. Knowing the lies we put out makes me more of a target, I always figured."

"Good policy, Andy. Come home safely."

Jane's advice had hit home, though. More than I ever liked to let her know. While I never told her as much, I had come to depend on Jane. Between the USIA teaching gigs and the CIA jobs, she had thrown me a financial lifeline.

The NatEx gig had brought me back to Poland from San Francisco less than a year after the Berlin Wall had fallen. It had saved my marriage. But within eighteen months after we started operations, the delivery service that had become such an American success story had turned into an utter failure in Europe. The corporate suits had decreed: NatEx would close up shop and head off the continent, leaving me high and dry. What would take its place was a mystery for me.

The NatEx Miracle

San Francisco had been my unsuccessful attempt to make dual citizens out of my young Polish-American family. But saving them from Communism and starting a fresh adventure in America made no more sense to Renata than trying to transplant palm trees from Hawaii to Alaska — in the winter. When the wall was breached on November 9, 1989, it freed more than all those East Berliners that night. It also set into motion Renata's plan to pack up our kids and head back to her homeland. And her version of freedom.

Breakfast, the morning after on November 10, began famously. I was getting ready to head to work at Bank of America headquarters in San Francisco. I was a new middle manager in the Stock Transfer Department of the bank's securities division:

"These aren't my people!" she began. "Why am I here? Having this baby was your idea! Why did I ever agree to leave? What can I ever hope to achieve in California as a PhD from Poland? Fucking shit! *Kurva!*" Renata was yelling at me after having spent all night on the phone talking to her colleagues in Poland. They were basking in the glow of enthusiasm and happiness at the changes happening all over the Eastern Bloc. They were also encouraging her to return.

"I am in fucking California exactly when I need to be in Poland! The most important event in a Pole's lifetime and I am cleaning, cooking, and taking care of two screaming kids for a husband that can barely support us in his new *fantastic* career at the Bank of America!" She always had a knack for heavy sarcasm.

I left for work feeling lower than whale shit. I called home several times. No answer.

When I got home that evening, their bags were packed. She had maxed out my meager credit card limit, flying out of SFO in three days. Her mother was already in the process of evicting her brother and his wife who had moved into our old flat in Nowa Huta, a suburb of Krakow.

"You can understand, I am sure, why I have to go," she said, not looking at me, as I came in the door. I glanced over her shoulder and saw she was busy making a to-do list: tasks for me, to make her departure easier.

"I guess I understand," I said. "But I'm $35,000 in debt after bringing you and the kids here." I was glum and feeling numb at the realization that another career and life path was going wildly off-course.

"You left the university with one of the most prestigious jobs in Krakow!" she shot back at me.

"Making less than $250 per month," I reminded her, as calmly as I could manage.

"What about the embassy jobs? That was a lot of money! All my friends were jealous of how I'd married an American. Little did they know how stupid you are!" she countered angrily. I was unable to respond to that cruel accusation, since part of that money, had come from the intelligence work I had to remain silent about.

After the longest and hardest three days in my life, my family walked onto that plane without even turning around to wave at me. The only thing she said on the way to the airport was, "Pay your fucking debts and join us. Sometime. If you want."

I drove back into the city and found a North Beach bar. As I anesthetized the hurt, I tried to contemplate a new path. Some pieces fell into place quickly.

Filing for bankruptcy was easy. And cheap. I found a Polish attorney in the city and got that done quickly. With my debts gone but my credit now in ruins, I knew that life in America would not be easy. But a fresh start was possible.

Part of my job at the bank was to manage the exchange of old stock certificates for new. Nearly all of that incoming and outgoing traffic at the bank's headquarters was handled by NatEx. The express document company of choice. Some days I had more than five hundred NatEx shipments going through my department. The next morning, looking at the stack of documents my people were sorting, I had a revelation about a chance to get back to Poland with a real job. But the Iron Curtain had barely begun to crack open. NatEx was not in Poland, I knew. But why couldn't I take them there? A corporation operating in a foreign country typically put a single executive in charge, a 'country director.' Why couldn't that be me?

The next afternoon, I braved a phone call to the VP of 'Global Expansion' at NatEx in Atlanta. Three reluctant secretaries eventually got me through to Ari Schlect.

"Mr. Schlect, I am your new Country Director for Poland, where I'm sure you are planning to start operations soon," I began.

He laughed. "We're putting a team together now for Poland." Then came the question. "Why are *you* our man?"

"I lived and worked in Poland for seven years. I speak the language." I had my spiel ready; much of it was the truth. "I manage all express document operations now at Bank of America." Well, that part was a lie. "And, finally, I have a plan to make your Polish operations profitable from the first month."

Ari was quiet for a long time. "Hold on. I'm going to patch us through to the CEO of Europe, Middle East and Africa. You tell him what you just told me and anything else you think will convince him to interview you for the job."

I gulped loudly and pulled a bottle of rotgut Smirnoff from the shelf as we waited for Mr. McGregor to get on the line. Two shots and some quick notes was all the time I had before he got on the call. Ari introduced me.

"So, Mr. Gold." McGregor sounded impatient. "Why are you the guy?"

"Mr. McGregor, after seven years in Poland I am already the 'Old Man' of the expat community there. Every business manager for every foreign firm in Poland knows me. I already know NatEx operations inside and out — from the standpoint of being one of your biggest clients. Finally, I will turn a profit within a month by using the express train system instead of domestic flights to deliver incoming and bring outgoing shipments into Warsaw."

McGregor rifled back at me, "You have papers to live and work there?"

"Married to a Pole with two kids. Something like our green card," I said.

After some other minor questions, McGregor addressed Ari, urgency in his voice. "Get Mr. Gold on a flight to Frankfurt. Jump seat him on a DC-10 linehaul if you can."

Three weeks later I was country director for NatEx in Poland. And heading back to what was now the *New* Europe.

***

If the NatEx miracle hadn't happened, I would have started divorce proceedings in San Francisco. Our resettlement effort in the USA came to an end but instead of splitting us up for good, the NatEx opportunity made it possible for me to be with my family and patch up our problems — for a while.

Operating out of Warsaw presented the next set of problems for Renata. She saw my good fortune with NatEx as only marginally a win for her. She'd returned to Poland to be a part of the grand new vision for her publishing projects, the Polish Studies Department and the university. My five days a week in Warsaw weren't much help for her to realize these dreams. My money was good, though, and my promises of an elegant modern flat kept her from screaming at me all weekend when I was in town. Living mostly away allowed me to focus on my job. I have to admit, my feelings were still hurt from being abandoned in San Francisco. No doubt this contributed to my tendency toward infidelity at times. It encouraged my willingness to work the intelligence gigs in hotels where the night life waxed till early mornings.

So as NatEx began to fade from my life, Jane came to the rescue. She was proposing a steady arrangement with the State Department's English Language Fellows program. It was exactly the kind of opportunity the wife would have promoted, but my deeper dive into the CIA contract work killed that career option. Even so, I kept my eyes open all the time for other options.

Leningradskaya Hotel — Moscow, Russia

Flights to Moscow from Warsaw were non-stop. Poland's LOT Airlines provided a very comfortable business-class service that included unlimited champagne. Warsaw had become the place to stage business start-ups in Russia, so business class seats were always filled with drunken execs, both Western and Polish, tending to their Russian operations.

"Hey, Andy! You doing NatEx work in Moscow?" the gentleman across the aisle called out over the stewardess. She was handing him a glass of champagne as we were getting seated.

"Hi, David," I replied, about four volume levels lower than he had bellowed, causing the rest of business class to look up. David was the regional head of American Paper and had been kind enough to bring his business to NatEx when we started operations. Things had gone sour quickly though, and when his shipments sat in customs far longer than he could tolerate, he switched back to the German express company he'd used before. "This trip's not for NatEx," I told him. "I'm ramping up the consulting work and trying to open up a new market."

A little more quietly than before, he leaned over and asked, "Is it true that NatEx is throwing in the towel over here?"

"It's true. We're wrapping things up soon," I answered. I was glad he didn't bring up any of the embarrassments we had caused him with late documents and paper samples that had disappeared in customs. "I'm sticking around, though. A lot's going on in Eastern Europe. Having a family in Krakow makes it a little harder to pull up stakes." I wasn't lying. My three-year-old daughter, Malgosia, waited for me at the window every time she knew I'd be coming home. We'd plan our weekends together as she sat on my lap after coming through the door. My son, Staszek, Renata's boy from her first marriage, was a genius. He already spoke English without an accent and loved to brag to his friends about his 'American father.'

"I'm sure you'll do well, Andy! Keep in touch," David offered sympathetically. He downed his champagne in one gulp and went back to reading his paper-trade magazine.

As much as I could have used a stiff drink at that moment, I rarely drank on the way to Moscow. Moscow trips had a complexion all their own. I expected unexpected 'adventures' from the moment I entered the jetway from the plane. The last thing I needed, then, was to be drunk if circumstances required a clear head; chaos or a dangerous situation could erupt at any time in this new eastern Klondike. Bizarre events had become common in the wild new Russian economy. Uncertainty about the future, not knowing the rules of the new game, brought out the worst in people in Moscow, which had already been a wild and xenophobic city before things changed. The best example might be that if a cabbie could extort more money for his services, who better to target than a foreigner?

I'd had exactly such an adventure on my first trip to Moscow for NatEx. The same snow lay on the ground that Gorbachev would have walked through fifty-eight days earlier on Christmas Day, 1991. That was when he signed the 'divorce papers'" for the Soviet Union. I wound up being three hours late for a meeting to discuss post-Soviet strategies at the company's offices, which were just off Red Square. Early on in the ride I sensed that the driver was, at best, taking a very circuitous route. I began trying to communicate with him.

Even though I was certain he didn't speak a lick of English, I started my protests in a loud New York accent, thinking he'd know I wasn't happy. "Hey, Buddy! I think I saw the sign for 'Red Square' quite a while back. We should've turned left!"

"*Khorosho*." Good. He spit out the word without even glancing at me in the mirror.

I took it to the next level and shoved a map of Moscow into his face. My finger was pointing at Red Square.

"This is where we're going. You should've turned off the ring road two kilometers back!" I crudely assembled my accusation into fragmentary Russian. I showed my concern by leaning far enough over the front seat that he could not ignore me anymore.

Continuing to look straight ahead, he pulled the car off the jam-packed highway and down an off-ramp. It led to an abandoned factory of some sort. Hitting the child-proof locks on the doors, he pulled over, stopped, and looked at me through the rear-view mirror. In Russian, he said, "The meter does not work properly. It is broken. I will take you to where you want to go for what is on the meter. Plus $500."

"What are you fucking talking about?" I screamed back at him.

Calmly, he replied, "You are businessman. Your company can afford it."

I probably would have paid the guy more money than the official fare, but the $500 'tip' seemed more than a bit too much to me. Scanning the decaying industrial site around me, I started to feel a familiar sick lump in my gut. *How the hell am I going to get out of here?*

As if to answer me, the cabbie started his car up again. In the same monotone, he began, "I will take you to someplace north of the city." where he dramatically demonstrated by showing me his fists, "and you will be beaten up and left naked in the middle of nowhere."

Trying to make a quick assessment of the level of danger I was in, I got the impression this driver was not used to pulling such a stunt. All signs were that he was a legit cabbie who was clumsily trying to break into the profitable new world of graft and extortion. Strewn across the front seat I saw all the proper, cute touristy pamphlets for Moscow that one would expect on a ride from the airport, along with ashtrays filled with cigarette butts and candy wrappers.

Nonetheless, the driver himself was enormous. He nearly filled the front seat of the older Mercedes sedan. But he seemed so intoxicated — and nervous about what he was attempting — that I worked up my courage and decided to wait him out.

"*Khorosho*," I said to him and sat back in my seat. I made a show of looking at my NatEx papers, anxious as hell that I had no idea what to do with the three-foot cord in my briefcase. Clint had said I should always carry it. For what? Wrap it around the cabbie's neck and ask him less politely to take me where I wanted to go? Without any real training in how to pull that off, it wasn't a real option. Next, I considered another item I always carried in my bag, a sixteen-ounce lead 'equalizer.' That *was* an option if I needed to smash the window out and get out of the car.

After an hour's stand-off in the afternoon heat, sitting silently, each of us waiting for the other to give in, I finally broke the silence. My business instincts were getting the better of my fear. I had come up with a plan to negotiate my way out of this. In a sympathetic tone, I tried to tell him in my best Russian, "I understand how bad economic conditions are for taxi drivers and the 'average Ivan' in Russia since the economic crisis hit."

I began to bargain the sum down. I opened the bidding, "Twenty dollars," I said, and showed him a crisp new bill.

"One hundred dollars," he countered. We were already down to a fifth of what he had originally been asking.

"Forty." I knew we were close to an agreement. By now, that knot in my gut had pretty much untied itself.

"Fifty!" he countered and shouted, "No lower!"

"*Dobro!*" I agreed. He smiled and tried to offer me a drink from the vodka bottle he pulled from his glove compartment.

"You first!" I gestured to show I wanted him to drink. I also imagined getting poisoned or drugged by whatever he might offer. I faked taking a shot from the bottle and handed him the fifty dollars, hoping he wasn't going to try to get more before we arrived at the NatEx offices.

That had been my precedent for the bribe-taking and corruption I would be exposed to in Moscow for the next ten years. Whatever outrageous sum someone was asking for, it could usually be negotiated down to about a tenth of the original request. Unless, of course, they already had a gun to your head or a torch to your foot. I could never completely forget about such possibilities. And, while I was at least lucky that this guy had caved so easily when the dickering began, it represents one of many early incidents in which I falsely attributed my escape to becoming more adept in the ways of spy craft and espionage.

***

On this trip, though, getting to the hotel had been mostly uneventful. My visa, secured while I was still the Polish country director for NatEx, was still valid. Getting through the maze of customs, passport control, and other security at Sheremetyevo Airport had gone exceedingly well — by Russian standards. My cab driver today was silent and didn't try to extort anything more than what his meter showed. We pulled up to the hotel's main entrance, under a huge awning that seemed to be welcoming guests for a media event that evening. It was around seven o'clock. Not so sleek but shiny black Volga limos lined up in the entrance drive; an inordinate number of beautiful women were milling about the doorways. I paid the driver and took my thick briefcase — a Russian-style *diplomatka* — with me past the crowd of women and into the hotel.

The Leningradskaya Hotel was in one of the seven Stalinist-style skyscrapers built in Moscow in the early 1950s. Many believed these buildings represented the ugliest of the socialist architecture that the Soviet Union bestowed on its Communist partners along with all the other cultural or educational institutions that helped entice those satellites to toe the line.

In Moscow, despite the hotel's grim architecture, my meetings were almost always at the Leningradskaya. I'd gotten used to the property's layout and knew the routine of the women who worked the bars. The CIA had informers there, working behind the scenes. They reported to unknown higher-ups that my disinformation packets would make their way to their proper target via the visitors I'd soon have in my room. I preferred the Leningradskaya because its lobby had a huge, wide-open bar area. That was where the women began their evenings in full luxurious style. Not only that, you could see the comings and goings of everyone around. As I started getting more acquainted with the clientele, I came to realize the Leningradskaya was Moscow's 'Spy Central Station.'

As was usually the case, I could see that the pimps were meeting with their handlers, all former KGB agents. The KGB itself was no more; after the Communist hard-liners' unsuccessful coup on November 6, 1991, that venerable Soviet agency had split. Its replacements were the FSB, Federal Security Service, and the SVR, in charge of foreign intelligence. These men and women were huddled at tables dividing up the 'available staffing' for the evening. 'Staffing,' in this case, meant the prostitutes working the bars, the Inter-Girls. Their job was to provide all the intelligence they could about foreigners and whatever they were doing in Russia.

As Clint had instructed me several years earlier, "Intelligence and disinformation work goes both ways when working with the women in Moscow's hotels. Do not underestimate their patriotic commitment nor their talents as spies. Some of these women are career intelligence agents or at least well-trained operatives."

During that same training session, Jane had chimed in. "Even the escorts without special training consider their work a patriotic obligation to the Motherland. They're called 'Inter-Girls.' They work the hotels both for money and to gather intelligence."

Jane watched my reactions closely and challenged me often. Based on what she knew about my early years in Poland, she zeroed in on one potential weakness. Often, she warned me, "Men who let their little head do the thinking for their big head do not fare well as disinformation runners in Moscow. They put our operations at risk." She added, "You must beware of all hotel escort contacts! No exceptions!" Jane was right about the little head and the big head while working. I was clearly an 'at risk' contractor.

Inter-Girls

All that was in the back of my mind as I checked in. My room was on the eighth floor. Knowing I was to receive several guests that evening, I had asked for a suite. Key in hand and carrying only my black *diplomatka*, I walked past the lobby bar's vast seating area to see if things were hopping yet. I didn't notice much. By this time, the staffing meetings were mostly over and the evening shift had yet to show up. That group usually made a grand entrance as the hotel waved off its day shift prostitutes. The night crew, the 'A Team,' earned its designation more from the increase in prices than for any kind of quality 'upgrade' in their services.

Once I'd asked a bellman about the shift change and the price differential. "It's something like paying $75 for half an ounce of caviar at lunch," he explained, "versus paying $225 off the dinner menu. Same caviar; just a few hours later."

I wondered if the limos I had seen outside were bringing in that crew for the evening. That seemed unlikely, but then I remembered something I'd seen the week before in the Russian insert of the *Warsaw Business Journal*. It reported that in a poll of a thousand girls in high schools and junior high schools across Russia, far and away they listed prostitution as the country's most respected and desired profession.

My 'promotion' to Moscow document running had coincided with my hiring as NatEx's Country Director in Poland. The company regularly put up its execs from Atlanta and Frankfurt at the Leningradskaya. That worked well for me. Meetings for NatEx's eastern European personnel were in Moscow, so Clint and Jane coordinated most of my dis-info drops with times I would be in town anyway. Renata expressed deep concern about my trips to Russia.

"They'll eat you alive over there, Andy!" she exclaimed after I told her Moscow would be a regular business trip. "You are a star here because people love your smiles, how polite you are, and that little bit of naiveté you use to get others to trust you. But that will be your downfall with Russians." She continued, "They will sense that possible weakness and do everything to destroy you! I guarantee it!"

"Thanks Renata. You really know how to build someone's confidence," I said flatly.

"I'm not finished, either. You will probably fall for those whores over there, too. They are like fleas in all the hotels. Christ! You are going to embarrass me again with your stupid American attitude. I know it!" Renata had, once again, given her cruel two bits to discourage me and show her disdain for the work I was now doing. Our arguments verged on theatrical as she mimicked how she thought they would approach me.

***

Sitting in a cubicle in the US Embassy in Warsaw, watching the Inter-Girls on camera, I got a good feel for how much of their intelligence-gathering — and our disinformation activity — occurred in the open, during casual conversations over a drink in a hotel bar. Not all meetings turned into sex. A fact that coincidentally defied Renata's claim that every man falls prey to the whores (*kurwy* in Polish) after they return from work.

In her part of my briefing, Jane became very numbers oriented. She gave me a lot of stats she and Clint had compiled over the years.

"An Inter-Girl's average catch rate — the tally of meetings that result in paid sex — is less than one per night." Jane paused to give me a meaningful look over the top of her horn-rimmed glasses. "Some, though, average five to seven catches a night, and get paid for each one." She cleared her throat and added, "We will do our best to keep you away from those types."

After I had spent some time in those hotel bars, I could see what was going on. Disinterest was the best cure for being harassed in this overheated environment. And by the time I'd become a two-year Leningradskaya regular, I also had some protections afforded by knowing the bartenders quite well. So the women were not inclined to be very aggressive towards me. They might come by and smile or check in with me when I would show up at the bar. "Is tonight the night?" they might ask, or "A drink for me or for us?" to see if I had any interest.

In short, the spy game in Moscow relied heavily on the sex trade as one of its main tools. The KGB had gotten a makeover, but there had been no major changes among the intelligence people in Moscow — at least as far as I could tell. Clint had secrets he would not share but he hinted that our side was much more deeply involved in the Moscow *sexpionage* world than was generally known.

***

Because of my promotion and the regular work in Moscow, my absences from Krakow were becoming longer and longer, and more and more frequent, which wasn't exactly helping the marriage. "You are staying in five-star hotels while I am in this shithole! It's like San Francisco again. Nothing in the shops these days. My mother isn't helping me. Being alone and managing everything is not a marriage!" Renata would frantically plead with me. "If you are such a big businessman now, then buy me a flat in the center of town where I can manage a life alone here!"

And the more I was gone on these missions, the more I allowed my imagination and untethered libido to consider some of the non-monetary perks that went along with certain CIA contractor work. It was true that I would soon be able to pay cash for a flat and fulfill that dream for Renata. But the debacle in San Francisco and our continuing problems in Krakow were not making it easy for me to shy away from the temptations I faced on my trips.

Up to now, my official work was about providing purely commercial disinformation. It had no critical strategic or military importance but might have turned Russian intelligence's attentions in some bogus direction. Examples included lies about this or that company investing in cloaking technology for ships or one of the big defense contractors developing a new type of booster rocket. Faked internal documents that were labeled "SENSITIVE" or "INTERNAL DOCUMENT NOT CLEARED FOR RELEASE" could always be found somewhere inside my deliveries.

If what Jane had warned me about this latest set of documents was true, tonight's drop was disinformation intended to redirect Russian intelligence efforts in aviation and aerospace defense. Jane's suggestion that I remain ignorant about what was in the package was her last-ditch effort to keep me one step away from ever turning 'black.' This is the term for an agent who is targeted for *removal*, likely never to be seen or heard from again.

***

The lobby's chairs and couches were filling up so I quickly found a seat. Twice I apologized to men who asked if the seat next to me was taken: I was meeting someone, I told them. Although I'd been briefed to expect three someone's, I decided that trying to hold three places in the Leningradskaya Hotel's crowded bar wouldn't be discreet.

I sensed an air of frustration in the lobby; there were more customers than usual and people seemed frantic to get a seat. I noticed a lot more West European women in the bar than usual, attending a post-fashion show reception. The show had just taken place in the main concert hall and everyone, Muscovites and foreigners alike, was maneuvering for a place to see or meet some of the star models from the pages of *Elle*, *Vogue*, and *Marie Claire*. Despite the crush, my waitress came unusually quickly. She smiled when she recognized me.

Her name was Alyona. She had waited tables and tended bar at the Leningradskaya for years. Originally from Ukraine but transplanted to Moscow twenty years ago, she was almost as striking in her close-fitting red hotel uniform as were the other women in their finest European designer clothes. To greet me, she leaned over and put her free hand on my shoulder and gave me a cheek-to-cheek kiss. Her bright smile always made me laugh. I marveled at how she was able to keep her massive shock of blonde hair held up so high on her head. "Andrew! Nice to see you again. Are you staying with us tonight? Someone came by the bar asking if Andrew Gold had arrived. Shall I point you out to her?"

Wanting to see my contact before she saw me, I quickly took her hand and asked, "Alyona, would you please discreetly point her out to me, first?" She frowned, maybe a bit embarrassed, and not so discreetly pointed to the woman in question. Who was already walking quickly toward us.

"Sorry, Mr. Gold," Alyona said. "She has been watching me the whole time and is coming this way now. That is her. She drinks coffee in the evening — since her workday has just begun." She gave me a smile and a little wink. "Shall I bring one for her on your tab? A glass of wine for you?"

Somewhat alarmed, I locked in on her and got a visual as she was approaching. I was almost convinced the woman she was pointing to couldn't be the Natalya I was expecting; she didn't fit the description I had been given. Nevertheless, I said, "Yes, Alyona. Do that, please."

I didn't like being spotted first if I was to meet someone I didn't know. More than once during my stays in Moscow, Alyona had been helpful in keeping my identity secret. I really liked how she worked with me, staging meetings the way I preferred. Even if she had fooled me into thinking she was in my camp, working for me, I always enjoyed spending time talking to her. The added benefit with Alyona was that she could speak Polish very well. If we needed to, we could 'escape' into Polish from time to time. That let us discreetly exchange information about people I was to meet or get details straight about other logistical matters in the hotel: who to avoid, who was a good guy, or ways to endear myself to the staff.

The guy who'd sent me here had acted uneasy when I asked if Alyona worked for us. He avoided answering me. As hot as the espionage game in Moscow had become during the late eighties, it was amazing that she had survived in her job for so long. The Soviets would take every opportunity to place a mole in positions that had frequent contact with foreigners — especially Americans. Alyona was a legend in the Moscow bar scene. There was not a foreigner in the city who didn't know her. She had earned respect for her ability to handle every possible situation that the nightly cauldron of European, Russian, and American businessmen — and spies — could stir up. And, for extra flavor, with fifty or sixty of the most beautiful women thrown into the stew.

Within seconds, the striking brunette Alyona had pointed out was standing in front of me. I stood up as she introduced herself. We stood eye to eye and very close to each other. "Good evening! Mr. Gold from Poland?" She waited for me to confirm that; a flicker of worry crossed her face when I hesitated. My delay was a response to my surprise that she didn't look like I'd imagined. Her hair was light brown, shorter than I had expected. In her low heels, I guessed she was about five feet ten inches tall. Most surprising was that she looked like a clean-cut American girl in a CoverGirl TV ad or a pretty Harvard exchange student. She was dressed nicely but somewhat conservatively compared to the others I'd seen: chic Paris-level catwalk beauties sporting a tidal wave of sultry Slavic sex, made up and dressed to bring every lobby bar patron to his knees. Natalya was just as beautiful — but different. Staring at her as I was, I remembered how enamored I had been with Eastern European women ten years earlier; how I fell head over heels with my Polish professor. With Renata. I was clearly still under that Slavic spell.

"Yes. Natalya?" I finally spit out.

"Hi! I am glad you are here. How was your trip from Poland? Did you get some rest after you arrived?" she asked. "May I join you?"

Natalya was extremely smooth. Her beautiful smile and round, dark eyes made her look more Middle Eastern than Russian. Her embroidered white peasant blouse, pleated gray mid-length skirt, and deep cinnamon-tinted shoulder-length hair, were pleasantly out of place. Here, extraordinary cleavage, slit dresses, and bleached blonde Vidal Sassoon coiffures were the rule.

I pointed to a chair across from me. Natalya quickly asked if the seat next to me wouldn't be better. I agreed and pulled the chair back. She slid smoothly under the low table, and seconds after we sat down, Alyona had our drinks to us: wine for me, coffee for my new friend. I think she'd noticed us sharing a moment of silence; sizing each other up, I suppose.

Natalya spoke English very well. She asked how long I had been in Poland.

I told her it had been nearly ten years.

She smiled. "Why didn't you greet me then with the traditional Polish three kisses?"

My answer was somewhat in keeping with tradition. "I was waiting for our first *bruderschaft* drink. Isn't that the rule? And besides, we are in Russia." Thoughts of Renata's *bruderschaft* lessons with me in Krakow crossed my mind as our introduction continued.

It was right then that Alyona showed up again, this time with two Moskovskaya vodkas. Natalya proposed the "call me by my first name" ritual at the table: "Natalya," she said, turning to me with her drink in her right hand, crossing her right arm slowly around mine.

"Andy," I replied.

We drank the shots in one gulp, as is the rule, and kissed cheeks: left, right, left. She brought her face back in front of mine and hesitated, our noses barely touching. Then, very lightly, she kissed me on the mouth to properly finish our *bruderschaft* introduction. Natalya's perfume, probably Chanel, was no part of the sweet, syrupy fog that filled the lounge. Her delicate scent lingered lightly around us as we talked about Moscow and my trip from Poland. During the first five minutes, she put her hand on top of mine several times. Also, in the first few minutes, Natalya was interrupted half a dozen times by men and women who seemed to be part of the fashion show crowd. Most said they'd been sorry not to see her there. Every time, she replied, twice in Russian and once in English, "I had an important date," and flashed me a smile.

Natalya asked how well I knew Moscow and if I would have a chance to do any sightseeing or shopping here. Then she got right down to business. "What have you been doing since NatEx announced its retreat from Europe?" She obviously had been well briefed for this encounter. "I was talking to your former colleague, Brian, here in Moscow, and he said you had left the company when its operations in Poland were suspended." Resisting the urge to go off on the chaos in the wake of NatEx's departure, I stuck to my game plan for the evening.

I smiled. It was time to play my own part. "Not the ideal situation for me, losing the NatEx gig, but the consulting office in Krakow is doing fine. This trip is the first of many to make sure I don't lose contact with folks over here."

"What kind of consulting do you do?" She seemed genuinely interested.

"Central European Exchange mainly works with Western firms that want to set up shop in the former Soviet bloc. We have some attorneys that do the technical work; it's my job to go out and find customers."

"Please let me know if there is anything I can do to help," she murmured. "I certainly hope this contact is secure." She flashed me another of her smiles.

"You seem well connected," I replied. "I'd be a fool to lose contact with you, I'm sure."

Natalya pushed her coffee away and slid over, very close to me, taking my left arm with her right hand and squeezing it tightly. "What time are you inviting us up to your room for a night-cap?"

"Us." There it was. She would be working with a team, just as I'd been briefed.

By now, her left hand was working its way slowly up my thigh, coming to rest comfortably between my legs. "And do you require that I introduce my friends first? Or do you trust me?" Her hand was now firmly resting as close as it could without actually lying on top of my rapidly growing cock. I paused before answering her, taking in a deep breath and letting it out as slowly as I could to try to bring my excitement level down. I needed to focus on the job I was there to do.

I almost choked on the words, "That won't be necessary, Natalya. Just come up before midnight, please. I need to be up pretty early tomorrow."

"I promise, we won't keep you from your early morning commitments. Just kick us out when you are ready." She laughed softly, kissed me on the cheek, and stood to leave. I admired the view as she walked away and disappeared around a corner.

Alyona strode past my table. Not stopping, she asked if I wanted another or should she charge our drinks to the room. I asked her for another. For thirty minutes I watched the lobby bar 'show' before retiring to my room.

This was shaping up to be a very unusual night. I was terribly curious about what it would be like being with three women. I laughed to myself, feeling embarrassed by my own excitement, and guessed I would find out very soon. I'd made it my *almost always* policy to refuse sex when it was offered and, instead, try to create a pleasant atmosphere. I didn't want to get too far out of control with the women at the Leningradskaya and felt my record spoke to that. Out of six disinformation runs so far, four of those times I'd turned over my materials in the bar. Only twice had I been forced to stage the heist from my hotel room, and both of those times was with two women. Dodging sex with one woman wasn't usually difficult. With two women, it *was* difficult. Adding a third seemed impossible. Natalya's spell on me didn't help, either.

***

A couple of hours earlier, I'd quickly showered, dressed in my usual gray sweater and black jacket, adjusted a few things in my room, and ordered two bottles of Russian champagne. Inside the liquor bar's glass cabinet, I'd stashed the packet of documents, making sure it was clearly in sight. The champagne arrived promptly so I slipped the bottles into the ice

41

buckets on my TV counter. So by the time I'd headed downstairs to meet Natalya, I was fairly confident everything in the room was ready.

Now, back in the room as 11 o'clock neared, I called room service for water and a couple of snack trays. Those wound up, being caviar, blini, lox, nuts and olives. At $125, I almost asked the attendant to take it back, but decided it would play better to keep the expensive snack. And the CIA rarely quibbled about my expense account… including the costs of 'doing business' with the women. It was reasonable to assume the food might serve some purpose, if only to stop my stomach from growling loudly — as it had been doing ever since I met Natalya.

Midnight arrived. She and her friends were no-shows. I knew it really didn't matter if they turned up late, except for one thing. I worried that I might rush the whole process of staging their heist. If things got going early, I might play more of a role in choreographing how they took the envelope. I wanted to know at which moment they grabbed the documents, who took them, and how long afterward they stayed. If the package went quickly and the women stayed, I worried that having them lingering in the room might expose me to greater risk from pimps or other agents outside the door. More than once in this line of work I'd had a woman open the door and invite an unwelcome stranger into my room. Once this job was done, I wanted the women out as fast as possible. Choreographing three women this time seemed hard to plan. As much as I was playing my awareness of how late it was getting, I worried that this might be the first time my drop wouldn't come off as planned. I had no contingency plan. That bothered me.

As I said before. I shouldn't have worried. Natalya took care of business.

***

The next afternoon, after my meeting with Natalya and her cohorts, I was taken by surprise at Sheremetyevo, Moscow's international airport.

"Mr. Gold, if you would kindly follow us, please. We have some questions we want to ask you." Two men in bad suits pulled me out of the line in Passport Control and asked me to go with them. I hadn't even gotten to the window to submit my visa and passport for inspection. This had only happened once before, when my visa application had been incorrectly filled out. That time, there was a discrepancy between my actual passport expiration date and what was written in the visa. But this time, I was pretty sure, there was nothing wrong with my paperwork.

Caught off guard, I found myself resisting their determined grip on my shoulders as they led me to a room behind the passport control booths. The loud click of the deadbolt locking behind me didn't help with the anxiety that was now beginning to overwhelm me. I couldn't help but start frantically reviewing everything that had taken place the night before. What had gone wrong that I hadn't noticed at the time?

"Sit down, please," the two said in unison. They immediately began firing questions at me. "How was your stay at the Leningradskaya last night? You stayed only one night and didn't go anywhere other than your hotel room... where you had a few visitors. I think you did some sightseeing in the city this morning. You must enjoy Moscow. The visa is a business visa. Did you do business? What exactly is your business?"

I was scared but hoped I wasn't showing it too much. I was feeling, I realized, a lot like I had on that long afternoon as a rogue cab driver's hostage. I responded, "Yes, I do enjoy Moscow, but my trip was planned to be very short. Just an evening meeting. And then I filled some free time before my flight out this morning. I do some consulting work here."

"Yes... yes... yes. Just as planned. Mr. Gold, we are concerned that NatEx has begun retreating from Europe and Poland is on the list to lose all NatEx presence. That includes your dismissal." This was the taller of the two — I made a mental note about his bad haircut and smoke-stained fingers — who was looking straight at me from the other side of the dark wooden table. He resumed the questioning. "Are you still employed by NatEx? Your visa is valid contingent upon your employment with the company. That is why we called you in to inquire about it. Now you mention consulting. What is your real business in Russia?"

"I'm still with the company. Some of us are investigating expansion in countries where we have profitable operations. Like Russia. That part is being done under the consulting agreement I have with NatEx," I lied.

The two men sat across from me, blinking their eyes in unison about every five seconds. Then the tall one said, "Very interesting." They both got up and left the room. I was alone for almost an hour. Twenty minutes before my plane was to depart, I knocked loudly on the locked door and told the guard on the other side that my flight was leaving very soon. I could hear his footsteps hurrying away. Within two minutes he came back, opened the door, and said, "Please go now."

I was the last passenger to get on the flight. In the business class section, my seat was waiting for me.

Cash in Advance

What was it that made me want to go back to Russia after all that? Sure, part of it was the chance to make some money. Poland in the post-Communist era was quickly getting more expensive and my wife's expectations were changing.

"I'm not going to drive a Polski-Fiat anymore!" she announced one day during one of my weekends in Krakow. "Opel, Ford, Peugeot, and Citroen all have nice mid-size cars that we can afford!"

"I agree, but in a couple of months we have to put a huge down payment on the new flat. I'm not sure now is the time, since Poland still doesn't have a decent bank loan program," I countered.

"You can't keep blaming Poland for why we aren't making more progress in our lives!" She was getting angry.

"Renata, the cost of living in Poland has more than doubled since we left. You want a new lifestyle with a new flat, a new car, a huge savings account and eight weeks off in the summer. Christ! It takes time! Please be patient!" I tried to reason with her.

"It takes *you* time—and too much of it! I have no patience for your business games! It's like we didn't exist at all for you!" Renata wanted a lot and she wanted it now.

Everything that I earned from NatEx and from my intelligence work went toward that end. She felt that she and the kids didn't exist for me. And I knew that I didn't exist for her except to deliver a lifestyle that she could showboat to her friends and colleagues. That realization furthered my desire to immerse myself in the covert world I was becoming more familiar with. Maybe it was the excitement over all — not just the sex part, but the adventure — that kept pulling me back in. Even as Jane kept telling me not to do it.

***

My first assignment had come before the Soviet Union collapsed. Before the wall came down, before the Iron Curtain was raised. There was still a Cold War on, and I didn't have a clue about how much trouble I might get myself into. Renata was in the midst of her divorce from a mathematician who had left her and gone to the United States. It was unclear if she and I were a thing for the future. That left me, at most, an interested suitor.

Jane was acting unusually nervous as she handed me an envelope with $50, my pay for teaching an English course the week before. "Sit down. I'll be back in a minute," she said, walking down a long, narrow room lined with cubicles. From one of them, a long arm appeared and handed her a manila envelope. All I saw was what looked like a grey tweed sleeve. She smiled at whoever the sleeve belonged to and returned to her desk.

Sitting bolt upright with the envelope in her hand, she asked, "Do you consider yourself a patriotic American, Andy?"

I remember a smile coming over my face; I suspected where the conversation was going. "I certainly do, Jane."

"I've made a recommendation to the CIA Desk Chief that you might be a candidate for doing some contract work for the United States."

"You mean for the CIA?" I asked, still smiling. I was giddy with delight.

"Yes, Andy."

"Is this something like what you told me about last year? When they asked you to pretend to fall asleep on a train? Then take pictures of what you found when the train was retired for the night?"

"Yes. I forgot I told you about that." Jane blinked rapidly and her eyes flicked back and forth. "Sit there. Don't get up. Read the first four pages of the document in this envelope. When you are finished, put the papers back in the envelope and we will talk."

With great interest I read the four pages and knew that I wanted to be the person to carry out the task that was described. I returned the papers to the envelope and set it on her desk. Jane returned to me and asked,

"What do you think?"

"I would love to be the one to do this work," I told her.

"The desk chief wants you to do it." She wrinkled her face. "I am not completely on board."

"I want to do it. It's perfect for me. I already have ideas about my coding and how I'll categorize my list. Please agree!" I almost pleaded with her.

"We pay $500 cash for these projects. That's a lot of money in Poland." Jane took the envelope, stood up, and led me to a conference room.

"Read the rest of the document. Study it. I'll tell the chief that you are in." Following Jane, I could feel my eyes tearing up with joy. *This* was adventure! *This* was what I had come to Poland for!

***

I was sent to Wroclaw, an industrial city in western Poland, to hang out in a distant suburban neighborhood next to a military base. I had to find a good vantage point to count and categorize all the vehicles and trailers that went in and out of the base's heavily guarded main gate. At that time, a lot of Soviet military vehicles and weapons were being deployed to the nearby East German border. Testing my creativity, my handlers wanted me to devise a coded method for keeping track, on paper, of everything I saw. While not a particularly complicated task, I had to do it for a full ten days and for as many hours a day as I could survive without nodding off or looking suspicious. Russian soldiers not liked very much by Poles who resented the Soviet 'friendship' that had been forced upon them for almost forty years, were crawling all over the place. They were sensitive to English speakers; probable spies, they assumed. In my case, of course, they would have been right. During that tiring mission, I had to concentrate on being very Polish. Drawing attention to myself was not recommended. One big reason for discretion was the suspicion that short-range missiles aimed directly at West Berlin were being deployed from this base.

Within sight of the main gate were a variety of public places I could go to do my watching. And counting. And categorizing. And reporting. I alternated between a café, a full-service restaurant, a neighborhood library, a cocktail bar, a meat shop with no meat — rationing was still going on — and a grocery store.

Until I got acquainted with a young librarian who worked from noon to closing time, nine o'clock, I averaged about two hours of sleep, wandering the streets each night trying to be inconspicuous. There were places I could hide, stay warm, and get some rest before the 6 a.m. rush of vehicles in and out of the military gate. After fourteen non-stop hours, though, of tracking movements in and out of the gate, by 8 p.m. every evening I'd have a hard time concentrating on the troop transport vehicles and missile launchers rolling by.

Then there was the additional factor that made it especially difficult to concentrate. It was that librarian, very pretty, sitting in her austere workplace and staring at me over the top of her white plastic-rimmed glasses. It wasn't hard to notice that this young woman looked a lot like Renata did when I first met her as my Polish language instructor the year before. Same white rimmed glasses, dark eyes and short cropped hair — and a stare that was hard to interpret. Was she thinking, "What the hell are you doing here?" or "Please come over and say 'Hi!'" Noticing the amount of time I was spending in her reading room, she finally introduced herself.

"Dzen dobry! Nazywam sie, Agata." Her name was Agata, she had just told me.

"Czesc! Mam na imie Andy. *Jestem Amerykaninem. Studiuje w SGPiSie w Warszawie."* I introduced myself as an American studying at the School for Planning and Statistics in Warsaw.

We hit it off quite famously. Soon she was allowing me to sleep until 5 a.m. on a sofa bed that had been set up in a back room for other workers. She would lock up the building and then quietly let herself in to visit me every night. On that first night, we talked, but it wasn't an hour before she took me by the hand and showed me where she made tea and fixed her sandwiches during the day. We had each other's clothes off in what, for me anyway, had been record time. Maybe I just had that TV spy spoof *Get Smart* on my mind, but I thought Agata looked a lot like Barbara Feldon, who had played Agent 99. She was medium height, had short black hair and dark eyes, and wore smart white blouses. She also had an amazing number of sex positions she was interested in trying out on that little sofa. My sex life with Renata had been pretty much governed by the rules of the Catholic Church and Missionary City. That had been fine for the short time we had known each other but Agata's rules made me want to run back to my teacher girlfriend in Krakow and show her what I had learned. Even for me, that didn't seem too smart. Our running joke was that Agata was doing *her* research in sexual pleasure and the female orgasm. She would usually leave me alone by 2 a.m., which was when I actually got some sleep during those 'research-filled' ten days.

Because I still had documents confirming my grad student status, I created a system of coded record-keeping that involved consumer products in Polish stores. If the Milicja — the Polish police — had asked me what I was doing, I would have indicated that I was doing research for my PhD. Also, to help me back up my 'research' story, Agata had pulled out a cart full of economic planning journals. My records looked like a huge shopping list, or a grocery store's inventory. When that mission was finished, I submitted my report, disguised as a grocery list, to Jane. She, and those above her, must have been impressed. After that, I was given work on a regular basis. At first, I had to submit my reports before being paid. But by the time I was introduced directly to Clint at the CIA desk, I was being paid in advance, with a per diem added.

My announcement back in Krakow that I would be getting more "teaching work from the USIA" should have been greeted with at least half of the enthusiasm and excitement I felt about regular gigs from the embassy. By this time, Renata and I were living together but her divorce was far from final. Instead of my constant travels, she preferred a baby sitter based in Krakow who could paint the small flat she owned, stand in the meat and toilet paper queues for hours, and pick her son up from school — preferably with dinner ready when she got back from the university. The value of Polish money before the wall came down was marginal and so was my value to Renata if I couldn't be a good partner where she lived. This was not a good sign. I should have been paying more attention.

Dima

Today's meeting in Warsaw's Marriott Hotel, on its surface at least, was supposed to be different. No sex, just business. That's why my Polish buddy Antek had agreed to join me as we met a mysterious character named Dmitri. I sensed an opportunity to wangle a new assignment from the CIA desk based on a fax we'd received. And maybe, I had to admit to myself, a chance to meet a new Agata or Natalya while I was at it.

Dmitri turned out to be a large, dark-haired, good-natured ethnic Russian from Kazakhstan. He wore a wide smile and thick dark glasses and told us he liked doing business in the Marriott. Here, without complication, he could bring professors and other academics from the universities and academies as far as Novosibirsk. A pedestrian tunnel under the street led directly from *Warszawa Centralna*. A first-time visitor to the West could get on a train in far-away eastern or central Siberia and make his way across the steppes in a week, without serious inconvenience. The trip involved just a couple of station changes and a pause at the former Soviet border to change the train's wheels to fit the narrower western rails. With even greater ease, businessmen could fly Russian Aeroflot airliners from a dozen Siberian cities like Krasnoyarsk or Irkutsk to Warsaw Okecie airport, though flying made for a somewhat more expensive trip.

Antek and I easily found Dmitri. He was sitting with his back to a wall of curtains near the hotel's north-facing windows. His legs were surrounded by black boxes — on closer examination, large briefcases. He had that look of a professorial type anxiously waiting for someone. Dima, as he preferred to be called, told us he had a small flat near the Marriott. He could walk there in less than five minutes. He'd had breakfast there this morning and was anxious for our meeting.

With brief introductions aside and some coffees ordered, Dima jumped with zeal into his pitch. He told us the "business opportunities" he represented were rather wide and were just now "beginning to avail themselves to the West." Having such a perfect place to do business, straddling the border of East and West, was his dream. And now, he said, he was beginning to live it out.

"So, Dima," I asked, "what are those business opportunities?" I tried to be upbeat with him. "Give us some idea of what's going on in Siberia with the emerging market economies and business there."

"Our meeting was for the high-purity aluminum and titanium mentioned in the fax you received," Dima began, excitement vibrating in his voice, "but perhaps a good introduction would be a short story of some of the people behind the deal."

"Perfect! Thank you!" I urged him. Antek sat beside me, staring at Dima, looking bored.

Dima pushed on. "Government officials from the former Soviet Union, managing directors of factories, and smart businessmen have crafted plans for marketing our product. People have been hired by this group to help carry out the plan at differing levels. These two groups make up the business side of this opportunity. These are people who had the vision to bypass the problems of our lagging infrastructure and non-existent market economy and go directly to buyers with a variety of products. For now, we are talking about titanium and aluminum and some other rare earth metals that were mostly processed and fabricated in the former Soviet Union." He told his story, memorized and recited like a business documentary, with considerable skill. Antek and I were looking at each other; we knew there was a very black side to what he was doing and to the products he was making available.

"Your fax mentioned academics in the business. What is their role?" Antek asked.

"I was just about to tell you," Dima responded.

"Sorry for interrupting," I said, giving Antek a joking "fuck off" look.

In the same theatrical tone, Dima continued his story. "It's quite all right. The academic side is the whole group of participating scientists and research people that have access to the materials or are knowledgeable about our products to facilitate a transaction. Their actual roles vary widely. Some will simply put together a proper product description and offer on letterhead. Others will coordinate permits, preparation, and transfer for transportation of material to a buyer. Because some materials may be very dangerous or toxic, their role can be extremely important."

When Dima finished, I couldn't help but wonder how much this dangerous activity had become regular commerce. "Would you be willing to say a few things about the dangers you just mentioned?" I asked.

"No. Not yet," Dima said.

"I think I'm starting to get it," I said.

Antek, by now, looked so bewildered I knew he was losing interest in Dima. He tapped me on the shoulder and said, "Gotta go! Miss World is calling." And, sure enough, there she was. The former Miss World, Agnieszka Krasinska, happened to be sitting a few tables away. She was hard to ignore, in a very short, tight, white dress and black Polish Army boots. "Give me a call later on," was the extent of Antek's farewell.

Dima was unfazed by Antek's departure and continued to build on his presentation. "So please let me tell you the real reason we are meeting," Dima said, arms outstretched.

"Yes! Please!" I encouraged him again.

"Our titanium and aluminum are a special case," Dima said. "Since the late fifties and especially starting in the mid-sixties, the first, second and third stages of Soviet-made Soyuz rockets have been falling back to Earth onto the steppes of southern and central Siberia. Some have also fallen in the forests north and east of the Baikonur Cosmodrome in Kazakhstan, where they are launched. Most of the material that can be gotten to relatively easily is in the Altai region. That is northeast of the Cosmodrome. If you go to that area now, you will find farmers tending their crops or building their barns from material they have taken from a booster rocket or the fuselage of a second stage that suddenly landed in their field or knocked their house over. This is an almost surreal image for a primitive and remote people; they have accepted that a twenty-ton piece of metal might at any time come raining down into the middle of their village, wiping out a whole family. Or even several families."

"I guess we don't have that problem in the USA since we launch from Florida," I commented. "And the boosters fall back down into the Atlantic Ocean."

"Precisely," Dima agreed. "But don't underestimate the Russian pride associated with being the bull's eye for the falling first-stage Soyuz rocket during an important space mission for the Motherland! It's kind of a good luck omen," he proclaimed, half seriously but also laughing.

I began thinking about the logistics of what Dima was proposing. "Who is the owner of that debris? Who would we be buying it from?"

"Andy, I'd like to say that there are ownership papers and a contract that can be drawn up. But that would be a lie. In most cases, where the Russians or Soviets haven't come around to secure the debris, it is for whomever claims it or disassembles it and takes it away. With a few exceptions, it is the property of the owners or caretakers of the land that it falls on. If it is in the middle of a village, then the village divides up what can be parceled out. But what's just as important as where it comes from is where it's going. The technology and facilities for recycling this high-purity metal are popping up in Western Europe. We just need to find it and get it there." Dima leaned closer to me and lowered his voice. "I have maps and precise coordinates of every piece of debris that has officially and unofficially fallen back to Earth and landed in the former Soviet Union."

"So. Are you suggesting that this is a deal without guaranteed terms and conditions? An offer to share an adventure? Seeking titanium and whatever else that has fallen from the sky?" I started getting dramatic at this point, facetiously paraphrasing him. "A fifty-fifty split on a treasure hunt in the far eastern Siberian steppes? And you have the treasure map!" I tried to play up his urge to describe this as an adventure.

It seemed to work. He gave me a broad smile. "I see that you are sometimes more poetic than I am, Andy," Dima said. "What a lovely picture you have painted of this expedition."

***

Paramount in all of my wild gyrations to secure contract missions, including the fresh relationship with Dima, was the need to assure cash flow for a wife who based her judgment of my worthiness on the money we were saving for the new flat. Dry spells in that cash flow precipitated arguments; I'd get blindsided by the kids asking, "How come you don't like us, Dad?"

"Why would you tell the kids that I don't love them, Renata?" I'd track her down and confront her with the question.

"They ask me why you are gone so much and I tell them the truth.

They aren't stupid. They can see you do this for you. Not for us."

With Clint the man who doled out both the assignments and the money, I was game for anything he sent my way. My new strategy was to try to sell him on my own projects. Jane, my USIA mentor, would soon be leaving the country. I was paranoid that without her support inside the embassy, jobs for me might dry up.

It was the day after I'd gotten back from Moscow and that threesome in my suite at the Leningradskaya. Clint was towering above us both. His face was hard to forget, with a handlebar moustache, bushy eyebrows, and thick graying hair that looked like it had been bowl cut. He was peering over the partition that divided his CIA cubicle from Jane's USIA workspace. He was talking about the short visit I had just returned from. "Sounds like it went well. Nobody was waiting for you when you left your room the next morning. We watched you throughout the rest of the next day before you boarded your flight. Looks like you made another flawless drop." He went on, "We also know that the target individual got your package. That was an A-plus job, Andy."

"What about getting pulled out of the passport control line at the airport?" I asked Clint. "That wasn't fun and games for me." I wondered if I was reading too much into the incident.

"You caught someone's attention, that's for sure. We didn't see anyone we would be concerned about tailing you that next morning. Too much stress on *this* one, Andy?" The tone of his baritone voice told me he didn't want to hear about my problems or worries.

"It wasn't an onerous job," I conceded, "and I've been pulled out of line before at Sheremetyevo. There is something else, though. Clint, I'm a little confused about the three women."

Clint got a funny smile on his face.

"The other times I've done this," I continued my query, "it was at most with two women; one of them was diverting my attention so the other could do the heist. That all made sense. So why the third woman this time?"

Clint leaned his arms on the cubicle's partition and rested his chin on his hands. "Take your guess who out of the three was working for us and 'invited' the other two — who happened to be connected to the agents we wanted the package to get to." Clint grinned theatrically and batted his eyes, waiting for me to acknowledge that I understood.

"Natalya works for us!" I blurted. "She coordinates these little heists! I should have known. Wow! She's incredible!"

"She is also in a very dangerous situation." Clint's demeanor turned serious again. "As a contractor just like you are, we've taken her to the limit of the risk that we can allow. These FSB pimps and agents are ruthless bastards. And Natalya, as you can see, is… well… special. She knew we hadn't told you about her and she played it exactly as we wanted her to." Now Clint sounded unusually proud of himself, clearly pleased that I had reacted as I did.

"All I can say is, Thank You!" I said, my erotic enthusiasm getting the better of my secret-agent discretion. "I'd take every opportunity to do the Warsaw-Moscow run if she was waiting on the other end!" I said that, of course, forgetting that my other boss, Jane, was sitting with us.

After I uttered that inappropriate remark, she chimed in, "Hey, boys! There's a girl in the room! Let's put our dicks back in our pants and talk about the future. Are you with me yet?"

I'd never seen Jane that way but wasn't surprised she could hang with the boys. I'd heard some incredible tales about her courage while facing real danger. I knew she was not one to mess with. Jane reminded us both that changes were coming to the whole setup of what I'd been doing for almost seven years now. The USIA had given me cover to do this work for the CIA desk by contracting with me for English-language teaching assignments throughout Poland. While the frequency of these assignments had diminished while I was employed at NatEx, I had ramped up my involvement with the CIA-assigned tasks, especially over the past five years.

During those early years, starting with the job that got me into that back room with the sexy Polish librarian, it was Jane who handed me the assignment notes out in the consular lobby. Every time, she said, "You really don't have to do this, you know!"

High Stakes Games

By 1992, things had changed. A lot. The Berlin Wall was down, Communist regimes had vanished from Eastern Europe, even the Soviet Union had ceased to exist. NatEx had charged into the region believing they could be the big players in the market using the US model — and had fucked everything up. My brief high hopes for a senior corporate gig to solve my money and marriage problems were quickly dashed. I was back on shaky ground with everything. And after all those jobs Jane had handed me over the years, she was about to be out of a job herself. That year, the United States Information Agency was disbanded, and the State Department — which had always controlled it — absorbed its responsibilities for English-language and cultural matters.

Jane, who had been the USIA's director in Poland, was given a ticket back to Washington. She hung on quite a while, as a lot of USIA programs needed to be rolled over into the English Language Fellows Program that the State Department was ramping up. During this transition period, Jane helped me get more deeply involved as a contractor directly for the CIA. And, when all was said and done, if there was anyone at the embassy who took the time and made the effort to teach me the ropes about things, Jane was the one. For the short time she had left in Warsaw, she continued to coach me.

***

It figured that just as Jane was leaving me on my own, I was getting mixed up in a game with much higher stakes. Clint was kind enough to connect me with a hush-hush new anti-terrorist program, but I was getting signals that the jobs coming up might be beyond my ability. That didn't sit well with my obsession to be part of the group. I needed these gigs. They kept me, and my family, living the lifestyle that Renata demanded. Otherwise, my name was mud.

The skills identified for these new assignments weren't high enough to require career spies, but they were beyond my abilities at that time. No one had to tell me that looking and acting innocent while keeping track of everything around me was not a highly prized skill. Renata, for her own reasons, had gotten suspicious of that act as the amount of time I spent away got longer and longer. Add NatEx responsibilities to CIA contracts and it was fast becoming difficult to get home at all on weekends. Being a resourceful and attentive dummy wasn't exactly something that read well on a resume. It *was* exactly that skill, though, and paying attention to the political and social unrest that was occurring, that might have saved me from a terrifying ordeal in Ternopil, Ukraine the previous year.

My accepting the job came after a particularly turbulent weekend in Krakow. Gearing up for our eventual move to a new flat in town, still many months away, Renata was tossing out everything old and/or making arrangements to buy new furniture and appliances.

"We're not going to fill the new place with old shit!" she started off one Saturday morning while we were trying to make a few decisions.

"Absolutely not. I agree. The washer is pretty new, though! Why would you just dump it?" I couldn't believe she had put our new Polish Predom Superautomat washer on her 'Toss this shit' list.

"Everyone at the new building has either a Bosch or a Siemens washer-dryer. Why should I settle for anything less than that? Remember, you're the fucking American in the family! How can an American family move in with a shitty Predom washer? That doesn't even have a dry cycle?"

"Renata, please! Just making the down payment on the new flat is stretching us! I'd hoped I wouldn't have to go to Warsaw next week. I wanted to get some things done here. You're making it so I *have* to go and beg for a teaching gig, just to pay to replace everything on your throw-away list!"

Clint had already approached me about a certain job in the Ukraine. I'd refused it. Jane had warned that there was risk of trouble at the factory the agency wanted to scour for technical data. As the enterprise was preparing for partial privatization, labor leaders had caught management, largely former Commies, siphoning off large amounts of money.

Clint needed someone to play the commercial manager for a bogus satellite dish antenna company from Arizona interested in doing business with the Ukrainian company. I had taken Jane's warnings seriously. But I'd left it with Clint that I'd call him if I changed my mind. Suddenly, with this new cash crisis looming, $500 sounded very good. I felt I had to accept, now.

I called him late Saturday after my argument with Renata petered out. With promises made for new appliances and orders placed at the Siemens store in Bronowice district, close to the new flat, Renata had gotten what she wanted. I asked Clint not to tell Jane about my decision until I left on Tuesday. Her calls and complaints sometimes undid me as much as Renata's.

Clint sent me to tour the Saturn Antenna Company. Ternopil was just a few hours by train from the Polish border—and quite close to Chernobyl. The mission was to get spec sheets and/or diagrams of antenna electronics. I was the American decoy, looking at primitive antennas in their warehouses and stockrooms. Other technical folks— much better at stealing the critical technical data—were to go out into the plant with low-level technicians. Everything was planned to the T. That is, until one of our guys had to go pee after a meeting. All my guys and the senior Saturn execs followed him into the bathroom. I stayed outside, saying, "I don't have to go. I'll wait here." No one noticed that I hadn't followed them into the bathroom. And when they came out, I was nowhere to be seen.

Looking back at events and my attitude leading up to this job, I probably attributed my series of mission successes and getting out of tight situations—like that threatening taxi driver threat in Moscow— more to my increasing skill on the job than to what was actually just plain luck. The question becomes relevant if my smug attitude contributed to my problems on this trip. Getting back to the basics of Espionage 101, the first rule of watching out for yourself as an undercover agent is: Avoid having your hands in your pockets. I happened to be violating that rule, standing with my back to all the doors entering the hallway, when a body condom came over my head. I later learned that was my abductors' name for a rolled-up piece of carpet with laundry bags capping the top. In less than a second, duct tape had sealed my whole head and face inside this thing, and a two-meter-tall Ukrainian ape with incredible strength clamped his arms around me. He squeezed until I lost consciousness some fifteen seconds later. My last memories, surrounded by white hot fear, were of being lifted and carried parallel to the ground. Any attempts to cry out were stifled by the orangutan's clamp that kept me from breathing.

It was a very smooth body heist. They had probably already driven away before my entourage had burped their worms and zipped up their pants.

Greeting the Saturn officials as they emerged from the bathroom was the local labor committee. They announced to everyone that I had been forcibly taken and would be kept until negotiations were successfully completed for a new work contract. That had to include, they specified, a percentage share of all revenues from international sales. It took five days for that contract to be signed. Despite all efforts to find me, I remained locked in a bedroom in a small villa on the edge of town. On the plus side, I got regular food and vodka deliveries. Not so pleasant: I had to use a chamber pot and any real toilet privileges or showers were infrequent. More frequent were the drunken apologies from my captors for having had to nab me in the plant.

A courier went back and forth daily between my 'house arrest' and the factory. My colleagues wrote me ten versions of "Hang in there. It's almost over."

It crossed my mind more than once during my detention that, as a contractor, my safety was probably not the highest priority during the CIA operation I was a part of. If they had wanted to, they could have quickly pulled me out. When it was all over, Clint never did satisfactorily explain the details. All he said was, "Extremely unfortunate occurrence but a very successful operation. Thank you, Andy!"

Clint and I agreed it would be best not to let Jane know about that particular unscheduled side trip. As it turned out, the diversion and hysteria that surrounded my kidnapping had taken the pressure off the agents performing the real mission. Unnoticed amid the commotion between labor and management, they came away with huge amounts of data and other material from the plant. Clint hoped I would just view my kidnapping as a promotion to hazardous duty. For that job, he paid me an additional $500.

Locked away during the week, I'd not been able to call home. When I finally got back to Krakow, I faced the music and the accusations as usual. Of course I couldn't tell Renata what had actually happened and where I'd been. Even if I had, there would be no sympathy for me and I'd have listened to a tirade about how "stupid you were for having allowed it to happen." Instead, I put a lid on the tongue lashing by quickly handing her the entire $1,000 for the week. It was a sum unheard of for the times and certainly covered the cost of the washer-dryer with quite a bit to spare for other luxuries. What pained me now wasn't losing the entire $1,000, but rather the realization that I no longer felt the joy I used to get from giving Renata special gifts and see her astonished, joyful reaction to my lavish presents.

***

By now, though, all that was way in the past. What had been a pretty terrifying ordeal at the time had mellowed into a good story. I had somewhat convinced myself that I could handle these dangerous situations — even though I hadn't done anything to keep myself out of that one, or to get myself out of it, either.

I'm pretty sure Jane was thinking about all this, too.

"Clint, I'm outta here sometime in the next three to six months," she said. "What's it look like for Andy? I'm not your go-between anymore; you'll need to find someone else to call him in to see Blake at the Marine Bar. And anyway, I'll be in D.C. a lot of the time. With all three of us here, now, give us an update. Can you tell us *anything*?"

Clint was brief but very official.

"An anti-terrorism team called AT Group is being formed. The guy who runs it is Joe. Just Joe. As the Soviet Union has disintegrated, strategic materials of all kinds, including nuclear weapons, are at risk of getting in the wrong hands. An American University report detailed that risk. That report was delivered to all the staff six months ago. It has given birth to this group." Clint ended it there.

We were curious: was there more?

Suddenly, that article I'd cut out from the *Herald Tribune* in the Marine Bar came to mind. The story was about the ex-KGB guy selling plutonium. Pulling it out of my wallet, I handed it to Clint. Clint nodded affirmatively. "Those are the guys we're after. When Joe arrives in Warsaw, I'll bring Andy in for an interview. That's what I can say now. Until then, we might have you meet Natalya again in Moscow."

"No complaints there, Clint," I assured him. I had visions of that LBD Natalya had worn that night when she arrived at my room. I also realized sadly that Renata hadn't even shown me the similar dress she'd gotten for herself from the extra cash I earned from that Ternopil, Ukraine job.

Jane growled at both of us. She forced herself to ignore our obnoxious fun and asked Clint, "Is this new group focused on nuclear weapons and missile sites? Or on the material for making bombs?"

"The contractors we trust — the ones we'll retain for the AT Group — will be assigned to projects related to the disappearance of plutonium and uranium or other nuclear related materials. So I guess it's the latter, Jane, as far as Andy is concerned."

"Let's take that article that Andy brought in. How much damage can fifty-seven kilograms of plutonium do, Clint?" Jane asked. "I'm trying to get an understanding of the urgency and scale of what this AT Group is going to be doing."

Clint squinted, acting like he was trying to remember details from his meeting about the new group. "Five kilograms is enough for a rudimentary 'Trinity' device that could kill a hundred thousand people. It's not a linear relationship, though. So fifty-seven kilograms could wipe out a city of more than a million. That depends, of course, on whether the buyer has conscripted the help of a team of guys who knew how to do the Trinity-style detonation. Sense of urgency and scale there enough for you?"

"Oh, my fucking God! I get it," Jane replied, clutching her chest. I felt my heart skip a beat, too. I realized I'd been seeing reports coming out almost daily in all the European newspapers about illegal sales of plutonium and uranium.

Clint shared with us part of the American University white paper he had mentioned.

Against the backdrop of the former Soviet Union continuing its implosion in an almost anarchic world of corrupt former communists, rich opportunists, and millions of disillusioned citizens, the U.S. government realizes that former Soviet strategic materials and nuclear weaponry are all at risk of being lost to outright theft or sale. Unpaid and hungry soldiers are posted at secure installations all over the former Soviet bloc. There are Russian military facilities that are not being financed to maintain their weapons nor protect them from outside terrorist threats. Strategic materials produced and housed at hundreds of facilities all over the former Soviet Bloc represent an unimaginable security risk to the entire world.

The CIA is well aware of the situation.

***

Clint had introduced me to the head of this new anti-terrorist program. "Joe, this is Andy Gold. Andy, this is Joe." No last name. Joe didn't volunteer it, either. The interview was uninspiring. He mostly asked me a lot of questions about my family and work situation. Toward the end, Joe alternated staring at me and scanning the file in front of him. "In 1927, your grandfather changed his name from Lick to Gold."

I was surprised he'd brought it up but just nodded.

"Any idea why?"

I knew why. "He started rough-necking the Oklahoma oil fields and took a lot of ribbing for his name. So when he chose a new one, he might have been doing some wishful thinking. You know: black Gold."

"I see. A Gold with blond hair and blue eyes. I don't know what I expected." Joe was still staring at me. To me, he looked a bit like an Italian hit man from the movies, but he seemed very composed. Without another word, he nodded to signal the discussion was over. He stood, smiled, and shook my hand.

During the several months since then, things had gotten more interesting. Even though I didn't go anywhere, I was having a lot of fun learning about high-end spy stuff. Joe had approved my spending time with his technical people, martial-arts instructors, and some seasoned CIA desk staffers who split their time between Warsaw and Moscow. Having been a pretty fair wrestler in high school, I especially enjoyed the mixed martial arts instruction, delivered CIA style. That meant an emphasis on ending a fight quickly — and permanently.

I had to learn how to plant tracking devices on people and in their bags. I would be carrying cameras and microphones. Taking photos of people and places would now be within my scope of work — if they ever decided to use me. I learned how to secretly set up parabolic microphones to record conversations across whatever room or bar I might be in.

Calibrating other instruments and setting up sensors came along with the anti-terrorist work, as well. Although, in fairness, after Chernobyl, I had already gotten very good at calibrating my own Geiger counter.

The biggest problem I had at the time, beyond my constant personal re-assessment of the sanity of doing this work, was dealing with and keeping my day job. When I had been NatEx's country director for Poland, staying on top of that responsibility had been a challenge. Even though my salary with NatEx had shot up to over twenty times the national average, that money was nowhere to be seen. Renata's obsessive program to change our lives had dramatically taken over. Most important for her was to high-tail it out of nasty Nowa Huta and move into Krakow's high-rent district. Just then, while NatEx was failing in Europe and sending signals that my days with them were numbered, a group of traders and marketing guys caught my attention. Most of the other get-rich-quick schemes from my early years in Poland had gone sour, but these guys had a way of making money from just about anything they got involved in. I decided to get to know them better.

Wanted: A New Day Job

In as much as I didn't see myself standing in bazaars selling underwear and t-shirts by the container load, I wasn't averse to doing international trade in goods. I knew there was a lot of money to be made that way and there were trading companies in Poland making money hand over fist. I didn't have a lot of experience at this, but the one caper I'd tried had turned out pretty well. So maybe, it occurred to me, I might just be able to invent some kind of wheeler-dealer gig for myself.

These days, I reassured myself, things weren't nearly as dangerous as they'd been eight years earlier, at the height of the Cold War. That was the time I'd grabbed an opportunity to cash in on a pile of old banknotes. I had smuggled them out of Poland and sold them at auction in Los Angeles.

It was during my first full year in Poland, just after martial law had been lifted. I was renting a room from an old woman with connections to history. Mrs. Malikowska, then seventy-eight years old, was the widow of a Polish Secret Service agent who had been killed on the first day of the German invasion, on September 1, 1939. As it happened, she had a large collection of old banknotes. Some of her bills dated as far back as the late 1700s when paper currency was gaining popularity. Mostly, though, they were Russian, Austrian, Prussian and German notes from the time of Polish Partition. Divided among Russia, Prussia, and Austria, Poland had been wiped off the map for almost 125 years. After her husband's death, Halina Malikowska had found his stash of old banknotes in his 'war chest.' She'd hidden it in the attic of their old country house. When the Red Army came through in the summer of 1944, flushing out the Germans, she had to move the chest to her apartment in Warsaw. During the long, cold winter four decades later, she had seen me fooling around with a little hobby of mine, buying up coins and banknotes in the flea markets around Warsaw. She finally got up the courage to ask if I'd take a look at her collection. She pulled the old chest out from under her bed and opened the lid. Wrapped, sealed packs of untouched notes from the early 1800s filled the case.

I called my brother, David, in Phoenix and asked him to find out what they might be worth. With my description of what I had, he found a buyer who was going to be at a big banknote conference in LA in a few months. Halina wanted to sell me the notes for one hundred dollars. She was embarrassed asking for so much money. I gave her five hundred.

So I knew there was a tidy profit to be made. I also knew that I'd have to take some pretty serious risks getting this illicit stash out of Communist Poland, into Communist East Germany and finally through the Iron Curtain, when that was still a maze of concrete walls, barbed wire, minefields and guard towers. But even then, ambition — or maybe you could just call it greed — got the better of my fears and I went for it.

Getting caught trying to smuggle the notes out of Poland would have been the Polish equivalent of a gross misdemeanor, punishable by up to five years in prison. I succeeded in getting them out by slipping a pack or two of the notes behind the headrests of forty seats on a train to West Berlin. The idea had come to me as I sat on the empty train an hour before departure trying to find hiding places for my contraband. Adjusting my own headrest as I sat and pondered my task, I saw a quarter inch gap between the wall and the fake leather pad. I easily slipped one of my banknote bundles into that gap. It disappeared nicely into the void. I'd found my hiding places.

Though I was nervous as hell going through East German customs and passport control, the only real hiccup came when I had to retrieve the packs. I'd inserted them behind the headrests hours before the train departed from Poznan, with no other passengers on board. In West Berlin, the train was now full of German passengers and about to continue on for Paris. I had six or seven minutes to enter seven compartments, apologize for disturbing the passengers, then visibly push the packs out of the spaces between wall and headrest. My tool for this was a thin Polish-language textbook, an annotated version of *Das Kapital* by Karl Marx, that fit perfectly into the gaps.

To cries of "Smuggler!" "Thief!" and "Drug addict!" I marched through the car retrieving all forty packs of bills before the train set off for Paris. In L.A. two days later, I sold my smuggled banknote collection for $25,000. Back in Warsaw the following month, I shared some of my profits with Halina. She was tickled pink.

**

Even with all that Cold-War intrigue behind us, I still had to figure out how to straddle the gap between Western corporate ways and Poland's lingering Socialist habits. Running the NatEx operation in Poland wasn't the typical overnight shipping job that one might imagine it to be in the United States. I doubt that many of my U.S.-based colleagues at NatEx, which had won a dozen awards for management and business ethics around the world, would have believed everything a country director would have to spend time on: arranging overseas study and travel visas for contractors and their children, as well as organizing and paying bribes to get help with customs clearance. But for our agent in Poland, none of this was out of the normal scheme of doing business. That agent was a company called POLOT, Poland's state aviation enterprise, which we had selected to carry out all deliveries and pickups in the country.

POLOT wasn't just a commercial operation. It had been a good Commie with a secretive military division, too. During the Korean and Vietnam Wars, it had worked with the North Koreans, the North Vietnamese and the Russians, taking American fighter jets that had been shot down and dissecting them for intelligence purposes. During one of my early meetings with POLOT and NatEx's European management team, a touchy question came up: Did anyone with POLOT know anything about American MIAs or POWs? As it turned out, the CEO for NatEx Europe had been a pilot in Vietnam. POLOT had been asked that question before. Its people had been trained to say they had no knowledge of anything like that. On that subject, POLOT's director always acted like he was one step ahead of everyone's thinking. Once he told me that he would eventually tell me about the MIA-POWs that he knew about. However, most of the other middle managers at POLOT thought he was full of shit. They told me to ignore him. From day one he made it clear that our relationship would get better every day if he and I took care of each other first, and only then worry about NatEx and POLOT. He had his own priorities.

As it turned out, though, it wasn't POLOT that was the weak partner. It became clear that NatEx's losses in Western Europe were going to bring down its whole operation throughout the rest of the continent. It was just a matter of time before pink slips would be sent out to the agents and country directors — the only real NatEx employees — in Eastern Europe.

All this weighed heavily on me. Keeping a real job in Poland was critical. Losing the NatEx position was devastating. I had the equivalent of a green card — permission to stay in the country — because I was married to a Polish woman. That wasn't as solid a pillar to lean on as it had been once, but I tried not to worry about that too much. Sure, she'd threatened to pull the plug on our marriage enough times that I could usually sense when arguments were getting ratcheted up for that ultimatum. I knew it wasn't a good sign that I was becoming numb to these attacks. What I couldn't imagine, though, was a state of affairs that would exclude me from being with Malgosia and Staszek. Practically speaking, and critical to my work, having a job with a major multinational provided the cover I needed to travel to Russia and other countries. The CIA contractor role depended on this; they were certainly not going to provide cover for me in the 'limited-liability' arrangement that we kept. That came only from having a credible position in the business or academic worlds. My work at the embassy was steady enough; Clint had kept his promise by getting me hooked into the new Anti-Terrorist Group. Joe encouraged me to stick with the team and suggested that I would be given an assignment soon. But I couldn't keep my travel visas active unless I had the cover of an official job. I began looking for ways to slide into another official role, preferably another corporate ex-pat job to get an American or British firm started in the region.

Sweet-Aire

So, without a real job in Poland now, I was afraid of losing the small nest egg I had accumulated in an account at Deutsche Bank in Berlin. I intended to keep the one promise I had made to my wife: to upgrade our living arrangement to a nice flat in Krakow. Regardless of whether the marriage was in a death spiral or not, it was an investment that would return very handsomely… for someone. In my short years with NatEx, at least I had made considerable progress towards accomplishing that, for my family if not for myself. I didn't want to put that money at risk. The idea of going into high-volume retail goods, with that nest egg exposed, brought on nightmares.

At the time, I didn't dwell much on the irony. That my urge to keep body, soul and marriage together was pushing me into more and more adventures in the wild East. And each new gig was pulling me farther and farther away, for longer and longer. Now, of course, I can see how this was exactly the last thing I needed if preserving my marriage was really my goal.

"Renata, when I was coming over on the flight after the NatEx miracle happened—" I began.

"Jesus!" she cut me off. "You start again! Miracle for whom? Promises of a new life and a chance for us. It is your promise of a life without us. And I can help put the icing on your fucking Miracle Cake!" She was trying to head off any attempt I might make to justify the sacrifice we were all making.

I kept trying. "This has been very difficult for me. It's not my favorite thing in the world to live my life in hotels and eat on the run."

"Let's say it's your second favorite thing. You are surely fucking everything that moves in all your loneliness!" she shot back.

"Renata! Please!"

Malgosia suddenly came around the corner, tears in her eyes, and threw her book at me. She ran to her room and shut the door.

"And you will probably say that you didn't even know she was home! Of course you didn't know! You are an idiot for bringing it up again."

My goal had been to reduce the anxiety at home in anticipation of an AT Group assignment. Once again, I failed.

***

Contemplating expanding my work search into sales and business development for a retail-oriented company, I think I was dazzled by the prospect of dollar signs, among other things. It was clear to me that the entrepreneurial activity, abuzz all over Eastern Europe and the former Soviet Union, was making a lot of millionaires.

I looked at the foreign firms operating in Poland, knowing my contacts with the hundred or more multinationals already here were quite good. Trying to find the firm that needed *me*, the abandoned NatEx guy, was my goal. Unfortunately, my NatEx failures and woes were common knowledge among the multi-national chamber of commerce members I schmoozed with.

Perhaps the NatEx experience and my resulting loss of personal credibility had put a bad taste in my mouth about another multi-national gig. On the other hand, I couldn't help seeing smaller companies making a go of it in Poland, doing international trade, and often signing cooperation agreements with big overseas firms. One of those upstart firms, Sweet-Aire, was of special interest. It was run by a young Polish guy named Antek Pakulski. Documents from Russia, Africa, the U.S., and Canada made their way to the small home-based office just off Ulica Nowy Swiat — New World Street — in an exclusive shopping district. I'd made a habit of keeping track of what they were receiving from around the world and how many express documents they were sending out. Something interesting was going on at Sweet-Aire.

I was first introduced to Antek as the co-author of a guidebook to Warsaw. I knew the team of Americans who surrounded him were assembling other guidebooks to cities throughout Eastern Europe and Russia. To me, that didn't sound like a millionaire-making business. Curious about what else he might be up to, I decided to get more closely acquainted.

One day, to catch the Sweet-Aire team a bit off guard, I showed up in my NatEx courier outfit. They all knew I was the big boss in Poland. They also assumed I was above anything like carrying packages in a delivery-boy uniform. Antek, Toby, and their latest sidekick, the very New York — very Brooklyn — friend, Nate, burst out laughing when they saw me. The laughter erupted again when I started handing out free NatEx model airplanes, T-shirts, hats, courier bags, and pens. Bribery, large and small, was everything in Poland, even among young Americans.

The laughter was short-lived. After they'd gotten their little bribes, all three returned to a heated argument about their tour guidebook business. They were talking over each other again, each insisting on his own version of how the upcoming St. Petersburg book should be done and who was going to do it. After about twenty minutes of this verbal free-for-all, Antek put his hands up and shushed the two Americans. "Jesus Christ! Andy the NatEx man is here! Can we stop for a minute and have a cup of coffee with him?"

Nate was the first to be the funny guy. "So… this Andy can't go over to Nowy Swiat and get a cup of joe on his own? He's gotta interrupt our doin' business?" After delivering this hyper-New York working-man monologue, Nate delivered a grin and said he'd make the coffee.

Evidently disgusted at such frivolity, Toby left the room.

Antek's lovely girlfriend, Agnieszka, went with Nate to make the coffee. Agnieszka struck me as the perfect partner: intelligent and beautiful, with a very good sense of humor in the strange world she and Antek were operating in. I pined away for such a relationship. At one time, I'd thought Renata had some of those partner qualities.

Toby stood nearly two meters tall — more than six feet — and with long, dark hair, was rock-star guitarist sort of handsome. But he was also one of those serious, 'Do it right and do it according to the plan' guys. That conflicted with his apparent weakness for beautiful women, which tended to come up in the middle of big deals. And this, according to Nate, was why Toby wasn't a twenty-five-year-old billionaire. Nate's story about Toby rang with a special tone for me. As he told it afterwards, he paused, looking at me with a frozen smile, knowing I was recognizing that weakness in myself. When I looked away, he broke up laughing, shaking his head and pointing at me, "Yeah! You better listen! Strike a chord, Dude?"

Now Nate, he was the hyper-intelligent, think-out-of-the-box, and 'Take no prisoners' kind of guy. He was also constantly saying, "They shouldn't pay anyone so stupid as to trust us." Which I thought sounded kind of ominous for me if I was going to be working with them. Nate's stocky frame, close-cropped, curly, light brown hair, and constant laugh — usually at times when others were mortified — made him a bit of a scary character.

Antek was slim, always stylishly dressed including a scarf, and sported long brown hair. He was handsome enough but had an unusually long chin that reminds me now of a younger Jay Leno. Antek saw art, opportunity, money, and stardom all wrapped up in Sweet-Aire's wide-ranging scope of activity. He spoke English with a flair and he could weave poetry into anything he was talking about.

Toby and Antek had been in business together for about a year but already seemed to be on the outs. Toby was convinced that Russia was where they needed to be. Nate, the outsider, agreed with Toby. While working for a famous ad agency in New York, Nate had been seconded to Poland with sound equipment to produce some events for high-value clients. Seeing bigger opportunities for himself, he had borrowed money to buy the equipment. Now he was looking for a way to collect the insurance money for it — but also to keep the equipment. Maybe that's why Nate agreed with Toby that Poland was going stale and they needed a change. Toby imagined himself in the lobbies of Moscow's hooker-filled hotels, doing business with the world's most beautiful women. Nate's plan, perhaps slightly more realistic, was to follow and use the insurance money to get them all set up in Moscow.

So I was huddled with Antek trying to get a pulse on how we might work together, using my AMCHAM contacts to help Sweet-Aire. After about ten minutes of this, Toby came back in and signaled that it was time to start round three of their argument. Antek grudgingly excused himself. He followed Toby to another room and the yelling started again.

With a better understanding, now, of how Sweet-Aire had started from advertising and gone to book publishing, with a few side trips into the world of black-market deals and now more legitimate overseas trading, I thought I could offer them some guidance. I had explained to Antek that I might help him in selecting a deal or several deals to get involved in, and could work to make them happen. And hopefully getting us filthy rich along the way. Antek suggested I look through their files and accumulated piles of paper and see if I saw anything interesting. Which is how, left alone in the fax room, I started looking.

***

There were three fax machines. This was top-of-the-line Panasonic equipment for 1992, all running non-stop. Each printed document, communique, or product image would emerge, automatically be cut, and fall into a neat bin at the base of the table. And no sooner did each fax slide onto the twelve-inch stack that it disappeared under the next one, right on top of it. A squeal followed by a shrill modem tone signaled that another potential million-dollar deal was being delivered to Sweet-Aire's International Trade Division, prestigiously situated in the heart of beautiful Warsaw, Poland. I watched this non-stop communication facility for a few minutes while listening to Antek and Toby screaming behind the door.

Satisfied that I understood how the production line worked, I decided to inspect some of the documents themselves. At random, I pulled out of the bin a formal sales offer in English:

"GOOD FOR 72 HOURS..." was emblazoned across the top of the cover page. It was for:

two 40 ft containers of raw Robusta coffee beans from Kenya... FOB Lagos, Nigeria.

Price: $25,000.

Payment by Letter of Credit to a bank in Switzerland or by cash at the port where the containers are located. Quality Inspection allowed only after Letter of Credit received or cash in hand.

Interesting. Antek was into coffee from Africa. That fit. He was on the right street; Nowy Swiat had the best cafes in Poland. He could sell the coffee right from his flat. A deeply cultural Polish guy doing some business in markets where Poland had lagged behind since all the changes began in the eighties. "Bet he's into wine, too," I thought.

Next fax: From Russia. AU. Gold! Shit! Twenty tons of it! It looked like something about the United Arab Emirates being in on the deal. "Delivery from UAE to any European port." The reproduction on this document was very bad. I would say the fax had been sent from a fax from a fax from a fax. The 'tail of intermediaries' in this deal looked like it was long. But then again... the commission from twenty tons of gold might cover the cost of THAT tail.

Next fax: "Ten Russian MIG fighter pilot helmets equipped with the latest eye sensor targeting material in the face plate." Unheard of, at least by me at the time, this technology apparently allowed the pilot to target weaponry using eye movements to activate the release of bombs or missiles or whatever. The English text was marginal but the document that came out of the machine looked very fresh, with Russian seals and old Soviet stamps complete with hammer and sickle. "Price: $10,000 per helmet... negotiable."

And there was so much more!

Heat-seeking missiles... ten truckloads of Lithuanian rough-cut lumber... ten containers of men's bikini underwear from China... 162 BMWs, model 320i... rare earth metals from Siberian research institutes... ten different requests for Portland cement from Turkey and Ukraine... steel from China... night vision goggles from Russia... a thousand AK-47s... high purity titanium. And then, for those looking for various inputs to the nuclear industry, the military, do-it-yourself terrorism, and possibly dirty-bomb making, there were offers and requests for plutonium in varying quantities... zirconium tubes for Russian-style nuclear reactor fuel rods... heavy water... uranium-235... uranium-238... depleted uranium in various forms and, the most disturbing of all, a short fax in Russian that could be translated as follows:

Available in any quantity:

Russian and former Soviet weapons of ANY type (including nuclear). Price and delivery NEGOTIABLE.

While Toby and Antek's argument raged, I collected about thirty of the most interesting and/or disturbing offers and requests for offers and tucked them into my NatEx courier pouch. Sensing that this round of fighting between the members of Sweet-Aire's management board was going to go on unabated for a while, I scribbled out a note to Antek.

'Antek, we need to talk about some stuff... possible cooperation in the future.

My NatEx gig is probably ending soon. I've got some ideas.

Oh... and I took a few of your more interesting faxes. By the way, there's some stuff there that you need to be careful with.

Please call tomorrow.

Andy'

My Own A-T Group Mission

Waiting around for Antek to finally call me, I had already been to the embassy with copies of my faxes. I also had my tried-and-true spy collaborator look at what I had taken from Sweet-Aire's 'trade communications center.' He was country manager for Techdyne and had been trading in strategic materials for a couple of decades. His top-secret security clearance gave him access to a lot of information I could only dream about having. Antek didn't need to know that I saw a CIA recruitment opportunity for myself among all the faxes he was getting about strategic materials and military hardware. I knew that intelligence guys from the U.S., Israel, and Germany were already in Poland sniffing out and sourcing the real sellers of this stuff. I thought I could open that door for myself by giving the CIA desk a heads-up on what I'd found.

One concern I had about using these documents was that if I was accepted as a materials tracker, the CIA would begin monitoring Antek's phone lines if they weren't already. It was an unsavory thought that I might be causing a good friend to be watched. But then again, if any of the stuff I saw was real, it was an opportunity for me to insert myself into the 'Track a Terrorist' game in Eastern Europe and Russia. Hungry for success in any of my work spheres, I was obsessed with hitting it big financially. I wasn't afraid to push the AT Group to get myself inserted into the game. Joe, the Anti-Terrorist Group's leader, was already very busy with dozens of reports about nuclear material making its way out of Russia and into dangerous hands. I saw my efforts at Sweet-Aire as my desperate attempt to get Joe's attention. He was running this show from Poland but managing teams all over the Eurasian world. My gamble with the handful of strange deal docs I'd pulled out of Sweet-Aire wasn't something Joe had any reason to spend time with. That was worrisome. I needed help to turn his focus to Poland.

***

Before I'd gone to the embassy with my 'magic' faxes, I decided I needed to make a call on an old friend in Krakow. This was Dennis, my spy buddy at Techdyne, whose official business was selling... the Hydra Floss. I knew Dennis could give me a reality check about a lot of the items the faxes described. I knew that most of them were bogus but there was a lot of information in them... including names and sources. While I disliked his telling me to stay away from stuff I don't know or understand, he'd usually relent and tell me things I needed to know. He'd also helped me get ahold of a Geiger counter during the Chernobyl disaster and set me up with some other devices he "happened to have lying around." Why he might need a radiation detector to sell dental-hygiene gadgets, I never asked him. Another mysterious thing about Techdyne's operation in Krakow was that it had the first fiber optic connection for communications and internet anywhere in southern Poland. No individual company would have paid the money it took to secure the permits to have the three-hundred-kilometer line run, underground no less. His telecoms and computer room looked like a major government contractor's NOC. That bit of tech jargon means Network Operations Center, and it looked like it could have been monitoring who knows what all over Eastern Europe.

Dennis decided he had to tell me that he and his wife had sex in the computer room almost daily. Their excuse, as he explained it, was the number of hours they had to spend in there, relaying data around the world. Dennis would always start with a crude joke, telling me not to sit here or put my hands there because that was where they had been doing it just a while ago. I could understand his wanting to brag. Ms. Jaworski was an attractive woman. Dennis always counted on me to affirm that fact. Still, I always got a funny feeling he would have killed me if I ever made too much eye contact with her.

Part of the reason I reached out to Dennis was that I knew he'd call or see the same people I was in contact with at the embassy. And in doing that, he'd give them a report about me. That was free advertising to the people who needed confirmation that I was still worthy to keep my job.

Techdyne was an American company that bought and brokered deals involving strategic materials of all kinds. It was filled with ex-spooks and techies who knew what all the systems integrators were doing and what sorts of materials were on the market or would be soon. It wasn't in

Poland to make money selling the Hydra Floss. Believe me, it was a front for the real objective: gaining access to some of the same materials I'd seen on those faxes. And you can be assured of another thing. Techdyne was working with my embassy folks at a much higher level of cooperation than I'd been granted. My narrowly tailored orders to do specific things were kid's stuff compared to the cooperation agreements Techdyne shared with the CIA. And while I was starting to get an itch to play in that league, I was also hearing a voice of caution in the back of my head. Maybe I was better off not knowing certain things. For the CIA, the company was one of its subject-area experts, helping to monitor so-called 'bad stuff' that might be coming out of Eastern Europe and Siberia. Techdyne was also a 'buyer' that could take ownership of materials related to the nuclear industry. And in so doing, it could take such things out of the hands of opportunistic sellers. That diversion would stop the potential outflow to terrorists or other unfriendly players who intended to use them themselves or to sell them to terrorists.

When I showed Dennis the faxes, he got excited. That night, he admitted he had become an active participant in the new AT-Group but wouldn't be going on missions. His contribution, he explained, would be made from his office in Krakow. I couldn't shake that image of him and his wife protecting the world from terrorism as they fucked like rabbits in their computer room.

I'd like to be able to say I was doing my best to force my big head to do the thinking in the covert world I was descending deeper into. The life that Dennis was living and the world that I'd regularly been taste-testing was irresistible. Renata and I were no longer mates; certainly not mating. Sad about it at times, but mostly mad about it, thoughts of Agata or Natalya or some of the other ladies I'd met in my travels had something to do with why this new life appealed to me so much. What had happened along the way that made a blanket, a bottle of wine, and a romp in the wildflower-filled meadows of Poland impossible now?

As I descended into my melancholy state, Dennis got serious, most likely because he guessed — or already knew — that I had an AT-Group mission in my future. That's when he gave me one of my first lectures on tracking terrorists.

The rules of the 'Track a Terrorist' game were simple. Adding Dennis's sugar coating to his high-school-level overview made it even simpler. His instructions were always either to "Follow People," or "Follow Stuff."

First, Dennis gave me highlights from the mission statement and ground rules. He motioned for me to join him in the Com Center. I immediately thought I smelled sex when I walked in. It was probably my imagination. He pulled out some files and started picking pages from a classified document on nuclear terrorism and handing them to me to examine as he spoke. "Stuff that people have and that we don't want them to have doesn't always stay with them." I nodded and he went on. "It's important to know who or what is being tracked. 'Stuff' is the general term for whatever material is being tracked. 'Bad Stuff' is usually poisonous or could hurt you in some way during transit. 'Hot Stuff' is the term for radioactive stuff that is — obviously — also Bad Stuff.'" He looked at me and asked, "Are you interested in this? Shall I go on?"

"Yes, yes! Please do!" I replied with enthusiasm — possibly hoping his wife might appear and demand a threesome right there in the Com Center. She was both Hot Stuff and Good Stuff at the same time I secretly mused.

He went on. "You will be instructed when you can touch or take stuff. Say, like removing something from a train that has reached the end of its scheduled service with no one there to receive it. You know what I mean?"

"Yes. Like the trains that empty at *Warszawa Centralna* and then sit on the sidings up the track at *Warszawa Glowna*?"

"Exactly." After a moment, Dennis changed the subject. "Do you do martial arts?"

"Some. Why?" I responded. The question gave me pause to think. *Am I ready for this?* I thought of myself as a lover, not a fighter. I could take care of myself and had been able to gauge the level of danger pretty well — so far. *Besides,* I tried to reassure myself, *they don't send contractors out on jobs with an imminent threat of harm lurking about. Do they?* Even that kidnapping in Ternopil had been pretty low key. *Sort of.*

"Just curious if you will be authorized to intervene in a bad situation," Dennis said. "Better to be able to take care of yourself if you do have to act."

"I see. I'll keep it in mind. Thanks." I didn't know how to respond to his curiosity but hoped he would continue.

Knowing that we were always allowed to bail out at the slightest hint of danger, I asked Dennis, "Will Joe want his money back if I ever have to abort a mission?"

Dennis shook his head and wrinkled his nose. "Nah. Unlikely. Valuable intelligence comes in all forms," he explained. "Even if all you can get is pictures and recorded data about the stuff and/or the bad guys, that will be highly regarded." I felt an enormous sense of relief with what Dennis was suggesting. It was becoming harder and harder to see a downside to taking on AT-Group missions. At this, Dennis gathered all the docs he'd been showing me. He returned them to his file and locked it.

Next to the filing cabinet was a small refrigerator. He reached in and brought out a bottle of *Wyborowa* vodka. I followed him to the guest room. Still no wife around. I was disappointed.

"Let's go over common situations the handbook doesn't say much about." He poured out two healthy glasses and sat down again. "Difficult situations might arise if you know the stuff is extremely dangerous and innocent passengers are unknowingly being exposed. On the other hand, radioactive material isn't always easily detectable. It might be transported in special containers that would make it relatively safe."

"I've been reviewing all the containers used in Europe," I told Dennis. "At least I know that much."

He seemed unimpressed. "Then again," Dennis continued, "It could be very dangerous if unshielded material is tossed into a potato sack and banged around like regular luggage on a three-thousand-mile journey across Asia and Europe. In a case like that, if the hot stuff is on a train or bus or sits in a station, you should consider finding some reason or another to suggest that passengers take other seats."

"Sounds like you've run into situation like this," I ventured.

"Joe told me about one of his star agents." Dennis downed a whole glass of vodka and waited until I followed him with mine. "He had to be careful and a little sneaky in a certain situation. Couldn't draw attention to himself. He spilled coffee on a seat that was directly under a brown paper parcel that had some hot stuff in it. Knowing it was unshielded, he was very effective in making that particular seat the worst place to sit on the whole train."

We were reaching a point with the vodka that we both knew it was time to quit. Dennis was pretty much a goner by then and I was having a hard time focusing after all the liquor we'd thrown down our necks, but his tutorial had set my mind to working. He made me appreciate a few key facts: balancing on the knife edge between fear of life in prison if caught and getting rich from one successful delivery can make people do crazy things. I could also see that, from the standpoint of the contractor, adrenaline and testosterone were a powerful fuel mix for pushing a mission into orbit. Adding alcohol and cash, though, could blind whoever had their hands on the controls.

By now I'd learned that the AT Group focused its efforts on North Korea, Iran, Afghanistan and Pakistan, plus some Muslim groups in Africa and the Middle East. All of them were trying to get their hands on Russian bomb-quality uranium and plutonium. Several of these groups had already pulled off some transactions to get the material they wanted. The AT Group was very busy now, along with intelligence agencies from other worried Western countries. Right along with what the CIA was doing, the Israelis and the German military had their own watch lists. Post-Soviet generals and other rogue military officers were viewed as particularly vulnerable to the temptation of stealing a nuclear device and selling it to whomever they could. When the Soviet bloc fell and its military machine ground to a halt, millions of soldiers and workers on military installations went hungry. High levels of resentment against Gorbachev's *Glasnost* and *Perestroika* were evident everywhere. And as Soviet state assets were being sold off to privateers, all those hungry military people saw their chance. Since the Fatherland had just caved in to capitalism and its assets were for sale, why shouldn't they take their cut? This incredibly dangerous time in the former Soviet bloc countries was, for me — despite the allure of adventure — the scariest of all during my years there.

***

Joe's review of the faxes I'd waltzed into the embassy with, together with a good recommendation from Dennis, got me at least part of what I wanted. The CIA accepted my plan to monitor the faxes coming into Antek's office at Sweet-Aire. It wasn't as exciting as playing cat-and-mouse with Russian prostitutes, but it was still pretty cool. And it helped solve my money problems. This became a paid job. As I was unable to tell Renata anything about my CIA contract work, it was called 'embassy work' at home. It included regular review meetings to assess and act on the most interesting information that continued to stream non-stop out of the 'triple-threat' fax machines. Antek's little company became quite the hot topic at the CIA desk in Warsaw. As a window into the darkest dealings of the growing nuclear threat in Siberia, it was monitored closely. Joe gave me very simple instructions. He asked that I collect all the faxes that came in. Others would decide which were 'actionable.'

Joe's time was being split between a lot of Eastern European and Middle Eastern countries. He was busy coordinating contractors throughout those regions. That meant sometimes I wouldn't see him for up to two weeks at a time. During one of these periods, I noticed a fax advertising "strategic materials and devices related to space industry and military science" that included a Warsaw phone number. I decided to check it out myself without telling Joe. Antek and I worked on it together.

By now, Antek probably knew I was less interested in this offer's business aspects and more interested in showing it to my embassy contacts. Antek could tell that I had no appetite for financial risk, especially when it meant I'd be even deeper in the dog house with Renata if I lost the money I'd been saving, for our big lifestyle upgrade. Even worse was the aspect of getting involved in risky international deals that required being away for extended periods. On the other hand, Antek and Agnieszka thrived on that thrill of the deal. Even more so if it was in a scary place like Lagos or Timbuktu. For me, the best mix of excitement, managed risk, and guaranteed income was exactly what I had been doing. And it could be even better, now, with the excitement of upping the stakes — and money — with the AT Group. I never admitted to Antek that I had a relationship with the CIA Desk—but all the same, he joked about it constantly.

This was the fax that caught our eye:

ATTENTION!

Russian Scientists and Team of Business Executives Offer:

1) Very High Purity Aviation/Aerospace Grade Aluminum and Titanium for Sale

2) Multiple locations in Russia for purchase and retrieval

3) Willing to provide a team of specialists to assist in operation.

4) Possible access to other strategic materials and devices related to space industry

Call 0-48-22-XXXXXXX

I hoped this would get more than Joe's usual raised eyebrows or non-committal "This is interesting" comments. But I also saw some interesting possibilities for myself. And that's how I ended up in the lobby of the Warsaw Marriott with Antek and that Russian wheeler-dealer who called himself Dima. Our apologies to Miss World.

Invitation to Siberia

"Interesting that there is a phone number and it's a Warsaw number," Antek noted. He suggested, "Let me call and speak in Polish. If they can speak Polish, that is."

The call went through. On the speakerphone, I heard a male voice answer in English.

"Hello, Dmitri here."

Antek replied in Polish: "Good day. I'm Antek. Can you speak Polish?"

And now Dmitri was speaking Polish. "Not well but passable. Better in Russian or English."

At this, Antek shifted the rest of the conversation back to English. "I am calling about the fax related to high-purity aluminum and titanium. Can you tell me more or can we meet to talk about it? I see you are in Warsaw. Or at least this is a Warsaw number."

"Yes, I am in Warsaw. Will you be representing yourself? And, if not, who is the buyer?" Dmitri, obviously a Russian, asked with some amount of doubt audible in his voice. "Are you an intermediary? What nationality are you and who is the buyer… or interested party?" It was clear he was dubious about talking to a Pole.

"If we can meet," Antek said, "there will be an American with me representing American interests here in Warsaw. He is the managing director of the Polish office of a multinational firm." And then it was Antek's turn for grilling. "And may I ask who you are and who you represent? Also, do you have something concrete we can look at? Something that will help us figure out if this is really something we want to pursue?"

"Just as the fax says, there is a group of Russian businessmen and some scientists, also from Russia, involved in the sale of these items. I am part of the business side of this deal and I am closely connected to the scientific interests that have made this opportunity available. I have papers, photos, and a proposed 'extraction plan' with me." Dmitri continued to push Antek with his questions. "So: is this American just an intermediary or somehow connected to the actual buyer? And what company is he the local representative for?"

"If you wouldn't mind, we can discuss this at the meeting. Where and when shall we meet?" Antek asked.

"Tomorrow. At 10 a.m. at the Marriott upstairs cafe OK for you?"

Antek agreed. "See you there at 10. With my American friend."

Hanging up, Antek shrugged. "He says he has papers, photos, and some kind of 'extraction plan', whatever the hell that means."

"So, we're meeting tomorrow. What's this guy's name again?"

"It's Dmitri."

"Good." I was very happy that I could now connect a person to this fax.

***

Several times before this, Antek had seen that my most recent trips to Krakow had been less about family and more about going to Dennis at Techdyne for advice and trying to connect him to a deal. Sure, I always told Antek that I was saving up my earnings for that better flat in Krakow, but he must have noticed that whenever I got back to Warsaw, I hardly ever mentioned Renata. Instead, he kept hearing about Dennis and his computer room and everything that was supposed to take place in there.

Cautiously, Antek asked, "How'd it go in Krakow this time?"

"Pretty well." I said. "Dennis talks a lot more openly with me these days as if he might think I could be useful for him." I knew I had to be careful with Antek about Dennis and HIS second life that I was starting to understand better. I joked, "He gave me some hints about the strategic metals trade. But not too much about the all-important Hydra Floss."

Antek acted like he was filing some papers, then turned and asked, "Did you get a chance to spend any time with the family while you were there this time?"

Antek knew more than most about my problems at home. He usually showed sincere concern about it. I knew he deserved an honest answer but it wasn't easy, so I told him, "I got lucky. Renata was doing a Slavic language conference so I was able to hang out with Malgosia and Staszek most of the day on Saturday. We did our American barbecue thing and played catch. I took the last express train back Saturday night."

He chewed on that for a while, nodded and smiled, but decided not to comment. We then went back to our Dima project. I was sure he was guessing the game plan when he asked, "So, are you interested in this because of Techdyne? Somehow connecting Dennis to it hoping he will be the buyer?"

"Maybe. I'll probably run this fax by him and see what his reaction is. He'll roll his eyes and say it's bullshit. Then run over to his teletext and squeal on me to the CIA guys two seconds after I walk out the door." Then I changed the subject. "By the way, where are Toby and Nate? It's so quiet in here. Strange."

"Nate and Toby left for St. Petersburg this morning," he told me. "They said goodbye to their girlfriends, picked up their stuff and left. Nate was all smiles. He got his insurance check for the equipment he'd claimed had been stolen. He's all good for St. Pete now for a few months, I guess." Antek had a hint of melancholy in his voice as he revealed this to me for the first time.

It made me think of the last time Renata and I had said goodbye on relatively good terms. She drove me to Krakow Glowny — the main train station in Krakow — and even walked me to the platform where the train was waiting.

"Is there any chance you could run NatEx from Krakow?" she asked me as I was making sure I had my ticket, keys, wallet, and passport in their proper places. "I've heard that other American companies are setting up their Polish headquarters in Krakow instead of Warsaw."

"Believe me, I ran that by McGregor the last time I was in Frankfurt. He just shook his head and said, 'Sorry.'" I was hoping not to see despair in Renata's face from my words.

Without any visible emotion she replied, "This is very difficult, Andy. I don't know if I can take it much longer. I'm being honest with you."

Instead of showing sympathy and coming up with magical words to reduce her anxiety, I just stepped forward and tried to hug her. She stepped back, put her hand out, and said, "Think about that. Please." And then walked away. I remember getting on that train very disturbed with her reaction.

My thoughts came back to Antek and his situation. "So, what will you do without Toby? Write and publish on your own?" I asked.

"Most likely back to the marketing and design stuff. My mother is leaving me this apartment so it's officially mine. I'd like to pull some money out of my hat because I have my eye on a coffee deal in Africa."

I already knew about the Kenyan coffee thing, but didn't say anything.

"It's kind of risky," Antek went on, "but I'm talking to a trade rep from China who's in town. He's a rich motherfucker. He knows how to pull off these scary deals." Then he made me an offer. "You are welcome to partner with me if you are interested."

I was flattered, but the deal didn't appeal to me. I was preoccupied with the prospect of creating my own mission at the CIA. I was carrying vivid pictures of Moscow hotel suites in my head, but even my mind's eye couldn't see anything comparable in Nairobi. I couldn't even imagine the ordeal of a coffee transaction in another corrupt country, one that I knew even less about staying safe in. Also, the prospect of losing $100,000 on a deal gone bad didn't sit well with me.

So I gave Antek a non-committal reply. "Let's see how this thing goes tomorrow. I may get a work gig out of it if I handle it right. I could use some of that deal training you'll be getting from your Chinese contact, though. Thanks for the offer."

When I mentioned the work gig to Antek, I'd already said too much. He was looking at me strangely. He probably wondered if I had used this opportunity to formally do something with my embassy friends. I'd need to be more discreet, I realized. Being able to work with Antek was important; the last thing I needed to do was put that relationship at risk.

***

The Warsaw Marriott had opened in that momentous month, October of 1989, just as the Berlin Wall was about to come down. It quickly became the most popular hotel and business meeting venue in Poland, and possibly all of Eastern Europe. The Warsaw Marriott was also a magnet for the money-making moguls coming from the increasingly Klondike-like East, with Belarus and Ukraine just across Poland's borders. In those early years, as many Russian Volga limos were parked around the hotel as there were Mercedes 500s.

85

Typical of the deals born within the hotel's walls were reorganization schemes hatched by nouveau riche Russians. These might offer one thousandth of the real value of a factory or industrial center to former workers who had been given ownership 'chits,' part of the half-baked efforts to privatize Soviet industry cooked up in the Yeltsin years. A growing number of Russian oligarchs treated Poland as a very friendly place to do business. And of course, whatever was going on in the Marriott, the CIA was watching.

And so, when Dima was well into his pitch about Russian rockets and titanium and underpaid Russian scientists, I had a pretty good feeling I had guessed right about that one particular fax. Looking around the Marriott's lobby, I was starting to think that maybe I really did belong here. Maybe I could be a player where all these big deals were being made. It was a tantalizing thought that always met and conflicted with my more conservative and less confident side. That was what told me to work within the relative safety of my competent embassy colleagues. Making a little less money with a lot less risk fit my personality. Still, I hoped that I could meet these two sides in the middle. I wanted to continue to grow into the new AT Group organization until such time that I'd read the big pitch right and knock the ball out of the ballpark.

***

In fear that our little love and Siberian poetry session was quickly going to devolve into vodka and singing, I told Dima that I had other meetings soon and hoped he could show me documents of some kind. I also apologized for Antek's disappearance but could sense that Dima felt more comfortable with my undivided attention — and my serious treatment of his fantastic plans. He had long ago guessed that I would not be the end user or buyer for the 'space wares' he was peddling. He also knew I had to show something credible to my buyer — whoever that might be. He kept asking, "Are we selling to the American *shpyony*?"

"No. Not to the spies. We are selling to American industry," I said, adding, "Best in the world!" just to get his goat.

He'd used that phrase so many times during the hour we'd just spent, bragging on the "Soviet Russian industrial complex: best in the world!"

With a long reach under the table, the giant Dima nearly

disappeared. He was busy gathering his three big briefcases filled with letters, photos, maps, and other quality-verification documents. Dima's diplomatkas reminded me of the kind of black leather bags that American doctors used to carry on house calls way back when.

Careful to pull out only what he wanted to show me and not to share too much, Dima was licking his fingers and checking a small notebook. It appeared to be his reference guide or index for what was in his cases. One diplomatka held mainly maps and detailed location descriptions for fallen Soyuz debris. Attached were names of local mafia bosses who needed to be bribed to gain access to some sites. He was mumbling to himself to be careful and make sure I got what I needed but not too much. At this point I realized Dima didn't know I spoke any Russian. In fact, based on his mutterings, I was already learning a great deal about the difficult logistics of the journey I seemed to be committing myself to. What Dima had already let slip told me I should continue to be a non-Russian speaker. It might save my life. In fact, it was becoming increasingly obvious that paying attention and doing what the professionals out of the embassy were teaching me was the best insurance policy for my continued safety. Unwise actions, out of a desire to fatten my wallet, could at any time put an end to the show.

The material he was letting me see all had clear stamps and seals from the Baikonur Cosmodrome. The data about the Soyuz launch vehicles came on the letterheads of a variety of industrial centers. Some other sheets, though, he quickly shuffled past without letting me get a close look. Those contained what might have been sensitive material. I could see stamps that indicated secret data, as well as pages with blacked-out paragraphs. On the pages he did show me, I tried to get locations by looking at the letterhead. I hoped to spot a name for the complex that I could remember: Samara/Jupiter; Chelyabinsk/Mayak; Khabarovsk/Cosmos; Novosibirsk/Universitet.

I left the meeting carrying one of Dima's diplomatkas. I also went away with the feeling that what Dima was attempting was way over his head. It appeared clear that the mafia and other controlling entities limited his access and his influence. I felt, strangely, like his kindred spirit. He, much like I, was thrashing about in a world he understood very little about. It seemed highly unlikely that he would become the rich man he had dreamed of being on the strength of his cache of information and his contacts in the scientific community. More likely, the scientists he represented were starving and hoped for their own big cash-out day, which was unlikely to come unless they personally went rogue. That, I knew, would mean selling the strategic materials from their institutes to a terrorist or some other cash-paying customer.

And so if Dima was in over his head, where did that leave me? When I left him at the Marriott, I was in possession of documents and materials that made me quite nervous. This looked like stuff you could get arrested for, even by my own country. Or maybe *especially* by my own country. I felt I needed to get it to the embassy as quickly as possible — but not directly. I imagined Dima could have had me followed. So I tucked the diplomatka into the backseat of my Peugeot 405 and drove around Warsaw for several hours, finally coming back to my flat on Juliana Bruna Street around 8 p.m. I'd called the embassy and asked to meet Joe at eight the next morning. He was arriving very late from who knows where, his staff told me, but had scheduled himself into his office early in the morning. When I coded my request 'urgent' they put me on his schedule. I did not sleep well that night.

New Mission

Eighteen hours had already passed since the train we were on had been elevated and Russian wheel carriages bolted into place. That was part of every crossing of what had once been the Soviet border, necessary to accommodate the wide-gauge rail system the Russian empire had adopted long ago, aimed to keep Western invaders — mainly the Germans — from overrunning the country using the railroads. I had often gone through this three-hour carriage retrofit operation at the Polish-Soviet border, but this was the first time, following the region's recent political and economic upheaval, that I had a chance to enter the new Russia by rail. Technically, now, I was officially in the CIS or Confederation of Independent States.

As first impressions usually stick with you, I sensed at the border a heightened level of fear and distrust toward the Westerners on the train. The negative vibes were reinforced by the rough crowd I found myself a part of as we continued east from Kiev. That feeling remained as the conductor came through checking our tickets for the third time, telling the disheveled and nearly toothless traveler across from me to get his foot off my seat.

His name was Yuri. He had poked his head into the compartment, briefly introducing himself, soon after we left Kiev. He'd boarded the train there and walked from carriage to carriage looking for me. Two other men materialized in the corridor behind him and all three crowded into the compartment. The two other men pulled down the compartment's top bunks, climbed in and quickly went to sleep. Yuri parked himself on the seat opposite me and fell asleep himself. He would wake up every twenty or thirty minutes, get up, and pace between our sleeping compartment and the luggage wagon where all of our expedition provisions were stored. The other two men in our group remained bunked out on the overhead beds as the train made its way to the East. Yuri spread out a bundle of maps, making notes about where we were to pick up additional supplies, and possibly a 'specialist' or two who would be necessary to carry out our mission. He often swore as he thought of yet another thing, we needed to do to minimize our risk in entering restricted areas.

His plan seemed to be about thirty percent worked out — or less. 'Specialists' in Chelyabinsk would have documents for him. Vehicles would have to be rented to get us out to the debris sites. He was almost certain the sites we were headed to had been taken over by very unfriendly groups, basically Siberian mafia. Another specialist knew the deep Siberian territory we were going to be traveling through and had offered us special maps. These were formerly Soviet, classified, and showed every possible road and trail in the zones around the debris sites. The closest I could compare these to, in the United States, would be Forest Service maps showing logging roads from a hundred years ago in the mountains of the Pacific Northwest. By the way he was acting, I concluded Yuri was most concerned about the danger posed by territorial gangs that had claimed certain Siberian regions as their own, and had established their own rule of law.

How the other two men in the compartment with us played into this fantastic mission, I was not yet aware of. Their names were Toshek and Vlad. Just from their looks, I would have guessed that the big guy was there to intimidate and beat people up and the ugly guy was there to scare the others.

Yuri's maps showed that the debris sites were several hundred kilometers from Chelyabinsk. They were near some lakes and scattered forests in the northern reaches of the steppes. Earlier in the year, three unusual orbital tracks from the Baikonur Space Complex had set off alarm bells at the NSA and CIA. The trajectories indicating a launch of atypical rockets, probably carrying a new type of spy satellite. From our own satellites, we had detailed photos of the second and third stages of these rockets lying on the ground. Even if we were unable to secure anything from the sites, we were to try to establish the beginnings of a network. Its purpose would be to bring out specific items for delivery to the United States or to U.S. interests. There was hope that certain instrumentation and other devices would still be attached to these rocket stages that had fallen back to Earth. Our information detailed probable targets, the priorities for each site, and some of the dangers we could expect. I couldn't help noticing, as well, a potential objective that went way beyond anything I'd heard about in Warsaw when I accepted this task. Hand-written notes on some of the documents suggested that we interview villagers in specific areas about rumors concerning U.S. MIA-POWs from the Vietnam War. Those American prisoners supposedly had been repatriated or sold from China and held for decades in the Siberian forest. So here's a third layer of intrigue and danger. First, tracing contraband nuclear materials. Second, tracking down fallen rocket parts. Third, hunting for American POWs! No wonder Jane had tried to warn me away.

It kept running through my head that this mission and the resulting trip had, in fact, originated as my brainchild, but the CIA had adopted and edited it. It had been my own initiative to deliver the faxes I had picked up that day in Warsaw to my contact at the embassy, so it made some sense to send me to meet the academic researchers. But as for the spy-satellite rocket boosters, and now for the alleged POWs, I had to wonder why more qualified agents hadn't already gone out to these sites. It all seemed curious. Why, I wondered, had it taken some faxes from a two-bit trading company in Warsaw to get the machine rolling on this mission?

***

Joe hadn't given me any answers to that question when we'd met at the embassy three weeks earlier. He had a lot of questions, though. "You initiated the contact with Dima?" he asked.

"No. Antek did. Based on a fax. At my insistence."

That told Joe that Antek knew about Dima. And I suspected Joe wasn't sure how much my Polish hustler friend should be aware of these latest developments. "Antek has done business with Dima?" Joe wanted to know.

"Not that I know of," I replied. "I'm sure that he hasn't. He would have said."

"How did you leave it with Dima?"

"I said I'm going to show the docs to my client and get back to him today. Possibly." I was feeling defensive.

"You should have let us know before you met him." The edge I detected in Joe's voice was making me feel even more defensive.

"I was intrigued by the way it mentioned scientific support and suggested unlimited military contacts," I answered. "The fact that there was a Warsaw phone number made it all the more enticing to meet them and find out what was up." I thought I should remind him of my qualifications. "Putting on the naive American businessman hat, is not very difficult for me, Joe." I said that despite knowing Joe was not in favor of that disguise.

"Give us the briefcase," he said. "Your diplomatka. We are going to analyze it. We'll know where it's been and what he's had in it since he got the thing in 1899." Joe shook his head but let a sly grin come over his face. He joked a lot but the humor was usually very dark, often based on the grim reality of losing agents he had been in contact with or on the parallel danger his current staff faced.

"Dumb American businessmen are disappearing too," he said, elaborating on why he disapproved of my act. "I'd rather not have you on that list." He gave me a meaningful look. "Since we can't do much about it if you get caught. Tell your Dima that you need until noon tomorrow to make a decision about working with him. I can tell you that there are some interesting things in this cache of documents, but probably not what you think." On that note, Joe ended the meeting and waved me off. "See you very early tomorrow morning. Please."

In hot water now with Dima — I'd told him I would return his materials today — I had to call him and ask for an extension. If he had demanded his briefcase and declared the deal off, I'd have had to make up a lie, maybe say I was out of town with the potential client. I prayed that Joe would do as he'd said and return the case early enough tomorrow, before I met Dima at noon.

As it happened, Dennis was in town from Krakow. It was something of a relief that he'd come to Warsaw. I wouldn't have to deal with the guilt of going to see him, and not spending time with Renata while I was in Krakow. I spent another evening with him talking about the AT Group and taste-testing some very good vodka. Dennis told me about at least six "material interceptions" the AT Group had performed this month on trains and at automobile border crossings all over Western Europe. Illegal export of radioactive material was happening more frequently. Dennis said he expected I would soon be involved in a mission. He also hinted that the stuff coming out of Russia was mainly from the areas that Dima represented. How Joe would react to Dima's off-the-wall space junk mission was anyone's guess at this point.

***

With a slight hangover and a deficit of morning caffeine to rouse me from my evening's meeting with Dennis, I struggled to concentrate as Embassy Joe filled me in on what he'd come up with overnight. First thing that morning, I'd told Joe that Dima had not been very happy about my keeping the diplomatka another day. I'd had to avoid his invitations to meet again to begin preliminary discussions about my trip.

Joe began bluntly, "Listen to me. Dima is basically a very low man on our totem pole of interests. But he has some heavyweights behind him that he probably doesn't even know about. Or if he does, he doesn't really understand who they are and what they are doing — or what they're hoping to do. Dima himself is who he says he is. He's an agent for marketing these materials to potential Western buyers. Whether he knows it or not, he's competing with a much darker gang of ruthless sales agents. They don't have any scruples about who buys their products. These guys are willing to do anything for the sale. Dima is a bit of a front for them. He's supplying an air of credibility and a bit of a diversion from the sinister work they're trying to do: to sell anything that can make them rich."

"What about the scientists? Are they bad guys, too?" I asked.

"From what we have now, we think the pure science folks aren't really involved so much. When Dima talks about his scientist group, he's lumping some other folks into the category. The general managers, technicians, operators, industrial/administrative staff from some of the nuclear facilities are in this group. That's because they still have signature power to go against procedures and release materials to whomever they wish. Throw a handful of former KGB agents and generals into the mix — some of them loyal and some of them resentful of the New Russia — and you have a very unstable situation." Joe's description made his concern obvious. He anticipated the next question on my mind: how did he know all this?

"Israeli, German, British, French, and even Polish intelligence contributes to the state of our understanding of what's going on," he said.

"The Germans are some of the most sensitive to all this. That's because the former East German military folks know a hell of a lot of what's going on in these facilities, including warhead-armed missile launching groups. The Israelis are concerned that they're a prime target of whatever could be fabricated from such material. So predictably enough, the Israelis have more of their Mossad agents wandering about than we can keep track of. Some of them will know you're being courted by Dima and that you're with us. That doesn't mean they'll be friendly to you if your paths cross, though." Joe wasn't done with his warning. "Trust is not commonplace among the anti-terrorist teams, even though they're all out there trying to stop the flow of radioactive material from Russia." He looked me in the eye and paused to make sure I returned his gaze. "We worry a lot about contractors getting hit by friendly fire. Please remember that."

I was pretty sure I would. Then I remembered something else that had been bugging me. I took a shot in the dark and asked, "I suppose you have photos or a film of me with Dima yesterday?"

"Yes."

"You're shitting me! That fast?" I was shocked.

As if I should have known, Joe explained with exaggerated patience, "The whole Marriott is bugged. Cameras are everywhere. We just don't have a way to know what kind of crazy shit is going to happen or when crazy people like you and Dima are going to show up. You told us you were there, so we pulled the camera and recordings to confirm."

"I must have a big file. Don't I?" My ego hoped the answer would be 'yes.'

"Which one?" Joe asked.

Laughing, I said, "I guess I meant the CIA's file on me."

"Let's say that you have an active file that has gotten rather thick. If you knew who was hovering around you from time to time, you would probably drop everything and go back to Kennewick, Washington."

"Meaning?" So much for ego. Now I was alarmed.

"I wouldn't worry about it. You've been a pain in the ass for the Poles from the beginning. Polish Intelligence is now hyper-Americanized but there are a few former bloc agents that would have liked to haul you in and scare you a bit."

"Let me guess. An agent based in Krakow who's a friend of my wife's ex?" I hoped he might confirm that particular suspicion.

"No comment. Back to Dima and his Siberian adventure. Or yours. We suggest the following general scenario with details to be worked out: "First: You accept Dima's offer conditionally and tell him there are three very northerly tracked Soyuz rocket remains that your buyer is interested in. We've located them on the maps he gave you, but he didn't circle them as options for you. We're somewhat interested in photos and whatever you might be able to bring back from any or all of these sites. If anything is left of the debris, of course. You get a big bonus if you can remove anything and pack it with you. We'll also have you do some soil sampling. Easy stuff. Put some dirt in a special bag and seal it up. A word of caution, though. There's an average of ten percent of unburned fuel that comes down with each jettisoned stage of a Soyuz rocket. That shit is very toxic. Do not approach the rocket debris if you see a lot of dead animals — or people — around the site."

I swallowed hard at this. It was shaping up to be a very different sort of assignment than rendezvousing with hookers in Moscow hotel rooms. I was committed. Even though the door was always open for contractors to back out, no way could I throw in the towel after having massaged this mission into being. It had been tailored especially for me. No letting these guys down now. Besides all that, I'd already committed the money. Every dollar I'd be getting from this trip had been promised to projects Renata had tasked me with to guarantee the move from Nowa Huta to Bronowice.

Joe continued, "Second: We'll give you names of people we want you to meet and deliver things to in Novosibirsk. Maybe some other places, too. I'll know more soon. We should have you build your presence in Novosibirsk to take the attention away from your 'camping' in the wild looking for third-stage Soyuz rocket debris.

"Third: Tell Dima you will meet him in Novosibirsk. You will travel there by train from here. In Kiev, two or three of our friends will join you. Get to know them a little. They know the dark counterparts to Dima and will have some involvement with this little journey. Trust me on that. Dima is not prepared to safely deal with the lawlessness you'll run into where you're going. But our people are, I believe. They also want to see if Dima's competition might show up. If they do, they'll want to assess you and see what you might be worth to them."

I caught myself swallowing hard, again. I started to feel nostalgic about all that flirting with beautiful women in the Leningradskaya's bar. But this was no time for daydreaming. Joe wasn't finished.

"Fourth: We need to get some tools of the trade to you and make sure you know how to use them. Tracking devices, bugs, cameras, drugs, hand tools for the rocket dismemberment. Just in case. And some light weaponry. No guns, though."

That got my imagination revving. I wondered who would play the role of 'Q' and show me how that 'light weaponry' worked. But my mind was driving again. I brought it back to Joe.

"Fifth: You can scrap the naive businessman shtick. Instead, you're a space travel enthusiast and a trader in special metals. You can use your friend, Dennis, as one of your potential buyers. He has agreed to that."

That part didn't surprise me. Dennis had told me as much during our vodka-and-beer-chasing session the night before. He'd also offered the opinion that the dumb-American thing was a no-go for this trip. To help equip me for my new role, he gave me a bunch of sanitized spec sheets — no company names — about titanium, aluminum, and some rare-earth metals needed for achieving super-strengthened alloys. He thought I should bone up on some of the technical lingo. He also offered a good idea: he suggested that I promote discussions with the university or any economics institutes in Novosibirsk, ask for cooperation in starting a joint MBA program there. I knew Dima would get excited about something like that. It would be like the early MBA Program the Krakow Industrial Society had negotiated in 1990 with the University of Detroit. It made a great cover, because I could be a legitimate part of it. For two semesters, I had taught general management and operations management courses at that institute.

"And finally, the sixth: 'Fifi sixty-six' from anyone's mouth, at any time, means they are with us." Joe said that so seriously it almost made me laugh.

I assumed he was joking.

"*What*? 'Fifi sixty-six?' Where did you come up with that?"

Joe's answer came without emotion. That, alone, was enough to make me laugh. But the rest was pure astonishment. "Your first pet, in 1966 in Guthrie, Oklahoma. You were living on Warner Street in what you've always called 'The Pink House'."

"Wow." I really was amazed. "You do know a lot about me."

"You talk a lot. You say more things to people than you realize."

Now Joe sounded accusing.

"And you are listening, obviously." I tried to make it a joke. "By the way, will I have a shoe phone with me?"

Joe ignored that. He stayed serious and his tone made it clear he expected me to get serious, too. "Not exactly a shoe phone." He described how to use a tracking device I actually would be carrying. "We'll know where you are if our guys lose you in the forest. If the signal goes on and off, we'll know you're trying to let us know something is wrong and need help. If it goes off and stays off, then something is really wrong. Like you've been cremated or buried. Along with the tracker, of course."

"Thanks, Joe. I feel a lot better." I didn't really, but I had to say so. Wasn't that how real spies were supposed to behave? Cool, with a dose of ironic humor? "How much are you paying me for this?"

"A little more than usual. This is a promotion." But then came another warning. "But you are on probation." That thought vanished from my mind when Joe asked me to come back later that afternoon. That's when I'd be set up with my tool kit.

***

As I left Joe's office, the negative vibes fled. More than exhilaration at the potential for danger and adventure, I was feeling pretty smart.

Elated that I had pulled together the intelligence for an AT Group mission — a mission that had been approved, and with me as the main actor — I thought I would see if Jane happened to be in the embassy. I wanted to tell her about my success. I also realized that, any day now, she would be leaving for good. This project might have me gone for up to three weeks. I needed to say a proper goodbye.

Her desk was empty. I scoured the Consular Division's back offices and finally found her. She saw me first and pulled me into a small room. I wasn't expecting to get an angry rundown, but that's what she gave me. She laid into me for taking another job "out of your league," as she put it. "Andy, please! This isn't your stuff to do. You aren't trained for it. They don't give a rat's ass if something should happen to you." She showed her teeth, like a vicious dog.

"But Jane, this seems like a different kind of job —" I tried to counter.

"You're goddamned right," she said. "It is a different kind of job, you idiot!"

"No, I mean it seems that there's a lot of folks that'll be interested in where I am and what I'm doing," I tried to explain. "In fact, I'm getting some tracking devices, bugs, cameras and other tools for this one. I'd say it's a promotion," I argued. But I knew it was hopeless.

She was still angry. She implored me to back out. "Shit. It *was* a promotion, but you're still a contractor. You're still carrying all the risk here." I knew she cared about me, but the way she expressed her concern just made me feel worse. "I'm not sure what you'll be doing." She pressed a finger against my chest. "But I will suggest one thing now. If you get into deep shit and sense that you're in grave danger, then hide. Give it up. Get out. And then take it slow, and use your wits to make your way back on your own. Before you leave, buy an open-ended train ticket. One that allows you to get on any train, anywhere in the former Soviet Union. Take a lot of cash. Or at least more than usual."

Her tone softened, just a bit, when she shifted away from the practical advice. "You've obviously won the trust of Joe and his crew," she said, "enough so that they're bringing you into this anti-terrorism group. But this is the type of work for… for… well, for someone different from you. That's all I'm going to say."

But it wasn't. She had plenty more to say. "I fly out this week. When you get back to Warsaw — if you get back to Warsaw —" and she poked her finger into my chest again for emphasis, "they'll have my office address in D.C. Write to me. By the way, I started out in Joe's crew before I went to work for the USIA. That was before he took the AT Group. I just couldn't take it. Andy." The anger had vanished from her voice by now. "That suggestion I gave you? It works. I know it worked in my case. Many years ago, when I got into trouble."

Jane hugged me, holding on for a little longer than usual. Then she let go and looked up and down the hallway before stepping out of the little room where she'd cornered me. Without another word, she walked away.

5.

New Tools

On the table in the conference room that straddled the old USIA and CIA desk areas were laid out the 'tools' for my trip. First were soil extraction scoops and sample bags. I had no problem understanding how to use them. Except that I felt like I was getting a lesson on how to do a prostate exam by the way the fellow was describing the preferred hand-finger extraction motion preferred for a soil sample. The gentleman was graying, slightly stooped, and wore an industrial apron with 'CIA' printed in big letters across his chest.

"Fine. Got it!" I assured him.

Next was a GammaData hand-held Geiger counter. Joe hadn't mentioned this. My instructor showed me how to turn it on and off. He said taking it on the journey was optional, but he recommended I do so, considering all the "riff-raff" I would be around. I had my own thoughts about it. I questioned how I would be received, carrying a Geiger counter when I was supposed to be looking for titanium and aluminum and maybe some rare earths, all non-radioactive. He shrugged and proceeded with a lesson in how to calibrate the thing. Which I would come to appreciate later that year while on a different tracking job.

One thing I appreciated about the agency-issued Geiger counter: it was about a quarter the size, and at least that much lighter, than the one Dennis had given me at Techdyne. That alone would barely have fit into my toolkit.

A little Olympus camera that fit in the palm of my hand lay next to a pen camera, which came complete with an instruction sheet. Next to that was what appeared to be a black glass button with sticky tape on it. It was also a camera. It could be placed almost anywhere and activated by touch. My teacher seemed to be getting bored after he showed me how to use it. He concluded, "Use your imagination when it might be appropriate. It can be used in the dark, too." Three similar but smaller button-like plastic rings turned out to be wireless bugs. "We like to eavesdrop. They are easy to hide. You should assume that they are always on," this non-glamourous equivalent of Bond's 'Q' told me. His comment conjured up images of my last mission to Moscow. Suddenly I wondered if Natalya, Danuta, Ela, and I had been filmed during our meeting at the Leningradskaya Hotel. And, if so, if somebody in a dark room somewhere was enjoying private showings of the footage.

The weaponry Joe had promised me amounted to two scary-looking icepick-like daggers. These were to be hidden in my clothing and my briefcase. I told the instructor that I couldn't imagine using them but he went on describing the three ways to kill or severely incapacitate someone. In simple terms, those choices were severing arteries, delivering a hatchet-like blow to the head and face, and inflicting the most lethal damage to blood-filled areas during close fighting.

I cut off that lesson as quickly as I could. "Thanks. Next."

The altogether expected super Swiss Army Knife was next. This thing was three or four times larger than any I had ever seen but still very light. Instead of blades and Boy-Scout-style implements, it included various advanced-looking tools for unscrewing, unbolting, bending, and whatever else it took to disassemble Soyuz rockets. The instructor only pointed at one implement with the comment that he thought I would need it. It looked like a high-tech Philips screwdriver with a curved head and an extension piece in the handle. I waited for further explanation. He said exactly what I expected: "Use your imagination."

Finally, perhaps the most versatile tool of all: fifty new hundred-dollar bills in an open envelope. I asked, "Mine to keep? I didn't know 'CIA' stood for 'Cash In Advance.'"

Not-Q, my instructor, frowned and said, "Keep track of where you spend it and who you bribe. Remember, a hundred dollars still goes a long way in the former Soviet Bloc. Unnecessary spending will come out of your honorarium. I would recommend that you get this money broken up into much smaller bills."

"And my shoe phone?"

Not-Q wasn't amused with my *Get Smart* joke. He was holding a pretty normal-looking pen. "This pen is your panic button. Removing the inside spring and then replacing it says to us, 'I am probably in trouble, something has happened, and I want to abort the mission. I will take action on my own.' Removing it and not replacing it for more than an hour says, 'I am being held captive and in extreme dire straits.' If you are being held captive and being moved from one location to another," he advised, "try to replace the spring after each move so we have a chance of finding you."

"How does it work?" I asked. "I mean, is it transmitting at some weird frequency?"

My trainer may not have had answers to all my questions, but did let me see that this high-tech panic button intrigued him. "A special satellite, of course, detects the transmissions. This has to be pretty new technology. The Russians are on their way to doing the same thing. Maybe that Soyuz booster you will be investigating lofted theirs into orbit."

Not-Q turned to his next item. "This big envelope is for you, too. Instructions, maps, the stuff Dima gave you, and whatever else we could cobble together for you to learn so as not to get yourself killed on the first day out." He handed me a large manila envelope bulging at the seams with material. Joe and his staff had pulled together about 250 pages of people, places, targets, alternative targets, goals ranked by priority, dangers and suggestions for mitigating risk, survival techniques from a CIA handbook, a topical Russian phrasebook geared to the intelligence community, and finally, as Joe had said, some letters. Those were to be delivered to faculty members at the University of Novosibirsk.

Then came a very unwelcome bit of news. My trainer Not-Q added, "Hey, Joe asked me to tell you that they're keeping that doctor's bag that Dima gave you."

I didn't bother trying to hide the shock on my face.

He ignored it. "After chemical analysis, it appears that Dima has, maybe unknowingly, transported some bad stuff. And relatively recently. They found trace amounts of plutonium dust, sarin gas, depleted uranium, and other 'funny' things. If Dima was expecting you to give it back, tell him it was stolen in the train station. Or something."

"Shit! He didn't give me the bag," I protested. "He loaned it to me. To carry all the stuff he'd given me."

"OK, let me tell Joe. You aren't leaving for a week or so. By the time you leave, he might have finished the tests he wants to do. There could be a few holes, though," he admitted, "or some pieces cut out of it that were used for the tests."

"I can say a dog chewed on it. Or something. Thanks for asking Joe. I would very much prefer to get it back to Dima if at all possible. It'll help my credibility with him. Even if it is a little radioactive and carries a light scent of nerve gas."

Packing Up

My tools just barely fit into the little leather backpack I always carried. From that day forward, that backpack became 'My Toolkit.' With that toolkit and a million thoughts racing through my mind, I had to organize my time. The most important task facing me was letting Renata know that I was going to be incommunicado for a considerably longer time than she normally would tolerate. After putting my story together, I called.

I started the conversation trying to kindle a little bit of excitement in her that this was the real deal. "This is the kind of consulting opportunity I've been hoping for. It combines my Krakow MBA teaching experience with the State Department stuff at the Embassy."

"San Francisco was supposed to be an opportunity!" She shot back at me.

I stayed calm. "Renata, I'll be back with several thousand in cash. It all goes to the new apartment."

"You haven't said how long you'll be gone this time." Now she was uncharacteristically calm. I was worried my answer would reverse the trend.

"It's at least two weeks but the new boss at the embassy told me to reserve three just in case we're able to identify an MBA partner quickly in Novosibirsk and begin negotiations."

Renata let out a barely audible gasp and was silent for a few seconds. "What else do I tell people here when someone notices that I have an *obecny nieobecny maz?*" That was one of her favorite descriptions of me to her friends: presently not present husband.

Irritated that she would probably use this as a chance to belittle my mission, I told her, "Tell them that your *important* husband is part of a delegation for the U.S. Government to help advise on a new MBA program in Russia."

"I'm sure that it was exactly *you* they were looking for. Right?" she interrupted.

I went on, pulling another lie out of my hat. "The Russian Academy of Sciences sent an envoy to Warsaw. He was asking for help in finding direction as capitalism and democracy take hold. They thought an MBA program in Novosibirsk would be a good start."

Renata calmed down. "Fine. I'm getting along better these days without you. Just promise you'll come back and take time off to help with things around here." I thought she was hanging up then suddenly she came back on the line and said, "Your daughter wants to speak with you."

Malgosia's sweet little voice replaced Renata's angry growls. In Polish, she said, "Hi Daddy! Mr. Marek says he's going to take me for ice cream and cake tomorrow at the café in front of the Lenin statue. I told him I had to ask you first."

Who the hell is Marek? I wondered, silently. "Of course it's OK," I had to say. "Give me back to your mother, darling. I love you!"

Before I said a word, she came on the line and stopped any further inquiry. "Marek and Danuta from my institute are working with me here on my new book. Without you to babysit, they have been spending most of the day in the flat. Marek was kind enough to promise Malgosia a little outing tomorrow."

"I see," I responded weakly. Somehow, I didn't like the idea of Marek being involved in her project, much less promising my daughter trips to the ice cream parlor in my absence. He was a young lawyer and Slavic language PhD, splitting his time between Polish language textbooks and family law. Renata had been working on writing a vocabulary textbook that covered a variety of topics—but I'd never heard that law was one of them. I did my best to hide my suddenly gnawing concern. "Tell him, 'Thank you' from me." A long pause must have told her how I was really feeling. "I'll try to send telegrams and call when I can." For the first time in a year, I'd wanted to say "I love you" but found that I couldn't. Renata hung up without saying goodbye. My send-off and well wishes from the family couldn't have gone worse.

In what was a superhuman effort for me, I swept the contents of that conversation under the rug. For the time being. I had too much to do. Becoming disconsolate over my family troubles could jeopardize the whole trip. I began telling myself, "Suck it up, Big Guy!" As much as I tried, though, I had the feeling that my commitment to this mission was seriously endangering my family commitments.

Returning to my mission checklist, I needed to study the materials I'd been given, work out a schedule with Dima, and coordinate the trip with him and Joe. That would also let Joe get his people — my people — hooked up with me for the trip to Novosibirsk. I wondered where in the world those people were. I wondered what their story was that qualified them for the role they would play. Most likely, I speculated, they would be as ruthless as the folks I would be up against.

It was beginning to dawn on me that, just like Jane had warned me, I might have taken on a bit more than I really had bargained for. Weapons in my toolkit, classified sensors, bugs, and camera equipment. Until now, I'd looked at everything I'd done for Clint as grown-up hide-and-go-seek games. And, I won't lie, sometimes with the added bonus of sex thrown in. While I always knew, of course, that I could get into serious trouble for what I was doing, it had always seemed the odds were in my favor to get done what I was asked to do without getting noticed or getting caught. And if I did get caught, I figured the worst that could happen to me would be deportation. I'd seen this in the late eighties, before the Berlin Wall came down. American college students in then-Communist Poland who were doing what I would later do were eventually getting caught. The Polish government at the time chose to make a big deal of this on TV, for their captive domestic audience, but the amateur spies were safely out of the country within forty-eight hours.

What I had been doing since then was more of a hide-in-the-open game, one that required little of me other than to be a lot more attentive than the average guy. The exception to that was when they sent me to Moscow on disinformation runs. This trip, though, was entirely different from any of that. Working for Joe, my new boss, I was out in the open, with an unavoidably high profile. I would be bait for Dima's competition and a target for those in Russia who looked for foreigners to kidnap and ransom. While I could laugh about some of what had happened to me that time in Ternopil, I wasn't eager to repeat the experience. As far east as I was going, it was unnerving to know, sanity was inversely proportional to the distance from Moscow. Whereas even in post-Soviet Moscow there were laws and a functioning system of government, the farther you got from the capital, the more hit-and-miss things became. After going through one strange kidnapping and another failed attempt in Ukraine, I had this strange feeling that I was setting myself up for the charmed third time.

***

"My briefcase feels lighter, I think," Dima said as I gave him back his radioactive, nerve-gas-tainted bag. We were at the Marriott Hotel again. This time, though, we were in the downstairs lobby bar, hidden somewhat from the crowds by the windows facing Ulica Jerozolimskie — Jerusalem Street. I purposely put my sweater and another coat and scarf on the chairs next to us to keep some distance from the other bar patrons. Evidently sensing that I was either nervous or gearing up for a serious conversation, Dima did what most Russians would in such a situation. He ordered a whole bottle of Wyborowa — Polish vodka — for just the two of us. *Shit!* I was trying to dry out a bit before my trip, but I knew it would be a big insult to refuse him. I begged him to avoid another pre-travel Russian tradition: the singing and dancing, kissing and hugs. So, we limited ourselves to talking… and drinking. He seemed disappointed to have to hold in his exuberance, but by about 8 p.m., with three quarters of a liter of vodka in him, he wasn't *that* upset.

We worked out that the three strange northerly Soyuz debris sites would be accessible, but Dima did not hide his disappointment that I had chosen exactly these. They weren't the ones he had worked out, which meant endless complications. Bribes and negotiations with the rogue locals and mafia were going to be necessary, he said. That would also require additional services from his man who arranged everything of that nature. And, of course, that guy would need to be paid, as well. I could see that my five thousand extra dollars had already shrunk to more like $4,500.

Our travel plans had been carefully worked out. I would go by Trans-Siberian Railway past the debris sites to meet Dima. We would get together in Novosibirsk. There, I would spend a few days under his guidance meeting some of the academics who were in his group. That would give me time to deliver the letters I had been given to the faculty at Novosibirsk State University. Dima and I would then travel together back to do the site exploration and extraction. These sites were at about the same latitude as Novosibirsk but far to the west of that city, and several hundred kilometers off the Trans-Siberian Railway. Photos of the sites showed mainly barren steppes with nearby patches of woods and wetland. I wasn't sure if camping in the open was preferable to being able to hide in the woods. Something told me I was in for some hide-and-seek in Siberia.

Dima loved the part about a possible collaboration with an academy or the university itself. Setting up an MBA pilot program would give him the visibility he wanted with the Economics Department at NSU. Up to now, the professors there had ignored his harping on commerce with the West and building relationships with Poles and Americans. To better gain this group's respect, Dima wanted me to deliver part of my introduction speech in Russian. *Damn!* Another nerve-wracking presentation in a language that was beautiful, sure, but not my own. I always worried that I would use verbs that in slang meant either farting or fucking. Renata had taught me quite a bit of that sort of wordplay but during parties with her university colleagues I almost never got things right. More than once, I had embarrassed everyone.

One particularly painful incident was at a party that Czeslaw Milosz, the 1980 Nobel Prize winner for literature was present for. I'd incorrectly used the verb *pieprzyc*, which means both to fuck and to add pepper to, in a joke I'd heard in Prague. Reversing the order of the verbs rendered the punch line meaningless. My closer friends laughed anyway and told me how I'd messed up the joke. Renata, instead of defending me or laughing with the others, made my blunder into a joke about how Americans don't understand the language. Therefore, she went on, we don't understand the culture and the essence of being Polish. She got the other half of the room laughing at me rather than with me. That wasn't the worst of the chronic issues between me and Renata, of course. But it hadn't helped matters. I still relied on her speechwriting and proofreading.

Not having her nearby, I reflected, would leave me vulnerable to other perils, too. My language skills and basic cultural understanding had come from her attention to my behavior. Even as she'd become the life of the party at my expense a half dozen times, I'd never taken advantage of the drunken female colleagues who had approached me with advances like, "You poor boy! She doesn't appreciate you enough" or "Andy! When you can't stand it any longer, here is my number." Now, I had too much important business on my mind in a world that was new to me. I couldn't let myself dwell on these sorts of distracting thoughts.

Visits to three other technical institutes were on our itinerary. These added several thousand more kilometers and endless logistical issues to our journey, which would stretch from Chelyabinsk in the west to Novosibirsk in the east. On our must-visit list was a weapons-related site in Novosibirsk. In Chelyabinsk, we had identified a weapons-related instrumentation facility as well as a nuclear plant that did fuel-cycle reprocessing. Other sites, somewhat more remote, were also nuclear related: a uranium enrichment plant and a fuel reprocessing facility. Despite considering Dima a small-time operator, Embassy Joe's folks had decided we should give him a chance to open the doors to these places. They viewed them as the most likely to lose nuclear material to bad guys. Providing an additional ticket in was really my goal — and Embassy Joe's hope, too. Grabbing anything from the Soyuz debris and getting soil samples was still an important part of the trip, but became secondary to the plant visits.

Dima and I tentatively agreed on a schedule for our meetings in Novosibirsk. One last shot of vodka for each of us was left in the Wyborowa bottle. I picked it up and poured our last shots into elegant crystal glasses. I facetiously asked Dima if this trip was going to make any money for anyone. He answered, "It all depends on the characters we meet and the strength of our character."

I nodded. That was worthy of a toast. *"Na zdrowie!"*

But now, through the vodka buzz, I started worrying about those characters we would meet.

Some Characters

As the slow train through Ukraine was now making its way toward Samara, Russia, I had plenty of time with my new partners. Embassy Joe had routed me through Kiev precisely to allow me to meet Yuri, Toshek and Vlad. Yuri, though he couldn't seem to sit still, looked suspiciously at everybody walking past our compartment, and was always tending to issues or taking notes, spent plenty of time talking to me. He was filled with information that he mostly agreed to share. The others, both Ukrainian, were just plain scary guys. Toshek was tall and thin with dark hair that stuck out on one side of his head and was matted down on the other. He had this half-smiling look in his eyes and face that almost never changed. He too, like Yuri, was tooth challenged. The combination of a shit-eating grin with spaces between his teeth unnerved me. I knew my feelings toward Toshek were a bit unfair; I figured I'd eventually get used to his appearance. But in the first four hours I'd been around him, I hadn't yet. As for Vlad, Yuri warned me to keep my distance from him and not to speak too much English when he was around.

In his own strongly accented English, Yuri suggested, "Even if he ask you question or tell you something, just move head or be silent. And don't make smiling too much."

"Why? What's up with him?" I asked, feeling defensive. "He knows I'm an American — I assume."

"He get very nervous on people sometime. He can shout easy and maybe try to hurt people if he think you are laughing at him. That's why no smiling from you. Americans smile too much. But I see you not making smiles so much. That's good," Yuri said.

After that, I was self-conscious about my American smile. "Thank you for the advice. I'll do my best to keep a serious face and avoid Vlad."

"One more something about Vlad," Yuri advised me. "He is still taking care of last job for someone. If he leaves sometimes, probably is taking care of things for his job."

I didn't exactly understand what Yuri meant, but I had witnessed

Vlad sneaking back to the luggage car and opening windows. My assumption was that he was smoking a cigarette there since we were in No Smoking compartments. Vlad was a powerful looking man over six feet tall who walked with a purposeful gait. He would scan all around himself, as he took half as many steps I would have to reach the luggage car. He wore a very dusty jacket with matching dusty pants. His clothes looked color coordinated with his dark sandy hair, which I imagined he had cut himself. And, to go with what Yuri had said, his chiseled Slavic face and deep-set eyes looked madder than hell all the time. His jaw was always clenched, the tendons taut in his neck and muscles of mastication on his head constantly twitching and writhing.

While after the first few hours I had hardly seen Toshek at all, and wondered if he had gotten off someplace along the way, avoiding Vlad wasn't as easy as I had hoped. With two days on a train to Samara, there were few places to hide. He and I found ourselves face to face more than a dozen times. The train was not packed tightly with people but very few compartments had any vacant seats. Every time I got up from my converted sleeping berth, Vlad would watch me. If I went in the direction of the luggage car, he usually stood up to see better. Twice I was held up next to the luggage car by passengers standing in the corridor talking. Both times, Vlad drifted out and stared at me until I passed the people and continued toward the restaurant car. He definitely didn't like me being anywhere near his things; I figured maybe he was hiding something in the luggage car. So far, the only thing I had seen him doing there was stand by the open window with one arm out and the other holding what looked like a sleeping bag or duffel bag. The bag was shiny and black, though, like a garbage bag for yard work. That seemed strange. On that occasion, I ran ahead quickly when I realized he might react to me watching him.

***

Our compartment had three bunks on either side. The top two berths would fold down against the wall with the middle bunk becoming a back rest during the day when we four were awake and sitting on the bottom beds. With my partners moving about all day, back and forth to the luggage car and the restaurant car, we were rarely in the compartment at the same time, except at night. I hadn't slept well the night before they joined me. On our first day together, around 2 p.m., I asked Yuri if he minded if I took a short nap on one of the bottom bunks. He nodded and pointed to the free bunk across from him. "Not a problem," he said, then gestured for me to lie down.

There were six blankets in our compartment and some pillows, without pillow-cases, that smelled bad. The odor was identifiable somewhere between armpit and old urine. I grabbed one of the blankets, kind of like an American furniture-moving pad or a quilt with half the stitching out or loose. The fill in the blanket was coming out, a strange, dark-colored sawdust. I stuffed the pillow into my jacket and zipped it up. As I was taking off my shoes and getting ready to lie down, Yuri handed me a small plastic cup with vodka in it. "Maybe you will get better napping if you take small drink. Please!" Surprised but not refusing it, I smiled at Yuri and shot it in one gulp. As I recognized from the flavor that this was *bimber,* moonshine made from sugar, it nearly came up as quickly as it went down. I'd never gotten used to sugar-based moonshine in Poland and had an immediate gag reflex when I smelled it. Miraculously, I kept it down, but my eyes were watering. Yuri said, "Not many Americans like our national beverage, I think. Rest for now."

It's hard to say how long I was asleep. The *bimber* took effect quickly and I was out. With a bit of a sleep deficit, I quickly started dreaming. It was a repeat of an absurd scene I'd witnessed leaving a small town in Ukraine the afternoon before. The train was slowly picking up speed and rocking side to side as we began passing small farms along the way. On a steep berm next to the tracks, I'd seen an older man openly masturbating with one hand and waving at the train with the other. I was standing in the corridor with a beer in my hand, staring directly at him through an open window. Others in the train, also looking through open windows, were laughing out loud and waving at him. The scene was the same in my dream except that two boys were sitting near him, watching and cheering him on. That dream faded and the next began. I was suddenly on a huge open plain with rockets and jets scattered on the ground as far as the eye could see. I was surrounded by them. Suddenly I was in a panic that I was going to die from the fumes of all the rocket fuel that the ground had soaked up from these behemoth boosters lying all around. In the dream, I started running but couldn't get anywhere as if I had hit the slow-motion dial on my brain.

With a start I woke up. For an instant, I couldn't see very well. I reached for my face and my vision came back, as a handful of three-inch long cockroaches went scurrying off. Realizing they had been on my face grossed me out. I tried to get to the WC to wash my face off but someone was inside. I waited impatiently in the corridor with my towel and a bar of soap. After a couple of minutes, a mother and daughter came out. Washing my face made me feel a little better. I joined Yuri back in the compartment.

"Why you look so upset?" he asked.

"I woke up with cockroaches on my face!"

"Probably thirsty. They were taking drink from your face. Maybe tears from your eyes or something from nose or mouth."

"Shut the fuck up. Jesus. I can barely take that." I slowly settled back into my seat but I was also upset about the first dream. Not the sort to engage in pseudo-Freudian dream analysis, I still had a sense of it being a warning about a pathetic future if I totally screwed things up with Renata. Maybe I already had. Could the dream be telling me that in all of the surreal life I had been living for the past ten years, the women and the adventure of it all, I was now in danger of sentencing myself to a solitary life? Had I now found myself in a land where morality no longer functioned and I was the amoral dick? Nothing but a prop in some kind of farce? The object of mockery from random strangers? An uncommon depression overtook the moment — until Vlad came back.

Just as I had been expressing myself in more colorful terms than usual when the cockroaches were taking a drink, and in English that was louder than my usual whispers, Vlad came down the corridor to the compartment. He had a very curious look on his face. After exchanging some comments with Yuri about my being a drinking fountain for cockroaches, and something else I couldn't quite catch, Vlad left again. And, of course, he was headed back to the luggage car.

I asked Yuri what Vlad and he were talking about.

Yuri thought for a few seconds about his answer. "Vlad hopes nothing bad happens to you while he's around."

"What the fuck does that mean?" I demanded.

"I don't know," Yuri said. He wasn't looking at me. Only then did I notice that he was counting a huge pile of cash. He had two plastic grocery bags on the bunk next to him. In one, I could see rubles. There were dollars in the other. Judging from the size of the rubber-banded packets of fifties and twenties, I could see that he had about ten times the number of dollars I had on me. With the devaluation of the ruble and the various black-market rates across the CIS, it was hard to say how much the tall stack of thousand-ruble notes was really worth. I'd never seen so much Russian money before, but I guessed it was worth another $50,000 in Moscow.

Courier for Cash

The first time I saw a large amount of money being delivered by the CIA was in 1984. I was studying the Polish language — and Polish women — in Krakow. I guess I was doing pretty well with both lines of study; anyway, one of those Polish women, my future wife, Renata, whom I'd known just six weeks, thought my language skills were good enough that she recommended me for a delicate bit of diplomatic work. That was to help with translation at a politically sensitive event. Three Catholic nuns from Chicago and a priest from Maryland had a confirmed meeting with Solidarity organizers in Gdansk. These Solidarity leaders, Polish steel workers at the Lenin Shipyard, were arguably the group most responsible for the ultimate fall of the whole Soviet Empire. They were still under house arrest after the martial-law crackdown a few years earlier. Even so, I was assured that the American Catholic reception in Gdansk would be just a 'well wishes' meeting organized by the Chicago diocese.

We set off from Krakow on a Saturday morning. It was a train trip of over six hundred kilometers, all the way across Poland, from the foothills of the Tatry Mountains to the Baltic coast. We got to Gdansk late, but on a summer evening that far north, it was still light. The nuns insisted that we go straight to the home where the union leaders were being held. The priest, whose brother happened to be a former U.S. secretary of state, quietly agreed, nodding anxiously to indicate that he, as well, wanted to get to their house. He also said he hoped to be invited to spend the night. That sounded really odd to me but I guessed such a gesture must be expected considering the circumstances: an American Catholic delegation making such a long trip just to meet them.

It was around 9 p.m. when we arrived. The military guards outside the home were uneasy with us strolling in. They wanted to frisk us, motioning for us to extend our arms to the side so they could feel us up for weapons or contraband. But the nuns insisted on entering untouched, swatting at the guards. Even under Communism, I guessed, ordinary Poles wouldn't dare show disrespect to a nun. Once inside, and after all the hand kissing and Hail Mary's were done, two of the Solidarity dissidents were very gracious. They immediately offered guest rooms for all of us.

Not long after we got our things into our rooms, we all sat down to a small dinner with vodka and other drinks. I noticed the priest was fiddling around with something under his robe and coat. As he came into the dining room to join us, whatever he was reaching for finally came out of wherever it had been hiding during the long train journey. It slipped from his hands and hit the floor with a heavy thump. I could see it was about the size of a loaf of bread and was wrapped in plastic. Along with everybody else in the room, I saw that it was a huge amount of cash. One of the Solidarity leaders started praying and thanking God for the gift to the movement. Embarrassed, the priest said, "I guess I ruined that surprise. I was going to hand it to you after we finished a couple of stiff drinks. Anyway, here is $300,000 from the U.S. Government — and mainly the CIA — to help you continue your good work against Communism."

***

Many years later, I learned more about how this worked. As a former CIA administrator confirmed to me, a lot of CIA guys and their operatives go around the world paying people money for things they do. That source, a guy named Bill, told me a couple of stories of being handed a bag of cash and a plane ticket.

"Basically, I was a bean counter for special operations groups." Bill said with a funny smile. His soft-looking exterior, short, with a thin balding top, didn't match the hair-raising stories he sometimes told. "We're in the middle of supporting Afghan rebels holed up in Pakistan," one of these began, "and my boss shoves way too much money in my hands to fly commercial. 'Get this to them pronto!' he says. 'Instructions are glued to the inside of this wallet. Don't open it until you get to Karachi!' he orders me. "I have to hoof it over to the State Department to find a diplomat to take it over by pouch so we don't have to worry about a baggage inspection. And then get on the next flight. I think I had ten Snickers bars and two clean pair of underwear with me when I left.

"In Pakistan," Bill went on, "I pick up the money from the embassy and open the wallet to get my instructions. It tells me to go to the Consular Office and ask for a letter waiting for me. The consular officer on duty hands me the letter. There's a map that shows a road and an X about five miles from the Afghanistan border. It says,

There will be a huge sign next to the road warning of the border up ahead and Russian inspections… in English. Be there between 1400 and 1500 hours today. Three nasty guys in very dirty turbans, probably with weapons, will see you and say, "Hi Bill." Just give them the package and return as soon as you can. Don't give the package to anyone that doesn't say, "Hi Bill."

"Everything went off OK but I had to correct the guy that said, 'Hyello, my American friend' instead of, 'Hello Bill.'

"Then there was the run to Honduras. I never even knew which rebels we were supporting there." Bill shook his head and laughed. "They flew me into El Salvador and drove me across the border to a little iguana barbecue hut. I had to wait until a blue Ford Bronco drove by and then walk about three hundred yards down the road where I'd see a Coca-Cola sign. There was supposed to be a KFC bag in the dirt. I was to put the money inside it then leave it exactly where I found it." Bill sighed. "Fucking bag wasn't there. I started looking for it and finally found it in a mud puddle. The money I had was in a sealed bag. So I followed my instructions. I put it back in that slimy mess and got the hell out of there."

"Did you know what the money was for?" I asked him.

"Not always," he said. "I rarely asked questions. Even if it didn't jibe with the bean counting I was doing. I preferred the money drops in Berlin. Usually those didn't involve human interaction. They did give me a belly full of beer; and the boss let me take my wife along."

***

The money that Yuri was counting turned out to be my signal that our mission had changed. Toshek and Yuri broke the news to me. We hadn't even gotten off the train yet. Already, they had the new money and new documents from Embassy Joe. They'd met him in Almaty, Kazakhstan where he had suddenly shown up with bags of cash for them to distribute and new instructions for me. The nuclear sites east of Novosibirsk had been scratched from my itinerary; after taking care of various business in Novosibirsk, I would start back west again. While the finer details were convoluted, the thrust of the change was that Yuri and Toshek would be with me as far as Chelyabinsk, get off the train there, and then we would meet up when I came back that way with Dima. That is, if Dima was, in fact, with me. Yuri would be the one making all the arrangements for me to safely get to the debris sites. Toshek, though, was the guy who kept the money. Maybe that faraway look on Toshek's face came from his possessing more money than he had ever seen before. He would use it for bribes and Yuri's arrangements— and probably keep a hefty portion for himself.

Neither Yuri nor Toshek mentioned Vlad. From what I could quickly gather from the amended instructions they'd delivered to me, Vlad was absent from the plans. So I asked, "What about Vlad? You said something earlier that he was finishing his last job and you hoped he would be leaving us soon." Toshek's unchanging smile altered slightly but could still be called a grin or at least a smirk. He said to me, "Vlad the Impaler might have to do something for money for us."

I laughed. "Vlad the Impaler! The original Count Dracula, I think. You said, 'do something for money'?"

"Maybe better to say he should be available to do something for money if needed," Yuri corrected me. I wasn't completely in the dark by this time. I'd figured out that Vlad was the 'hatchet man' for the group. The U.S. Navy Underwater Demolition Team used the term to describe the one guy who carried a lethal weapon. He would quietly neutralize someone if required while the team carried out its mission. Vlad certainly looked the role.

Yuri went on, "These places you are going with Dima are not picnic places. Money talks there. And also, there are strong eyes from Moscow everywhere. Eyes sometimes want money too. These eyes can only respect similar strength. Your Dima is not strong and his small money would only insult them. Our job changed when Joe came to Almaty. Now we are spending a little time with you and we are watching for some more important people that might be around Chelyabinsk. Vlad will be needed for you to be successful with your photos and dirt collection and disassembly of Soyuz. We — including you — need to get used to his dirty looks."

"So can I ask you how much money Joe gave you for this job?" I asked Yuri, knowing he probably wouldn't answer.

"No! It would be very rude question. But I will say that it was a lot more than the five thousand dollars you were given." His reply did give me some useful information: it showed he knew a lot more about me than I knew about him.

Yuri and Toshek weren't exactly talkative characters as that slow Russian train made its way eastward but, when approached by other travelers and coaxed into a conversation, they could hold their own. It sometimes seemed like they had rehearsed their 'good cop/bad cop' routines to be able to get information from people or, as in the case of casual train travel, get ordinarily quiet Russian or Kazakh travelers to open up about things they might not normally talk about to strangers. Such was the case with a family returning home to Kazakhstan from L'viv in Ukraine, a formerly Polish city that had been forfeited to the Soviet Union when the borders shifted at the end of World War II. Interestingly in this case, this family could speak Polish since they had been uprooted from their original home — the Poles called it Lwow in those days — and forcibly sent to Kazakhstan during the Stalinist terror of the thirties and forties.

***

As Toshek and the family exchanged stories about Stalinist wrongs never righted, Yuri leaned over and offered up a few details about Poles and forced migration to Ukraine and Kazakhstan. This was a subject my mother-in-law in Krakow had always spent more time talking about than I really had the time to listen.

After listening to the Poles' story in our compartment, he said to me, "America prides itself on its multi-racial population. I think you have been welcoming immigrants for a long time."

"You're right, Yuri. Each region in the U.S. has its own history of early settlers, many of them directly from overseas."

"Many Poles, Lithuanians, and other ethnic groups were forced to uproot themselves and head to the East," Yuri said. "I grew up with a lot of them. Your immigrants came by choice. Ours did not. Big difference." He seemed lost in his thoughts and a moment of melancholy.

"You have any idea how many were forced to move?" I asked.

"Stalin 'transferred' huge populations in my own country. That number probably will never be known. I've seen numbers for Poland that were about a quarter million. And 100,000 didn't survive the terrible first winter in Kazakhstan."

"Reminds me of the American Indian removals perpetrated by President Andrew Jackson in the 1830s," I said.

"Interesting word for it. 'Removals.' Sounds very Soviet to me," Yuri commented.

***

Yuri and I joined the broader discussion. Between my Polish and their Russian, we all had a lively talk about life on the steppes of Kazakhstan and the occasional arrival of twenty-ton Soyuz space boosters falling on farms and villages around their own property. This family of four, with what I thought were classic Polish features, blondish hair and blue eyes, was composed of a mother and father around forty and a boy and girl in their early teens. They were all unusually tall and thin but not unhealthy looking by any standard. They lit up as I spoke, realizing they would be able to practice their Polish with me. It was hard not to see Renata, Malgosia and Staszek in these faces. While the distance between me and my family was steadily increasing as the eastbound train continued deeper into Siberia, I felt stronger about the importance of the mission. I felt a greater bond with the people we were trying to protect in this forgotten part of the world. This also encouraged me to try harder to salvage some aspect of my rocky marriage. Even if it was just the kids.

The young boy looked at his father and excitedly started telling one story. "We were sitting down to dinner and suddenly we heard a strange whistling sound. Lena, my sister, was outside and started yelling to us to come out. A piece of flaming metal, as big as a house, streaked across the sky and crashed into a barn outside our village. We saw the explosion when it hit the barn. It started a fire that burned up several houses. Many animals were also killed in the fire."

The father continued the story. "Fumes from the fire, I guess the burning rocket fuel, killed another family that lived downwind from the crash site."

I asked the family, "Were you ever informed by authorities to be on the look-out for these man-made meteorites?" Everyone in the compartment laughed. What a suggestion! That the government might release information about impending launches.

Lena, the young girl, tugged on her father's sleeve and reminded him about the volunteer fire team and their experiences. He nodded and explained, "Large swaths of steppe would often be consumed by fires started when a Soyuz rocket stage hit the Earth. How bad the fires were depended on the time of year and how dry the grass or timber was. We were always most afraid of the fumes from the rocket fuel. Lots of animals usually died. Farmland would be useless around the debris." The farmer paused. His eyebrows rose as he described more action scenes. "So, you can imagine finding these strange smoking hunks of metal on the ground. Farmers would usually jump in their vehicles, drive to such a site, and strip them of anything removable that might be useful around the farm."

"Would you just leave the 'monster' lying there?" I asked.

"Most farmers wouldn't have the equipment to remove them. So for years, we plow around them until the dirt piles up. That would create a strange mound in the middle of a wheat field." He figured that he knew of nearly fifty or sixty such buried space fossils within ten miles of his village. The children chimed in to tell their father that there were others only children knew about and were keeping secret. They smirked and giggled as their father's eyes got big with surprise.

Toshek changed the subject slightly. "Do space part pirates come to your village?" he asked.

The father reacted immediately. "Caravans of cars and trucks come," he confirmed. They would show up to take away these man-made meteorites or, sometimes, to claim them and then guard them. When that happened, he said, "We could never take rocket parts. Never even see them. Nobody else would see, either. Or photograph."

"Who are these bastards?" Toshek asked. "Locals? Riff-raff from Moscow?"

The father didn't hesitate to discuss this with us. "We have our own locals that try to control who gets space junk, but we don't fear them. We fear the guys from Chelyabinsk and other bigger Siberian cities. They come in and set up their camps. They have guns and feel comfortable in our village. This causes a lot of fear and pain. Small battles are fought all around us, sometimes, as the groups fight for control. We are told that some of the people are from the government trying to reclaim things that are rightfully theirs. I sometimes have my doubts about that. They seem just as willing to kill people as the riff-raff from Chelyabinsk."

"Does anyone have the ability to lift a whole ten-ton piece of metal onto a truck and haul it away? Do you see this happening ever?" Yuri asked.

"That happened a few times. One of our richest neighbors in the next village has a trucking company. He hired a crane from a state construction company not far away. They rigged up chains and cables on several pieces of space junk. They were able to lift these pieces onto a flatbed truck he owns and haul them away. He has them on his property with guards and cameras all around. He is afraid that a space part pirate will come and try to steal them." The father's voice trembled with excitement as he told us this.

"Would a farmer who has a piece of space junk on his property be willing to sell it if someone offers them money?" Toshek asked.

"Everything has its price. Of course!" the father replied.

I laughed and nodded in agreement, and secret embarrassment, perhaps more keenly aware of this fact than the others could have known. All the talk of dirty dealing and corruption kindled a thought. I wondered if our Siberian family had ever heard stories about American prisoners of war turning up in the Siberian Gulag. I shared this, in whispered English, with Yuri.

He rolled his eyes a bit and asked, "Is this a Joe request?"

"Yes. He's had you on the POW-MIA detail before?" I asked him.

He nodded and spoke up immediately to our Polish friends as if to get this on and off the table as quickly as he could. "What about the legend of American soldiers from Vietnam being 'sold' to the Soviets and held in camps or prisons? Any rumors flying around about that for the past twenty or thirty years?"

The father acted like he was digesting the question slowly and thinking of an answer; mostly looking at me, since he assumed I was the interested party. "We know there are theories about that," he said carefully. "The closest thing I can say for sure is that if there was ever an opportunity to do it, the Soviets of the sixties and seventies would have done so." I nodded in agreement after Yuri translated the man's answer. That led him to mention something he had heard: a kind of folk-tale in the form of a song about American hippies living in a commune somewhere between Vladivostok and Harbin, China. He couldn't remember the words or the tune.

"Really!" I exclaimed. "Any possibility of it being true?" I was almost laughing.

"I don't think so," He said. "Vodka and religion can make you see and believe in things that aren't there. We don't have a lot of religion. But we have a lot of the other thing."

Yuri's look meant, I think, that he hoped the POW question could now die, a ridiculous rumor collapsing of its own weight. I let it lie, for now, but reminded myself to push the issue with Dima and his contacts when I got to Novosibirsk.

The train rolled on. The monotony of sounds, the sights that changed very little through the dirty windows, let my mind return to the money, bribery, and the question of how much cash it might take to get anything done when I returned from Novosibirsk. Also, I wondered if I'd be doling out money to Dima's people before I ever got back to Chelyabinsk. Would I have enough left? Would Yuri and Toshek take care of 'arrangements' as they said it was their job to do? Would I even find them when I returned with Dima? And would Dima be upset that I didn't trust his arranging things?

This trip was wearing me thin emotionally. Beyond the mission details, I was beating myself up with my own dilemma smoldering 2,500 kilometers west of this lumbering train. Was it over with Renata? If destined to separate or divorce, was that the end of my life in Poland? Would I see my kids again? Follow through with the new flat, step away and bid farewell honorably? And yet, as the train rumbled ever eastward, I was only heading into my fourth day.

Progress Rocket Factory Samara, Russia

The train pulled into Samara after forty-eight hours of 'rough-riding' the rails from Kiev. The short rail lengths still in use in that part of the former Soviet Union made for a rhythmic 'duggity-dug... duggity-dug... duggity-dug.' At the train's speed, the intervals between track joints were about two seconds each. I wouldn't guess that we had ever gone faster than eighty kilometers per hour the whole way, if that. Stops at nearly every small village also slowed our progress. Then long waits on side tracks for priority trains going the other way, where there was only a single track for two-way travel, added what I calculated to be more than eight hours to the trip.

Once in Samara, Yuri suggested that he and I go to the factory that makes the Soyuz rockets. It had a predictably optimistic Soviet name: Progress. It offered some watered-down tours for foreigners. At least it might get me somewhat familiar with the unclassified versions of the booster and upper stages. Yuri also wanted to show me in person where some of the more interesting 'bolt-ons' would probably be found if we actually got to any debris sites. I was happy to be off the train for a couple of hours and in a pleasant enough city where the Volga and Samara rivers meet. The rocket factory had a long history of space vehicle production, on top of fabricating and assembling civil and military aircraft, going back even before World War II.

Industrial cities in the former Soviet Bloc all smelled the same, at least to me. Way too much coal was always being burned in cities where humans in fact needed to breathe to stay alive. An often-overlooked aspect of the Soviet planned economy was that factories, refineries and power plants, producing the most unpleasant of exhausts and pollutants, were in walking distance from residential areas. Planned residential communities with names like 'First Proud Five-Year Plan' or 'Defense of the Motherland' would be within two or three tram stops or right next to an extremely dangerous chemical plant or steel mill. A notorious example was the Nowa Huta suburb of Krakow. The Lenin Steel Factory there was just five minutes from the flat where my wife and kids and I were living.

Samara seemed the same. It was a mere ten-minute walk from the train station to the coal-fired generation plant that belched tons of unscrubbed sulfur and soot into the air every day. The Progress aviation and rocket fabrication plant was a tram ride of just ten minutes from the downtown post office. Yuri and I had walked there to pick up some post cards. How convenient! A ten-megawatt power plant on the Progress site took care of any problems with interruptions in electrical power. This added a nice gray-to-black patina to everything around the plant, especially downwind to the east and the south.

The most damning of circumstances, just like in Krakow, was that these plants were upwind from the major residential areas.

We spent our first five years in Krakow in Nowa Huta. I knew what breathing dangerous levels of coal dust, sulfuric acid, and chlorine gas could do to you in a short time. Forget about outdoor clothes lines to dry your sheets. They'd be black in less than an hour. Two bouts of pneumonia in the summer of 1986 took jogging off my list of activities. Growing herbs or tomatoes on the balcony for your salad? Forget it! We had plenty of good reasons to want that better flat, in a much cleaner part of the city. Renata had been part of the Solidarity demonstrations there in the early 80s when tear gas and live ammunition had been used to break up protests. Commie tear gas caused permanent damage to eyes and lungs. She wasn't the only one with breathing problems. My daughter had inherited my asthma. Our fast-track program to get the family away from this Soviet-created blight was serious.

One must wonder what kind of city planning or urban development decision-making had gone on. In the case of Poland's Communist leadership, decision-making, and industrial planning, it served the government well to employ a hundred thousand workers who had been moved to Nowa Huta from the penury of Poland's rural south. It also benefited the regime to locate the plant upwind from a concentration of Poland's intelligentsia, which happened to include a language instructor and her foreign-born husband. Many saw this as an effort to literally smother us and silence any resistance.

Renata's own dissident activity mirrored her father's heroics as a Polish partisan during the Second World War. Solidarity had been crushed but shortly after martial law was imposed, she had successfully escaped to Sweden. That two-year experience had opened her eyes, making her hungry for something better in her life. When we married, I had promised to be part of that. That commitment had carried a lot of weight in my decisions about career choices and living arrangements.

I put all these reflections aside when our tour guide greeted us in the Progress Rocket Factory's visitor reception area. He introduced himself as Sergei. He was tall, with long silvery hair and a face that reminded me of Leonard Nimoy's Spock on *Star Trek*. His combed-back pompadour reminded me of the teacher in my intensive Russian class at the University of Washington. Just as intense as that teacher who I couldn't get along with — I eventually dropped his class — Sergei acted like he was unaccustomed to leading an unannounced American through the factory. Although he said he'd conducted "countless American official visits," after a pause to emphasize his surprise at my arrival, he qualified this. It turned out that those American visitors were either relatives of high-level Progress employees, astronauts, or NASA officials. People who had already been carefully vetted. He finally agreed to take Yuri and me only on a short tour and asked us not to photograph anything. We signed a strange-looking non-disclosure agreement in Russian. Yuri joked that it was worded in such a way that our just being in the plant was grounds for an espionage case. "Let's be careful," he said, "since we have been tried in court and are already convicted on paper."

Indeed, the tour was short. We were allowed to view production areas only through windows on second-level mezzanines. And while we were forbidden to take photographs, cameras were everywhere, pointing at us wherever we went. A lot of mirrors, too. Probably these mirrors were one-way glass.

Sergei answered a question I had always pondered as a kid, having an interest in U.S. booster rockets and engines. I asked him, "Why do Russian rockets seem to have a lot of small engines compared to the United States Atlas, Titan, and Saturn rockets? Those have, at most, five on each stage."

"It is very common question," he answered. "First stage of our Soyuz rockets, now use four identical conical liquid-fueled booster engines. Each booster engine has a single rocket motor with four combustion chambers, two Vernier combustion chambers, and one set of turbopumps."

Sergei pointed to an area on the assembly floor below us. "See all those conical nozzles over there? They correspond to each combustion chamber."

"Wow! I get it. Four rocket engines, each with multiple combustion chambers. That makes it look like nearly two dozen engines — if you think like an American." Sergei seemed unenthusiastic about this. I turned to Yuri. "I hope I can see such a configuration within the next couple of weeks, during our debris site visit."

"I think we should finish this tour pretty soon, Andy," he responded. "Maybe after we get through the production areas." Yuri showed no emotion but was acting a little rushed.

Soon enough, we were taken to have tea and cookies in a large room that displayed scale models of famous rockets that had carried the world's first humans to space. Sergei excused himself for a few minutes, allowing Yuri and me to walk around the room on our own reading the labels on the museum exhibits.

"You see interesting things? Get better idea what Soyuz rocket look like?" Yuri asked.

"The stuff in the information packet from Joe is pretty detailed but it was good to see these things in person. I'm glad we took this little side trip."

"Not saying too much now, please," he whispered.

Sergei had come back. He asked us, bluntly, "We are interested in where you are going now. You said Novosibirsk earlier. Are you scientist, businessman, or government person?"

"Novosibirsk is my final destination. I have some meetings with a man to introduce me to Novosibirsk State University officials. We are going to discuss a business program cooperation project. And maybe I will visit some more factories." I noticed that I was starting to talk like my host and Yuri. That was inevitable. It happened whenever I wanted to avoid confusing someone when speaking English, unsure how proficient my audience was.

"Very good idea!" Sergei gave me a broad smile. "I am former faculty member at NSU. Political Science and Information Management; kind of propaganda expert." Sergei laughed at his own joke. "Your train is leaving soon. Best to be on your way."

We thanked Sergei, who presented us with a bag full of Soviet and New Russian pins and brochures about the factory. The propaganda chief also gave us a brochure about the beautiful area around Samara, campgrounds on its rivers and other vacation sites.

Sergei waved at us as we were leaving. "Much luck and be careful! Don't be too curious out here in Siberian back country. Curiosity is not good for survival here. Except in the laboratory."

As Yuri and I walked back toward the tram stop, I asked him what he thought Sergei was really trying to say.

He replied, "Sergei is not sure what he smells but he wishes he were involved in it. It's a good thing he works here. If he worked in a uranium enrichment plant, every bad guy would get what they want with his help." Yuri prided himself on being able to read Russians well.

Katerina and Zhenia

I wished I was better at reading Russians as I fumbled with the old-style skeleton key, trying not to panic. Just a few hours after leaving the rocket factory, I was fearing for my life back on the train. I'd gotten the key from a woman in the dining car. Finding car seven was easy; it was the first one next to the restaurant car. The seventh compartment was clearly marked, too, and the key easily opened the door. Breathing heavily, I closed it as quickly and quietly as I could after I looked to see how close Vlad was behind me. There was no mistaking his murderous rage; I hoped his equally obvious drunkenness had slowed him down.

I also needed to know if anyone had seen me go into the sleeping compartment that Katerina and Zhenia shared.

By my guess, no one had seen me, nor could anyone know where I'd gone after I rushed out of the dining car. Except, of course, my two new lady friends. Holding my ear to the air vent on the door, I listened for any sign that Vlad was making a scene in the restaurant car. Quite the opposite, though. Everything was strangely silent. After about a minute, I finally heard people talking normally and assumed that Vlad either had left or was sitting quietly at a table. My heart had been racing wildly the past five minutes and I finally felt myself relaxing as my breathing slowed.

I took a moment to look around and noted that the women had a much more comfortable space than I was sharing with Vlad, Toshek, and Yuri. It was the Russian version of a first-class sleeping berth that you would get in countries like France or Germany, but with a bit of the Russian flair. Nice embroidered sheets on a real — almost real — mattress that was properly made up with down pillows, even chocolates on turned-down sheets. Chai sachets, a refrigerator, nice china cups and plates, and three champagne flutes waited behind a small glass door next to the private washroom's doorway. These women had also stocked up on juices, bread, and other food that was neatly wrapped and stored on the shelves of their mini-pantry. The wardrobe was open. Several dresses, all floral prints, hung neatly on the right side with sleeping gowns, underwear, and some sexier night wear on the other side hanging from pink padded hangars. There were only three bunks, all on one side of the compartment.

I was already contemplating asking my new friends if I could offer some money to take the third bunk in their compartment. Yuri and Toshek might deem it best for me to stay out of sight from Vlad till he sobered up. Considering whether to leave now and return my key to Katerina, I heard a knock at the door and assumed it was the women coming to reclaim their private space. In fact, it was.

Katerina, the older of the two, had an arm around her niece Zhenia, who appeared to be feeling unwell. She smiled weakly and excused herself to the bathroom.

I moved toward the door to leave, and Katerina stopped me. She suggested I stay for a bit. In a slightly hushed voice, she said, "That crazy man chasing you will probably sleep now. Zhenia and I shouldn't have had so much to drink but we don't want you to leave yet. Stay and have something to eat. Zhenia will lie down but I think we can all talk in this small space without feeling cramped." She could see I was a little surprised that she was welcoming me to stay. "Don't worry," she assured me. "We don't take your money on first date."

She didn't have to ask me again. I admit, at that moment it wasn't just the danger from Vlad that motivated me. In that cozy compartment, my cramped apartment in Nowa Huta and the unhappy wife I had left there were the last things on my mind. Very willingly, I stayed.

***

I had first spotted them, having soup with bread and a drink, as we were about to pull out of Samara. Yuri and I had made it back to the station well before the train's scheduled departure, but as we waited in a small cocktail bar near the platform, we heard the whistle and announcement that the train would be departing in two minutes. We hustled over to our car, number four, and got aboard. While hurrying down the platform, I caught a glance through the restaurant car's windows. The two attractive, well-dressed women were already sitting at a small table. I realized, based on my adventures in Moscow, that they had a different look about them. Very pretty, but made up a little too much, maybe, for the dust and dirt they would now be 'swimming' through on the train. I wondered where they were from and where they might be going. Chelyabinsk was twenty hours away. If the schedule was right, we would be arriving around noon tomorrow.

My curiosity was up and I decided to investigate. A minor pang of conscience might have momentarily slowed my exuberance as I worked my way through the crowds on the train. Pushing family faces away from the work I did was clearly something that even Jane back at the embassy promoted. Being around attractive women and sensing opportunities for capturing unexpected intelligence were part of the job. Even the chance meeting with the Poles on the train the day before had revealed things about rocket debris we weren't aware of. This *was* an interesting opportunity, I thought. The guilt faded and I continued to our compartment to get cleaned up a little and see if I could find our newly embarked travelers in the restaurant car. Then, I walked right into Vlad. He was clearly drunk and talking to himself when I stepped into the compartment. Yuri had already disappeared and Toshek was not around. So I was forced to deal with Vlad myself. He muttered something in Russian to the effect of, "You fucked up, asshole." He looked right at me as he said it. While I wasn't positive he was directing his comment at me, it did seem likely. He was shaking his head and still staring at me.

"I'm finished now," he said, "and I can deal with you... however I like."

That made me just a little uncomfortable. I was changing my shirt and putting on my jacket as he said this. I knew exactly what he had said but tried to act as if I hadn't understood him. He poured a huge shot of vodka into a green bell pepper he had cut the top off, making a three-or-four-ounce shot "glass." He downed it quickly and looked away. The half-liter vodka bottle was almost empty. Judging by how drunk he was, I guessed that this was the second bottle he'd been working on since we'd arrived in Samara. I was ready to get away from him and did so as fast as I could. The dining car was on the other side of the luggage car and I sprinted there, hoping Vlad would not follow me. The last thing I wanted was to have him barging into the dining car with a knife, screaming obscenities.

The two new women were still sitting where I had seen them through the window. It was an elevated table for two with stools bolted to the floor. I had no chance of inviting myself to their table unless I stood. Suddenly, I felt a small amount of ironic humor; I was plotting for a way to introduce myself to two women. The tables were turned and I was now the 'Inter-Guy' on the train, scheming to meet them. That made me laugh. In a funny way, it also justified my actions as part of my work. I asked the waiter if I could sit near the window closest to them. I also asked him if the women had ordered anything alcoholic to drink. He said they had ordered one vodka each, but thought it was time for a second shot. He asked if I was buying. I told him I would be glad to buy for them. And for him. He smiled and thanked me, tipping his hat a little.

"Do you mind if I sit over here by the window?" I asked the women in English as I passed them. I noticed they weren't wearing the typical bad Russian perfume. Both smiled slightly. Now that I was up close, I could see that one of them had little lines around her eyes and other subtle signs that she was somewhat older, probably well into her thirties, at least. She's the one who answered. "Not at all. Please do. We are leaving soon."

"I'm sorry to hear that. I asked the waiter to bring out two more of whatever you were drinking," I said, exaggerated disappointment in my voice.

"Have you already paid him?" the younger woman asked. She looked first at me and then back at her companion without any change in expression.

I lied and said I had.

"In that case," the older woman said, "we will have one more if you will join us here."

"The table does not allow a third person," I pointed out. "Maybe you will come to my booth here and join me?"

Without a word, they gathered their few things and slid into the booth, the younger woman next to me and the older directly across.

"What is this word 'boot'?" the older woman asked. "Are you saying 'boot' like shoe for our sitting place?"

The younger woman was beginning to laugh a little as her friend queried me about 'booth' and 'boot.' I was pretty sure the older lady was having fun with this language lesson and being playful, but she was a good actor, playing the part seriously. "Why would Americans or British use 'boot' to describe a place to sit and have a meal? Boots are dirty!"

The younger lady put her head back, softly laughing out loud.

"I am Yekaterina," the older one said, "and this is Yevgeniya, my niece." As she held her hand out, I suspected she wasn't sure whether I would shake it or try to kiss it. I knew I was right as she started with her palm down, but then turned it perpendicular to the floor as she saw I was reaching my hand out, too. It was an important moment, I thought. Shaking her hand would be more American; I wasn't sure if I wanted to play the Polish card yet. A Pole would always opt to kiss a woman's hand if it was offered.

"May I call you Katerina and Zhenia?" I asked.

Their faces both registered surprise that I had suggested an informal shortening of their names so quickly, but Katerina replied, "Yes, it's OK. You said our names very well. I think you know some Russian."

"Not much," I said. "I know Polish pretty well." At that moment, our drinks came out. The waiter put a bottle on the table with four glasses. I was looking at the fourth glass when the waiter said, "I will take my shot and go. Thank you, Mr. Gold."

"Mr. Gold. Now we know your last name. Shall we know your first name? You know only our first names," Katerina proudly exclaimed.

"Andrew. Or Andy," I said.

"Nice to meet you, Andrew or Andy," Katerina replied with a smile.

I frowned at this. "Let's make it Andy."

"OK. Nice to meet you, Andy."

"Very nice to meet you, Katerina and Zhenia."

"He has a nice voice, Auntie, don't you think?" Zhenia whispered in Russian. It was quite loud enough for me to hear.

***

The conversation went very easily. It was as pleasant a time as I have spent getting to know strangers. My conscience was clear. A friendly conversation with strangers on a train. Nothing flirtatious about it — mostly. I had nothing to feel guilty about. They had the air of being on vacation and seemed unusually happy for Russian women traveling alone, especially on a train that was *not* headed to a vacation spot. Like sisters sharing a few secrets with a stranger that might have never been told, Katerina said, "Three-year journey is coming to an end. We are going home to the family estate between Chelyabinsk and Yekaterina. Small town, Dalmatovo."

Zhenia added, "It is beautiful there. My grandfather made it an oasis in Siberia."

Katerina looked at Zhenia and said, "Needs a lot of work, though. We saved enough in three years to restore it to its original beauty…I hope."

Andy asked, "It was your plan from the beginning? How did your journey begin?"

Katerina answered quickly, "Difficult times for all of us in Dalmatovo so I went to Moscow where I could find a good job.

Zhenia explained further, "My mother started to become sick. Kidney disease and a transplant was necessary but difficult to organize. I graduated from Novosibirsk State University and went to live with Katerina. Some things I could help her with. Sometimes she didn't want too much help." Both Katerina and Zhenia laughed obviously sharing another secret thought about their adventures together.

Andy asked Zhenia, "Was your mother worried about you going to Moscow?"

She trusted her sister to take care of me…and she did. My mother died waiting for a transplant with no chance for dialysis. After the funeral we went back to Moscow. A few years later we went to Kiev.

Katerina had never had a child. As a doting aunt, she had always participated in raising Zhenia. Now that her niece was in her mid-twenties, they were best of friends. I guessed that Katerina was, at most, maybe five years older than me. She wore her natural blonde hair short, and while not super thin was quite muscular, standing about my height. I detected slightly Asian features in her face. Zhenia was a tall, thin, true redhead with long hair and had no sign of the Asian hints I saw in her aunt. In fact, if I'd seen her on the street in Dublin, I'd have thought she was a local.

"Please, what do you do, Andy? Businessman maybe?" Katerina asked.

"A little bit of that. Do you know the company National Express? It is in Moscow, too. Until recently, I was the country director for National Express in Poland."

"Really? I know the country director for National Express in Moscow. His name is Brian."

"Oh, my God! You are kidding! No, you aren't. You know his name!" Inside, I was a little afraid that I had made a mistake by letting slip my connection to NatEx. I regretted saying anything about it.

"I am no longer working for them," I hurried to clarify. "I also do some teaching at a business school in Krakow. We want to discuss setting up an MBA program partnership with NSU," I explained. Katerina's charm was working on me in an overpowering way and I could feel my interest in her growing. Of course, Renata's eyes also forced their way into my mind. I visualized her staring at me as I was doing an in-class quiz in her class. "Can't think about her now, damn it!" I screamed to myself.

"Poles with Russians?" Katerina asked.

"Well, sort of. But with the University of Detroit or some other American university as the main partner."

"That is good idea, I think. Russians and Polish people don't always see eye to eye." It occurred to me without effort that some Polish people don't always see eye to eye with Americans, either.

"And you two? What did you do in Moscow and Kiev for three years? And what do you have planned upon your return to Chelyabinsk?" I asked. I looked directly at the women, without blinking.

"We worked as escorts," Katerina answered, also without blinking. "Now it is time to return to our home and do something for ourselves with the money we saved." When Katerina said this, they, too, focused on me and waited for my reaction.

I struggled to avoid showing my surprise. It wasn't so much that Katerina was or had been a prostitute. It was more surprising for me that 'Aunt Kat' had admitted they were both escorts after they told me the story about Zhenia's mother dying. I had imagined an academic position for Katerina at Moscow State and Zhenia doing translation work at Aeroflot's Tverskaya Street offices in central Moscow. Instead, I listened as they told their actual story. Katerina began to describe her Moscow experience, "When I saw there that jobs as secretaries pay so little, I decided I would make big changes in my life and take risks... something that gets in your blood when you are in Moscow." Andy just nodded and let her continue. "Sex business is really big business for some people.

Making sure you are safe and being smart with your money is part of the job. My niece came to protect me… and became my best friend." Zhenia smiled at Katerina and put her hand on her aunt's arm resting on the table next to mine. We continued to sip from the bottle of vodka and ordered fish and some beers as we talked.

Katerina jumped into the conversation again, "Mafia and government control of sex in the hotels, especially in Moscow, makes it difficult sometimes. Staying focused on making your bank account big is not easy…especially when others are trying to control you. We had some problems in Moscow and decided to go to Kiev. Another year of making money in Kiev was like a fresh start in a new place. Now we are going home with plans for a real life."

These two attractive women had escaped to Moscow from the Siberian steppes, worked their way into the elite world of Moscow prostitution and its high-end escort services, and in three years socked away a cool $900,000. The money was now sitting in an account on Cyprus.

Knowing how dangerous a life that must have been, I was intrigued with how a mature woman, taking on the care and mentoring of a young niece, could choose to become a prostitute — and somehow enlist the young woman's help. I fumbled with my words as we were all a little drunk, but they understood what I was trying to understand. Katerina interrupted me.

"After seventy-five years of Communism, the freedom to make what feels like unlimited money becomes very obsessive. Also, seeing a goal for our future — where there was no future at all — made us very determined to be successful with our plan. Living in America, you must understand something about these feelings. Don't you?"

I could only smile and nod in agreement. I put my hand on Katerina's arm and squeezed it as I thought about what experiences they must have been through during the past three years.

"So, now a question for you, Mr. Andy," Katerina asked, breaking the silence of my surprise. "Why is an American living permanently in Poland and traveling in Russia on a train that is going to Novosibirsk and our famous closed cities? Why aren't you in New York or Los Angeles being a typical American?"

The vodka fueled a see-saw of images of the results of my risky affair with Renata so many years ago. The crowded apartment in Nowa Huta. The walks in Golden Gate Park with Malgosia. Renata's ultimatum and escape back to Poland. Her relentless attacks on me now. I let them fade and then told Katerina, "Students become lovers and lovers become fathers. Fathers have to support children and life is complicated."

"Complicated it is," Zhenia agreed.

***

While I'd nearly forgotten about Vlad and his drunken threats a little earlier, a disturbance behind me broke up my conversation with my new friends. It was coming from the corridor in the direction of our car. Hearing Vlad's voice and the vulgarisms he was spewing as he loudly worked his way towards us, I came out of my own slightly inebriated state. I won't say I was scared, exactly, but I certainly felt on edge. OK, I admit, I was kind of scared. About several things, only one of which was Vlad. But I worked up my courage to ask Katerina if I could hide in her compartment that night.

She could see I was reacting to Vlad's approach. Whether she could see everything else I was reacting to, I had no idea. "Is he looking for you? I heard him say something about killing someone before he started vomiting and fell on the floor. Someone is helping him up now."

She handed me her key and, urgency in her voice, directed me. "Seventh car, seventh compartment. Go quickly!"

I couldn't help but notice Zhenia giggling again, her hands over her mouth, as I struggled to get out the dining car's opposite end unseen by my predator. For the moment my challenge was to avoid knocking the waiter down as he served the evening's steak tartares and pickled herring to customers reacting with horror to Vlad's drooling entry behind me.

***

"Why did you leave Moscow and go to Kiev?" We were comfortably settled into the first-class compartment. Since Katerina seemed in a mood to talk, I decided to indulge my curiosity. "Oh, and since you said you were working from many Moscow hotels, do you know my friend Alyona? She is a bartender at the Leningradskaya Hotel lobby bar."

"Interesting you ask these two questions together, because there is a little connection between them." Katerina responded slowly as our discussion turned from events in the dining car to how we had wound up on this train together. Zhenia was in her bunk, fully clothed. She lay on her side, her head on her left hand, listening to the conversation and only occasionally chiming in. Whenever I looked up to see if she was dozing off, she would catch my eye and smile sweetly.

"Moscow hotels and the women working there are completely controlled by the police now," Katerina said. "But for the first two years, we did our business without anyone controlling us."

Zhenia spoke up with a dissenting voice. "Not completely true. We also had an organizer that arranged for our rights to be in certain hotels. He arranged our entry cards and kind of license to do our business."

"License?" I asked.

Katerina continued, "Because the Russian mafia controls who can be an escort — or prostitute — at all the Moscow hotels, it is necessary to pay them regularly and to be sort of 'registered' with them. Our 'agent,' I call him, did this kind of work. He was closely connected to them and to the Russian government. He was not too unreasonable. But after two years of being our agent he disappeared. We were not allowed into the hotels anymore. We left Moscow since we had no 'license.' Every person we tried to find to be our new agent was only an asshole. When Zhenia's mother died, I made a kind of promise to Zhenia that, as bad as everything was, we would eventually be free of working for bad people. We would have money to do what we want. The situation in Moscow would no longer allow me to keep my promise."

I hesitated but asked her directly, "Were you an Inter-Girl in Moscow?" Zhenia broke out laughing but quickly quieted down. As I've mentioned, Inter-Girls were the prostitutes who officially entertained foreigners while the KGB or FSB looked on or listened in.

"I am sure that we were," Katerina said, "but we never agreed to it officially." She turned to Zhenia with a slight smile as if they had shared secrets.

"You said my friend Alyona the bartender is somehow connected to all of this." I reminded Katerina that she had linked Alyona with her problems in Moscow.

"Rumors were that Alyona is connected to whoever killed Mikhail, our agent. Alyona is very slippery. No one can figure out if she is Russian spy or American spy or just another mafia-controlled employee. Maybe you know something about her?" Katerina returned the question to me.

Alyona was just as enigmatic for me as Katerina described her. She had an uncanny sense of managing her huge bar so that everyone, regardless of who they were, felt that she was operating undercover for them. Instances where she seemed to know who I was meeting with and who would be going to my room later had been just too well played. So why and how would a rumor get started that she was connected to getting rid of someone? That was probably the result of some customer, like me, who came to believe she was absolutely on his team.

"No, she is very secretive," I said, "but the best bartender, concierge, and personal assistant I've ever seen. She never told me anything more than her interests in business, her hopes for a new great Russia, and her desire for Americans and all Westerners to feel safe in Moscow."

"Kind of bullshit answer that Americans are very good at giving," Katerina countered. "Sorry, Andy. I am sure she works for someone that has power. She's too good at what she does. And she has kept her job much longer than anyone I have seen after all the political changes."

I didn't mind her cutting response. Actually, I felt more respect for her analysis since she, too, had seen that Alyona was operating at a different level from the other players in her bar.

"So, you escaped Moscow and set up shop in Kiev. Why Kiev? And how did you do there?" I continued my questioning.

"Not sure what is it 'Set up shop in Kiev' but I think you mean moving and living there. *Pravda?*"

"Exactly. Sorry about the English slang."

"Family... not so close... helped us find a place. We quickly were able to build our contacts and business. Almost like in Moscow. Similar atmosphere but on smaller level." She thought again and added, "Quieter in Kiev but sex is always something that can be sold. Same customers. Businessmen, government officials, teachers. Professors and scientists, too."

"So now retirement for you, Katerina? What about Zhenia?" I asked.

"Teacher or travel agent I would like to try some time," Zhenia interjected from the bunk above me. "I have the Russian license to be travel agent and I did a small course for teaching English in Kiev."

Against my efforts to steer away from it, I used what I knew of Renata's teaching experience to comment, "Teaching your native language to foreigners can lead to interesting things. I guess I'm a good example of it. With the changes going on in this part of the world, you'll be inundated with interest. It's not difficult getting certified, either."

"Really? You think so?" she asked.

"I am certain of it." I added, "I am impressed, Zhenia." I looked up at her with a smile. I hoped to give praise to a young person who had faced innumerable ugly nights and horrible experiences in her last three years. At the time of this conversation, I was only thirty-three, but I was moved to see that these two women were neither demoralized nor unwilling to return to their homes. They were confident and ready to make new lives for themselves.

I succeeded at that, I thought. I had done what I originally set out to do. I'd learned one of the planet's most difficult languages and then catapulted myself into a corporate executive role in a foreign country. But then I thought about Renata in San Francisco. Why had that been such a failure? Unlike Katerina and Zhenia, she had been demoralized and afraid of the U.S.A. Ignoring all we'd agreed to, she had gone back to an old life. I'd been the one who came up with a plan to keep the dream going — according to her new terms. *Why can't she be more forgiving with me?* I brooded, the vodka helping me to feel sorry for myself. Through the alcohol fog, I looked admiringly at these two women. *Look at their resilience, courage, and humor!* They had faced adversity ten times worse than Renata ever had.

My drunken musings got me wondering. "Are you sure that going back to Siberia is really where you want to be?" I asked. "Having had a taste of the big exciting world beyond these barren steppes?"

Zhenia gently applauded my question.

Katerina responded, "There are things to take care of that have been waiting three years since my sister died. After that, maybe we will travel. Zhenia won't always be with her aunt. Soon she will marry an American and live in Chicago. I hope."

Zhenia acknowledged her aunt's prediction only with raised eyebrows. Otherwise, her expression remained unchanged.

"And you, Mr. Andy? You did not mention a beautiful wife and I see no ring."

"There is a Polish wife. For now. The ring was lost long ago, on a trip to Yaroslavl. Probably stuck between cushions on another Russian sleeper car going back and forth between Yaroslavl and Moscow for three years." My brief consideration of how much to say about Renata gave way to a fond recollection, memories of one particular late-night sales trip from Moscow to Yaroslavl in 1989 during the NatEx startup. Resentful about Renata's escape and continuing inflexibility, I fell prey to those feelings and my lingering thoughts that she'd stolen from our lives what I considered a fairy-tale-like existence in Sausalito or San Francisco's North Beach. How could she have given that up for a gritty, polluted little workers'-paradise dump downwind from the steel mill?

So I was ripe for temptation when a pretty young physicist from Dubna, Russia's theoretical physics town, got on the train late in the evening. We talked together until we wrapped ourselves around each other, then slept. She kept saying my wedding band made her uncomfortable. I woke up without the ring. I always wondered if she had taken it or if it simply fell off during our four-hour wrestling match. I preferred to think that it was still deep inside the fold of the upholstery on that couchette.

Katerina offered no comment to my edited version of the story. After a moment, she changed the subject. "Come back to the dining car. It looks like Zhenia is almost asleep." She held her hand out and waited for me to assist her in standing. She looked at me differently for a moment then opened the door to the corridor. With no sign of Vlad and only normal-sounding voices coming from the dining car, we walked in holding hands. Finding seats side by side in an empty "'boot,' we had two shots each of vodka with some orange juice. Katerina ordered a bottle of water to take to her room. She kissed me twice during the fifteen or twenty minutes we sat hip to hip in the dining car. I felt no desire to resist. For an instant, I also remembered Malgosia asking if it would be OK to go to the ice cream parlor with Marek, the attorney. Marek. I wondered if he was wearing my slippers and robe right now.

When Katerina got her water, she suggested I come back with her.

Katerina opened the door to their compartment and quickly shut off the light. As the main light went out and a night light flickered on, I could see that Zhenia had closed the curtain to her bunk space. Katerina whispered that we should be very quiet. Zhenia would be wearing earphones from her Sony Walkman, she told me, and would not want to hear us. That worked for them and it worked for me. And what Renata doesn't know won't hurt her. All of these thoughts were in an untidy ragged mess — and were forgotten — for the rest of the night.

Katerina took off my jacket and gently pushed me down onto the lower bunk. She whispered, "Please be here when I come back. If you want to wash yourself, you can do it after me." She disappeared to the compartment's private bathroom and I could hear water running for what seemed like half an hour. After she emerged, I did, in fact, take that quick shower she had suggested. Then, naked, I slid into the bunk on top of her, laying my clothes outside on the floor.

"Zhenia will see my clothes," I said into Katerina's ear. She moved slowly under me, stirring even greater excitement.

"Not a problem," she managed to whisper as I pulled away and caught my breath for a moment.

She whispered, "Be silent," guided me inside her, and then kissed me for what felt like an hour nonstop. We were tightly clamped to each other, moving ever so slightly in her body's vise-like grip. Finally, I could hold it no longer. I felt my body overcome with an almost electrical wave and then a shiver that lasted for what might have been five minutes.

We remained in our locked embrace but rolled over so we were both on our sides. Within about two minutes — admittedly, my sense of time isn't perfect in these situations — she was snoring lightly. I don't remember much more from that night except the rocking of the train — and fleeting thoughts of what I would do if Vlad should try to kick down the door.

Farewell

Katerina stirred before I did. Early morning light was breaking through the curtains around our bunk. I heard Zhenia humming as she boiled water for the morning tea. Katerina smiled at me as she got dressed in the confines of the cramped bunk space that we were sharing. I remembered that my clothes were on the floor just below me. Reaching down to pull them in and get myself dressed, I discovered that Zhenia had folded them and laid them on a foot stool. Katerina slipped around me and dashed off to the bathroom. I pulled the curtains and sat on the partially made bed.

"Good morning, Mr. Andy! How are you?" Zhenia asked in a pleasant voice, a smile on her face.

Through the window behind her, I could see that the sun was shining brightly. We were stopped on a siding in the middle of flat, grassy countryside. From the time, I guessed we must be about three hundred kilometers from Chelyabinsk. I remember thinking about Buzz Aldrin and what he said when he stepped out onto the moon after Neil Armstrong: "Beautiful, beautiful, magnificent desolation."

After gazing across the magnificently desolate steppe for a few seconds, I finally answered. "Thank you, Zhenia. I am well. A little too much vodka but I slept very well — considering these bunks are not designed for two people. And you? I hope we didn't wake you last night when we came in. Are you feeling better this morning?"

"You were both very quiet. I didn't hear anything. I am fine, thank you for asking," Zhenia said, nodding convincingly. "Will you face this crazy man this morning? Are your friends going to help? And, by the way, where were they when all this was happening?" Zhenia was right in asking these questions. They stirred my concern, as well.

The fact that Yuri and Toshek had been nowhere to be seen during Vlad's meltdown probably meant something else related to the mission was going on. Once I got some tea or coffee in me, I wanted to face whatever was awaiting me with Vlad. It seemed completely strange that he viewed me with such disgust. Inasmuch as he couldn't possibly care about who I'd slept with last night, the pleasant experience I'd had would not be anyone's reason for disgust—at least not anyone on this train. For God's sake, I'd never met the man. Yet after a few drinks he was ready to decapitate me. I wanted to — had to — find out what was up.

Katerina came out of the bathroom and went to work with her niece on a mini-breakfast for the three of us. She and Zhenia had a dozen open-face sandwiches made up in less than five minutes from their own cupboard. Rye bread, sardine paste, farmer's cheese, olives, roasted peppers, plum jam, canned ham, and slices of yellow cheese. Katerina divided it up into three each for herself and Zhenia and left six for me. I ate four and pushed my final two back at them. Gulping my tea and standing up, I gave them both a hug, thanked them for their kindness, and promised to be back soon: to treat them to a proper lunch before our arrival in Chelyabinsk at around noon.

Pausing long enough to take note that the sounds from the dining car seemed normal — laughter and spirited conversation — I walked straight in and saw Yuri and Toshek. They were in a booth that had enough room for me to join them. Yuri wore that expression he'd had when I first met him: he was worried and trying to figure something out that was troubling him.

"You are alive. It is good. Vlad lost his glue last night," Yuri said as I sat down. Confused for a second, I realized he meant, "Came unglued."

"That's for sure! Do I have to run if I see him this morning? And what the fuck is up with him? What on Earth have I done to piss him off so much?" Hoping for some answers, I wanted Yuri to explain a few things.

"Remember I told you that he was finishing up a previous job?" Yuri asked me in a low voice.

"Yes."

"He has been… let's say… nervous about this job. Ever since we left Almaty, he has been tossing parts of a body off the train. It was in the luggage room in a triple-lined body bag. He finally got rid of it all yesterday. And then he started drinking." The disgust that spread across Yuri's face as he told me this paired well with the horror of the story he was telling.

Thoughts of Embassy Joe giving Vlad such a task suddenly gave me

142

pause. And now I was wondering what I was doing with these guys. "Please tell me that Vlad's 'job' wasn't assigned by Embassy Joe." It was more a demand than a question.

"No, Joe isn't the direct customer in this case. But the customer is in bed most of the time with your country. So, Joe probably knows what's going on."

"Can I guess who it is?" I pushed Yuri. "Would you tell me if I am correct?"

"No." And that was all.

***

I was left to imagine what country might be behind Vlad's unpleasant task and had a few choices. Because the Mossad was known to be unforgiving when stalking suspects in its growing anti-terrorism efforts, the Israelis were my first choice. Also, in the post-Soviet era, vendettas extended across all the former republics. The United States tended to distance itself from the smaller Central Asian states but was beginning to take sides when nationalist fervor started to breed terrorists. As Zbigniew Brzezinski, Jimmy Carter's national security advisor predicted and then saw happening not long after the Berlin Wall fell, all of the ethnic conflicts that pre-dated the October Revolution re-erupted as the Soviet borders were re-drawn. A dozen and more countries found themselves once again autonomous and free to return to the nationalist battles or internal jihads they had waged before the First World War.

Just as the CIA was taking sides in Latin America, folks from headquarters in McLean, Virginia were now taking the long flights to the former Soviet republics. They were busy recruiting and supporting candidates for the eventual establishment of democratic and free-market mechanisms in those largely anarchic territories. And just as Poland had its influencers from the U.S. embedded with Solidarity during the seventies and eighties, so the southern Soviet republics, prime candidates for upheaval in the nineties, had American businessmen working both undercover and in the open, searching for new leaders for the future. Compared to Embassy Joe, who might deliver a few thousand dollars for some work to be done like I was doing, the guys from Virginia doing candidate recruitment or regime change work were much more formally organized. They also got a lot higher level of support.

Also, with so many countries operating in the region, people like Vlad, Yuri, and Toshek could pick up intelligence work from a host of Western players. Vlad had been given an unpleasant task with very significant payment at the same time he accepted Embassy Joe's request to go meet and work with me. I don't know if Vlad killed the person whose remains were in his bag. All I know is that he had to dispose of it. And he chose to do so bit by bit as the train made its way from Almaty in Kazakhstan to where we met in Kiev, then on across the steppes toward Samara and Chelyabinsk.

***

Once we'd established that he wouldn't discuss Vlad's disposal mission any further, Yuri had more to say. Once again, it turned out, our plans were changing a bit. "Vlad and Toshek are leaving the train now," he informed me. "Some people that know them got on the train in Samara. We noticed them yesterday in second class. It would be bad to have a confrontation. I will meet up with Toshek and Vlad in Chelyabinsk tomorrow or the next day. These guys are glued to their seats back in second class and are behaving very strangely. Since they do not know me, I spent my evening yesterday, while you were hiding from Vlad, planting some bugs and putting a small camera in place. I know who these people are; they are notorious for taking radioactive materials from weapons installations and nuclear sites. They come with cash; they leave with bad stuff."

Knowing such sinister characters were on the train gave me the jitters. What made me even more nervous was Yuri's surprise announcement: that my backup team was backing off.

"Does this mean you won't be with me for the Soyuz site trips?" I asked. "That's just ten days from now."

"We will see you when you return from Novosibirsk, I am sure," Yuri assured me. "Our task until you return will be to see where these guys on the train are going and find out what they are doing in Chelyabinsk. I am expecting to hand them off to someone when you arrive with your friend Dima."

"Where and when do we meet, Yuri? I can force Dima to stick to my schedule." I guesstimated now much time I would need in Novosibirsk. "So… let's say exactly ten days from now, if that is OK."

"Give me a two-day window, Andy, in case I have difficulties. Let's say ten to twelve days from today. In Chelyabinsk, if necessary, check into the Hotel South Ural. It is a hotel that has been for academics and government people since the thirties. Not super comfortable but clean. Also fully bugged."

"That sounds funny," I said. "Clean and bugged."

Yuri got the joke but didn't react. "No discussions about 'business' in the room, please, and no names! I will see you when I see you."

"Not unless I see you first!" I countered, but, once again, my attempt to be funny was lost. Yuri's focus was strictly on matters at hand.

Vlad and Toshek got off the train directly behind the locomotive, stepping down from an exit that was marked 'Forbidden to Exit Here.' Since second-class cars were the last, farthest from the locomotive, that afforded the new passengers the least chance of seeing them. They chose to get off at what was only a short stop for changing the train's crew and delivering mail to a small village. Toshek was wearing his usual crooked grin and Vlad still looked mad as I sneaked a peek from a corridor window just a few feet behind where they alighted on the platform. As the whistle blew and we began to move, I dashed back to my carriage and took as thorough a sponge bath as the little washroom permitted. Katerina and Zhenia would be packing soon and getting ready for their arrival in Chelyabinsk in a few hours.

Watching me putting on a clean shirt, Yuri said, "Those two ladies you were with are OK. It was last year in Kiev that we had them checked out. Your Embassy Joe has information about them. I think they moved from Moscow to Kiev about a year ago."

"Jesus Christ, Yuri, you must have more information for me — or about me — that you haven't told me, I'm sure." I was flabbergasted that he knew Katerina and Zhenia. Who else might know them? No. Crazy. What happens in Siberia stays in Siberia.

"That is true. My instructions came with some information, as usual."

"Well, for fuck's sake, please let me know if there is anything I should know, to keep me out of trouble! Sinister Russian Mafia types, for example!" I was tempted to test the waters and ask him about any formidable Polish academic types out there to ruin my life, as well.

"That is part of my job," Yuri said with a shrug.

"So, if you have to choose between helping me stay alive and doing your intelligence work, which one will you choose?" I asked. I had to wonder where his loyalties really were. It seemed like everyone I ran into had divided loyalties. I was certainly beginning to understand my own.

"Don't ask me stupid questions." He said this without looking at me. "Go to your ladies and say them goodbye. See you when I see you in ten or twelve days. Because I will see you first."

For the first time I saw Yuri smiling. I realized he had pasted both lines together from the film *Gallipoli*. I also saw a small glass of vodka sitting next to him on the windowsill. He was a little more relaxed than I'd seen him since I met him. We shook hands and said goodbye, me in Polish and him in Russian: *"Do widzenia!"* and *"Do svidanya."*

***

On the way up to first class, I stopped at the dining car and asked our chef if he had something special, he could have delivered to car seven, compartment seven. In our battle between Polish and Russian, I understood he could have some blinis and caviar and three small steak tartars with a bottle of Russian champagne delivered in about an hour. For that, he said, "No charge if you give me twenty dollars now." My confusion must have showed; my face told him I thought "no charge" and "twenty dollars now" were somehow in conflict. But the details didn't really matter. It was an incredible price to pay for what we were getting, so I turned my frown to a smile and agreed. Then I had another thought, turned back around to him and asked him to include a nice flower in the deal. He knew the Polish word for "of course" and loudly exclaimed, *"Oczywiscie!"*

Katerina and Zhenia were packing their bags as I tapped on the door and let myself into their compartment. I could smell an aromatic tea brewing and gladly accepted a cup. Trying not to be a nuisance, I waited quietly for them to start the conversation.

"You are best buddies with your killer-friend Vlad, now?" Zhenia asked me.

"Not exactly. He just got off the train. I will have another chance to make friends with him in a couple of weeks. In Chelyabinsk."

I had the women's full attention. They had stopped their packing and tea making.

"What about you two?" I asked. "What are your plans?"

"We are going soon to our family farm near Kamensk-Uralsky," Katerina answered. "Is in a small village called Dalmatovo. Here are some photos I got recently from my cousin who lives near there. It is a wonderful place. But it is so far from everything that has been in our lives for the past three years. I feel anxious about planning to live there." Katerina was showing a side of herself I had not seen. Fully confident and always positive since we'd met, she now sounded apprehensive about a new life back where she had spent summers with her grandmother so many years ago. She went on to explain that she planned to completely renovate the family home. She had already transferred $100,000 from her Cyprus account to a bank in Chelyabinsk, which was about 180 miles away from the farm. I couldn't help but think of my own upcoming move from the wastelands of Nowa Huta to Krakow's city center. This would be the third move for me. Two of them had been filled with optimism, the return to Poland a mixed bag. Regardless of my own history, I could only feel excitement for Katerina and Zhenia.

I looked at her photos. Even though it did, in fact, seem run down from neglect, the farmhouse itself appeared to be well built. I told Katerina the house looked "solid."

She smiled and said her grandfather was a talented metallurgist and refused to build anything quickly or without forethought about design and structural safety. She laughed. "My grandmother blames him for living in the barn for three years while he perfected his castle."

"So how was your grandfather able to put together such a fabulous place on a farm in the midst of collectivization? During all the rest of the terror Stalin inflicted on landowners?"

"My grandfather was a very good Communist and a scientist. He had over forty patents in non-ferrous metallurgy. Against what your government's propaganda might suggest, smart or valuable people were well rewarded in the old system." Katerina's answer sounded well-rehearsed. No doubt she'd been asked this question before by Westerners who didn't understand that there *was* a privileged class among Communists, people who were truly valuable in building their nation.

I just nodded and said, "I would love to see your place sometime. I wish you luck with restoring it to its full glory someday soon." Leaving unspoken the other half of my thoughts. I wanted to make love with her again.

Zhenia, quiet up to now, spoke up. "You can come after you finish all your work in Novosibirsk and wherever else you will be for the next two weeks. Katerina will invite you. Besides, we want to talk to you about an invitation to the United States."

Katerina didn't interrupt Zhenia but flashed her a stern look, as if she wished she would keep silent. In Russian, Katerina told her niece, "I wanted to ask him about it!"

Zhenia's response was also in Russian. "You were starting to get sentimental about home. I was worried you'd forget and not get around to it."

A sharp triple knock signaled that our special little lunch had arrived. As the chef had promised, three of everything except the one bottle of champagne. Zhenia devoured her blinis and caviar in three bites and mixed her tartare before Katerina and I had even taken the blinis out of the warm basket. Zhenia then spread her tartare on slices of rye and set her plate down where she was packing. We pulled the glass flutes from the pantry shelf and split the champagne equally. A little buzzed and happy to return to the subject, we discussed the American visa process.

"First step is finding out where the nearest U.S. Consulate is to you," I explained. "I'm sure there are plans to open one up in this part of Russia, but I don't think that's scheduled for another year."

Instead of waiting for that to happen, Katerina said, "We can fly to Moscow, then. What do we have to do there?"

"There is an application for a visa. It's not very complicated, really. You need to show that you have enough money to make the trip and take care of yourself. Or show that you have someone in the U.S. that agrees to sponsor you. It also helps to show you have a job and a husband you'll be coming back to," I explained. That hit an unexpected raw nerve as I said it. I wondered if I had a wife to return to. And, if I didn't, would I also begin 'massaging' things so I could stay.

Zhenia jokingly lamented, "So, I have only one of the four requirements: I have money but no sponsor, no husband, and no job to come back to. Or at least no official job."

"You don't have to fly to Moscow. We'll get the forms mailed to you within a week or two." I was feeling generous. I suppose that altruism is a convenient cover for self-interest. I may have felt I was genuinely helping someone, but was I papering over a strong longing to cultivate an exciting new love relationship? "I'll write a letter of support as your sponsor. But it would be good to have an official job," I suggested. "Nothing too glamorous, just a real job, with a salary, something that can be confirmed."

"During Communism everyone had job," Katerina said. "Job was easy. But official job with good money was almost impossible." She turned to Zhenia and the two women began to plan what sort of job Zhenia might get connected to. "Cleaning lady or secretary will be easiest to arrange," Katerina proposed.

"Perfect," I said. "While I'm in Novosibirsk, I'll get started on writing the letter of support. Within a month or two we'll have all we need to apply." The champagne was making me show off just a bit. "Maybe we can meet in Moscow, at the U.S. Embassy. Have a visa party at the Leningradskaya Hotel!"

Katerina's frown told me I might have taken a step too far. "Your Alyona will bake a cake for us, I am sure."

Zhenia's mind went back to matters of commerce, too. "Visa help in Moscow and in Warsaw is very expensive," she said. "How much you expect, Mr. Andy?"

I'm not sure why I said this. I liked to think I was feeling fatherly to this beautiful woman who was only eight years younger than me. It didn't hurt that I'd enjoyed an exciting evening with her attractive and still-youthful aunt. Whatever the motivation, I blurted out, "The happiness of giving you away at your wedding in Chicago will be enough."

The funny look on Katerina's face made me wonder if I was taking her place in this imagined wedding. I don't think she entirely disliked the idea, though.

***

The train pulled into Chelyabinsk on time. Crowds were waiting on the platform, scurrying about and rushing to line themselves up with their assigned car. Those of us getting off the train had to push our way through the crowd after stepping the meter or so down onto the platform. I looked for Yuri getting off but did not see him. Zhenia and Katerina were behind me. Katerina handed me an envelope with an image of the Romanov Museum in Yekaterinburg. She whispered in my ear, "Thank you for everything. And please come see us. I have the address and directions in the envelope. And some other things, too. If you really can start the visa application, we will both be grateful." With two kisses on each cheek from both of my friends, they floated down the steps into the boiling crowd and disappeared.

I felt terribly alone. Over three thousand kilometers from the wife and family I was supposedly providing for on this latest escapade; would I go back? Should I go back? After a minute of staring blankly into that mass of people, suddenly Katerina's face came into focus again. She was standing near the station's main entrance. She was waving at me and I think I saw some mascara running down her cheeks. She was crying.

I dabbed at my face. So was I.

Chelyabinsk to Novosibirsk: A Glowing Report

I hoped I was looking casual and inconspicuous when I stepped into the crowded third-class car. Luckily, all the men in their matching jumpsuits were engaged in banter among themselves and had no idea about the trickle of sweat inside my shirt or my hammering heartbeat.

Hand in my pocket, I touched the 'ON' switch on my Geiger counter. *Damn.* I got a loud barrage of clicks. In my haste to grab it, I'd completely forgotten to turn the machine's volume down. I wasn't even anywhere near these guys and already the instrument was making the positive sound for radioactivity. The 'flow' of particle detection sounded more like a firehose on high.

I thought about it for a moment and then decided to take a detour into the bathroom. There, I turned the 'squelch' down so the response to background radiation would be minimized, and only relative increases would register. I turned the volume down, as well. Testing the GC, I pointed the sensor wand hidden in my sleeve at various things in the bathroom. It gave me extremely high readings, especially from the floor and in the trash receptacle.

Coming out into the corridor, I put my hand up to fake a stretching movement, touching the wand to a bag that carried the same symbol I saw embroidered on the men's work uniforms. I clearly heard the crackling 'flow' of the GC's sensor going off as the wand brushed the bag. I noticed that these workers, apparently on their way home after a long work week, were drinking steadily, which meant they were also frequently going to the bathroom at the corridor's opposite end. I planted myself on a seat nearest the spaces they were crammed into and easily allowed five or six guys to pass. As each one squeezed past, I let his pants leg brush lightly against the wand. Three of the first half dozen I tested were hotter than anything I had seen in 1986 in the Krakow markets that catered to Russian traders; that was right after the Chernobyl accident. By comparison, the other people going by me were registering about the same as when I'd tested myself. The lower I got to the floor, the more radioactive I was. One lady passed with potatoes and some other tuberous vegetables in her bag. Her bag was just as hot as the floor: off the scale.

One of this particular Geiger counter's features was automatic recording. It was keeping a record of the measurements I was taking so I didn't have to memorize anything other than WHAT I was testing. After satisfying myself I'd established a clear pattern, I stopped my experiment. By now I was convinced that when the sun went down, we would all be glowing brightly in the Siberian night. All of these men looked to be blue-collar factory workers. Their hands were likely not pushing pens very much. Machinists, material handlers, millwrights, steam fitters, carpenters, steel workers, operators, and who knows what else they did. I had no idea when they would be getting off the train but decided to go back to my compartment. My guess was that, since this train would be stopping soon in some little village or another, they'd likely be getting off there. I'd seen enough.

***

My chance encounter with the radioactive workers in third class had begun with a little homework. With another day ahead of me on a dirty train filled with cockroaches, very little water to drink (orange sugar water didn't count), and that non-stop 'duggity-duggity' sound, I'd decided to pull out and read some of the materials Joe had given Yuri to deliver to me. The train had finally pulled out of Chelyabinsk at 4 p.m., which would put us in Novosibirsk tomorrow around noon. A youngish-looking woman with two boys had planted themselves in my compartment, immediately unhooking the upper and middle bunks and allowing them to rest against the wall opposite mine. She looked at me and suggested I do the same so no other passengers would be tempted to take the upper bunks, especially if the train didn't fill up as the afternoon progressed. This was always the time I disliked the most about traveling by train without a private sleeping compartment. While I could survive sharing a compartment with almost anyone or anything, there were others who would go through extreme gyrations to avoid having other people sharing their compartment.

Passive techniques for discouraging fellow passengers ranged from spreading smelly food everywhere to placing baggage in such a way as to make others think the compartment was full. If someone ignored those signs and asked if there was a free space, you'd answer "No!" and say the others are in the dining car. More aggressive tactics included putting a sign up that said, 'NO MORE PLACES' or 'BUSY.' If the conductor came by and you gave him a few dollars, he might put the official sign up himself — and then at some point in the journey deliver a nice cup of tea and cakes for you. That had happened to me several times traveling on Russian trains from Berlin to Warsaw. On one of those occasions, the conductor had advised against coming out of my compartment until after the border crossing into Poland. Against the conductor's advice, I peeked outside and saw the sleeper car being systematically disassembled. All the smugglers on board were filling every possible hidden nook and cranny with contraband goods to avoid detection. In so doing, they avoided paying customs duty or taxes. And whatever they'd paid the conductor was surely less than the bribes officials at the border would demand.

Without borders to cross on this leg of my journey, I wasn't worried about customs issues. But judging from the crowds on the platform and the amount of luggage they dragged aboard, this track looked to be a major route for informal commerce or the 'gray market.' Much of what people were carrying seemed to be destined for flea markets in towns around Chelyabinsk. While we were traveling on the same line as the famous Trans-Siberian Railway, it was a far less elegant local service. Also, two third-class cars had been attached to the end of the train to accommodate local commuters. Those cars had un-upholstered wooden bench seating in half of the car.

The smells of Asian and Russian foods carried aboard by travelers mixed in the dusty air. The temperature had gone up quite a bit. Passengers were forcing open the train's windows and vents where it was possible. My fellow travelers' faces were reflecting the changing ethnic groups as we rolled deeper into Central Asia.

The boys in my compartment had been arguing non-stop since they arrived. I suspected that was why no one else had ventured in. But the heat and the 'duggity-duggity' finally put them to sleep. That was my opportunity to pull out my 'PLEASE READ' envelope from Embassy Joe. The first pages gave me a lesson on the ethnic makeup of the region I was traveling through, largely the result of forced removals from other republics by the Soviets.

Equally interesting to me was the next section. It described the information the CIA was getting now about the relationships between two groups of entities. On the one side were those that had access to nuclear materials. On the other were the groups that would be vying for the materials and collaborating with local criminals to get them. A list of those materials included the possibility of complete bombs.

Beyond the broader educational material, Joe's informational packet included specific instructions. This material was also organized in sections.

The first part was for contractors like me who'd been recruited into the AT Group.

MEMO:

TO ALL AT GROUP MEMBERS

***

"We know and are tracking organized terrorists actively engaged in using various criminal groups and corrupt connections to gain access to nuclear material and transport it to their desired locations.

You are now involved in this tracking and reporting activity.

Much like the US programs that developed the atomic bomb, the Russians have organized and managed 'closed cities' for decades. These cities are industrial towns that are organized to carry out the design and manufacture of weapons of mass destruction that includes nuclear bombs during the Cold War. Within these closed cities, the criminal elements that could be motivated to sell materials to a terrorist include:

- Convicts who have returned to the city
- Ordinary workers motivated by non-payment of wages
- Drug couriers/university students
- Workers from the Tatar or Bashkir communities
- City officials
- Guards and disgruntled military and/or scientific personnel

Once secured, nuclear material can be transported out of the cities via:

- Corrupt soldiers among the military conscripts surrounding the city
- A multitude of growing criminalized elements including 'taxi

services' and the so-called Russian Mafia groups
- Construction industry transportation
Once outside these closed cities, material can be transported by:
- Truck, rail, uncontrolled Russian airlines
- Experienced drug and gun runners supplying to southern republics for Muslim terrorist groups
- Other ethnic criminal groups
- Customs brokers

What is most important for you is that this material is already flowing out of these cities. Through bribery and corruption at extreme levels, the security systems have been bypassed or disabled. The criminals within the closed cities and the terrorists are wooing each other for their goods and money. This capacity for working together is growing. Exacerbating this problem is the fact that law enforcement in these cities and in Siberian regions has deteriorated to the point that it is as corrupt as the criminal organizations we are talking about. The current political instability also adds to the uncertainty of the situation and the anarchy that law enforcement officials are working in. While we are attempting to work with the former KGB in finding common ground for controlling this huge risk to the civilized world, we are not yet able to say that we have a good working relationship."

The next section was more narrowly focused. On me.

Instructions for Andrew Gold

"Your role should remain passive and exploratory with the contacts you are going to make in Novosibirsk.

• Remain somewhat aloof while there and do not become a television personality. PLEASE!

• Listen for opportunity. Don't believe everything that Dima says but be especially attentive to the nuclear group(s) and try to assess if they have information on the growing threat of criminal/terrorist marriages.

• Stay clean in Novosibirsk and then when you meet Yuri in Chelyabinsk, we will ensure your safety going out to the Soyuz debris sites.

• Yuri, Toshek and Vlad will take full responsibility for safety.

• Do not risk your own safety if the sites are under criminal control — of any kind.

• If for some reason your security team doesn't show up at your appointed meeting time and place, give them a two-day window and then leave if they have still not shown up.

"Vlad is also a little 'on the edge' with an unpleasant task to complete that one of our partners threw in at the last minute. Give him some space for now."

As I read this, I understood Yuri's two-day window request. And I wished I had read it before Vlad set out to decapitate me the day before.

Thoughts of Antek and his magic fax machines in Warsaw began to come into my head. He'd said all the non-stop faxing into his office had taken nearly a year to develop. The crazy nuclear material offers had started coming just a few months back. There had been one 'special' Pole who had come to his office. He lived in Przemysl, next to the Ukrainian border. He called himself Scooby. Antek said he never knew his real name. He seemed filled with knowledge of which factories beyond Samara were producing high-value materials and acted willing to help Sweet Aire get involved in a deal. He'd described "major upheaval in military circles throughout the ranks in Russia" that had resulted in rogue officers offering up weapons for sale. On one occasion after having been absent for quite a while, he showed up with a Russian version of a DOT 'transport pig container.' In it were several vials of cesium-137. He had claimed it was a delivery for a Polish government client. It's very likely that this shipment had been the work of someone behind the scenes at a Siberian plant who had made it available for illegal sale. Watching the way Scooby behaved around others, Antek had surmised that his poor social skills and arrogance precluded him from getting very far in big transactions. Antek's assessment, in the end, was that he knew what he was talking about and probably had been approached by intelligence officers from at least one Western country who wanted to share his knowledge. Scooby spoke fluent German and Russian. After turning up with the cesium, he spent all day on Antek's phone, calling to Russia and to Germany. After about three more months of routine appearances, Scooby mysteriously disappeared. It was shortly thereafter that the faxes from Samara, Chelyabinsk, Novosibirsk, Ozyorsk, Mayak, and other places started up. If that was Scooby's work, it wasn't the only legacy he'd left. Antek soon discovered he'd been saddled with a phone bill of nearly five thousand dollars.

As I was getting up to speed on geography and demographics concerning these plants and the closed cities around Chelyabinsk, it started to make sense that Antek would eventually have started getting such offers of strategic material. Just about all of the metal refineries and chemical plants that Scooby had been going on about, ad nauseam, were located nearby. Scooby had probably given Antek's fax number to a lot of his agent contacts. Then, as the nuclear material market started to develop, Antek was on plenty of lists as an agent. An agent with possible buyers somewhere in his chain. Sweet Aire became the 'lucky' recipient of these dubious offers and an honorary black-market club member.

***

My roommates in my compartment had woken up. They were eating sandwiches and sardines as I tried to study my paperwork. The adult company was quite OK, in fact, an elegant woman in her late twenties or early thirties probably, very slim and wearing a scarf with dark hair tied in back. I understood in her why the Slavic sense of beauty included deep-set dark eyes. I felt I should give the young mother some time without my scowling at her little monsters. I had already had to ask them — twice — not to bother my bags when they climbed up on the seat to play with the straps. Joe had given me a lot of technical data to absorb and that evening my absorption rate had gone to zero. I took off for the dining car for a snack.

The soup of the day was goulash. Whatever meat was in the goulash, it didn't look, taste, or behave like any meat I had ever eaten. Nevertheless, it was a large portion and I ate it all. After an orange soda and a small package of sugar wafer cookies, I was ready for a walk. As I stepped up to the window to hand the bus-boy my bowl, I noticed a young guy sitting alone. What caught my eye was the interesting jumpsuit he was wearing, with an emblem that looked a little familiar. He was wolfing down several sandwiches, washing them down with a Russian cola. His eyes had that half-liter vodka look. I guessed he had the post-alcohol munchies. I didn't think too much about it as I set off to maneuver my way through the length of the train, toward second class, for a little exercise.

Despite the frenetic crowding as passengers mobbed the train in Chelyabinsk, most of them had been able to get a proper seat in the compartments. Only a few passengers were sitting in the aisles, balancing on their luggage or perched on pull-down seats. It was quite easy, then, to make my way through the five second-class cars.

It was a normal looking collection of passengers for a slow train carrying a mix of long-distance travelers and short-run commuters. Some had lots of luggage; others only a briefcase, some tools, or a lunch bucket, evidently on their way to some quiet village perhaps an hour outside of town. Then, in cars eleven and twelve, the third-class carriages, I could see twenty to thirty workers, all in similar coveralls or jumpsuits. Most of them had the same emblem on their left breast as the guy in the dining car. Looking a little closer, it dawned on me that I had seen that emblem on faxes I had picked up in Antek's magic room in Warsaw. I got even more excited when I then saw that, while not all these guys wore that particular emblem, *all* of them had the international symbol for radioactivity above their belts.

I guessed I was in one of the commuter cars used by the workers who had just come off their shift in one of the secret towns outside Chelyabinsk. It might have been Mayak or Ozyorsk, maybe

Chelyabinsk-40 or Chelyabinsk-65. These were all part of the Soviet Union's equivalent of the Manhattan Project. Ozyorsk, for example, was the opposite number to Richland, Washington. Those two cities have the distinction of being the first places to produce plutonium for the Cold War's nuclear bombs. Later, back in my compartment, I dug back into my 'homework' materials. Comparing the emblem I'd seen, with maps of the rail route, I figured out that these workers were from the Mayak facility in Ozyorsk, still a closed city due to the sensitive nature of the nuclear material produced there.

Observing these men, busy getting drunk while headed home to villages outside the closed city after a week at the plant, it hit me: these were exactly the guys who could be pulling out material from the plant. That got me excited. Now, instead of enduring a mix of boredom and irritation with the kids in my compartment, I could actually start performing my mission. I decided to go back just long enough to pull my trusty 007 Geiger counter out of the toolkit that was safely stuffed deep in my bag.

Huffing and puffing by the time I finally made it to my compartment, nine cars forward toward the chugging locomotive, I saw the young mother was napping with the smaller boy asleep on her lap. The second boy, though, was looking through a bag that he had pulled out of my suitcase. Startled, I let out a loud, "HEY! Get out of there! Goddammit!" to which the little boy started crying. He jumped on top of his mother, who had already snapped back to wakefulness and was looking for something to swat him with. He tried to hug her, not an easy task as she was vigorously slapping him across the face. I turned my attention back to my things on the floor. I was relieved to see he had only gotten to my clothes and toiletries. Much further and he would have found my cute little leather toolkit. I didn't want to think about what would have happened if he'd tried to play with my ultra-sharp self-defense tool or other spy delights. He'd have probably cut off his own tongue if he'd put the scalpel-like blade in his mouth. Or maybe badly sliced a finger if he'd so much as run the blade along his hand.

The mother calmed down after giving her son what seemed like about enough punishment. As I heaved my bag up onto the highest bunk, I gave a double finger to the offending little boy, saying "*Nyet-nyet!*" I left the compartment with my Geiger counter stuffed in my coat. The cord to the sensor wand ran down my sleeve; in my hand was a control where I could turn the machine on and off without being seen.

***

Armed with all the data the GC had recorded, I went back to my compartment, trying hard not to rush, strolling as casually as I could. I took out Joe's 'CHELYABINSK BACKGROUND INFO' sheets and looked for material on the industrial facilities still operating in these closed cities. Three-by-five data cards offered some hair-raising details about Mayak's and other local factories' activities:

"Chelyabinsk-65 produces tritium and other special isotopes. At present, tritium and other isotopes (plutonium-238, cobalt-60, carbon-14, iridium-192, and others) are produced by the nearby reactors 'Ruslan' and 'Ludmila'.

"Tritium is transferred to the Mayak tritium plant, producing tritium components of nuclear warheads. The isotopes are transferred to the radioisotope plant, which manufactures alpha-, gamma-, and beta radiation sources, plutonium-238 and strontium-90 thermal generators, and a wide range of radionuclides.

"In addition to reprocessing of spent fuel, the RT-1 plant is a storage site for approximately 30 t reactor-grade plutonium, and is involved in radioactive waste management, and research and pilot production of uranium-plutonium MOX fuel."

No finer dirty bomb could be made than from the materials these guys were around. The accidents that have occurred here and at nuclear generating facilities nearby are legendary. Joe's notes detailed some of those tragedies, as well.

I was tired of wayward neutrons and all the thoughts of alpha, beta, and gamma radiation. Without eye covers to hide the glow I imagined all around me, I put a T-shirt over my face and went to sleep for my last night on the train to Novosibirsk.

***

As I guessed, by the time I got to the dining car at around seven the next morning, all the nuclear workers were gone. My chef friend had been replaced by a younger cook. He smiled at me as I sat down at the same booth where Katerina, Zhenia, and I had first met. Just like everything else, the farther east we got, the menu was evolving into more Asian flavors. The chef knew I was American and offered scrambled eggs and toast with a special off the menu cup of coffee. I gladly accepted. He was from Uzbekistan. He told me he had a Ukrainian wife who spoke Polish. It was helpful that he understood everything I said in Polish, since I was trying hard not to reveal how much Russian I understood. Besides our ability to communicate, he was happy to be serving someone who smiled at him.

Taking him my empty plate and cup, I asked if he was living around Chelyabinsk. He nodded and said he was from a village an hour out of town. I asked if he knew much about the radiation accidents that had occurred around Chelyabinsk over the years. No sooner had I asked than a stricken look crossed his face. The fear was unmistakable. He told me he and his parents had been forcibly relocated after one of those events. "No one in my family has felt the same since. We are chronically tired. Always sick. All my aunts, three of them, died mysteriously before they were sixty years old."

I asked him, "How did you know that there was a problem?"

"There were emergency vehicles everywhere with men in suits going from house to house telling us to stay inside. For weeks we could only go to town for shopping and then were told to go home and to stay inside with our doors and windows closed. Finally, they said that 'for our safety' we needed to move. My family was sick with sadness as well as sick from the radioactivity."

This sounded exactly like one of the incidents in the CIA reports describing well-known radioactivity releases that occurred near Chelyabinsk."

One of Joe's NUCLEAR ACCIDENT DATA cards read as follows:

"...the September 1957 explosion that occurred in a radioactive waste storage site involved some 20 million curies of material. A cooling system of a radioactive waste containment unit malfunctioned, and some two million curies spewed across Chelyabinsk, Sverdlovsk, and Tyumen Oblasts covering a total area of 23,000 square kilometers inhabited by a quarter of a million people. Massive evacuations of the population were taken. Significant radioactive contamination covered an area of more than 800 square kilometers, and there are areas where the concentration of cesium-137 and strontium-90 are still hazardous to human health."

If there were any moments that put the importance of the mission into perspective, it was this conversation with the dining car cook and my monitoring of the red-hot nuke squad the night before. Two generations of careless management of Cold War nuclear bomb production had left large swaths of Ukraine, Kazakhstan and the Russian Urals uninhabitable. According to reports that were coming out, much more should be so designated. Dozens of nuclear facilities across the region were filled with this dangerous material but now in management limbo. That left them susceptible to outright sale or theft of weapons-grade uranium and plutonium, as well as isotopes that would be perfect for a dirty bomb. In fact, it was already happening. Joe included articles much like these in my document package:

"While the USSR is Disintegrating, Uranium and Plutonium are Leaking Out

Abstract: Italian police are reportedly investigating the shipment of uranium and plutonium from the former Soviet Union into Europe. According to the deputy prosecutor of Como, Italy and head of the Italian investigation, the Soviet fissile material was to have been delivered to Iraq or Libya. News reports indicated that shipments of Soviet fissile materials of varying amounts, from 4 grams to 40 kilograms, were seized in Vienna, Prague, Zurich, and Como between October and December 1991. The radioactive materials were stolen from the Irkutsk mining-processing plant and the theft was assisted by Vitaliy Fedorchuk of the Ukrainian KGB and Colonel Oleg Petrovskii of the GRU.

Date: 30 December 1991-6 January 1992

Bibliography: *Kommersant*, No. 1"

"Nukes for Sale?

Abstract: Red Army troops in Eastern Europe and the Soviet Union are reportedly selling conventional weapons for cash to the highest bidder, and nuclear sales may soon follow.

Date: 10 December 1991

Bibliography: *The Toronto Star*, p. A19"

"Fears Grow that Soviet A-Arms Are on Market

Abstract: A Russian Foreign Ministry spokesman confirmed that arms sales to Iraq are under way. An Egyptian newspaper reported that

Iran purchased three nuclear weapons from a former Soviet republic for over $150 million. Shevardnadze is concerned that nuclear weapons could fall into the hands of paramilitary groups. An administration arms control delegation is scheduled to meet with leaders of Russia, Kazakhstan, Ukraine and Belarus to discuss export controls.

Date: 11 January 1992

Bibliography: *The Los Angeles Times*, p. A1"

"Continuing Smuggling of Radioactive Materials

Abstract: Four foreign nationals were detained in Milan on 8 January 1992 for attempting to sell 2 kg of red mercury of Soviet origin. Italian investigators say they have evidence that nuclear substances and materials for their purification are being smuggled through Austria, Switzerland and Italy to some Middle Eastern countries. The four arrested in Milan arrived from Budapest with mercury kept in two containers made of special glass with Cyrillic inscriptions. The mercury, thought to be a sample from a large shipment of radioactive substances, was being offered for $800,000, much less than the usual asking price for red mercury, $50-100 million.

Date: 10 January 1992

Bibliography: FBIS-CENTRAL EURASIA

Orig. Src.: TASS, 9 January 1992"

"Outlaws in Search of Nuclear Know-how

Abstract: Spector sees a danger of nuclear material leaking out of the FSU. He points to an episode in which Soviet weapons-grade plutonium was intercepted in Italy. [See also Arms Control Today, 1-February 1992.]

Date: 9 January 1992

Bibliography: *USA Today* (Interview with Leonard Spector) p. 13A"

"Nuclear News on Uranium Pellet Seizure

Abstract: 261 uranium pellets enriched to 5 percent reported to come either from the Ulba (Ust-Kamenogorsk) Metallurgy Plant in Kazakhstan or the Atommash Production Association plant in Russia were confiscated by the Austrian police in Vienna.

Date: July 1992

Bibliography: *Nuclear News*, p. 55"

Intourist Siberia Hotel, Novosibirsk, Russia

"Your friend left you. He was very rude. You will invite me to your room soon?" A brunette, on the tall side, wearing a shiny polyester leopard-print dress, materialized at my table. I was sitting in the main restaurant of the Intourist Siberia Hotel, finest guest accommodations in Novosibirsk, dirty dishes from dinner still on the table.

While the place fell far short of the elegant hotels I'd patronized in Moscow, some things were very familiar, including how the women worked the room. I couldn't help but feel a pang for the spectacular Natalya and her two friends from that night in the Leningradskaya. But this woman, though perfectly attractive, was no Natalya.

She laid her hand down next to mine. "Perhaps a drink for us first?" she added. The bartender was watching me over his glasses, waiting for me to signal my approval. I agreed, but as soon as we were served, I stood up and took my drink with me towards the bathroom. The woman sat down at my table to sip her drink… I suppose waiting for me to return. I did not. Before I even got to the bathroom, I was hijacked.

Quickly homing in on me from the right was another woman who could have been among the predators, but I hadn't really noticed her before. She looked quite normal — without overdone makeup — with naturally dark features, sandy brown hair to her shoulders, and a simple dark maroon sleeveless dress. Her gait told me she was not wearing high heels. And that we were on a collision course about five meters ahead. I slowed down and caught her eye. She slowed down too. She stepped up to me, looked at me very intensely and said, "I am Fifi sixty-six. Can we go to your room to talk?"

It was very difficult to hide my shock. I suddenly felt weak; I nearly dropped my glass of vodka. That was the AT Group code name Joe had told me to remember.

"Fifi sixty-six. Do you know it?" she repeated.

"Yes. Of course." My voice came out somewhere between a whisper and a croak. I had a hard time remembering exactly what Joe had said about 'Fifi sixty-six' but I knew it was the group code. I also knew I had to treat it seriously.

She said she would knock on my door in five minutes. I went straight to my room and sat down to wait. For some reason, I noticed I was breathing hard and sweat was starting to form under my arms. I couldn't stop shaking.

***

By the time 'Fifi' knocked at my door, I had calmed down enough to think about how I was going to behave. I was trying to decide what I would say and not say. The fact that she had the code name and wanted to talk to me made me assume that she was legit. If after talking with her something seemed wildly out of sorts, I'd decide what to do at that time. As the folks at the embassy had told me more than once, "Get as much information as you can and give as little as possible."

As she stepped inside my room, I noticed her jaw was working and her eyes flicked from side to side. I thought I detected a tremor in her hands, too. She seemed deathly afraid of me. Was that real fear? Of me? Or fear of the situation? Maybe she had bad information to tell me. Or was she planning to do something to me? A dozen scenarios flashed through my head as she came in, but outwardly, at least, I stayed calm. I pointed to a chair next to a small table with a lamp. She was carrying a small cosmetics bag or something similar and had nothing else on her that I could see. She'd said only "Thank you" when she walked in and went straight to the chair I had pointed to.

"So. Those words opened my door here for me to listen to you. What words were they, again?" I asked this just in case I had completely misunderstood down in the bar.

"Fifi sixty-six," she repeated, carefully. "Did I pronounce them badly?"

"No. Who told you that these words are important?" I asked her. "And who are you?"

"My contact told me that you are like me," she answered. She sat with her arms folded in front of her, little signs of resistance to my interrogation. "I sometimes do things for money and I don't talk about it." That didn't answer either of my questions, but it made me laugh.

"So, you are talking to me for money, I assume," I said.

"Well, I think that probably it is not just money that makes us do what we do. Do you agree?" She let her hands drop into her lap; her shoulders relaxed a bit, too. Since I was having some fun with this situation, she may have thought she could, too.

"You are here meeting Dmitri the trader and businessman? Many meetings in Novosibirsk are planned? You are planning to go back to Chelyabinsk with Dmitri to do something there with him? You also have some meetings with other important people in Chelyabinsk? Am I correct so far?"

To each of her statements that she'd formulated as questions, I nodded and replied, "Uh huh."

"Your man is named Joe?" she asked.

Again, I nodded. "Uh huh." By this time, I was really wondering where, if anywhere, this conversation was going.

"So, I have three instructions from Joe. Listen carefully.

"Number one: Joe has something for you to do that is very important for him. On Thursday this week, two men will check into this hotel. Their names are Anatoly and Georg. These men probably have some 'bad stuff.' You know what is 'bad stuff'?"

Another nod, another "Uh huh."

"Joe wants you to do everything you can that is safe to take pictures of them, their baggages." She rattled this off as if painstakingly memorized and rehearsed.

Remembering some of my first assignments, I felt a pang of sympathy for her.

She wasn't finished. "See who they meet with and try to use your radiation detection machine to test them and their baggages."

"We say 'baggage' and not 'baggages,'" I corrected her, gently I hoped. "It is correct for both one bag or many."

Staring at me for a moment after I said that, she said, "No one correct me before. Why I not know that?"

"It's OK. Your English is great. Please continue," I urged her.

She continued. "Anatoly and Georg will check out after one or two days. We find out where they are going if possible and someone, maybe, will follow them. Joe wants every information quickly when we get it."

I'd already started calculating what this new job might mean to my

166

schedule, especially the meetings with Dima. With the time I had in Novosibirsk and the plans Dima had laid out, I was glad we had trimmed the meetings he'd arranged down to four. I also realized that even four meetings might be a problem if the timing wasn't right. Or if dealing with these two fellows according to Joe's new instructions got complicated.

As this went through my head, I realized I didn't know the name of this woman sitting right here in my room. "You already know that my name is Andy," I said. "I don't know your name."

"Cindy," she answered.

"Oh, come on." *Too transparent.* I frowned and shook my head. "Your real name is…?" I countered.

"I am known as Cindy here in Novosibirsk. I don't want you to accidentally use my real name." The look on her face was deadly serious. She had crossed her arms again. "I am Cindy until we finish Joe's job."

"But Cindy isn't a real name here. Russians don't use that name, do they?" I asked.

"Prostitutes do." At this, Cindy relaxed her posture again. "I will be 'working' in the lobby and around the hotel. You do your photos and your radiation testing. And I do my photos, interviews, and recordings."

She was looking straight at me, so seriously. I tried not to smile at this, but I am sure I let her see how astonished I was. I had a flashback to Clint revealing Natalya's true role for the Agency in Moscow. That had shocked me, as well. Another distraction from my hopes for getting serious about the things on my to-do list in Novosibirsk. *Damn it*! *In the service of country, home, and family,* I thought, looking at another attractive colleague. Maybe this was a 'mission from God' as in *The Blues Brothers*. What else was going to come between me and my wavering dreams of making everything right in Krakow?

"You said there were three things from Joe," I reminded her.

"Number two is that you should give me the envelopes from Joe that you were supposed to deliver. Number three is for you to do everything possible to travel back to Chelyabinsk without Dmitri."

I dug out the envelopes I had stuffed deep in my toolkit and gave them to Cindy. And I tried not to think about letting Dima down on the expedition for our Soyuz debris. As Cindy slipped the envelopes into her dress, she began to stand. I hadn't seen a pocket, so I got the feeling she had just tucked the papers inside her underwear. She really had a way with me, already. *Focus, big guy!*

"These guys arrive in two days," I said, before she could start toward the door. "Will we meet again to coordinate our activities? I still have a lot of questions." These new instructions had left me ill at ease. The rapid heartbeat and the sweat were back, I realized. I wasn't very confident about how to do everything Joe was asking.

"Of course, we will have a lot of time. Until they arrive, you are my only 'customer.' We have this room to plan and coordinate."

Sheepishly, I asked, "Do you have your own room?"

"Yes. I have a place," Cindy said, "but I am trying to play like prostitutes here. I should follow their rules, so no one thinks I am different." I, for one, could see that she was different. My earlier thoughts were almost embarrassing now. This woman was unique.

I knew enough about their world and how they talked about each other. That helped me understand that if Anatoly or Georg wound up with one of these women and she talked Cindy down, then her chances of success in this little adventure would be greatly reduced.

Cindy asked if she could take a few minutes to put on her makeup before going to work. I nodded and waved her toward the bathroom. While waiting for her to come out, I started making notes for my first speech at the Academy of Sciences. It was about ten minutes before she emerged. Her transformation told me she knew what she was doing.

"My God! You are a different woman!" I exclaimed. Now my heart was going a little faster yet, but it was a different kind of nervousness. Cindy had stepped out of my bathroom looking twice as beautiful as any woman I had seen at this hotel so far. I convinced myself for the moment that what was happening, and my feelings, were all part of the job I was doing—and was expected to do. Not an easy argument to make at that moment but distracting thoughts of Renata, guilt, or loyalty needed to be cast aside.

Feeling a little uncomfortable at my question, I asked, "I am your only customer, you said?" I imagined prolonged scenes in the hotel portraying a businessman alongside his contracted escort. That wasn't how I'd envisioned things. But I could deal with it — I supposed. *Just business.*

"Until Thursday, Andy. Let's make some business together." She gave me a smile, now, that I realized was positively dazzling. "Please come down later and begin our acting. I will make it easy for you. Don't worry. I am waiting." Krakow, again, faded into the mist.

***

Earlier that afternoon, as the train pulled in to Novosibirsk, Dima had arranged to have a man waiting for me on the station platform. He was holding a large sign that read, '*Wilkommen* Herr Gold' as the train pulled up. I saw the sign a half mile before the train got to the station. The damn thing was six feet long and four feet high, decorated with American flags — but written in German. I asked him why it was not in English (*Warum nicht auf Englisch?*) and he answered, also in German, "I don't speak English. Why would I make a sign in English?"

The driver's name was Sergei and he let me know, in Russian, that he was working for Dima. The drive from the station to the hotel wound through what he referred to as "the scenic part of town." I hoped he was wrong. From the back seat of his Volga limo, all I saw was demolition of old buildings and construction of new.

Among the newest construction in Novosibirsk, though not the best quality, was the Intourist Hotel Siberia. It was a lot like all the other services that had been cobbled together by the Soviets, under their Intourist agency, for international travelers seeking to visit the USSR.

Comparing conditions for foreigners now to what it was like ten years ago, I should have had no complaints. The hospitality industry had gone from worrying about hiding the surveillance wires and microphones in the walls in 1981 to putting bidets in the bathrooms of nicer hotels in Moscow by 1992.

By 1990, it became obvious during my early NatEx trips, Moscow was getting close to striking a balance between its outdated Communist propaganda and satisfying Western expectations of quality. The objective was to attract Western visitors and their cash. While it was easy enough to attract capitalist entrepreneurs to Moscow, including hotel chains, it was extremely difficult to get them out into the boonies. Like Novosibirsk. Even as the Cold War raged, the Intourist chain of hotels, haphazardly conceived and rolled out by Communists, had attempted to offer the services international visitors might expect from a big, powerful country. After ten years, though, it seemed that government-run businesses like Intourist still didn't quite get it. Evidence of that was dreadfully obvious at the Intourist in Novosibirsk. Nevertheless, Dima remained very proud of what the Soviets had accomplished. He wasn't shy about his opinion that Gorbachev had ruined his country. So it wasn't surprising that Dima put me up in the Intourist Siberia.

Just inside the lobby entrance, I saw a shiny placard that listed the hotel's offerings. I took a quick inventory: multiple restaurants and cafes, a swimming pool, a sauna, a game room, a bowling alley, lounges, and entertainment in the form of a night club and bar with live music and dancing. It took me a little longer to discover that most of those did not operate during my stay. What the hotel should have focused on, I realized once I had checked in, was getting running water to its bathrooms, ensuring lamps contained light bulbs, stocking its restaurants with food and drink, and putting clean linens or duvet covers on its beds.

In the short walk from registration desk to elevators, I noticed that the walls in the common areas were mostly unpainted, made of unplastered cinder blocks. To brighten up these bleak expanses, Intourist posters were randomly hung in dark corners. The posters were the most interesting of all the artwork on display around the hotel.

I was surprised by how bad it was, considering what I'd experienced in Moscow. Even during the worst of times in the capital, the Ukraina and Leningradskaya Hotels had known how to do things right. *Central Siberia has some catching up to do,* I told myself, to accommodate the post-Soviet influx of tourists arriving by train and plane. Eventually, Novosibirsk would become Russia's third largest city. Its visitor infrastructure would also catch up, with more than a dozen four- and five-star hotels there now. That was fitting; the city was already famous as a center of science and technology, mainly through Novosibirsk State University. NSU can proudly claim itself as the producer of much of Russia's academic elite. In 1992, when I was there for the first time, those same claims were freshly being made.

The Intourist, Dima had enthusiastically informed me, had been built for both tourists and professors and researchers visiting NSU. Once I got there, I didn't have any difficulty telling the difference between tables where physicists discussed high-energy physics in English, businessmen speaking Italian vented their frustrations about banking in Russia, and a family from Germany planned a sight-seeing visit. Of the

Intourist's guests, my sources would tell me, seventy-five percent were academics and scientists. The remaining quarter were businessmen and tourists. This overabundance of scholarly types did not stop prostitutes from camping out in the hotel's common areas and lounges at all times of the day. That was one bit of intelligence-gathering I was well equipped to do after my experiences in Moscow's hotels. I had no trouble identifying the working women on the premises. As I entered my room, number 738, for the first time, I felt the door being held for me as I carried my bags inside. A tall blonde woman in a yellow dress I had seen sitting in a chair by the elevator had followed me to my room.

"Hello. I am Lena. I am waiting for you near the lift," she thoughtfully let me know.

I kind of laughed and said, "Thank you," but quickly closed the door to make sure there was no doubt about my action or body language. I felt so dirty after four days on the train that I couldn't even imagine taking her up on her offer. And anyway, after nearly a week of what amounted to free time on the train, it was really time to get down to business. I needed to concentrate on all the reasons I was here, and it wasn't for dalliances with prostitutes. *Focus, Andy!* I told myself. *You're a pro. Sort of. Do your duty!*

From what I'd understood from Sergey, Dima wanted to have dinner at around six. He would be meeting me at about five in the lobby bar. That gave me quite a bit of time to get cleaned up and relax.

A knock at the door interrupted my unpacking. I opened the door the two inches the safety chain allowed, and the room filled quickly with a cheap perfume I had smelled in flea markets in Krakow — and sometimes in hotel lounges in Moscow. The woman at the door this time was a redhead whose eyeliner and mascara were extremely over-done. She asked if I would invite her in for tea or a cocktail.

"No, thank you. I am having a meeting soon. Good-bye." I closed the door but had to push hard; she was pushing back. A call to the front desk followed this encounter. "Please ask the nice ladies in the hallway to leave me alone. I will not be needing their services." Not now, anyway. "I am in room 738. Thank you."

A man speaking British-accented English replied, "Right, right! We'll let them know, sir!"

The next knock came about five minutes later after I had already started to undress. I didn't open the door this time, but shouted, "What is it?"

"A gift from the front desk, Mr. Gold," a male voice answered in English.

I asked him if he could leave it by the door.

"Not a good idea. It is champagne and some biscuits. It would be stolen in five minutes," the man replied.

Surprised, I opened the door to see a young bellman in uniform. I took the bottle and box from him. I gave him the two dollars I had in my pocket. He acted surprised that I wanted to tip him. He seemed pleasant enough, like a student type. He looked to be about my height, with closely cropped brown hair and the sort of Slavic features that might be Russian or Polish or any other Eastern European nationality. It occurred to me he might be useful. I needed to make a friend here; the hotel was already presenting me with challenges.

"How late are you working today?" I asked him.

"Until midnight, sir."

"Maybe I will see you later, then. Thank you! What is your name?" I asked.

"Vincent," he said.

"OK, Vincent. Thank you again." I gave him a smile and closed the door. Then, silently, I opened it again to watch him walking away. He didn't look back. Depending on how long I stayed in Novosibirsk, a helpful assistant might be needed. And since thanks to Embassy Joe I was cash 'heavy' these days, I thought about Vincent as a possible candidate.

***

Around 5:30, the front desk called up to say Dima had arrived and was waiting for me in the lobby bar. I was ready and headed out. By the time I got halfway down the corridor, I saw three more women had joined the blonde I had first seen sitting by the elevator. They were all either smoking or putting on makeup, sitting around a knee-height table. I'd come out of my room quietly but one of the women already had an eye on me. She alerted the others that I was coming in their direction. I looked around to see if there were stairs I could take, to avoid any unpleasant confrontations. No chance.

"My friends have come so now you can choose," said the blonde I had met earlier. "You prefer blonde or brunette? A little big like Basia? Or small like me?"

"Thank you." I offered her a slight smile. "Good night, ladies."

"Why he said 'Good night'?" I heard someone ask. The elevator door opened and I stepped in.

***

"How was your trip, Andy?" Dima loudly greeted me. "You covered thousands of kilometers going through the beautiful Russian countryside! It must have been a wonderful experience for you! Are you tired?" He was sitting one table away from the bar, where the bartender was busy polishing glasses and putting ice cubes into a bowl. The bar looked strangely different from when I'd come through earlier that afternoon. I'd been snooping for a place to get a beer or any drink for that matter. Nothing was available, and it had looked deserted. That was just a couple of hours earlier. Now actual liquor bottles stood on shelves; cartons of juice stood side by side: cherry, blueberry, elderberry, pineapple and orange. And the ice — that really confused me. It was like seeing a loaf of bread in China: out of place with the prevailing traditions and conditions I thought I understood.

"If you want your beer, we have Budweiser for you. Would you like?" Dima asked me.

That gave me another mild shock. But deciding not to act too surprised, I said, "Yes, a beer please. And a shot of chilled vodka."

"Chilled?" the bartender looked at Dima, evidently confused.

"*Kholodno,*" he answered in Russian. The bartender nodded.

"Never too early for business," Dima began, "but I want you to know that we have many official invitations to meet. Maybe too many. Some will be disappointed, but I understand you have only five days for this part of your trip. It is really a shame. You have come to a real miracle of the mixture of Soviet and Russian history, tradition, and innovation."

I sensed a patriotic lecture coming on from Dima and hoped my drink would come soon. I was right.

"You probably don't know it so I will tell you. Novosibirsk's rise to become the Silicon Valley of the Soviet Union, and now Russia's center of learning and academic excellence, did not come easily."

"Because of all the drinking in the Siberian cold, I imagine," I joked.

"Funny — but no. The town's growth and the success of its eventual academic Techno-Park took considerable planning and thought from a lot of visionaries." He was dead serious.

I couldn't resist the opportunity to play with him. "Dima, the story I've heard includes a handful of self-serving tsarist decrees, a smattering of enslavement by autocrats, and a good dose of plain old Communist tyranny."

"OK. Mr. Wise Guy." It looked like I'd actually hurt his feelings. "We should get our drinks. Anyway, we will get a lecture on this subject tomorrow during our visits."

"I'm sorry, Dima. On the subject of timing, maybe I have more than five days for my stay. If it is worth our time." I could easily appear accommodating; my return to Chelyabinsk to meet Yuri and the others wouldn't happen any sooner than ten days from now. On the one hand, I really hoped I could come away from this part of the trip with good leads for Embassy Joe. On the other, I was scheming about a very specific way to fill the time until I met Yuri. That would involve sneaking back to find that over-built family house in the countryside. The one where Katerina and Zhenia were staying. A foreign feeling had settled over me since arriving in Novosibirsk. For once, I wasn't thinking of Renata at all. Maybe the 3,000-kilometer distance from Krakow, and even the smell of cheap perfume from the seventh-floor hookers, had triggered an unambiguously longing emotion. For something completely different. Something completely disentangling.

"So, Dima, tell me who is dying to meet with us? Also, give me your opinion about who we *should* meet with and why. Let's assume we have one full week here before we head back toward Chelyabinsk." I picked up a couple of olives from a bowl on the table. Dima munched on peanuts from an identical dish. So far, we were the lobby bar's only customers.

Dima motioned for the bartender to bring us our drinks. He looked at my beer, a Czech Budvar — an authentic, original Budweiser, actually brewed in a town called Budweis — and laughed. "Breakfast drinks during business are bad luck but I'll let you have one first."

To set him at ease, I chuckled at his joke. I had noticed during our first meeting in Warsaw that he seemed more relaxed when I drank vodka with him. As much as I hated to drink like this in a place I didn't know very well, I had a few shots. But still drank a lot less than he did.

Dima rattled off a dozen institutes, academies, and educational departments. Each of them, he assured me, would pay five hundred dollars to have me sit and listen to their 'dog and pony show' as they bid on a chance to set up a joint MBA program with a Western university. While I couldn't imagine not working with NSU's economics department, I thought it could be worthwhile to hear out a few of these other possible candidates. Dima, on the other hand, was thinking more mathematically: along the lines of multiplying twelve by five hundred dollars to equal six thousand. His fifty-percent cut of the deal would be a nice week's pay of three thousand dollars for the privilege of being treated like royalty. He also imagined being wined and dined for another week after that as whichever groups we short-listed continued to battle for our favor.

"Dima!" I needed him to back off a bit. "How many of these disappointed candidates are going to be mad enough to hop a cheap flight to Warsaw six months from now," I asked, "and put a bullet through my head? I'd really prefer it if we could lower expectations a bit."

"Lower expectations? Mine? Hmmm." I could almost see the wheels turning in his head. "Two hundred fifty per meeting is OK?" he countered. "We each get fifteen hundred dollars, plus food and drink for a week. Still pretty good." Dima wanted a quick win from my visit to Novosibirsk. Cash was his preferred prize. He couldn't get it off his mind.

"Can we come up with a short list of candidates?" I suggested. "Say, four of them? The others we can ask for whatever marketing collateral they can come up with. That will let us seriously review it all. Then we'll see if something floats to the top that actually sounds interesting." Dima was staring at me like I had pissed on the fire and called in the dogs, way too early.

I gave what I hoped would come across as a patient sigh. I explained to Dima, "My friend, I am not here to take money from them, just to have the right to meet and talk. If they are expecting to have to pay something, then you take it all. You have done all the work to get things set up. I just don't want a dozen enemies. I don't want to burn my bridges; I'd like to keep open the possibility of returning to Novosibirsk in the future." It seemed best to say it in Polish since other customers were finally showing up all around us.

I wasn't really paying attention until I finished my little spiel to Dima. Only then did I notice that the people at the adjoining tables were the women I'd encountered up on the seventh floor, plus plenty of others I hadn't seen before. All their makeup looked freshly applied. The old standby, mixed cigarette and perfume scent, was wafting through the bar. Of course. Now it was the beginning of their workday. Watching the Intourist brothel come alive for the evening, I was acutely conscious of the stark contrast between the women in this bawdy scene and what I felt for my friends Katerina and Zhenia.

Dima reluctantly tore his eyes off the women, pondered what I had said, and with a smile, started to come around. He poured two more quick rounds of drinks before he spoke. "I can work with that. We've got the Krakow-University of Detroit materials. So I will create a Request for Proposal from those." Keeping an eye on me, as if hoping for my approval, he rattled off a string of details. "We will be asking for candidate schools to detail everything they can contribute; what the goals of their program would be; estimated student enrollment; marketing; funding; administration and teaching; facilities; and maybe proposed cooperation with local businesses and other institutes." He caught his breath. "That should keep them happy for a while. I'm almost tempted to keep it at five hundred dollars, since I'll be working my ass off reviewing this stuff."

That was better. "Sounds like you have the makings for a pretty good RFP," I told him approvingly. "I can also give you some things from the initial meetings in Krakow," I offered. "That should help you see how they contemplated assembling such a jointly run program."

Dima and I sat a while longer chatting about our plans for the next seven or eight days. Finally, two women walked over to our table and asked us for a light. Dima immediately obliged but then quickly shut them off, asking them not to bother us. I saw that change of atmosphere as an opening to question Dima about the POW-MIA rumors.

"Hey, Dima. I have a question for you. It's a completely different subject but one we could make a little money from." That got his attention.

"Of course, Herr Doktor Gold! What is subject?!"

"American soldiers captured in Vietnam. Prisoners of war. Many of them are still missing. This subject is still very sensitive in the United States."

Dima tilted his head up and looked down his nose at me.

I pressed on. I tried to avoid making this sound like an accusation. "Do you have any personal knowledge of this? Or know of anyone we could talk to that might know if any of those prisoners somehow came to the Soviet Union?"

Dima cleared his throat and pulled his chair up to the table. He leaned closely toward me and asked, "We are making money for doing research. Is this correct?"

I thought a moment about my answer. "It's not going to be millions of dollars. But if we found out something that can be proven — any evidence for the truth — we can be paid handsomely."

Dima's *I'll do anything for a buck* face appeared. He threw back another drink. "Leave this with me. I do not promise I will find a Gulag with these men all alive, playing baseball and singing patriotic songs." I could almost see him doing the math in his head. "But I have some ex-high military officials that might make some comment about this history for small fee. We can add fifty percent for ourselves."

I was beginning to regret I had said anything. Knowing Dima, I guessed he would happily create a history to guarantee he got money for his efforts. I also worried about this far-fetched project getting in the way of our higher priorities.

Without warning, dinner appeared, but I think it had been pre-planned. Dima ate quickly, glancing alternately at his watch and me, before excusing himself. We shook hands, deciding where to meet tomorrow. Now, with him gone, I needed to think about preparing for talks at the Russian Academy of Sciences and at NSU. Then there was the prospect of talks about finding a common ground for a pilot curriculum, leading up to eventually offering an MBA. Even if all this was complete bullshit, I knew, I needed it to sound entirely credible. Embassy Joe had promised me that if anyone needed references about me, they could contact the U.S. Embassies in either Moscow or Warsaw. The cultural attachés would know what to say.

I couldn't concentrate on this yet, unfortunately. Dima's abrupt exit had left me exposed to the predators who were gliding their way around the room, angling for the kill. I wasn't the only prey for these Russian cougars, thank God. Luckily for me, a large group of Dutch men arrived who seemed to have more receptive thoughts on their minds about such a hunt. Nevertheless, the ratio of women to men was perilously high. That encouraged the more aggressive stalkers, who were starting to become annoying.

And that, of course, is when I found an excuse to get up, and when Cindy found her excuse to approach me. And so, not long after our get-acquainted conversation in my room, she and I were ready to go to work. Together.

Partners

For our first action together, Cindy went first. I was to follow within about fifteen minutes or so. None of the seventh-floor harem was hanging around the elevator, so we seemed to be in the clear to act as if we had met for the first time down in the bar. Cindy was the director for this scene. She told me to go straight to where she was sitting and ask if I could join her. She said that would be a clear sign that I had staked out my claim. It would reduce the chance of any other woman trying to get between us.

Things worked pretty much as we had planned. As I made my entrance and delivered my opening line, Cindy said, "You are very welcome to join me; sit here." She uncrossed her legs, motioned for the bartender to come over, and pointed to the end of a booth. My assigned seat allowed us to sit close and have our knees touching under the table. She reached her hand out and grabbed my leg. She pulled me slightly toward her as if to say, 'Good. Keep close.'

The bartender, the same fellow who had served Dima and me before our early dinner, came over and asked if I would be having beer or vodka this time. Cindy suggested vodka. As the bartender departed, she added, softly, without looking at me, "After your drink, we will say goodbye and you go to your room. I will make arrangements with the hotel, so I have my 'license.' It may take some time. Your seventh-floor ladies are trying to block my activity here."

I understood what she was suggesting. Directly behind us, I saw, two of these ladies were already sitting. I resisted the temptation to reach over and thump one of them. Cindy could sense I was not happy with what she had said. She made a face that I read as, 'Not a problem, they aren't worth it.' At that same moment, I saw my young friend, Vincent, the bellman who had delivered the champagne and biscuits. He was walking toward the bar carrying a tray. He didn't seem particularly rushed, so I waved to get his attention. He saw me and smiled, put down his tray, and came over to our table.

"Hello, Mr. Gold! How are you this evening?" The smile never left his face. His eyes, I could see, were on Cindy, as if he was hoping for an introduction.

"This is Cindy, Vincent. She is having some issues with the hotel. I would be grateful if you would help clear things up. Oh, if necessary, could you direct her to someone who can do that quickly?" Casually, without looking at it, I laid a five-dollar bill on the table.

"Why, of course, Mr. Gold. We'll help Cindy immediately. I am on break now! I can escort her to the assistant manager for the evening shift." Just then, he may have feared he'd overstepped his bounds. He hastened to add, "Whenever she is ready." His gaze at Cindy was eager as a puppy's, I thought.

She told him, "Just a couple of minutes, thank you."

It was hard to tell in the low light, but I thought Vincent might have blushed. He gave a little bow, discreetly palmed my five-spot, and went back to the bar, where he stood waiting, his eyes still on Cindy.

I leaned into Cindy's ear and said, "I hope that was OK."

Her reply came instantly, and with a sexiness I hadn't heard in her voice before. "That was perfect, Mr. Gold. See you soon."

I downed my vodka in one gulp. Cindy and I went through the necessary motions, kissing each other on the cheek, as I left for my room. Cindy and Vincent disappeared toward the front desk. By now, the seventh-floor harem appeared to be losing interest in her — and in me. Luckily there was quite a crowd now. Ninety percent of the men, I estimated, were on the prowl. Cindy and I would soon fade from the harem's memory. As I made my way up to my room, I was also thinking about Vincent. If he, in fact, was going to painlessly help Cindy and would keep taking my money for little jobs, why not ask him to help us with something important? He could signal me when Anatoly and Georg arrived. Also, somehow — I hadn't quite worked that part out — assist in monitoring them. I had some ideas for getting Vincent motivated without revealing who our targets really were. Or, for that matter, who *we* really were.

***

"Your Vincent is a hero." Cindy stepped into my room no more than fifteen minutes after we'd parted downstairs in the bar.

"Good. I have some plans for him, if you agree."

Cindy smiled. "Let me guess. He will help us with the Anatoly-Georg project. No?"

"You are absolutely right. We will have to see how much we can trust him but, at a minimum, he can signal the minute they arrive. That will let us go into action with the other parts of the plan," I explained to her. But then I remembered. "Other parts of the plan — that we haven't worked on."

"That's why I am here, Mr. Gold." She sat down at my desk and began writing on the cheap-looking hotel stationery. The Intourist letterhead was scarcely more than tissue paper, but at least it didn't take up much space.

As she wrote, I sat in an armchair and we organized our plan. By the time we finished, we had multiple sheets outlining several alternative plans for how we would go into action, depending on how and when Anatoly and Georg would arrive. Whether by one of the two of us or by Vincent, the lobby would be covered starting at 6 a.m. Lots of places in and around the lobby afforded a good view of the entrances and the reception desk. We considered everything we could think of.

* Which door would they come in through?
* We'll bug the public phone in case they use it.
* How will they be standing at the reception desk?
* Where will their luggage be sitting and what type of luggage will they have?
* Bags on shoulders are harder to test with the Geiger counter than bags in their hands.
* Pay attention to which room(s) they will be assigned to.
* Will they use bellmen? Doubtful.
* Will they be wearing coats?
* Could we be found out or suspected and how do we react if we smell that they are on to us?
* How much should we try to accomplish in the short time we will have between their arrival and getting to their rooms?
* Think about the possibility of additional people being in their party or in tow who could notice our interest in them.
* How should we behave with each other? Completely

181

independently with separate tasks or as a couple?

As we talked through and argued about the safest and most efficient way of getting things done, I realized that Cindy had done this type of surveillance before. Her attention to detail, I had to admit, was far more developed than mine. At one point she asked me to bring out everything Joe's people had given me. She wasn't very impressed with my toolkit and its contents. Probably realizing I was no professional, she commented, "We'll make do with what we have. It's not much, but it could be worse."

Finally, the question of involving Vincent became critical. We took a long time considering his role. In the end, it was our decision to limit his involvement so he thought the intelligence he was supplying us was aimed at gaining the upper hand in "business competition."

These questions were all posed, discussed, and answers laid out on the flimsy stationery that Cindy was working on. I could tell that she had written more than one letter on such fragile paper. Never once did her pen rip any page throughout the long hours we worked. Only about an hour before we finished did I pull out the champagne and biscuits Vincent had left that afternoon. I was proud of my professional discretion. Was there any real difference between the vodka shots with Dima earlier as we discussed our business plans and the champagne with my other business partner? I'd even held off until Cindy had asked if there was anything to snack on.

At 3 a.m., we put the paper aside and quietly sipped the Soviet champagne — decent enough tasting — while munching on the rather dull biscuits. By American standards, they were something between a cracker and a cookie. Not especially salty, not very sweet.

Not long after we broke for our snack, Cindy began to doze off. I offered her the bed, feeling pleased with myself for my uncommon chivalry; and for my ability to disregard the fact that a highly attractive young woman, in character as a prostitute, would be spending the night in my suite. I said I had some things to do and would just use the extra blankets and pillow from the sitting room's chest of drawers. She waved her hand, "No" and said she wanted to stay on the couch until morning. The afghan blanket on the couch just covered her. Only slightly deflated from her refusal, I handed her the extra pillow. She reached up, grabbed my arm, and said, "Thank you, Andy. Our first night together!"

With a little laugh, I leaned over and kissed her on the top of her head, "Thank you, Cindy. See you in the morning."

***

My alarm went off before seven. Suddenly I realized I was unprepared for two very important meetings today, one with the dean of economics at Novosibirsk State University and the other late afternoon cocktails with the Novosibirsk Branch of the Russian Academy of Sciences. I bolted to the bathroom, not realizing Cindy was inside, also getting ready for the day. She was wrapped in a towel but didn't overreact when I nearly ripped the door off its hinges.

"Oh, shit! I'm sorry, Cindy! I'll use the water closet. I panicked. I haven't even prepared for my meetings at NSU and RAS today. I promised Dima that I would do a part of it in Russian." As I was babbling, she was calmly rubbing lotion onto her arms and shoulders.

"Write in English what you want to say in Russian," Cindy calmly offered. "I will translate for you and give you a pronunciation guide. Do it quickly this morning and I will finish it before you leave with Dima." She added, "Close the door so I can finish. *Pizhalsta*."

Cindy stuck around that morning after I handed her an abbreviated version of my speech. She patiently helped me with improving my Russian pronunciation.

"Talking too close to the front of your mouth. Swallow it a little." She advised as I was reading my introduction. "Oh! Very good now!" she smiled and stroked my face. "Good student!"

After two dry runs, she offered some suggestions for how to behave: more Russian and less American. "No smiling except to receive compliments or when they are clapping for you," she advised. "Shake your head slightly like you know what you're talking about and they should be agreeing with you." I laughed imagining Khrushchev or Brezhnev in front of a huge audience spewing lies about the West. She laughed and said, "They will think you were kind of boss of capitalist propaganda. You will for sure get extra points of respect." It was impossible not to reflect on how Renata had similarly coached me on acting more Polish. The similarities ended there, though. Renata rarely encouraged me, was always impatient, and never congratulated me on my successes.

Cindy finished her coaching with a critical eye on my clothes. She approved of my suit and choice of tie so, in that category at least, I was OK. Her only comment was, "You look good in suit. But if you were at least 190 centimeters tall, that would be the best."

Not long after I'd been found wanting, short of 190 centimeters, the front desk called up to say Dima was waiting for me in the lobby. As I left with my favorite diplomatka and the notes Cindy had prepared for me, I hesitated at the door. "One hundred ninety centimeters is good... for whom?"

She was backlit by the sun shining through the window behind her. I couldn't see her face. Instead of acknowledging my question, she only waved goodbye. "Good luck today."

The Russian Academy of Sciences & NSU

By the time of our visit, the Techno-Park — in the modernistic academic city called Akademgorodok — had already signed cooperation agreements with institutions all over the world in dozens of fields of study, all part of Russia's growing interest in commercializing research for business pursuits. I kept in mind that it was this uncontrolled access to the raw sciences that Western intelligence-gathering agencies were most concerned about. The newly formed Russian Federation had very little influence on these untethered and unfocused teams. The CIA and similar spy agencies were making inroads to monitor and intercept the outflow of strategic materials, especially those that shouldn't be in the hands of terrorists. Embassy Joe had accepted my guise as a scholar-businessman to make contacts in Akademgorodok. This worked with my chief ally, too. Dima wanted the prestige of bringing in an American academician and businessman.

As for me, I wanted to make my speeches, hand out my cards, and get back to Cindy at the Intourist as quickly as I could because Anatoly and Georg might show up any time.

Our first meeting was supposed to be at the Economics Department of Novosibirsk State University, with the dean and his invited guests. Stan, as the dean wanted to be called, rushed us into his enormous conference room.

I whispered in Dima's ear. "This is the fucking largest conference room I have ever seen!" I'd never seen a conference room that could seat three hundred people.

Dima cocked his head over and covered his mouth to tell me, "Next door is an auditorium that seats several thousand."

We had arrived late. Thirty or so dignified looking men were sitting around the huge table. They stood when we approached. I made a quick assessment of the types I saw: Trotsky revolutionary socialists, Lenin political visionaries, and Karl Marx philosophers.

Stan bellowed, "Please sit down, my illustrious guests! We have a packed house next door going through the agenda of our monthly Academy of Sciences meeting. We have some time to fill you in a bit on this fine institution. The other colleagues in this room are department chairmen at the university. They have excused me from introductions but are hoping to talk to you later in more intimate surroundings during cocktail hour."

Dima stood and made one introduction. "This is Professor Andrew Gold. He has had a marvelous time traveling by rail from Poland to be with us. We thank you for this opportunity."

I stood up, waved in a friendly fashion and nodded in agreement. They probably took it to mean, "What he just said."

Stan took over with a history lesson. "You must know a little bit about this place. I will tell you some of the highlights of the historical journey to this moment — if you allow, Professor Gold."

"Oh please! By all means!"

"Delightful!" Stan smiled, scratched his goatee, and began. "The early seeds for development of this region were planted in the late 1800s by Tsar Alexander III. He is referred to as the Peacemaker or the Construction Tsar. Did you know it?" He stopped to look at me as if I was a student expected to answer an oral exam.

This, at least, I felt prepared for. "I think I've heard something about it, sir. The Trans-Siberian Railway? That might be attributed to him? Or something."

"Very good, Professor Gold!" Stan continued his lesson. "Despite his accomplishments, tsars were not universally liked. After a plot to assassinate Alex III, its leaders were executed. One of them was named Ulyanov. He was the brother of a fellow whose later revolutionary name you might recognize: Vladimir Lenin." Stan raised his eyebrows with what he expected to be a surprising bit of information. He waited for me to acknowledge my amazement. I nodded, hoping that was enough for him to continue.

"Alex III stayed alive long enough to build railways all over Russia. He worked to modernize his country instead of getting it into wars that weren't really its business. The tsar imagined a network of railroads that would crisscross the steppes and mountains. The Trans-Siberian Railway from Moscow to Vladivostok, though not completed until after his death, is one of those rail routes that came to be." Stan stopped again and waited for my sign of astonishment.

I was ready to play this game. "Isn't the Trans-Siberian Railway visible from earth's orbit?" I asked.

Dima interrupted. "I think that's the Great Wall of China."

Turning to thank Dima for correcting me, I noticed that a dozen of the department chairmen, were fast asleep. Stan must have noticed this, too. He cleared his throat and shuffled past several pages of his presentation, fast-forwarding to Soviet times and Stalin.

"In 1926 the town here was given a new name, Novosibirsk. Means 'New City in Siberia.' Soon Josef Stalin's grand plans for industrialization and electrification gave focus to Siberia's development. The five-year plans granted this booming city major facilities for manufacturing, food processing, and power generation. Novosibirsk earned its nickname, 'Siberian Chicago.'" Stan had given up on pausing for me to acknowledge each wonderful fact. He plowed steadily ahead.

"By the late 1950s, Nikita Khrushchev had the idea to build a scientific powerhouse in the middle of nowhere. With all its challenges of geography and climate, the region around Novosibirsk certainly fit that description." Before I could signal my agreement to that proposition, someone opened a door, stuck his head in, and called out, "Five minutes, Professor!"

"OK. OK. *Spasibo!*" The gentleman backed away and shut the door. Stan flipped ahead a few more pages. "I will begin to conclude. Where we sit, though just thirty kilometers from the center of Novosibirsk, is more than an academic compound; it is a complete town. Complementing its institutions of higher learning and the Siberian headquarters for the Russian Academy of Sciences are libraries, restaurants and cafes, hotels, stores, hospitals, houses and apartments, cinemas and clubs. Here we have all the luxury amenities Russian culture can provide. All are designed to serve the town's highly educated residents. Akademgorodok even has a man-made beach on the Ob Reservoir. Sand brought here by the hundreds of truckloads for the benefit of our workers." Stan looked at me and then added, "If you, Professor Gold, brought your swimming trunks, we can take a swim after your speech!"

"Thank you, Stan!" I stood, hoping this indicated the end of his presentation. "I didn't bring my swimsuit but I appreciate the offer."

Thankfully, I was right. Stan gathered up his papers and sat down. After a few pleasantries and some mineral water, Dima and I thanked him and made the rounds to shake hands with the other men in the room as they began to wake up, anticipating my own speech.

Stan clapped his hands and motioned to the rear door. "Professor Gold! And Dima! You are the special guests today of the Siberian Regional Academy of Science. For this special occasion, everyone has shown up — all 2,500 members."

My gasp must have been audible. The recently awakened department heads were laughing at my gaping jaw. Launched into the grand hall, I saw the vast space was standing room only. Every face looked anxious for a chance to cash in on the American invasion of Akademgorodok. My heart jumped into my throat. Even Dima, equally focused on cashing in, gave me an anxious look. He could see I was sweating this one in a big way.

Stan was ahead of me and Dima behind as we quickly walked to the podium. He directed us to chairs just below the main speaker's lectern. As we sat down, I whispered to Dima, as calmly as I could manage, "This might be a disaster. Please help me if I am having problems."

Dima nodded. He said something along the lines of "No mentioning that you are happy about political and economic changes!" His next words sounded only like

"Blah blah blah. . ." and I didn't catch them.

I was carrying Cindy's Russian translation of my speech. She had written the entire text in easily legible block letters and included a phonetic pronunciation guide for my introduction. The rest of the speech was my description of how cooperation might be carried out. It was borrowed directly from my Krakow experience and included a list of 'desirables' an American university might want in such a partnership. My planned conclusion was simply a promise to report to those American colleges and universities that might be interested. That, and an offer to follow up through Dima within a month.

The crowd got quiet.

Stan introduced me in a very simple way. "Please welcome our guest, Andrew Gold. He is an American with business experience, living in Krakow, Poland. He is on the faculty at the MBA pilot program in Krakow. It is sponsored by the Krakow Industrial Society and the

University of Detroit."

I stood and thanked Stan. I don't know that I'd ever been as nervous as I was standing at that microphone with several thousand Russian academics expectantly watching me. My voice shook during my first sentence. "Good afternoon, professors, administrators, and friends. My name is Andy Gold. It is my great pleasure and honor to be here in your beautiful country and to be invited to meet you in this legendary city of science and learning."

That line in Russian was greeted with a blast of applause that lasted ten times longer than it had taken to say those words. I could hear some comments from the front rows, something like, "The guy actually spoke some Russian. Not the usual American accent. Spy for sure! Ha! Ha!" Whoever had said that, it was rewarded with laughter, more clapping, and more joking.

When the crowd quieted, I got into the rhythm for what I hoped was exactly how Cindy had written it for me. Her script even offered prompts in two places, "PAUSE HERE FOR SECOND. SMILE AT AUDIENCE," after particularly affectionate claims to love the Russian language and people. She was right. They were waiting for opportunities to show their appreciation for my speaking more than a handful of words in Russian. The audience gave me two more standing ovations before I even got to the meat of the speech. At the end of the Russian lovefest that was my introduction, I apologized for having to escape into English. I took a long drink of water and then pulled out the rest of my notes.

With that change, the audience cooled off. I got lukewarm stares as I described the Krakow-Detroit program. I remembered that Dima had advised me not to suggest that cooperation here be anything like how we'd done it in Poland. At that moment, I knew exactly what to say. I dropped any further description of the Polish model. I also felt a Russian accent beginning to slip into my English.

"The much better Russian model of cooperation will therefore be our guide to a successful collaborative effort. What that Russian model will be, I am confident that the members of this most prestigious body in the world will quickly formulate and our program will be repeated everywhere."

The line seemed like a cop-out, but it was received with thunderous applause again. And then, as the clapping began to slow down, memories of a time that seemed long ago drifted into my head. In a debate class at the University of Washington, I had won a competition by, of all things, extolling the virtues of Communism! In that winning speech, I had memorized all the lines of propaganda the Albanian leader, Enver Hoxha, and his government used to describe their great Marxist-Leninist state. I had also mastered how the Albanian Communists had described the 'imperialists' from the United States and its Western 'stooges.' I'd even practiced my delivery and cadence to match the rare available footage of Hoxha's speeches. For some reason, on that podium in Novosibirsk, I was overcome with the desire to recreate that atmosphere. I started talking without my notes to build up these scientists' patriotism. My objective was to offset their feelings that post-Soviet Russia would not have a good atmosphere for science and learning. I cringe now, remembering my bad Russian accent and exaggerated tone.

"This incredible institution, the Russian Academy of Sciences, came into being and was forged to what it is now over decades. It is the foundation for a great nation; perhaps the greatest nation. It is that framework of greatness that will guarantee that our Russian-American MBA program model will carry itself as worthy of emulation by other countries that are seeking a grand model for success."

Those grand but empty words produced the last standing ovation, but it was the longest. Already, Dima was frantically shaking hands with people in the front rows and with men and women crowding around to talk to him. I had planned on saying more to Dima and Stan for their invitation, but the audience had interpreted my patriotic blather as my final statement. In the end, it all worked out well. The Academy of Sciences asked us only to attend a small cocktail session afterward and did not put any of us on the spot to speak again. Everyone had been present to hear what I had said. Now they all just wanted to drink — and get us drunk.

***

"Hello, Dr. Gold. Lev Meyerkov from the High Energy Physics lab here at Akademgorodok. Very nice speech today. I am interested in discussing sometime the American model for commercializing high-tech innovation. Would you be interested in such a discussion?"

Bingo! Embassy Joe's kind of guy! *Good hit Number One*, I thought, as I told Lev that I wasn't a PhD but knew a little bit about the subject. I explained that my own father was involved in nuclear fuels fabrication in Washington State.

"Oh, probably your Hanford Nuclear Reservation," Lev said. "Where you make weapons-grade fuel. I think your Japanese bomb material was done at Hanford, too."

"You are absolutely right!" I said, and proceeded to take advantage of the opening he'd given me. "I guess we are surrounded here by many institutes and factories for similar fuel reprocessing and weapons grade fuel fabrication, isn't it true?"

Lev didn't hesitate to answer me, but seemed melancholy. "At our highest production level, it was a busy time in the sixties and seventies. The economic crisis of the eighties and complete system collapse now in the nineties has us at a standstill. But you know that. I would one day like to visit University of California at Berkeley and maybe MIT sometime."

"I am sure you could get an invitation just by reaching out," I assured him. He smiled, and we exchanged business cards before I moved on. I wondered who else with access to nuclear material and potential bad stuff I could meet today. I then had an American-style idea that didn't go over super well, but did get some results.

I found Dima talking to a local celebrity, a man who had been a famous weightlifter in the sixties and seventies. During a break in their conversation, I asked Dima to try to announce that we would be delighted to get business cards from all the guests present since there would not be enough time to talk to everyone. Stan made the announcement, which generated an audible sound of disappointment. Even so, a lot of the people complied, and we had quite a large handful of cards by the time the evening began to draw to a close. One other discussion had struck me as important. I noticed Dima seemed to have been cornered by several men who were arguing about money. I couldn't tell what the context was, though.

"What was that all about, Dima? Seemed serious," I asked after he'd broken free.

"Some of my closer contacts from administration of a specialty metals facility near here," he said, with what sounded like consternation. "They want to know if we are going to talk about Soyuz debris with you.

They are disappointed that your contacts chose to go back to Chelyabinsk for the three wild debris sites so far north. They are thinking that it would be good to talk about other subjects while you are in Novosibirsk."

"What other subjects would they have to talk about, do you think?" I asked him.

"Specialty metals I am sure, but it might be on the edge of legal," Dima answered. "That means probably illegal until we pay someone money to make the paperwork legal." That sounded strange.

"Make the paperwork legal? Or make false paperwork look legal?" I asked.

"Maybe a little of both, my friend. But it is enough money for us, in my opinion, to take risk if there is buyer you can find." He said this slowly, as if he was thinking about every word before he let it come out of his mouth.

I had a reply in mind, too, something I almost actually said, as if Dima was part of the terrorist team: *Sounds like bad stuff to me and we're in the business of bad stuff.* But I thought better of it and kept quiet. Instead, I raised my eyebrows and asked him to find out more. I also told him I would probably be busy all day tomorrow doing work in the hotel.

If he was able to set up a meeting with his colleagues, he agreed, he would deliver a message to me through the hotel concierge.

With a quick run-through of the cards we'd gotten, I estimated that seven or eight individuals were promising candidates to supply information about strategic materials. Another fifteen or twenty seemed like they might have close ties to people Joe was interested in. That alone seemed like a winning evening for me. Add to that Dima's disappointed 'admin guys,' and I thought we weren't doing too badly.

Still, things were getting a little convoluted for me on this trip. My to-do list for the next few days was getting longer by the minute.

1) Cindy was waiting for me to initiate our plans for dealing with Anatoly and Georg, but I had no idea how that might turn out or what the dangers were.

2) Dima was acting on his own managing the RFPs and also developing a short list of potential MBA partners willing to pay bribe money for his scheming. Was this going to get me in trouble?

3) The real NSU MBA proposal was coming soon, which meant I'd need to figure out who the lucky American partner would be.

4) I hadn't yet told Dima that he wasn't going with me when I returned to Chelyabinsk in another week.

5) Would I be meeting Yuri, Toshek and Vlad in Chelyabinsk?

6) Katerina and Zhenia. I knew my interest in them didn't involve business, but I needed to know: Would I be able to see them again?

7) Would anyone be able to safely provide passage to Soyuz debris sites that were closely guarded by mafia thugs?

With that array of worries closing in on me, I hopped over to Dima and asked him if I could head back to the hotel alone. The NSU cocktail gathering had become a full-fledged party and I was able to sneak out without a problem. I'm glad I did.

When I got back to the hotel, Vincent and Cindy were all over me: Anatoly and Georg had arrived just a few minutes earlier. As tired as I was, I had to rush into action, grab my toolkit, and start gathering information.

Welcome to the world of following bad guys with bad stuff.

Welcoming Committee

Vincent had spotted our guys first. During the evening, it was his job to greet arriving guests in front of the hotel, sometimes opening their car doors for them as they rolled up. Awnings covered the driveway, which was marked 'For Checking-In Guests Only, Please!' At about 7 p.m., a cream-colored late-model Volga had pulled up. Vincent's courteous greeting as he opened the driver's door was met with a gruff Russian warning, "Shut the fucking door or I'll cut your nuts off, you little prick!"

To which Vincent immediately responded with an apology. He did this as he was shutting the door, but not before he heard the passenger tell the rude driver, "Georg! Calm down, you idiot!"

As he told me in breathless detail a few minutes later, Vincent quickly bowed out of any further greetings or bellman activities for this delightful pair. To a young assistant bellhop, he whispered, "We need to delay these guys as much as possible. We will get a big tip if we can do it without being too obvious." He then darted into the lobby and grabbed a house phone. "Cindy, they have arrived! I am ninety-nine percent sure that Anatoly and Georg are in a cream-colored Volga in front of the hotel."

Cindy thanked Vincent and slammed the receiver down, racing to the desk to review our notes, and then pulled my toolkit from under the bed. She didn't open it but was praying I would arrive soon. Leaving it ready at the foot of the bed, she ran downstairs carrying a purse-load of cameras and bugs to carry out some version of the surveillance routine we had been practicing for the past two days.

When I arrived at our room ten minutes later, I spotted the toolkit first thing when I opened the door. I was back in the lobby in ninety seconds.

Cindy had already started her filming session. First step was taking photos of these guys in 'Self-Parking,' removing their bags from the car's trunk and the back seat. She then got several shots of Anatoly ducking into the lobby to retrieve a bellman's cart and rolling it back to his car.

Georg, according to Vincent, had been swearing non-stop as he moved the bags around next to the car. We had told Vincent we needed close measurements of their bags and he had done his best, offering them help with their luggage. They had refused. Georg had again made reference to Vincent's testicles being at risk if he touched anything of theirs. Understandably, Vincent sought other means of getting close enough to measure their bags.

Anatoly and Georg both had a darker complexion than normal for Russians. As Cindy put it, "These guys look Romanian, but their Russian is absolutely Moscow Central City dialect."

I suspected that Cindy had misspoken, confusing 'Romanian' for "Roma," meaning she thought they looked like Gypsies. Both needed a haircut; both greased their hair down quite close to their heads. Both had sideburns that were not typical of the times. Cindy began to suspect they were residents of Turkmenistan or Uzbekistan, backwaters of the former Soviet Union. She had noticed their shoes and workman jackets were typical of the Central Asian region. Watching closely as she recorded a two-minute video of the men piling their bags onto the bellman's cart, she noticed a huge difference in how they handled their luggage. They casually carried what seemed to be two normal travel bags. But two other bags, obviously heavy, they placed much more carefully onto the cart, laying them on their sides instead of standing upright like a regular suitcase.

Vincent's earlier suggestion to his young assistant gave the boy some pause. He had to consider how to delay their progress getting to their room. The plan he came up with was very good, but did involve some risk. Without us knowing it, he removed several metal pins that kept the wheels on the luggage carts. All three of the hotel's carts had at least one pin missing, he told us later. The cart our targets were using had made it out to their car and back, loaded with their things, without incident. By then, Cindy, Vincent and I were each watching discreetly from different parts of the lobby. The weakened cart was next to the registration desk. Its load of Anatoly and Georg's things including at least fifty pounds of something very bad. At this point, none of us knew what the boy had done; he hadn't had a chance to tell Vincent about removing the pins.

In the time that it had taken them to get inside through the hotel's parking lot entrance, pass through the lobby by the business center, turn left at the concierge desk, and stop briefly at the convenience store to discuss where they would be getting food and drink, Cindy and I managed to place bugs on their shabby coats, photograph them from all sides, swab their bags for lab analysis, make two passes with the Geiger counter, and get measurements of their bags using the swab stick and the Geiger wand as rulers. For camouflage, Cindy and I fussed over a pile of luggage, acting like we were tourists trying to get organized, about twenty feet from the registration desk. As Anatoly and Georg pulled the cart up to check in, Cindy was listening in to the conversation at the desk. Hidden in a suitcase she had a twelve-inch parabolic antenna hooked up to a microphone. It was good that we had the antenna, because Anatoly was speaking very softly to the hotel clerk. For Georg, however, we certainly didn't need it. He was pissed off at everything and everybody, and loudly threatened everyone's testicles — even those who weren't equipped with any.

"I know the reservation was for a regular room with two beds," Anatoly said, "but a larger room would be best. If you have a suite separated by a door, we would be willing to pay for that."

The desk clerk looked through his list of vacant rooms before politely responding, "We have something like that, but the second room is quite small. It has only a couch, coffee table, and TV. It is not appropriate for sleeping in. The couch is not a sofa bed."

Cindy smiled and gave me a wink as she heard Anatoly say, "The luggage will go in the second room. We don't want to be in the same room as the luggage. My colleague's dirty clothes are in it." I found that both humorous and appalling when Cindy played that back to me later. It was obvious that these bad guys didn't want to be too close to bad stuff that might make them sick.

"How will you be paying?" the clerk asked Anatoly.

"Cash now," he answered.

"If you want to use the phone in your room during your stay, we will need to have a deposit or a credit card on file," the clerk reminded him.

To which Anatoly responded, "Oh yeah. We have to make a call later." Georg loudly offered six or seven violent swear words and told Anatoly to hurry up. It was at this moment, without warning, that Vincent's young buddy went into action. Vincent's instructions to earn a big tip by delaying these men had been big motivation for the boy. He told us later that he was standing with his back to them, watching in a mirror for the right moment to pass by them without being noticed. At the precise moment he thought was best, his toe tapped the cart's wheel, knocking it off, and at the same time he ran his hand over the top of one of the regular suitcases, tripping its snap release and opening one side, just as the cart was falling over to the side where the wheel had been. The loose wheel was rolling directly toward us at the opposite side of the reception area.

Even Anatoly began to swear as the cart toppled, starting to dump all four bags onto the floor. "Oh, Jesus Christ! Georg! Fuck!"

Georg grabbed the upright on the cart and yanked it, but that just jerked the bags loose, guaranteeing that all slid off. The opened suitcase spilled clothes and toiletries over the rest of the bags. When one of the suspiciously heavy bags hit the floor, it clanked like a scuba diver's oxygen tank. Sliding two or three feet, the bag stopped when it hit a wall. Cindy and I could now clearly see it was made of something like burlap or hemp, wrapped with cheap shipping tape. Whatever was inside had shifted and ripped the fabric. Clearly visible through the tear was the radioactive hazard symbol. Next to it but less readable was some kind of logo or symbol. Next to the parabolic antenna in Cindy's microphone bag was a hidden camera. She stepped back quickly to snap a photo. We both hoped her camera was high enough to see inside the tear we were staring at.

It was Anatoly's reaction that said the most about what was inside that bag. It scared me to death. Rather than move quickly toward his fallen luggage, he covered his face with his hands and forearms as if he was afraid something would explode, or maybe go critical. Something like enriched uranium. Everyone noticed this. The night security guard jokingly called out, "You act like you just dropped nitroglycerin." Now, for a change, Georg didn't launch into another tirade about ripping someone's balls off. With a weird look on his face, he waved away both Vincent and the boy as they hurried to help. In a tone that might almost have been polite, he said, "Thank you. I'll take care of it. Sorry for the problem."

Both Georg and Anatoly straightened out their mess, repacked the suitcase that had popped open and took their keys from the desk clerk who was holding them out.

"Room number 605," she said. "Junior suite. Elevator is over there." She pointed for them. "Do you need help with your bags?"

Vincent had already run to bring his guests another cart. His young accomplice discreetly pointed to one whose wheels hadn't been tampered with. After delivering the new cart, Vincent casually picked up the wheel that had gone astray.

Georg successfully resisted his urge to threaten anyone else's gonads as he gingerly pushed the new cart, loaded with its ominous cargo, toward the elevator. Anatoly followed close behind, slowly shaking his head.

"Well, that was certainly a strange incident," the desk clerk said after the elevator door closed.

Vincent appeared in the lobby with a broom and dustpan. As he swept his way toward us, he quietly asked if he and his colleague had delayed them enough for us to do what we needed to do.

"Absolutely yes," I said. "Thank you! And please don't clean up yet where the baggage cart fell. Let me do something first."

I still had my Geiger counter handy, taped inside my heavy coat, with the wand inside my sleeve. I ran a washcloth over the area where everything had fallen to get a final swab for testing, simultaneously doing a quick check with the Geiger counter. The counter wasn't screaming, but it told me the floor was hot from whatever had just spilled out from the men's bags. I moved the counter over to a spot about five feet away and the crackling calmed down to a low growl.

Hot stuff had indeed just passed this way.

***

"We need to inventory what we've got and what we still need to get from these guys," I said to Cindy while we removed film canisters and tapes from our toolkits. "Do you think we need to keep an eye on their room tonight?" I asked her as we tucked the kits back under the bed.

Cindy smiled. "Vincent and his little buddy will come to the rescue for that type of work." Just as she spoke, there was a knock at the door.

I opened it. "Speak of the devil! Hi, Vincent."

"Sorry to bother you," he said, standing at attention in the hallway.

"But I wanted to ask you for a favor. I told Ben, the guy that was helping me earlier, that you would tip him for his involvement. I hope that was OK?" Poor Vincent looked sheepishly at the floor, as if I might be angry with him.

"Not a problem." I laughed, to let him know I was pleased with how he and his apprentice had performed. "If I give you four twenty-dollar bills, is that enough to distribute between yourself and Ben?" I offered.

"Wow. That seems like too much!" Vincent said, surprise in his voice.

"Well, maybe not. We are also hoping someone can let us know if anything unusual goes on down at Room 605 tonight. Also, we need to know how many nights they have reserved." I extended the eighty dollars to him. "Would that cover what you did today, finding out their length of stay, and watching the room tonight?"

"Yes," Vincent said with a broad grin. "I'll call if anything happens." He saluted me but peered over my shoulder, apparently checking to see if Cindy was there.

"Bye, Vincent!" Cindy said in a monotone as he turned to leave.

"Oh, Vincent!" I called after him, starting to think about giving him better instructions. "These guys may get super drunk, have women over, get in a fight, order food, and cause general mayhem here at the hotel. None of that is cause to wake us up in the night. What *is* cause to contact us, is if they both leave. Either with or without the luggage. Also, if any of those bags are taken from the room. By anyone. In fact, if any bag goes out, let us know. It's possible, after the whole hotel witnessed their embarrassing mishap downstairs, that they've transferred things to other containers."

"Got it." Vincent said.

"Thank you, Vincent. Good night."

About ten minutes later, the message light on our phone lit up. I punched in my code and heard Vincent's voice.

"Vincent here. Our guests are staying on a day-to-day basis. They said it could be one night and it could be up to five nights. They also said they are waiting for a phone call from Switzerland to be patched into their room. Good night, again."

"Switzerland. That could be the money guys or the consignees," I thought out loud.

"Or both," Cindy added.

We began to theorize. "Novosibirsk," I mused aloud. "Crossroads east-west and north-south. Makes sense they are waiting here for further instructions. Go west! Go south! Go southeast! Militant Islamic buyers and you go south, maybe. Arabic terrorists hiding out in Switzerland call to arrange a letter of credit if their reps confirm delivery. But where will delivery be?"

Cindy chimed in, "That's what Embassy Joe wants us to find out. That is why he sent me here to say 'Fifi sixty-six' to you. Looks like we are only halfway to finish line."

"Hey, I've been curious about something." I caught Cindy's eye. "I hope you won't be mad at me if I ask."

"You want to know if I am really a prostitute," she answered quickly. My face must have given me away; she smiled when my expression told her she had been spot on.

"Jesus Christ! Yes! That's what I was wondering!" I couldn't believe it. Once again, she'd read my mind.

"And I am wondering," she countered, "if you are a real businessman."

For some reason the question had hit me hard. Glumly, I said, "I don't know what I am, Cindy." I thought about it a while longer and then gave up. Both on answering her question, and on getting an answer to mine. "Good night."

Cindy watched silently as I collected my things to move to my room. She stood motionless a moment and then said, "Let's get up early and talk about next steps."

"OK. I'm up at six."

Cindy reached out and touched me for the first time since we'd been together. With both hands, she stroked my face and head. Silently, we hugged for about two minutes. Pulling back, she looked me in the eye and said, "Good night, Andy."

I lay in bed a long time thinking about the convoluted world I was creating for myself. Even when I slept, I couldn't get conflicting ideas out of my head. First, feeling attracted to Cindy. Working so closely together in this incredibly important mission laid us both bare. I really liked what I could see of her. She was intellectually challenging and proficient in a world I was in awe of. It wasn't that I'd never felt that before with other female colleagues; but Cindy took it to a new level. Our lives might depend on that critical level of trust. The conflict, though, was unbearable for me. Once, I'd felt great camaraderie with Renata, too. I respected her intellectual prowess; I felt grateful that she'd taken me in and given me the intensive academic version of *Everything You Need to Know About Poland and Europe to Be a Superstar... and Avoid Being an Idiot.* And I had to admit, I had recently seen signs that Renata could soften her attitude toward me. Was I not giving her enough credit? Staring at the ceiling, I rehashed what she'd said in that last conversation before I headed east. Had her words been more about hoping for a better relationship instead of a threat to leave me, as I had taken it? This trip and my perilous secret life with the CIA had all come about so I could stay in Poland. Stay with her and the kids. It was about getting our family into a better home. *Christ!* I tossed and turned. I'd come back to Poland to give my best shot at repairing something that had been important to me once. I wondered if it could be again.

An Old Friend and New Plans

Six o'clock in the morning came with an unwelcome jolt and a muffled scream. I awoke from a dream, hanging on to a cliff and about to lose my grip. Dressing and thinking about the day, I could see that Cindy was up as usual, doing her bathroom routine. I could already compare Cindy's routine to Renata's. I decided it wasn't worth ramping up my emotions on that front so early in the morning. I decided to take a stroll and passed the bathroom without disturbing her. Pulling the door shut, I took off quickly down the hallway, gravitating toward room 605.

Padding down one flight of stairs and then following the long, plain corridor as quietly as I could, I noticed that the door to room 608, about twenty feet past number 605 on the opposite side, was open about four inches. I slowed and saw Ben, our young friend from yesterday, sitting on the floor holding a notepad. I stopped and pushed the door open a little. He looked a little shocked, but I smiled and whispered, "Thank you. But please be careful." I returned the door to the position he had left it and continued down the hall. I took the end stairwell up to the seventh floor and returned to my room. Cindy was toweling her hair dry. She turned with a smile when I came in.

"Having breakfast with Georg and Anatoly this morning?" she joked.

"I wanted to. But they were still snoring. By the way, I saw our young hero, Ben, from yesterday. He's on duty. He's in room 608 keeping an eye on 605 and waiting for something to happen," I told her.

"I have some important news for us." Cindy's tone had turned serious.

"Interesting. Please tell me."

Cindy appeared to be organizing her thoughts, maybe choosing how to say what she wanted to say in English. "Looking at the negatives from when the bag tore open yesterday, I would say the container is for enriched uranium. The symbol we saw next to the radioactivity warning definitely starts with 'U-2.' The rest is not visible. I know a little about the standard cases used to transport fully enriched uranium-235. I would say that they are in possession of a weapons grade uranium container with almost no shielding. Does that mean U-235 is inside that container? Not necessarily. But I don't know."

That did sound serious. "Should I call the embassy and try to talk to Joe?" I asked.

"No. Not necessary. I already got some information from him," Cindy admitted.

"I guess you didn't get much sleep, then." My voice must have sounded as unhappy as the frown on my face implied. I was realizing that a lot went on when I least expected it.

Cindy chose not to react. She continued, "We are waiting for the call from Switzerland or wherever it will be from. There will be extra ears on that call, and we will know what to do soon after. It is likely that we take the stuff from Anatoly and Georg."

"Somebody's likely losing their balls, then." I said this very seriously, remembering Georg's favorite line from yesterday.

Cindy rolled her eyes.

I thought about what she had said. It all made sense. The call gets successfully traced and enough information is gleaned to understand who the intended buyers or financiers are. Tracking them down will become a job for somebody else. But the hijacked material needs to end its journey here. Now that we—or, more accurately, our side—knows everything, why continue to expose people to the dangers? I was relieved to see this job would be ending soon. The last thing I wanted was for Joe to tell me that I am assigned to be the stupid American businessman heading to Uzbekistan in a sleeping compartment with two guys, who happen to be carrying enough fissile material to blow up a city of one and a half million people.

Cindy interrupted my thoughts as they drifted towards mushroom clouds, dirty bombs, and Armageddon. "Another little detail for you: We will probably have to share the room for a night with one more person you know. Your old friend Toshek is arriving today, late in the evening. He is coming here from Krasnoyarsk. It is possible that you and he will travel together back to Chelyabinsk. If the call comes from Switzerland, he will probably help with taking the uranium. It is his specialty."

"Uranium is his specialty? Or taking things from people is his specialty?" I asked, quite seriously.

"Definitely the second thing you said," Cindy replied with a vigorous nod.

Very surprised by hearing that Toshek was coming through Novosibirsk from Krasnoyarsk, a day's trip to the east, I was having trouble believing it. "But wait a minute. I left Toshek about two hours the other side of Chelyabinsk, in the middle of nowhere, just three days ago. Now he is coming from Krasnoyarsk? He would have to be traveling almost non-stop to be here in Novosibirsk heading west, going back to Chelyabinsk!"

"Sounds exactly like Toshek's usual program. Not unusual at all," Cindy said, trying to sound nonchalant. But I had a feeling she found him nearly as unnerving as I did. "Toshek is the king trader of *ichthyol* ointment. Between jobs for Joe or whoever, he is always transporting or arranging transport for ichthyol concentrate going to the West. You asked me about his specialty? Ichthyol is definitely one of them."

"*Masc ichthiolowa*?" I asked, using the Polish for ichthyol salve. "That gooey black stuff for boils and other skin problems that's in every Polish grandmother's medicine cabinet?"

"Correct! Toshek is famous as the 'Ichthyol Man,'" she promptly agreed.

"Weird stuff," I commented. "I'm surprised it has a market in the West."

"Western European doctors have been using it a long time but the concentrate in raw form is best from deep inside Russia and China." Cindy knew something about it, I could see.

***

Even after all these years in Eastern Europe, I hate the stuff. Reading the label on my own tube of it: "Natural substance from the distillation of sulfur-rich oil shale. It is purified and with an ammonia additive, becomes a viscous, water-soluble substance with a characteristic bitumen-like odor. Use on eczema or psoriasis or use as a drawing salve." As the 'Valley Girls' of the eighties liked to say, "Gag me with a spoon!"

***

With these new developments, what was even more impressive to me than Toshek's fame as the 'Ichthyol Man' was Cindy's up-to-the-minute knowledge of so many things. She had developed all her clandestinely shot photos, without a lab, while I was sleeping. She stayed in constant contact with Embassy Joe. She somehow knew about Toshek's whereabouts and impending arrival, and now was part of a plan being formulated to seize the uranium as soon as she got the green light in a phone call from Switzerland. I started to realize that my unspoken question the day before, about her being a prostitute, was quite stupid. What a super-spy she was! I didn't have a lot to compare her to, since she was the first real spy I had collaborated with, but it was clear to me that her skills were impressive. My own awkward efforts were greatly overshadowed by what she was capable of — and was already doing.

I'd been strongly drawn to other uber-proficient women in my life. Renata had also impressed me — and a lot of other suitors she'd sent packing. She'd opened doors for me and greased the skids (and palms) of scores of influential people to get me welcomed into Krakow's close-knit and pretentious business and academic community. I'd surely be cast out of that clique if I chose to close or alter the ending of my long chapter with Renata in Poland. And finally, Katerina! The Soviet/Russian version of the self-made woman with drive, courage, and compassion as I'd never seen. At that moment, having no idea what I wanted most, I got back down to business.

Cindy finished with her 'ready routine'— shower, hair and makeup — and said she wanted to talk to the boy in 608, as well as to Vincent, if he was in yet. After she rushed off with a quick wave in my direction, I decided to give Dima a call. I wanted to find out when our next MBA dog-and-pony show would be. Those meetings were producing good contacts for Embassy Joe and I wanted to get as many of them done as I could, up until that call from Switzerland came in. On the other hand, I'd nearly missed out on the action here at the hotel during my last meeting at NSU. So I knew I was risking the same by leaving again. We had no idea when the call would be coming in. Yet it was becoming certain that Anatoly and Georg would move quickly whenever they got their instructions.

I ordered the call to Dima through the front desk. It came back within five minutes. From the beginning, I begged Dima to keep our meeting short. That ran contrary to his instincts, which was to spend as much time as he could drumming up business. He was already acting on the RFP idea for dozens of institutes and collecting money for each one. His earlier idea to personally meet with dozens of institutes was now dying. Fortunately, I no longer had to fight his over-exuberance to meet and greet every academic group in town. Nevertheless, today we were scheduled as guests during the weekly board meeting of the Novosibirsk Regional Techno-Park. It was the group Embassy Joe's advisors had identified as Dima's core people, the ones who could be suspected of plotting to sell radioactive materials for big money. In spite of the danger of events unfolding at the hotel without me, I really needed to attend this meeting. It was my best way to get as many contacts as possible. Dima promised to organize things so I could exit early if I needed to. I was starting to get the impression that he liked having me come and go quickly. That left him alone to hold court with his regular bunch of club mates, free to make unrealistic promises in return for upfront payments.

Cindy came back as I was in the last stages of getting ready for my meeting. She was tightly focused on details that would be important when the call came in. She filled me in on her meeting with Vincent and young Ben. The assistant bellman keeping watch in room 608 was completely asleep when she knocked on the door. She suggested that he go back to sleep so he'd be rested up for later. He was happy to comply — and to get paid for it. She had found Vincent was behind the reception desk bright and early, and talked to him about the hotel's ancient phone switching gear. After the manager on duty went out for a smoke, Vincent immediately slipped her into the phone room. She patched the line for our room phone into the one for 605. When she reported this to me, I asked how she had done this without making *our* line accessible to Anatoly and Georg. She gave me a pained look. I assumed that meant I needed to learn something about tracing and bugging calls.

"We'll know exactly when the call comes in and be able to listen to it," she explained.

"That call will be heard in Warsaw, in Washington D.C., Zurich, and somewhere between Afghanistan and Kazakhstan. Wherever Joe has his southern team working. "

"And Room 738 at the Intourist in Novosibirsk!" I added. "How did

Vincent react to you messing with the hotel phone system?"

"He let me do it. Didn't say anything," Cindy answered. "I think he assumes that everyone is doing dirty business. Since he kind of knows now that there is something terribly wrong with these guys, he's happy to help for now."

"Do you think the rest of the hotel staff suspects anything about us?" I asked.

"They do. But just like Vincent, there is so much corruption around here, they are happy that guns aren't being used. They are grateful that people aren't dying in the hotel. Yet."

I wondered if she was armed and, if so, whether she was prepared to shoot someone. And after hearing those sentiments from Cindy, I thought I might just extend today's meeting with the Techno-Park guys.

***

Dima admitted that this was the group he had been talking about when we first met at the Marriott in Warsaw. He had described academic professionals and businesspeople working together on projects. On this sunny day, he had decided to show off his pride and joy, a new Volga. As he drove me through Novosibirsk's potholed streets towards Akademgorodok, he got sentimental. He told me about his "sadness of the falling of the Soviet Union" and the power vacuums that created in all the state-dependent science and technology organizations in this part of Russia. I got brave and asked him if the nuclear weapons and the industry that produced them had in any way been compromised by what he'd called a 'power struggle.' He admitted that he knew there was talk about this in the West, but he couldn't believe anyone in the inner circle of weapons bases and weapon building could ever betray the Motherland.

"Not even for huge money?" I asked. "A million tax-free dollars goes a long way in this part of the world."

Dima was silent. It dawned on me I may have gone a bit too far. After all, lab testing on his own briefcase had detected traces of nerve gas and plutonium that had recently been carried in that diplomatka, whether he'd known it or not.

Dima eventually responded to my 'huge money' question. "Big money can make most people do stupid things," he said. "That is what government is for. Scare you enough to be good and not try to do *numer stulecia.*" He added, "I think you know this phrase, '*numer stulecia*' in Polish."

I did. It describes an enormous deal or transaction. The best translation might be "deal of a lifetime."

"I do know that expression, Dima. And sometimes it worries me that the economy here is so bad that even your closest friends — the people we're meeting today — are capable of something stupid. Possibly."

This time Dima did not comment.

We parked in a reserved space and were whisked up to the main conference room on the Techno-Park building's tenth floor. Thirty or more men and women — more women than I had expected — were sitting in high-backed leather chairs. Everyone was talking loudly and passing around bottled water and soda. Everyone had a place around the huge table. Lenin, Marx, and Engels hung on the wall but so did Einstein, Tesla, and Abraham Isahakovich Alikhanov, Russia's number one particle physicist. I liked this kind of meeting. It allowed me to meet and possibly talk to every single person, far more useful than the mob scene in the auditorium the day before.

Instead of making formal introductions, Dima spent two minutes pointing out who was who. Most of this crowd were physicists, chemists, metallurgists, research engineers, and aeronautical engineers, with some business people, too. Those were labelled as responsible for marketing, finance, or operations at the various institutes. As I had come to realize over the years, scientists in Russia were a lot more fun to be around than the bureaucrats and party *nomenklatura*. Those were the people with power, but not necessarily competence, who had been elevated to their positions by appointment from the Communist Party. I think I would have been able to guess with at least a ninety percent success rate who was a scientist, who was an engineer, and who was *nomenklatura*, just by looking at them. My first clue was that scientists usually knew how to laugh and tell a good joke.

As we were getting seated and shaking hands, some around the table still laughing and sharing a joke, Dima suddenly announced that we should begin. The Techno-Park's director, Sergei, stepped up to the lectern, thanked everyone for coming, and introduced me. He preceded our session with a short summary of the history of Akademgorodok and the supporting TechnoPark.

"Welcome! For our special guest, I should give a short introduction to the work we do here and how we came to be." Sergei started. "In short, along with the Akademgorodok, the TechnoPark is focused on the hard sciences to support, among others, the Soviet — I should say Russian," he corrected himself — "military, the nuclear weapons program, Cold War pursuits, and the space program."

Someone loudly corrected Sergei at this point, "Cold War? Is there a Cold War?" The group laughed and waited for my reaction. I just laughed with them.

"Without any further interruptions, I am sure, I will continue," Sergei reacted sternly, looking over the top of his round, black plastic-rimmed glasses. "Akademgorodok, over several decades, grew to house and support several hundred thousand people. With generous state support, scientists and others who could contribute to the cause were more than happy to escape from, let me say, complicated circumstances in Moscow. And here we are, 'hiding' in the frozen steppes."

Much to Sergei's dismay, a hand shot up. An older colleague interjected, "Do you mean staunch totalitarianism instead of 'complicated circumstances' perhaps, Professor? So that our guest better understands?"

"Thank you," Sergei said and quickly went on. "It was a great privilege to live here after, hmmm, such circumstances in Moscow. The conditions here were quite unlike the, um, the difficult housing situation and..." He paused, as if searching for the right words. "... The career stagnation in the capital and other Soviet cities." He turned to look directly at me. "This special city offered a level of freedom unlike anywhere in Soviet Union, perhaps in any socialist country. Here we had freedom to talk about difficult subjects. Like economic reforms, Western literature and a free press. We were able to listen to poets and to music that was not, shall we say, officially sanctioned. Here, it was all OK." Now he scanned around, making eye contact with his colleagues. "Even the sciences themselves were freer," he said. "Genetics, cybernetics, and other new fields were not approved elsewhere in Soviet Union, but welcome pursuits here in Akademgorodok."

I noticed this got vigorous nods of agreement, especially from the man who had raised the 'staunch totalitarianism' question.

Sergei looked at his watch and began to wrap up his introduction, "And so today, well-funded by at least a dozen academic groups and close to a hundred business interests in Novosibirsk, the Techno-Park is a public-private partnership that attracts cooperation in the sciences and helps commercialize the technology that we develop here. Professor Gold, please come up and tell us about your interests here."

Unlike yesterday, very little in the way of juicy patriotism entered my talk. Dima had advised me that probably half the people here had been at the NSU session and so didn't need to hear another inspiring speech about their Motherland. After stepping up onto the podium, I spent fifteen minutes describing the courses required for an MBA in the U.S., how students decided on a specialization, and how elective courses work. I finished with an example of the cooperation with business and the employment recruiting that go hand in hand with MBA programs.

When I asked for questions, the discussion became heated, bogging down into a dispute about whether the program should award a master's or a doctorate in business administration. Much of this was just confusion over terminology. But since in Russia, the master's degree is the first earned after high school, some argued that this new program should offer only a PhD, as "master's in business administration" didn't sound impressive enough. It was all very Russian to me. The arguments were hyper-rational and uber-logical and loud. Amid the animated discussion, I suddenly recognized a face from Poland. Wladek Kruk had been the operations director for NatEx's Polish agent, POLOT. There he sat, smiling across the table at me. How I had missed his distinctive high-rise haircut and toothy smile earlier, I don't know. The argument about degrees had left me behind, so I got up, walked around to Kruk and shook his hand. Even though he insisted on the traditional three-cheek kiss, the gesture barely caught the attention of those sitting around him, busily waving their arms and extolling the virtues of a DBA versus an MBA.

I happily ignoring the uproar. "What the hell are you doing here, Kruk?" I used his last name, as I always had when we worked together.

"I flew one of our Antonov 2 planes here yesterday," he explained, starting off in English, "delivering something from the Polish government." Then, apologetically, he switched to Polish as he had always done while working as my operations guy. "I saw your name on an announcement in the dormitory where I am staying. They said I was welcome to come and see you."

"ANT 2? Isn't that the old Antonov that was like a 1930s biplane? Two wings? Upper and lower?" I asked. I couldn't imagine flying such an antique all the way here. "It was also built by POLOT in Poland, wasn't it?" I added.

"Yes, exactly!" Kruk seemed delighted that I remembered. "I stopped four times along the way. Beautiful trip! Maybe you will ride back with me?" He was even more excited at the thought of us hanging out a while together.

***

Kruk had been such a hard worker at POLOT/NatEx in Warsaw, I was very sad for him when NatEx backed out of its contract, leaving all those people in the lurch. He was particularly fun to be around when we would travel on the job. His favorite line in English when he was excited was, "Oh my God! I'm going to pee all over myself!" Try that on for size: imagine you are having dinner with the CEO of the European NatEx group and your colleague gets excited, telling about a work-related incident. He probably heard the phrase from a child when he visited America years ago. Obviously, he thought it was a great line.

Other than that, the only real problem with Kruk was that when he got nervous or upset, his sweat glands went into overdrive. And not ordinary sweat glands. His produced an odor that made him very difficult to be around. One time, we were having considerable success clearing packages from customs for on-time delivery. The atmosphere was light, and he smelled like an ordinary guy. But within half an hour, the customs agent suddenly became difficult to work with and frustration set in. We had slowed down so much it became clear we wouldn't get the packages on the train to Krakow before it departed. Kruk's sweat glands got to working and for the rest of the afternoon it was impossible to be in the same room with him. The customs agent shut down our clearing space and told us to come back the next day.

Kruk had been especially hard hit by the fall of NatEx in Poland. The general manager for POLOT fired everyone connected to the NatEx contract when news broke that the American express delivery company was high-tailing it out of Europe. Kruk had worked for POLOT for nearly

211

thirty years. He had expected eventually to leave on good terms. He had been a flight engineer turned pilot and probably had done some work for the Polish intelligence agencies, flying near the Western borders taking pictures of whatever the Soviets' partners were taking pictures of in the seventies and eighties. When I had packed my things, Kruk was the only POLOT boss who bothered to come into my office to say "Goodbye" as I was leaving. He told me he had been fired and would gladly work for me if I "started some kind of business." He said he liked the adventure of business startups and had thrived on all the action associated with NatEx's beginning. As it turned out, POLOT did hire him back to run its own air delivery service throughout the former Soviet bloc. This trip to Novosibirsk had been one of his important deliveries for the Polish military.

I had a real soft spot in my heart for Kruk and was very happy to see him that day. Unable to spend more than a few minutes getting caught up, he quickly jotted the phone number of the dormitory where he was staying on a wrinkled scrap of paper.

As I had the day before, I left the event early, without Dima, after someone handed me a phone message. It read:

"The 'Swiss Show' has started at the hotel. Please come quickly!

Cindy"

Kruk, who had come just to see me, wasn't interested in anything going on at the meeting. As I was running towards the taxi line in front of the Techno-Park building, I realized he was following me. I had apologized profusely to as many of the folks at the meeting as I could when the message had come through. I had also, once again, thanked Kruk for his appearance. When he saw I was going to hail a cab he called out, "Hey, Andy! I can drive you! I've got a car for the day. It's here! Let me take you wherever you need to go!"

"Kruk! You are a savior! Thank you! It's the Intourist Hotel. Do you know where that is?"

"Yes, yes. No problem." I folded myself into a tiny East German Trabant and Kruk sped off, ignoring lights and stop signs. I'd forgotten that he was the worst driver I'd ever ridden with. I then started thinking about my fear of flying and wondered if I could ever imagine flying with him as a pilot.

"How long are you in town, Kruk?" I asked him over the racket of the Trabant's two-stroke engine.

"Two more days only," he yelled at the top of his voice. "My plane threw a piston rod on the way here. I am having the engine redone."

"I will call you late tomorrow and invite you here for a drink," I offered.

As we approached the hotel, I pointed to a side entrance and said, "I have to run! Thank you, Kruk!" With that I jumped out and was in a full sprint toward the hotel. I hoped not to get caught in the middle of something unpleasant or unplanned now that things were heating up with our radioactive guests. I also wondered if Toshek had arrived and if he was already engaged in his 'specialty.'

Bushwhacked

Toshek and Cindy were talking so fast when I burst into the room that I could hardly pick up on the details. What I could decipher of their Russian was that they were coordinating who would do what with our uranium-laden buddies in Room 605. When I rushed in, Toshek acknowledged me with a nod and his best, almost toothless, smile. After years of adjusting his mouth to show the couple of teeth he still had, his smile curved to the left, like a wise guy in an old movie. Based on my experience on the train last week, I figured that was about as gracious or friendly a greeting as one could expect from him.

They went on talking. It was sounding like there were four or five scenarios that let Toshek feel confident enough to enter our friends' room and safely take out the U-235. He would need X amount of time if we initiated scenario one, or Y amount of time if we opted for scenario two, and so on. With each scenario Toshek offered, Cindy said "*Da.*" She took no notes. They referred to previous events I knew nothing about, with lines like this: "You remember when we got the hot stuff from the Kazakhs in Almaty? We'll do it similarly. That's right. You did the diversion. I acted like a custodian getting into the room."

I could also tell that others were involved, waiting somewhere outside the hotel. Those included policemen or law enforcement of some kind. A hazmat truck was mixed in somehow. It would be my job to call Vincent when the operation began. He would be waiting in the lobby. When he got my call, he was to step outside the hotel in plain sight and raise both his hands. That would be a signal to whoever these other people were.

As the rapid-fire conversation slowed a little, I dared to interrupt with a question about the Swiss phone call. "What exactly happened during the call? Any surprises?"

"Call was from Zurich," Cindy said. "It has been traced and we were given the OK to pick up the hot stuff. There will be a hazmat truck from the Physics Institute at NSU. Some fucking Americans are waiting too."

I was surprised. "Americans?"

"They never tell me. I am always confused," Cindy complained. "You have too many intelligence agencies and you think you can send your legal people anywhere in the world when there is a crime." She shook her head. "I just hope they don't fuck this thing up if it gets messy."

"Legal people? Like DOJ?" I asked. I had never heard Cindy complain about Americans going around policing the world. Still, I was glad to hear she was aware of the Department of Justice or whomever she was referring to.

"That's it," she confirmed. "DOJ."

Just as Dennis from Techdyne in Krakow had told me some time ago, DOJ guys are everywhere looking for evidence of international crimes. I thought it extremely brave of them to be throwing their weight around in the heart of Russia's nuclear weapons belt. If, indeed, that's who these mysterious Americans were.

The phone rang, interrupting the conversation. Cindy snatched the receiver off the hook.

"Da? Georg? He is downstairs in the bar now?" she repeated what Vincent was telling her. As quickly as she'd picked up the phone, she threw the receiver down and ran into the bathroom, shutting the door behind her and yelling for me to pull a dress from the closet. *"Daj mi sukienka najbardziej seksowna wedlug ciebie!"* Asking for what I considered her sexiest dress was something she thought was best said in Polish, as if only she and I would understand. But, of course, Toshek could understand Polish, too. He gave me the biggest and crookedest grin I had seen from him yet.

I dashed into the walk-in closet, which was now doubling as Toshek's warehouse for his Ichthyol, looking for a killer sexy outfit. Since it was still late afternoon and the sun was high in the sky, I avoided what appeared to be a faux-leopard-skin suit trimmed with lion fur. I opted for a skimpy LBD. She smiled approvingly at me as I opened the door and handed her the little black dress. Of course I couldn't help smiling, myself, at seeing her completely naked for the first time.

"Would you want me if I had this dress on?" she asked, sounding a little bit coquettish.

"Oczywiscie!" I said in Polish, as I stepped out. Of course.

In three minutes, the door came flying open. Cindy was ready for the kill. Compared to her morning ready routine, she was out in a tenth of the time and even had on a decently done face, albeit a tad sexier than usual. If I could be the judge.

"Call Vincent and make sure he stays in the lounge!" Cindy barked her orders. "I'll be down in two minutes. Tell him to have an orange juice waiting for me at the bar!"

Wow. I found myself turned on by Cindy's aggressive, take-charge approach. And ready to follow her orders.

Pausing at the door, speaking more softly now, she described to Toshek how she intended to keep Georg in the bar until either we called down to say it was over or she saw Anatoly and Georg being hauled out.

At this, I thought Toshek's twisted grin looked a little scared. He told her to be careful, then mumbled something else. I couldn't be sure of it, but I think Toshek asked Cindy if she needed anything to put in Georg's drink. She emphatically shook her head, "No."

As soon as Cindy was gone, Toshek stood directly in front of me face on, which I interpreted as his 'Listen to me and don't fuck up' stance. "I am going into Room 605," he told me, "and will try to open or unlock the outside door to the little room where the uranium is." We had established, with Ben's help, that the door to the suite's second room could not be opened from the hall. "When I enter the room, call Vincent. He will signal to our outside help. When they arrive, wherever you are, just get out of their way. They will take the uranium from you. Some other fellows with guns will take care of our bad guys. Anatoly will probably try to fight or argue with me. You will hear us. Go into the room and get the bags and take them downstairs. You must act very quickly. But do not disturb the bags too much. Like dropping them. You understand why?"

"Possible criticality, I suppose." While I meant to sound confident about my knowledge, this came out with a squeak that revealed how uneasy I was feeling.

Toshek's reply was silent but eloquent. He just made a movement like slitting his throat.

As a last step before beginning our part of the mission, Toshek grabbed a big towel from my bathroom and a floor mop he found in the shower room. I noticed the handle was considerably stouter than an American version. He removed the mop head, kept the four-foot wooden handle, and soaked the towel. We sprinted down the hall to the stairwell, down to the sixth floor, and straight to 605. Toshek put his ear to the door and checked to see if it was locked. It was. I backed up and partially hid inside a linen closet that still gave me a full view of what Toshek was doing. From his pocket, he pulled out an interestingly shaped metal rod and slipped it up his sleeve out of sight, all the while keeping his ear glued to the door. The moment seemed to last forever: Toshek standing there, me hunched over looking at him. And then young Ben, still hiding in 608, slowly opened his door. I suddenly decided I should tell him to call Vincent the moment Toshek entered the room. Watching Toshek listening at the door, I'd broken into a sweat realizing I would lose precious time if I had to run back to my room to make the call and then hope I didn't get back too late to grab the hot stuff from the suite as Toshek had instructed me. Or worse, come back from my room and find Toshek had been beaten to death by Anatoly — who looked like a bigger version of Vladimir Putin and about five times meaner. Even with his shirt on! Even so, Toshek's confidence in being able to handle the situation was infectious. In the back of my mind, though, I knew that he depended on me to be his backup if things went awry. That kept my motor running at high RPMs.

I put a finger to my lips and whispered into the boy's ear. I instructed him to keep an eye on what Toshek was doing and the moment he entered the room to call Vincent. I also told him to close Room 608's door behind him and not to come out until all the commotion ended. For good measure, as my mother said to me many times during tornado warnings in Oklahoma, "Go lie down in the bathtub and don't move until it's safe!" Somehow this tickled me. Ben's look told me he had no idea why I had started to giggle.

"Why are you laughing?"

"I'm sorry. You wouldn't understand if I told you," I replied.

I returned to my crouched position at the linen closet. After we'd waited several minutes, Toshek had not moved an inch. In one hand he held the wooden mop handle and the wet towel. In the other was his door jimmy tool. The towel was dripping on the floor. In that tense silence, I could hear the 'plop... plop... plop' as the water began to form a puddle at his left foot. After another minute, Toshek turned to me and mimed that Anatoly was on the phone. He returned to his stance with his left ear

217

glued to the door. Another minute might have passed and then Toshek started to bob his head up and down. He turned, winked and slipped the jimmy tool into the crack where he guessed the door's bolt would be. My heartrate went up another twenty beats per minute; I could see that things were going to start happening very soon. I was surprised by how quietly Toshek had been able to jimmy the door open. I turned to see if Ben understood this was the moment we had been waiting for. Eyes wide, he nodded. He understood. The boy disappeared into the empty room to call Vincent, closing the door with a soft click. At the door he had just opened, Toshek stood listening for about five seconds. That's when I understood why he had chosen that moment to enter. I could hear the sound of water running in the bathroom.

***

In those ten minutes leading up to Toshek's entry to room 605, things in the lobby were going well enough for Cindy and her attempt to keep Georg busy. While she had not said what she was going to do to keep him busy, I assumed that she would play her part as one of the women of the lobby and come on to him, holding out the promise of something lovely to come later.

Events unfolded quickly, I was told, as Cindy entered the lobby bar lounge.

"Vincent!" She called out as she approached the bar.

"There." He pointed to her drink and nodded as she made her way to the bar, scanning the room to find where Georg was sitting. Vincent pointed with his other hand in Georg's direction. When she spotted him, she realized he was at a table looking out the window that would probably be the best vantage point to see the SWAT team and hazmat van that would be approaching in about five minutes.

Cindy paused, knowing that as paranoid a guy as Georg was, he would quickly put two and two together and cause a far bigger problem than the one she had prepared to manage. She knew she had to act quickly to get him re-positioned, somewhere else in the bar. According to Vincent's admiring account, her methods to entice Georg elsewhere were extremely effective.

"Hi! Why are you sitting here alone?" she said in a sultry low tone, placing her hand on his head and caressing the back of his neck. She moved in front of him, blocking his view onto the street, and whispered something into his left ear. He immediately stood and fled with her. Cindy pushed Georg down into a chair in the darkest corner away from the windows that she could find. She straddled him on the chair as quickly as she could, pulling the top of her dress down and unsnapping her bra while pulling his head into her chest. With this move, she knew he would not be able to see or hear the emergency vehicles approaching. Georg frantically began searching for her hand… any hand… and finally shoved her right hand into his pants to jack him off as he was licking her breasts like a ravenous grizzly bear startled out of hibernation. Cindy thought, "He smells like a sick animal." But kept up her action to divert his attention. Within minutes, he finally ejaculated with a force that left them both covered in sticky semen that added to the horror of the moment as Cindy heard the SWAT team approaching. Knowing the end of the nightmare was upon her, she pushed herself off of him and began to cover herself with a tablecloth that was folded on the table next to her. One of the para-military SWAT team members yelled at Georg, who was now staring in surprise at the armed group that surrounded them, "Get down on the floor! Face down! Now!" Georg hesitated. The nearest soldier snapped his three-foot Billy club across his face and nose. With that well-placed blow, dark red blood splattered all over Cindy, who was trying to get away from Georg and the SWAT team now taking over. She told me later that she was glad I had picked the little black dress, since the blood splatters weren't noticeable. And because dry cleaning in Novosibirsk was risky for a Chanel dress.

***

But all that I wouldn't learn until later. For now, my attention was focused on Toshek as he entered room 605. He moved away from the shower sounds, going directly for the door of the suite's second room, where we assumed the bags of uranium were. But to my horror and dismay, just then a naked and surprised Anatoly stepped out of the bathroom.

Feeling like a linebacker waiting for the opposing quarterback to call the signals and take the snap, I rose up slightly, poised for the moment to go into action. Anatoly's early appearance had caught us off guard. I waited for Toshek's response. As Toshek reached for the door handle, Anatoly screamed something unrecognizable. Toshek whirled around, swinging the mop handle at Anatoly's head. Trying to block the wooden shaft, Anatoly caught its full force on his forearm. He screamed but continued to rush toward Toshek. Toshek tried to bring the stick back to jab Anatoly in the stomach but never got into position to deliver that second blow. Anatoly got his hand on the wooden handle and grabbed Toshek by the neck. It was time for this middle linebacker to react to the situation and get Toshek out of trouble. Aiming for somewhere between Anatoly's knees and his waist, I had about ten meters to get up to full speed and tackle him. I kept my feet under me, lifting him up and away from Toshek, who was gagging from Anatoly's grip on his throat. When Anatoly and I fell hard onto the wooden floor, he kept beating me on the back with both hands. Toshek recovered quickly. I managed to roll over on top of Anatoly. In quick succession, Toshek snapped him in the head with the wooden handle, wrapped the wet towel around his face, and then stepped on his neck. I now had control of both arms. Anatoly, unable to breathe, stopped resisting. Toshek motioned for me to go after the uranium.

All this time, the door was open. To our misfortune, Anatoly's yells before Toshek's towel and foot silenced him had gotten the attention of the hotel's one security guard. We had all forgotten about him as we planned our action. The alarmed guard ran into the room and blocked the door, declaring that he would kill anyone who tried to leave. I am sure a choking, naked man lying in the middle of his own room, writhing in pain, with two guys standing over him looking like thieves, did not weigh very heavily in our favor. A few words told me the guard spoke no English. I told Toshek to tell the man to call Vincent downstairs, which would make everything clear. To get the security guard to act quickly, Toshek added a bit more to the story. "OK, hero," he said, "there is a bomb in the other room. It is going to explode in a moment. Call Vincent downstairs and you will save your own life." Within two seconds, the guard was on his walkie-talkie.

A tense thirty seconds ensued. When the guard finally understood from Vincent that the whole hotel was now involved in an anti-terrorist action, he motioned that I was free to go. At that, I slowly entered the little room. On one side, the two bags lay on the floor next to a sofa. I gingerly lifted them, surprised by how heavy they were. I didn't relish the thought of hugging them close to my body but as I tried to get a good hold on them, keeping them out and away, they would begin to slip. Clutching them tight to my chest was the only way I was going to make it all the way to the elevator and to the lobby. I got into the hallway, grunting and straining. My exaggerated yelps were more from imagining how many rads I was taking than from the weight of the U-235 I was lugging.

Luckily, the hazmat team met me as I was approaching the elevators. Their voices muffled inside full coverage suits that made them look like Apollo astronauts, they communicated with gestures. They motioned for me to set everything down on the floor, return to my room, and shut the door. The police, or whoever they were, came right behind the hazmat guys. They nearly ripped the door of room 605 off its hinges. Two SWAT team guys were dressed in gray camouflage, arrayed with a variety of hand weapons on their belts and carrying an AK-47 each. By now, Anatoly had worked the towel off his throat and was screaming again. The armed men grabbed him and threw him back to the ground, wrenching his injured arm behind his back. Taking an arm and a leg each, the camouflaged SWAT guys lifted Anatoly and manhandled him out of the building, screaming the whole time.

Toshek and I grabbed the towel and wooden handle and scurried back to my room on the seventh floor. Toshek turned to me after we got inside and asked, "Was it American football or rugby skills you used to help me?"

"American football, Toshek. It was a classic tackle. Once he had your neck in his hand, I knew it was my turn." I patted him on the back. I could see bruises on Toshek's neck and dried blood that had oozed from where Anatoly's nails had dug into his throat.

Toshek shook his head, "Not too bad, Andy. Thank you! Bad guys bushwhacked!" It didn't take him long, though, to return to his real passion. He made a beeline to his ichthyol boxes and asked, "You know anyone that wants to buy a ton of ichthyol concentrate? I can have it delivered FOB Krasnoyarsk or CIF Kiev. No better quality. No first aid kit should be without it!"

Yes, above all, even after saving the Western world from another terrorist threat, I could see the real truth about Toshek. He was, most importantly, the Ichthyol King of Central Siberia.

Cindy was not far behind us. She got back to the room during Toshek's ichthyol sales pitch. Knowing exactly what the miracle ointment was for, she joked that she might need it rubbed all over her body after what she had just been through with Georg.

"Not a good idea," Toshek said, deadpan. "Not recommended for large areas of skin."

Cindy rolled her eyes. "Maybe a shower would be better. May I?"

I nodded and pointed to the bathroom. I hoped, if it would help, that she would take a long bath. Before she'd returned, Vincent had phoned to tell me Cindy and Georg had been quite "engaged," as she did whatever she could to keep him downstairs and occupied until the SWAT team arrived.

"Give me thirty minutes?" Cindy grabbed fresh clothes and shut the bathroom door behind her. Toshek and I nodded in unison.

"So, Toshek. I have a couple of questions." I was curious about a few things.

"About ichthyol?"

"No. Not exactly. Who were the SWAT guys?" I asked. "They didn't say much, and they didn't show any badges or credentials."

Toshek pondered this for a moment, "Let's call them locals with both Western and Eastern anti-terrorist training. Your Joe guy at embassy has paid them in advance for services. More than once."

"So, this anti-terrorist activity is all underground? Nothing official? But who is leading it?" Now I was really wondering who was pulling all the strings.

"No leaders. Not yet. Yuri knows more than I do," Toshek said. "But it seems to me that three or four very strong actors sometimes make quick decisions. One who decides, then informs the other three. Might be something happens that Israelis are coordinating, then Americans come in and help or take over. It's like your Navy SEALs get called for action and go. No questions asked. Problem for me is I worry someone might get confused. Think I am bad guy. That's why I take money from everyone." Toshek's description of the AT Group's early activity matched what Yuri had told me on our train trip from Samara. He added, "Risky business like this makes me hope for big success selling ichthyol."

"Good luck with that ichthyol stuff!" I didn't have the heart to tell him I had a real aversion to the black oily shit. Instead, I said, truthfully, "I've had to use it a couple of times myself."

Toshek laughed. He'd realized I was talking about some terrible boils I'd had on my butt in Warsaw. I hated that stuff. It took a long time to work and, in the meantime, the experience was very unpleasant as pressure built up in the sore.

With a call through the bathroom door, Cindy interrupted my delightful conversation with Toshek. "Andy. Can you come in, please? We need to make some decisions."

"OK. You... you are decent?" I asked, slowly opening the door.

"Why do you ask if I am decent?" Cindy asked. I could have sworn I detected a tinge of shyness in her tone. "In this case does it mean 'good' or 'not naked'?"

"Not naked," I replied, my opinions on the subject definitely mixed.

"You won't see much. Come in, please," Cindy urged me.

This is all business, I reassured myself as I entered. *I'm sure.* Though a little bit out of character for Cindy, it occurred to me. But after what we'd both been through, like the jock that I'd been once, I had the attitude that colleagues can do business in the locker room.

"OK. Can I sit here?" I pointed to the toilet, where her little black dress was neatly draped over the seat. I picked it up and laid it on the towel rack. A flashback to long-ago bathroom sex with Renata caught me a little off-guard as I carefully transferred Cindy's stained dress, onto the rack. I'd been well trained. Renata insisted that I treat her finer clothes with some respect.

Cindy was naked but completely covered by bubbles, only her head showing. Very seriously, she said, "Joe says we have some problems in Chelyabinsk with Yuri and Vlad. We need to be there, latest time, tomorrow afternoon, but we already missed the night train."

"You and Joe have been talking here? While you're taking a bath?" I was more than a little confused; I guess I raised my voice a little.

She stayed calm. "I get messages during the day," she explained, as patiently as a kindergarten teacher talking to a five-year-old. "Joe gave me a magic message machine. My message says we three should all go together to Chelyabinsk. Flying is better if we can do it." Now Cindy spoke like she was telling me more than Joe would have liked me to know.

I refrained from asking anything more about her 'magic message machine.' While I never confirmed that this was her magic message machine, I did later find out that she was getting coded telegrams from the hotel office.

As she'd been soaking under the bubbles, Cindy had been thinking about trying to charter a flight. Or maybe going to the airport and bribing someone with a plane to fly us to Chelyabinsk.

That sounded to me like an extremely risky ploy, especially in Siberia. Then I had a better idea. My good fortune of just having encountered Kruk at the Techno-Park meeting couldn't have been timed better. Now I wondered what were the chances of flying with him. After all, he had just invited me to fly back with him in his old Antonov 2. If those engine repairs he'd mentioned, were complete, and if he could leave tomorrow morning, we could be in Chelyabinsk by noon. I told Cindy about it.

She sat up a little straighter, but sadly not enough to dislodge the bubbles. What I did see was her confident smile again. "Maybe you *are* a businessman after all. There are no commercial flights to Chelyabinsk until late tomorrow afternoon. Please try with your friend Kruk."

"I will call him now. But wait. I didn't ask. Why do we have to be in Chelyabinsk so quickly? And why are you going? I thought we were going to say goodbye soon, now that you've gotten all your guys here." I was full of questions as I started to worry about what was up, what was so critical that Yuri and Vlad — and Joe — were rushing me to get there so quickly.

Cindy began squirming a little. The bubbles hiding her body were rapidly disappearing, and she noticed this as soon as I did. Using her hands to pile them back up onto strategic locations, she said, "Doors open and close sometimes. Door to your three Soyuz sites may close soon. Yuri and Vlad are keeping it open for another day or two. I might be able to help with other doors, Joe thinks. He already pre-paid me. Means it is important."

What little I knew about how Yuri, Vlad, Toshek, and Cindy worked, I had a feeling that the element of anarchy was at play here and that of all his operatives, Joe trusted them the most to deal with it. I'd read of the Central Siberian mafia and the other mini-mafia spin-offs operating everywhere. The criminal gangs showed up wherever there was money to be made or influence to exert. I assumed that access to these Soyuz sites was difficult to get and that there were no open tickets.

With a little pang of regret, I left the bathroom before Cindy's bubbles all popped. Fishing out the crumpled note Kruk had given me, I went to make a phone call. I was hoping his creaking old biplane was fixed, that it had enough room for all of us, and that my friends would all be welcome to fly with him. It seemed a lot to expect in a place where disappointment was the rule.

Bold, ambitious Vincent came to the rescue again. I called down to the desk and asked him to try to find Wladek Kruk at the Techno-Park dormitory. In about ten minutes, the phone rang. It was Kruk. Excited to be playing pilot and host to me and my friends, he said, "Oh my God! I've got to get it gassed up, cleaned up, and ready for first class passengers! Flight departs for Chelyabinsk at eight o'clock sharp!"

I knocked and then tried to open the bathroom door to give Cindy the good news. Jiggling the handle, I yelled through the door that we were going First Class on the POLOT Express to Chelyabinsk.

"I am happy to hear it," she answered.

After one last jiggle, I gave up on the bathroom door. It was locked. By now, all of Cindy's bubbles must have popped.

Cindy

Toshek's response to our change in plans focused on how it would impact his business ventures. "It is good for me. If I can work through the night, I can get things done and Ichthyol Magic Mousse gets to market faster." He babbled on about his noxious black goo, seemingly totally unfazed by the day's events.

Cindy, on the other hand, said she was happy about doing something out of the ordinary; flying to Chelyabinsk. But once again, she became preoccupied with the new mission, and probably knew a lot more about things than she was willing — and possibly allowed — to say. She suggested that we go down to the bar and have "dinner or drinks or something." Very little eye-contact all day, uncharacteristically unfocused, and thinking of food and drink constantly, told me that she was on edge. It was probably more than just the upcoming work in Chelyabinsk, but it wasn't obvious to me what exactly was troubling her. I could see she was very good at hiding things.

The Intourist restaurant's sharply limited menu had already been the butt of jokes in just the two days we had been staying at the hotel. Hoping to lighten the atmosphere a bit, I said to Cindy, "Tonight, let's take advantage of the delightful gourmet menu of squid and Pacific Northwest halibut cheeks at the restaurant downstairs." That didn't work. I gave up trying to cheer her up and got back to business. I told her it was time to finally tell Dima he would be on his own from now on. I had to tell him, as I explained to Cindy, "I need to cancel our grand expedition in the Siberian wilds." That finally got a smile out of her.

"OK, do it," she said, impatiently. "I am waiting. I am a little hungry and I want a drink."

I excused myself to go down to the lobby where I could call from a phone booth. When I reached Dima and told him we were leaving town in a hurry, he wasn't mad at all. In fact, during the call he was so busy that he put the phone down several times to take other calls. He would be talking to me about how he was managing the RFPs, milking clients of money they would never see again, then suddenly put the receiver down and answer another phone — without any warning.

My years of high level, and not so high level, meetings in Poland and Russia had told me Dima was the sort of middle manager who had at least four phones on his desk. Because of our decision to use an RFP to extract information from the dozens of participants interested in a joint MBA program, Dima had been able to create all kinds of money-making competitions, and to get away with charging academic institutes fees to get them on short lists for MBA program cooperation. Those competitions included trips to see satellite campuses or cooperating private sector businesses, trips that he would insist he must take, too. He might just flat-out say he needed a vacation and that if someone would pay for it, they would be in a more favorable position to win.

I'd never seen anything more blatantly corrupt than the way he was doing this. I really worried about how I would be received the next time I showed up in Novosibirsk. I thanked Dima for all he had done, and was doing, and promised I would be back in ninety days or less. And that I'd bring my own short list of American MBA programs that were interested in forging alliances with Siberian academic institutes.

Dima asked one last question as I was getting ready to hang up. "Are we still doing doctoral dissertation on American prisoners of war from Vietnam in Soviet Union?"

Doctoral dissertation. Clever. I'd almost forgotten about our conversation at dinner. I replied, "Yes, Dima. Please be ready to report on this when I return. There will be seed money available by then."

"Good word! *Seed money.* I am thinking it will grow if we feed it properly! Have a good trip, Andy!" That was the last thing I really wanted to hear from Dima, but at least he, and that odd conspiracy theory, were both on ice for now.

When I finished with Dima, I stepped over to the house phone and called up to let Cindy know I was free for "dinner or drinks or something," as she had suggested.

"Wow," she said. "I thought you would escape and be out late like a Russian man, leaving your *date* in room to be mad all night. It is good you are fast." The word 'date' caught my attention. I heard some kind of shuffling sound like she was organizing or putting things away. "Get me something to eat and drink," she came back on the line. "I don't care what. See you in a minute. Thank you."

Again, 'date' was a word I had to mull over. Of course, that was just a joke. This wasn't a date; it was a business meeting — over dinner. A review of a successful operation, a mission accomplished; and planning for the next one. And indeed, something I could take a lot of satisfaction about, myself. Toshek had gotten into serious trouble. There was no way to deny that I had saved the day by tackling and taking Anatoly down. I entertained the thought, half seriously, that I'd be coming back home a hero, with a fat wad of cash for my troubles. Could I even imagine that rare thankful smile on Renata's face when I entered our little Nowa Huta flat? Instead of the skeptical (or even scornful) looks that had been too frequent, lately? I was still thinking about that last phone call with Renata. But then, a more immediate memory was clouding the issue. I couldn't help imagining what had been so poorly concealed under Cindy's bath bubbles not so long ago.

Vodkas, juice, and water were waiting on the table, along with some stale pretzel sticks, when she met me near the window. The day's last bit of light was coming in. I'd made sure we were sitting as far away as possible from the booth where she and Georg had had bar sex. It was somehow in the back of my mind that her experience with him was part of why she seemed out of sorts. I couldn't imagine anyone being so brave as she had been to do such a thing. If that was what was bothering her, I could certainly understand.

"Do they have food in the restaurant tonight?" was her first question when she saw the pretzels.

"Yep. Filet mignon for you, my dear!" I informed her. She was turned away and craning her neck to try to fetch Vincent. *I called her 'my dear.' Is that what I meant?* No, just a little playful irony is all. *Honest. That's all.* Whatever she might have thought about that, I knew she didn't believe that something delicious was coming from the kitchen. Not until the wonderful smell of fresh beef grilling came wafting out of the kitchen. Vincent knew we were leaving in the morning and he was working his magic for one last big tip. He also had some wild mushrooms that he'd had sautéed and served with the meat. That, and not so fresh rye bread with butter, made for a fantastic meal by Novosibirsk standards, all washed down with a very average vodka and a bland orange-flavored drink.

Cindy, happy that she'd eaten real food, made an attempt to steer our conversation back to Chelyabinsk and Yuri and Vlad. This was unsuccessful. Without warning, my friend Kruk suddenly showed up carrying three huge POLOT gift bags for his "first class passengers," as he called us. When I spotted him, he was walking through the bar towards us faster than I could run. His hair, combed high and back, was rocking side to side with each stride. That was the old Kruk I remembered from when he'd been introduced as my operations man three years earlier. That first day, he had wept from happiness to be wearing a 'real American business uniform,' proudly admiring the NatEx polo shirt I had given him.

On this day, in the bar, Kruk's one-man show was also memorable.

"You are Cindy! Andy told me about you! Americans aren't as polite as Polish men. So… let me introduce myself." I really hadn't hesitated so long in making introductions, but Kruk always loved the opportunity to compare rude Americans to uber-polite Poles. "I am Wladyslaw Kruk, former operations director for NatEx on the territory of Poland, and currently the chief operating officer of POLOT's new operation for European and Asian air express delivery services. We don't have a good name for it yet. So I give you the full description." At this point, Kruk kissed her hand. "Of course, our unfortunate experience with NatEx was our chance to study this business. And now we will compete against them in a difficult market. I am a pilot and tomorrow I will be your pilot and travel assistant to Chelyabinsk. My good friend Andy, who, by the way, was my boss for a while, has given me this opportunity to serve you. My gift bag is more than a gift bag. It includes your necessary flight jackets, goggles, and hearing protection as well as some snacks and small gifts from POLOT: the Polish State Aviation Works. We also have included a small first aid kit that contains motion sickness tablets if you might have that weakness in your system. They also will make you sleep. So be careful! Will you please deliver the third bag to your colleague, Mr. Toshek?" By this time, Kruk was out of breath.

That let me slide in an invitation for him to sit with us and have a drink.

"Don't mind if I do. But only one drink. I must be fresh for flying tomorrow!" He was happy to accept our invitation and smiled as I'd never seen him. Kruk's body odor issues were on the edge of breaking out, but for the moment, he was quite tolerable. And he was being so nice to us. There was no way we couldn't invite him to have a drink.

Of course, that also amounted to an invitation for him to continue his monologue. He started right back in.

"At eight o'clock sharp we have flight tower approval to take off with a slight northwesterly bearing to avoid some nuclear missile sites directly west of the city here. After we get past them, we will cut back a little south and west to put us on a direct flight pattern for Chelyabinsk. There will be a few sightseeing opportunities along the way so I will vary my altitude to give you the chance to see some interesting things."

In Russian, Cindy asked him, point-blank, "Will all these tourist things slow our arrival time in Chelyabinsk? We have important meetings tomorrow afternoon."

Undeterred from his mission to show us we would all be having a good time, he fielded her question and resumed his pitch. "Our delay will be minimal. You will all be given a chance to fly the airplane and we will practice using our parachutes before we depart. I have some delicious things — or maybe not so delicious since they might be old—but that will be OK." That finally got a laugh out of Cindy. I was glad to see she was starting to like Kruk. "If we are ahead of schedule, we'll land for a picnic lunch and refuel at my favorite farm. This is where many Polish families have been living for almost seventy years."

"Is that one of the Gulag camps?" Cindy asked.

"Not exactly. But half the residents at this place were forcibly moved there. A few of them were in Stalin's camps, as well."

"Great! I bet that is a happy place. I know exactly what kind of lovely atmosphere that is." Cindy said. While this was obviously meant as a joke, it got me started wondering about Cindy's past. Through the sarcasm, I could see she was beginning to open up a little.

In a way that only Kruk could do it, he smiled at Cindy despite her ribbing, toasted to her health, and drank his shot in one gulp. He'd ended up sitting between me and Cindy, which gave him the opportunity to pat us both on our knees. Then he stood up to say, "Thank you! I must be on my way. Please be at the airport by 7:30. Looking forward to a nice day of flying with you! Good night!" But before leaving, he couldn't resist. In parting, he leaned over and said, "You two kids be good!"

"Good night, Kruk!" I gave him my broadest, friendliest smile. "And thank you very much for taking care of us. I am very lucky you found me in Novosibirsk! See you tomorrow!"

Kruk departed through the bar at the same speedy pace as his arrival.

Cindy commented, "Seems like a reliable guy. I wouldn't doubt if he has connections to Polish Intelligence Agency." I had never doubted that possibility, either, but I thought it was very interesting that after just a few minutes with him, she'd come to the same conclusion.

But then Cindy's mood took a darker turn. She asked me to talk seriously about the dangers connected with our Chelyabinsk mission and whatever "unknown elements of surprise" that might await us there. "I want you to think about ending your activities now on this trip. You have big success with me and Toshek here in Novosibirsk," she said, not a hint of a smile on her face anymore. "And Joe can do without your involvement in his Soyuz debris trip, I think. It is your connections with Dima that you are best at. Your protections disappear when the bad people are all around you."

Has she been talking with Jane? I wondered, only half in jest. Once again, a woman was trying to talk me out of a mission. "So, you think that Yuri, Vlad, Toshek, and you are not enough protection?" I asked. Her steady gaze was unnerving me; I stared at her finger, which she was running around the rim of her glass. This got under my skin. I had to wonder, why have women all my life tried to talk me out of decisions I'd already made? Even my mother, back in Guthrie, Oklahoma! She couldn't keep me from watching through the window as the roof of the nursing home next door got blown off. No way was I going to stay in the bathtub during a tornado!

Cindy interrupted my thoughts of Oklahoma and the tune she was playing on the rim of her glass to say, "I only know for sure that Yuri and Vlad feel very insecure about it, too." She was still staring at me. "That tells me to be careful. Also, we have never done this kind of thing in the open wild country. If we get separated, we can get lost or, even worse, bandits who know the countryside can have a big advantage over us. There is no morality in places like that. The Russian-style mafia is different from Italian. There is nothing ethical in Russian version of organized crime. When you met Vlad, he was getting rid of a body. Someone who was killed in a place like where we are going."

"OK. OK. Let's give it a rest for a moment," I urged her. "Let me think." I had no intention of bowing out of this trip. Maybe I was still a little high on the adrenaline from today's excitement, and having earned myself a Bronze Star for exemplary service. Trying to step outside and look at it objectively, one might suppose I didn't like having women tell me what to do. But, honestly, the idea of the bonus money attached to hazardous duty was probably the biggest driver in my decision making. An extra-large down payment on that flat in Krakow and finishing off the terrace with Italian marble sounded pretty good to me. I didn't like the idea that Cindy and I might be about to part company. But I didn't have any ready answers for her, either. I could see she was seriously challenged by a new and potentially risky set of circumstances.

Cindy grabbed my arm and added to her argument. "If you are now going to think, then please think about this: I want to remind you that we are not employees and can accept or reject work whatever we want. If we don't do something completely stupid or take jobs from Russians or Chinese or terrorists, we will still be asked to do more work. In other words, if we view the risk as too much, we should not accept it. We should go home."

Cindy didn't realize that with her impassioned plea to be rational, she clinched it for me. I'd made my decision. Of course I'll accept the risk. For the thrill, for the ego boost, for the money — and for the chance to experience it with *her. If I'm with her, I'm up for this.* It didn't take too much additional effort to come to the additional conclusion that I had too much invested in this mission. At this point, I couldn't very well go home without a big cash payoff, anyway.

We were talking quietly but the lobby bar women could see we were discussing something intensely. Two of them came over to our table and stood there looking at me, shaking their heads. The taller of the two blondes said to me, in English, "What are you discussing? Maybe she is too expensive for you! Come over to our table instead."

I laughed. Bantering with hotel prostitutes was nothing new for me.

But Cindy responded with a little scowl. In Russian, she told them, "My fiancé wants to fly me to New York to get married. I want to be married in London. That is what we are talking about. Now get the fuck out of here!" I knew Cindy could stand toe to toe with these women. That she would do it by describing what had happened with Renata and me, USA versus Poland, was a bit unnerving.

The shorter woman shook her head. "I don't believe it," she said in English. Both turned and walked away.

"That was well done," I told Cindy. My feelings toward her were getting stronger at a speed I couldn't control now. It encouraged me to take the chance of asking after her bold lie to the lobby bar "bitches," as she called them. "So now we are engaged and can't decide where to get married." But I decided it was time to get an answer to another important question.

Sofia

I looked Cindy in the eye. "Maybe I should know your name, finally."

Without hesitation, she answered, "I am Sofia."

"Thank you for telling me, Sofia. Very nice name. It fits you a lot better than Cindy."

"You are married, and I am not," Cindy — Sofia — said bluntly. "Tell me about your wife. You never talk about her." She hadn't seemed especially interested in the topic, so I had steered away from the subject.

"Joe and others at the Embassy say not to talk about family," I said. "That is why I haven't said much. My marriage is dying. Her name is Renata. She was my teacher when I was learning the Polish language. We've been together about ten years. It might end soon. But then again, if I can give her what she wants, at least a bigger, better, cleaner place to live, I might be able to turn things around." I checked for Sofia's reaction before going on; her expression was neutral. "I took on this life to try to give my family a better life. But I've discovered that it might turn out to be fatal to the relationship. When my daughter and son find out what I do, they will disown me."

"What does it mean 'disown'?" Sofia asked.

"They will be upset and say to me, 'You are not our father anymore,'" I explained.

"I see. Not good." Sofia frowned and then asked, "You like to have an official job, don't you? Does it help?"

"My corporate shield was very difficult to maintain. Keeping a responsible job, when this kind of work is also important to me, is almost impossible," I told her. Revealing more than I might have without the vodka, I went on, "I'm always trying to take time off or I'm getting 'sick' or family members are dying, all excuses to leave my work for these things that we do." Sofia was listening closely. "The same is true with Renata. I have to make up jobs and reasons to leave her for this work. And because of our sick relationship." I finished with, "I'm not very good at this masquerade."

She liked 'masquerade' and said it was a good word to remember.

Despite my having painted my world as I had, she lightened up again. I decided to ask about herself. "Can you tell me more about you, Sofia?"

What Sofia told me did not come out in one unbroken monologue. It took some time and questioning to understand how complex her life had been.

Unaccustomed to talking about her past but willing to share some of it in bits and pieces she began to open up a bit. "My family, originally from Russia, moved to southern Ukraine in the fifties."

"Moved or relocated by the government?" I gingerly asked.

"Forced to move — of course — and we lost everything near Leningrad. Or St. Petersburg. Whichever." She paused and then added. "By the time I was born, things were still difficult but stabilized. We lived among Poles who had been in Gulags and were forced to work on farms without hope of returning to Poland. My Polish came from that experience."

"Wow. This is a recurring theme here, I'm finding. No wonder you seem to be comfortable with my Polish," I said.

"My whole life was a mix of Polish culture and some of our Russian traditions. But mostly, I grew up with children running around the village. It was officially forbidden to speak Polish but my friends were secretly learning Polish at home."

"What sort of profession did your father have?" I asked.

"He was an educated miner. It means he was a mining engineer. I saw very interesting places when I was young. He took me on working trips all over Asia and Middle East."

"So, you speak some other languages?" I ventured to ask.

"A little Arabic, Chinese, and some Mongolian."

"And... so... as an adult, you studied espionage," I joked.

"Physical education and martial arts," she corrected me. "I have been a teacher, a mixed martial arts instructor, and a massage therapist." Looking me in the eye with a naughty little smile she added, "I have never worked as a prostitute except when role-playing for jobs. Like with Georg this afternoon. My life since working with Joe has been crazy. I have lived in twelve countries in three years." Sofia's role playing as a prostitute turned me on; I imagined her playing the game like Natalya did in Moscow. It was a cold shower, though, when I realized the horror that she'd felt today playing out that role for our mission.

I tried to drive our discussion elsewhere. "So, what about the future, Sofia?"

"Sometime soon I think I want to slow down. Maybe I will live in the British Virgin Islands. Living modestly in Russia let me accumulate a healthy bank account in the BVI. But still not healthy enough."

"Yes, there is a difference in buying power between here and that part of the world."

"Friends in Miami wanted me to accept an invitation to visit three years ago," she said, "but that was when the anti-terrorism team was organized. Now I want to get that bank account up to a more respectable level. Within the next two years." It sounded like she was pondering her future out loud.

"And the question of men in your life? I must ask." I felt a little heat in my face as I stepped into that perilous territory, for the moment leaving behind thoughts of the perilous territory I still thought of as 'home.'

"Men have come and gone," she readily answered, "but luckily I have never been pregnant. I am hoping I can find a normal person in BVI or Miami." That explanation came with a shrug and a smile.

"BVI and Miami may not be the best places for finding normal people — in my opinion. No more than, say, Moscow or Novosibirsk or the Trans-Siberian Railway." Then, with an effort of my conscience I moved the conversation back to professional matters. "What was your first job for Joe?"

"I was supposed to sit in a bar in Bucharest and record a conversation between two men," she told me. "I had parabolic mics and a camera built into my purse. I got extra money for helping to steal a briefcase."

"How much did he pay you for that?" I asked.

"Five hundred dollars. Cash in advance," she said. Now it was her turn to ask. "And your first job?"

"For seven days, I sat in a cafe, a restaurant, a library, a grocery store, a meat shop, and a bar outside Wroclaw. I counted trucks going in and out of a military base." I decided not to mention my recreation in the back room of that little library. That would have drawn too sharp a contrast between how much I'd enjoyed myself with Agata the librarian and how little Sofia had enjoyed her encounter with Georg.

"How much did Joe pay you?" Sofia asked with a smile.

"It wasn't Joe that time, but same as you. Five hundred dollars. Cash in advance." I returned her smile.

It had gotten late. We both had told each other many times that it was time to go to bed and finally we did head upstairs. One reason I'd hesitated so long before returning to the room was the certainty that Toshek would be frantically getting his ichthyol ready for the trip and probably wanting to discuss his miracle salve. As we walked in, we were signaling to each other over Toshek's head that neither one of us wanted to talk about it. But Toshek was driven.

His marketing questions were mostly directed at me. "Which is better: 'Miracle Ichthyol Salve for Treatment of Infected Staphylococcus Sores' or 'Ichthyol Ointment: A Cure for All Pus-Filled Sores?'" Toshek was scribbling out possible pitch lines for his smelly ointment.

"Actually, Toshek, I don't like either one, to be honest."

"Me either. Not descriptive enough." As Toshek pondered this, Sofia and I slipped out of his earshot toward my bedroom and the bathroom.

Another awkward 'Good night' was building up. Sofia motioned that she was claiming the bathroom first. As usual, I gathered my sleeping things and toiletries bag and left them by the bedroom door, waiting for her signal that she had finished and I could go in for my shower. I'd gotten accustomed to hearing the bathroom fan running during the moment before she closed the door behind her. Tonight, I heard neither the door nor any fan running. I was startled to see the bedroom door open. Sofia silently stepped in, just six inches in front of me, and shut the door.

She turned around and whispered hoarsely — clearly on the verge of tears — "I feel very dirty tonight. Even after washing myself. This time in the restaurant with Georg was a short hell for me. He started to get up to call Anatoly, so I had to stop him. I had to touch this dirty man who was stinking terribly. He made a big mess all over me. If I go to bed alone, I will cry all night. If I can have you beside me and you will be nice company for me, I will be better tomorrow. Can you let me sleep next to you?"

What could I do but smile? I had a fleeting thought of the similar invitation I'd gotten from Katerina in her first-class railway compartment just days before. I don't remember thinking at all about anyone in a faraway apartment in Krakow. I placed my hands, as softly as I could, on Sophia's head and face the way she had done to me the previous night. And now I couldn't think about anybody else. Her straight hair fell across her face. Before I could say anything, she looked through it at me and said, "If that is 'Yes,' then please go to bathroom and come back soon. Don't worry about Toshek. He is occupied with his get-rich scheme."

I quickly did what I needed to do in the bathroom. Although Toshek was almost always quietly talking to himself, when I stepped out of the bathroom, I could tell his mumbling was a little louder than usual. He looked up and waved me over. Just like he had earlier, before we set out for Anatoly's room, he squared himself up in front of me. I could tell what he had to say wasn't going to be an ichthyol sales pitch.

"Cindy probably told you Yuri and Vlad are not feeling completely safe taking you to the Soyuz sites. Yuri is afraid because Vlad is afraid. Yuri knows some people that are asking for money and asking too many questions about our 'customer.' There are other ways for your Joe to get what he wants from rocket trash. You don't have to be the American businessman we are protecting. Risky mix. Very bad men around an American and a woman. For me it is a fatal combination." Toshek held my gaze for a long moment. "It is only my opinion."

He paused for another moment, and when he went on, he turned away, no longer looking me in the eye. "Good we are flying with your friend and get to Chelyabinsk quickly. Ichthyol to market faster means more cash. I have another question. How big bottle should smallest bottle be for selling in America? Two ounces, three ounces?"

Even though I was trying to wrap my head around what he was warning me about Yuri and Vlad, I decided Toshek's ichthyol question deserved an honest answer. "Your smallest size should be what you can get ten to fifteen doses or applications out of. I also think that half-ounce sample packs would be good for selling at holistic pharmacies." Toshek took this in silently, but smiled and nodded as if digesting what I had said. He saluted me with a cheerful "Good night."

Once again, I was being warned to reconsider this final part of my mission. Having seen how proficiently Sofia and Toshek had assessed and handled the situation here at the Intourist, I probably should have recognized that, other than my timely use of brute force against Anatoly, my success in this was mostly luck, in having them to do the dirty work.

It certainly was not from any particular skill of my own. I should have considered backing out. But I didn't.

So, Cindy — now Sofia — and I ended up together in the same small bed. As I remember it, after I quietly let myself into the room, Sofia opened her arms to me. She was wearing a loose-fitting sleeveless nightgown, yellow, with little ribbon bows in front. On top, it revealed well-toned tan shoulders. Below her knees, it let me see she had beautiful, athletic legs. She wore nothing underneath, which meant I had no difficulty noticing her full breasts. As I looked at her, I immediately had an erection. I had pulled out my best clean black and white polka-dot boxers for the occasion and asked Cindy if I could go without my shirt for the night. She only said, "Shut up and hold me."

We held each other so tight I was sure I was smothering her. As she was doing to me. With only a thin layer or two of fabric between our bodies. Aware that my arousal — that protrusion in my boxers — might be keeping Sofia from sleeping, I tried to turn myself to lessen its press against her body. The last thing I wanted was to remind her of her unpleasant encounter with Georg.

"You are suffering at this moment, Andy," Sofia whispered in my ear. She felt me squirming.

"Quite the opposite. I'm worried that I'm bothering you."

"You mean your erection?" She laughed softly. "It is nice to know it is available." She put my earlobe in her mouth.

"Are you having trouble sleeping?" I asked her.

"I just want to forget. Sleeping will come later," Sofia said, continuing to tongue my ear.

I thought about it for half a minute and then ventured, "Will you let me try to help a little?"

"You are no sleep doctor," she said, "but I will let you try if you have an idea." She began to loosen her grip on me. "But no drinking," she added.

I didn't object to that; vodka was the last thing I wanted in my mouth just then. I began to kiss her on the neck and slowly worked my way down her chest, around her breasts and further down. I paused.

"Anything wrong with my plan so far?"

"I don't feel sleepy, Andy. I feel better, though." She took my head in her hands and, with gentle but insistent pressure, led me slowly to where I had intended on landing anyway. I put my mouth and tongue to work. I stayed there as long as it took to feel her begin to tremble, and then delicately arch her back and finally shake uncontrollably for just a few seconds.

She pushed my head away. Breathing like she'd just done a hundred-meter sprint, she murmured, "It is fine sleep therapy, Andy. Can I give you such treatment?"

"It was my present for you, Sofia. You don't have to." It wasn't the only lie I've ever told in bed. Secretly, I did hope she would return the favor.

"If I don't, I'll never get to hug you closely with *that* between us." With a laugh, she grabbed on to *that* and slid down on me, closing her mouth tightly on the bothersome barrier between us. I was a much easier task for her than she had been for me. After my own body shudders ended, she whispered, "I enjoyed both jobs, Andy. Thank you." Then she kissed me as she had never before.

We quickly returned to the bear hug we'd started with. The sleep therapy worked for both of us.

Through the night, each of us released our grip on the other only enough to roll from one side to the other. If my back was to her, then she held me firmly, even as she snored a little. When she turned away, she took my arm and wrapped it around her with a tug that told me to hold her tighter. Even when we faced each other, she was able to sleep while holding me, with my full weight resting on her arm.

***

It was about six o'clock by my guess, from the light filtering into the room, when Sofia began to loosen her grip. I allowed her to slip away to the bathroom. She came back to the room fully clothed but wiggled her way back between the sheets, nestling her back against me. Once she was settled, she whispered, "Did you decide something about Chelyabinsk and our new mission? Will you continue or will you quit?"

I didn't hesitate. If I had, I might have reflected on how mixed my motives really were. "I want to continue," I answered.

It took her a while to respond. When she spoke, it was businesslike. "OK. Time to get started." Her tone softened just long enough to add, "Thank you for the night of good sleep." Sofia turned, looked at me and gave me a kiss. Then she rolled away, stood up, and was gone.

POLOT Flight 42

A knock at the door at 6:30 was the only interruption while the three of us did our final packing, getting ready to head to the airport. In his relentlessly thorough way, Kruk had, of course, requested a wake-up call for our room. Vincent, also diligent as usual, used this as a chance to deliver breakfast. He strolled in with an unusually colorful tray of smoked meats, cheeses, fish, and carp roe — an economical alternative to caviar, called *taramosalata*. All this was surrounded by fresh vegetables and bread and accompanied by hot tea, served Russian style, in glasses with silver holders. Eating quickly, we asked Vincent to wait as we pooled our spare cash to cobble together a proper final tip for all he and his young friend Ben had done for us. It amounted to about a hundred dollars, U.S. His eyes grew wide as he blinked back tears. With a sad smile, he wished us well. He had already made sure the Hotel to Airport Shuttle was reserved for us and that we were ready early enough that we could finish the tea and sandwich fixings he'd treated us to. An expectant air of adventure filled the hotel room that morning. I'd not felt this since the trip had started some ten days ago. It didn't hurt that my elation was layered on top of a lingering afterglow from the night before. And while our farewell breakfast was only a short respite from the danger we knew was coming in Chelyabinsk, it was a welcome sense of relief to have a break from the mission.

Toshek had spent all night preparing his sample bags for his ichthyol marketing blast. He was busily putting the final touches on packaging the whole mess for our flight today. Sofia was already packed, as if she knew what it meant to be on the run. Both had a lot to say about the upcoming week. It was obvious to me that Sofia was the detail person, wanting to hear that defined procedures would be used to manage our risk. Toshek, on the other hand, was trying to say that we needed to be flexible enough to react to the unexpected. Having seen Toshek at work when he prepared for and finally confronted Anatoly, I could appreciate his desire to work things out as they came. Knowing we would be out of our element, I also wondered if Toshek and his two partners were ready to run if we were overwhelmed. I think that was the main thing Sofia wanted to hear from Toshek: If the situation deteriorated, at what point would we bail? And as we escaped, how would we protect ourselves?

When the time finally came, Ben appeared in the hall with three bellman's carts to carry our bags. Toshek, in an unusual display of humor, asked Ben if all the wheels were firmly attached. He hadn't seen Anatoly and Georg's famous entrance, but we had joked about it enough that he he'd been looking forward to kidding the boy.

Ben and Vincent stood under the awnings waving as the shuttle van pulled away from the Intourist. Sofia sat next to me on the third-row bench seat. She leaned over and handed me an envelope. "Open it." Inside, I found a thousand dollars. Fighting the afterglow of last night with Sofia, I imagined how far that would go in Krakow.

"For me? What for?" I asked.

"Joe wired it to us. Says it's a bonus for hazardous duty." She spoke just loud enough for me to hear over the shuttle's Russian diesel engine, clattering like an old tractor.

I had to wonder if the hazard pay was for work already done or for our upcoming duty in Chelyabinsk. "For which work are we being paid extra?"

"Don't ask me," Sofia said. She shook her head and grimaced. "I am worried about that, too. He also wrote something in the teletext I don't understand. Here: I wrote it down." The note Sofia showed me said, "TELL ANDY GOOD JOB FOR HIS GAME SAVING TACKLE." Sofia could see it made me smile. She smiled back at me but didn't ask for an explanation.

Sofia quickly returned to her serious face, a sign she was engrossed in the logistics of the danger we were fast approaching. "I know that you and Toshek have been talking about things," I said, as softly as I could so Toshek didn't overhear. He was two seats away, busily tending to his baggage and moving things from one pocket to another. "Are you really worried?"

"Yuri, Toshek, and Vlad don't usually carry a lot of guns," Sofia said. "We'll see what kind of 'camping' protection they have collected for this trip. In my opinion, it is one of the few things we can do to keep our hosts from doing something crazy. All these guys are dreaming of is *'numer stulecia.'* A chance to get rich from one fantastic deal."

I told her we couldn't do much until we saw Yuri and Vlad later today. Sofia just smiled and nodded in agreement.

The driver knew to take us past the passenger terminal and straight to air cargo. That was another half mile into the airport zone, amidst enormous warehouses and hangars. Silhouetted against the large white Quonset hut that served as a hangar for POLOT's planes, I could see Kruk, halfway into the engine space of his Antonov biplane. He was in a set of gray mechanic's coveralls, but I could see his shoes were shiny. It figured, I told myself, that for our trip Commander Kruk would have his best uniform on under those coveralls. Hearing our van approaching, he looked over the top of his glasses and pointed to where he wanted our driver to stop. As we jumped out, he also pointed to where he wanted our luggage to be offloaded. Always the operations manager, Kruk was thinking ahead for our comfort and convenience.

"One more carburetor adjustment and I'll be ready for you!" he yelled, with a smile and a wave, before sticking his head back inside the engine cowling.

***

The Antonov 2 was not the sort of plane that inspired great trust when looking at it. To me, it looked like a cross between a World War I biplane and a DC-3 from the 1930s. Most of the people I had talked to said it was an extremely safe plane. I also learned that POLOT was very proud of its fleet and took extremely good care of it. It was this fleet that the director of POLOT had proposed to use for package delivery throughout the former Soviet Bloc. I remember the faces on the NatEx directors who had flown in from Atlanta and their European headquarters in Frankfurt, expecting a proposal for a modern fleet of new vans and couriers to support its services in Poland. Instead, they discovered, shipments would be loaded onto ancient looking ANT-2s and parachuted into the cities where deliveries were to be made. POLOT's senior management felt badly insulted by the laughs the NatEx bosses gave to their presentation. After that day, the relationship between POLOT and NatEx was never the same.

***

Famous for white-knuckle anxiety while riding in any small plane, I was not feeling especially good about our trip. Still, I knew Poland had a history of both wartime and civilian aviation to be proud of. So I was going to do my best not to allow myself to get wound up in unjustified worry about our eight-hundred-mile flight from Novosibirsk to Chelyabinsk. Sofia and Toshek never flinched or showed any concern as we prepared to take off. They seemed even more amused than I was that we were being treated to this very special air transport experience. Kruk's formal, official approach made them laugh, but even so they listened closely and obeyed his orders as he got us ready.

"Since I will be flying at low altitude to facilitate your sight-seeing, I want you to have your parachute very close to you the whole time! If you go to the bathroom, take it with you. Also, here is the ripcord: this metal handle near your chest. We don't have time to practice but please raise your hand if you have ever parachuted before." Both Toshek and Sofia raised their hands. Sofia looked at me, anticipating that I would be surprised and might have a question for her. I didn't. I just gave her a thumbs up. I never did ask her about it.

Kruk taught us how to fasten and unfasten the seat belts and harnesses. He warned us that he might request help during the flight if we ran into weather problems or the cargo shifted. We had brought all our baggage into the passenger compartment with us and strapped it down. So any other cargo we didn't know about was in the hold or someplace else we didn't have access to. What started to trigger my small-plane jitters was his basic instruction about the instrument readings and what we might feel if we had to take the plane's controls. When he started to go over the history of Polish aviation, I decided I'd better cut him off before he got too long-winded.

"Poles have a stellar record in military and commercial aviation," I interrupted him. "That, we know about. Thank you, Kruk!"

"OK. OK. We'll get started." I could see he was disappointed that he couldn't deliver the rest of his carefully prepared lecture. He relented and finished his pre-flight checklist.

I remained outside as Toshek and Sofia finished their last cigarettes. Stepping away from them, I wandered alone around the apron, circling

244

the plane looking for the obviously forgotten bolt or latch or open cowling that would bring us down in flames if I didn't make this last inspection. To my relief, I found nothing. I was making my way back toward the entry door where my colleagues were standing when Kruk caught up to me. He asked me who Toshek and Cindy were. That was the only name Kruk knew for Sofia, and that was the way she wanted it. She didn't explain why she wanted to remain 'Cindy' on this mission, but I complied with her request.

"What do your colleagues do? Are you in business with them? What shall I put on my passenger record for 'occupation'?" I detected a bit of panic in Kruk's voice. He always was a stickler for detail, especially when working in foreign countries.

"You have to record our occupations?" I asked.

"It is kind of dinosaur question from socialist days that the Russians are obsessive about," he explained. "I am sort of curious, too, though."

"Toshek is a businessman. A trader. Cindy is a project manager," I told him.

"Project manager with skydiving experience is interesting profile. Maybe she is former KGB," he suggested. Then he offered a bit of advice. "Be careful!"

It was time. Our excited pilot gave us a wink and a 'follow me' gesture and we all climbed on board the Antonov 2 and strapped ourselves in. As Kruk got the lumbering gooney bird's engine started, I wondered what it had sounded like before all his tinkering. It was knocking loudly and even took Toshek's attention away from his ichthyol notebook. He unstrapped himself from his chair and tapped on Kruk's shoulder. I couldn't hear what he asked, nor what Kruk said back, but Toshek seemed OK with his answer. After we taxied to the runway and Kruk throttled up the Commie biplane for takeoff, Toshek pulled our heads together and yelled, "Knocking is normal after the piston rod work. It will quiet down once we get into the air."

That didn't sound like a very good explanation, but I didn't have much choice but to accept it. Kruk released the wheel brakes and we were on our way.

Sofia crossed her fingers as the plane bumped down the runway. I put my palms together and mimed as if I was saying a prayer. We all laughed as Kruk pulled back on the wheel and the Antonov 2's nose lifted. The bumping stopped and we were airborne, finally on our way to Chelyabinsk on the POLOT Gooney Bird Express.

The skies were mostly clear that morning. Temperatures were a comfortable ten degrees Celsius, about fifty Fahrenheit. Winds were light, which contributed to a smooth takeoff. After going about five miles west, Kruk took a long, exceedingly gradual turn to the right, heading almost due north. As he'd explained before, we were avoiding restricted airspace over a huge nuclear missile base. He pointed out what he said were the buildings servicing the active missiles. For my benefit and amusement, he added a bit of historical perspective.

"As long as the imperialistic West continues to threaten the peaceful Eastern countries of the former Soviet bloc, Russians will be forced to defend themselves and their loyal brothers!"

We all laughed. Sofia took my coat collar to pull me towards her and yelled in my ear, "He says these things very much like the propaganda minister would say on television. I think he was responsible for POLOT propaganda program. Or he is a good actor."

"I know he was a good socialist at one time. He helped me at NatEx. He is a good man. I don't really care what he believes in," I told her, "unless he decides to crash the airplane to save the world from us."

Sofia knit her brows, unsure how seriously to take my wisecrack. She responded, "It is sometimes important to know what people really think. Caring about it is what is paying my bills. For now."

"So, tell me," I asked her, "if you had your choice between being an employee at a bank or continuing to do this crazy work, what would you choose?"

"I am doing what I want now, and I am proud of it," she answered, a determined look on her face. By now, as we gained altitude, the wind picking up inside the unpressurized cabin was making her hair fly wildly about.

Kruk leveled the plane off at an altitude I guessed was somewhere around ten thousand feet. I could tell the air had thinned quite a bit, but I knew we were considerably below fourteen thousand feet, the height of Mount Rainier in Washington. I had climbed that mountain and remembered my labored breathing as I summited. All three of us huddled against the plane's left-side windows until Kruk turned around and motioned for us to split up. "Always have at least one person on each side," he asked, to keep from unbalancing the little plane. We complied, switching sides for about an hour as Kruk took us in a western direction, heading straight for our destination. After about ninety minutes, he signaled for me to join him in the cockpit.

"We are fighting a headwind that is a little stronger than I expected," Kruk told me. "I will land at my usual refueling place in an hour and a half and give my friends their presents. To stay on schedule, we will have to quickly take off after refueling. So, we will have a much shorter picnic lunch with Polish people than I promised." His face showed how disappointed he was. "We will call it a long bathroom stop."

"Don't worry about it! We are enjoying the ride. A short break will be nice. Thank you for telling me." I smiled to reassure him it was all right.

I went back to my seat where I had been watching the desolate country below slowly pass by. It looked just like parts of the Dakotas or Wyoming or even Eastern Washington, unending grassland across small hills. The only patches of trees were scattered here and there, seemingly at random. I saw very little in the way of rivers or bodies of water. Sofia was watching, and, like me, seemed mesmerized by the unending panorama of the steppes. I interrupted her blank stare with the news from Kruk: that we'd be landing in a bit to refuel but our greatly anticipated picnic with the Poles was to be abbreviated. Despite the headwind we were bucking, it hadn't been a particularly bumpy ride. Even so, after four hours we were all starting to get a little airsick and welcomed the idea of a short break. Sofia wanted to be in Chelyabinsk as soon as possible but would have to tough out an hour on the ground and three more in the air. According to Kruk, if we could stay on schedule, we would be landing around five in the afternoon.

The passenger cabin in the AN-2 was little more than a cargo bay equipped with unpadded leather jump seats. The only backrests were straps attached to either side of the fuselage. As the plane drifted in flight, we would all swing right and left in unison. Despite the discomfort, the ride was also very loud. Under those conditions, sleep was impossible.

Thirty minutes after my announcement to Sofia, Kruk cut the engine down to idle. The biplane began to tilt downward toward a landing strip at an unnamed village that promised fuel for us and Polish treats for the airstrip's tenders. These were a mostly Polish extended family that had been living nearby for decades since a forced removal from near L'viv in the 1920s. While the landing wasn't smooth, it was under Kruk's control the whole time. A huge banner with *Witamy Panie Kruk!* "Welcome Mr. Kruk!" painted in red, with a crude Polish flag, hung from a strange cylinder halfway down the runway. I noticed it as Kruk turned the plane toward the crowd and taxied about fifty meters in their direction. Quite the welcoming committee was waiting.

Poland on the Steppes

When the plane stopped, Kruk jumped from his seat to greet the dozen or more people running from a little building on the edge of the runway — if you could call the grassy expanse a runway. Their smiles were visible a hundred meters off. Considerably more women than men, their colorful skirts were flying up and flapping in the wind as they raced toward us. A young man, possibly a teenager by the look of his face, but tall and husky, was pulling a cart behind him. I guessed he would be loading Kruk's presents to haul back to wherever they all lived. I hadn't noticed any houses. I wondered how these people could live so far out in the steppes without visible signs of agriculture, industry or any other economy. We all clambered out and greeted the excited little crowd, getting hugs and kisses from everyone. Toshek fell very handily into his fair Polish. I could hear Sofia speaking better than I could in the language I thought I was fluent in.

With everyone getting acquainted, I turned my attention back to that strange cylinder that the welcome banner was hanging from. I had this disturbing hunch I had recently seen something like that. About thirty feet tall and eight or nine in diameter, I guessed. As I started to recall that rushed factory tour in Samara, Toshek noticed me staring at the object and broke away from the crowd. "I believe that's a Soyuz meteorite," he said

"The numbering is still visible. I believe you're right, Toshek." I was getting a funny feeling that Kruk and POLOT Flight #42 had just brought us to an unexpected twist in our journey.

A short, stout man with a self-important air stepped up to speak. "I am Darek. Let me welcome you to our own little Polish town, Nowy Wies!" The name meant new village. "This is Zofia, and that is Bartek. My wife Magda. Our children, Danuta, Benjamin, and Stanislaw. Are you tired and hungry? Surely you will stay and have dinner with us! Can you spend the night? Hello Wladek! Thank you for coming again! We look forward to every visit that you can spare for us. Tell us what is happening in the world. What is going on in Poland? Russia? United States? These guests, are they your friends? They look very nice. Oh, please come to our little shack on the airport property and have lunch with us!"

Watching the Mayor introduce his family with such pride and seeing the bright faces of his children, I began to experience an emotional meltdown like I'd never felt before. I was feeling the same way about my own family. *My family!* I was screaming silently to myself. My ten-year FAMILY mission, I was mentally admonishing myself, should put any other job or CIA work in the back seat. I thought. Had I torn my family apart for money, the desire for adventure, narcissistic recognition? *Maybe even for sex?* I walked away from Toshek and the crowd, my eyes tearing up, a huge lump in my throat and stomach, not wanting to cause a scene. Toshek saw me pull away and followed, several steps behind. He'd likely seen me wiping my eyes and decided to make sure I was OK.

Just loud enough for me to hear, he said, "I think you are homesick or something."

"Yeah, something like that, Toshek," I uttered as best I could without sounding like I was bawling.

"We all get that way. From time to time," he offered as consolation. I turned and put my hand on his shoulder. We started walking back toward the mayor.

"Maybe it is good for you to think: your journey east has ended," Toshek suggested. "And now we are quickly moving westward. In direction of your home and family."

I smiled, appreciating Toshek's attempt to make me feel better. "Let's go catch the mayor before he disappears."

Toshek and I pulled the mayor from his crowd and took him aside to talk. "*Panie Darku! Czy mozemy rozmawiac? Mamy pytanie.*" We were asking Mr. Darek if we could talk, to ask him a question.

"*Oczywiscie!*" Of course! He followed us toward the tall cylinder and the welcome banner.

His arm around Darek, Toshek asked, "Is that what I think it is? A piece of a rocket?"

"It landed right there where it is standing now. It took a small army to get it upright." Darek answered, his arms folded and a serious look on his face. "That was a scary evening. The wind was blowing from toward our village." He pointed east where a low hill kept us from seeing anything but grass. "We heard a screaming noise as it was dropping, then an explosion as it hit the ground, luckily bouncing over the landing strip. The fumes from the fuel nearly killed us."

"Can we take a look?" I asked him.

With a smile, Darek waved his arm toward the Soyuz debris. "Please do! I will get back to my people."

Toshek and I jogged the rest of the way to the looming cylinder. I had brought my toolkit and pulled out one of the miniature cameras to get photos from all angles. I took close-ups of any numbers and other identifying markings I could find. By this time, Sofia had broken away from the crowd and joined us. I wondered if she had seen my earlier meltdown. While I was feeling better at the moment, I knew it was time for making a big decision. An uncharacteristic feeling of clarity about my dilemma descended around me. It wasn't yet clear to me what that decision would be, but I knew that this trip and the events I had experienced were having their effect.

"Kruk is a hero here! He's sneaking vodka shots with all the ladies!" she announced. She stopped in her tracks, suddenly recognizing the behemoth from Baikonur. "Holy shit! Rocket stuff!" I got ahold of myself and my emotions before Sofia got too close. Fishing my photography, I joined her and Toshek for a quick pow-wow.

"Guys, we can't stick around for very long." I rummaged into my toolkit and pulled out $100. Handing it to Toshek, I said, "Please give this to Darek and come up with a plan to cooperate with him on any data we can get about Soyuz debris around here."

Toshek kept his hand extended. "For another $100," he said, "I'm sure he'll disassemble and deliver anything he can find."

I pulled out another hundred. After a moment's thought, I handed it over. "Tell him we're also interested in any stories about American prisoners of war that might be floating around after all these years."

Toshek smiled, took the money, and offered, "Everyone has something to say. Nobody has any proof." Stuffing the cash into his pocket, he mused aloud, "Maybe I can sell them some ichthyol. No doctors out here, for sure."

Rejoining the group, we saw Kruk's attention had finally returned to his passengers and cargo. For a moment, I thought, he looked extremely sad. Then he stiffened up and apologized to the expectant crowd that we could stay only for a short pee-break and a snack. There was a general murmur of disappointment but Kruk tried to manage that with an announcement: he had a trove of supplies for them that needed to be offloaded.

"Get me fueled up," he barked, "and bring the cart for all the goods in the cargo bay!"

I caught a glance at Sofia. She was talking to one of the older girls, probably fifteen or sixteen. The girl wore her blonde hair in long braids that hung over a white peasant top. Her plain pink skirt had probably been bright red when it was new. Around her neck was a colorful kerchief with a Polish embroidered design. I guessed it was a traditional Krakovian scarf, since that was the most popular style. Smiling and laughing, Sofia stepped back to the plane, reached inside for one of her bags and pulled out a pen and paper. After writing something, she tore her paper in two and gave half of the sheet to the young woman. Sofia folded up the other half and tucked it into her rear pants pocket. The two hugged and kissed in the Polish style: left cheek, right cheek, left cheek… or is it the other cheek first? I could never get that right. It wasn't the only Polish thing I could never get right.

Sofia waved at the girl then started walking my way. Staring at me as she got closer, she slowed down and stopped in front of me, "Why do you look different? You know something I don't know."

Again, Sofia's intuition, or whatever it was, told her something was up. I wasn't too surprised. If I looked like I felt… enlightened… I'm sure it was noticeable. I replied, "Just getting smarter every day." She raised her eyebrows, then winked and nodded. *No way she knows what I'm feeling!* So I tried to believe. But Sofia had been full of surprises from day one.

Surrounded by all the colorful Polishness with scarves, flowers, traditional Krakovian costumes, and the smell of food wafting from the terminal, I took advantage of the last few minutes we had on the ground and ran to the dusty-looking building at the end of the airfield. The mayor had invited us in for treats and a chance to shop for folk art or baked items.

Like a mini-bazaar, tables were covered with embroidered sheets and table cloths. The walls were adorned with woven kilims and small tapestries representing all the regions of Poland. Memories flooded the moment. Memories of walks in Krakow's famous Cloth Hall when I was a new student and a pretty young professor of mine was showing me around, giving me a private tour of her city. It was after one such walk through the Cloth Hall that I suggested a coffee and brandy. That was all it took. That night, my life's direction had changed.

I spotted an icon that I'd never seen before and asked the merchant what she wanted for it. *"Dwadziescie zlotych, prosze."* Twenty zloty, please.

"How about five dollars?" I countered.

"Dobrze, moze byc." OK, that's fine. I gave her the smallest bill I had, a ten, and waved away the change. I'd expected a smile or a thank you. I got more of a 'You're crazy' look.

I'd known immediately that Renata would like the icon. She'd specialized in Ukrainian iconography and I suspected this specimen, very well preserved and probably very old, would be special for her. I tucked it in my jacket and ran back to the plane, where everyone was gathering for our departure.

The big Polish boy we had seen pushing the cart earlier passed us on his way to unload the bounty Kruk had brought. He pulled ten or twelve packages from the rear cargo hold and stacked them on a cart. I saw canned goods, ultra-pasteurized milk in cartons, medical supplies, some clothing, shoe boxes, lots of candy and chocolate, coffee and tea. The big boy also wrestled some sort of machine, screwed to a wooden Euro-pallet, onto the bottom shelf of his cart. I guessed it was a small generator.

Knowing we were special guests, flown in by Poland's own POLOT Air Express, it was probably a disappointment for the Polish community of Nowy Wies that we couldn't stay and enjoy more of their hospitality. After the plane was offloaded, the young man topped off our tank and yelled to Sofia and me, *"Juz, gotowy!"* It's ready.

Sofia let out a big sigh. "Enough. Go get him. Time for us to go."

"Kruk! Plane's ready to go! Wind's a-howlin' against us! All aboard!" For the last leg to Chelyabinsk, we had a full tank of gas and empty bladders. Cindy's new young friend rushed out a bag of sandwiches for us. The hugs and kisses were mixed with tears and Kruk's promises to come back soon. Piling into the Antonov 2, I realized Toshek was missing. Still talking to Darek about the missiles and MIAs?

Through the plane's windows, we finally spotted Toshek hurrying around the corner of the strange little terminal. He waved at our new contact, Darek, mayor of Nowy Wies. In his other hand, he was carrying something. I offered him a hand up into the cabin. Once he'd buckled himself in and Kruk had fired up the engine, Toshek handed me a long, heavy military knife. Seeing it, I got a chill up the back of my neck. Engraved on the blade was "J.B. LONGAKER — U.S. ARMY." He yelled at me over the roar of the backfiring engine misfiring, "Mayor Darek is ready to gather all the rocket trash in Siberia and send it to you. As I was leaving, he gave me this. Here is your evidence: American soldiers in Siberia!"

Stunned, I looked more closely at the knife. My initial thoughts then turned to doubt. I had seen similar knives in every flea market in Eastern Europe. For all I knew, some GI in West Germany had traded this one for a bottle of schnapps and a night with a hooker, and it had been part of a long chain of barter and bragging ever since. But that wasn't for me to decide. I stashed this tantalizing clue in my toolkit and got ready with my colleagues for the final leg of our journey. However, the POW angle might pan out, the missile debris was unquestionably real. Kruk's refueling stop had proven much more fruitful than we could have imagined.

By the time Kruk finally got the mighty Gooney Bird running smoothly, we lined up on the uneven track that served as the runway here at Nowy Wies. In less than a hundred meters of motoring into the stiff wind, Kruk had us airborne. Next stop: Chelyabinsk!

***

Getting us back to altitude, Kruk tried to find alternative heights that would be less bumpy than what we found at around nine thousand feet. Experimenting with five-hundred-foot intervals, he brought us back down to around six thousand, but everywhere he tried was turbulent. Basically, the wind was there for us to fight, and would not be evaded. I wouldn't have minded the bumpy ride so much but Toshek and Sofia both were getting greener by the minute as the Gooney Bird tossed their stomachs. At this pace, we wouldn't get into Chelyabinsk until 6:30 or 7 p.m. That was starting to get close to Yuri's absolute deadline. Our ticket into the Soyuz debris site was valid only until midnight tonight, and Yuri wanted some extra leeway besides. That would allow time for scouting out our site before we set up camp for the night. With a three-hour drive after we arrived, that was cutting it close.

"No chance for flying lessons today!" Kruk yelled back from the cockpit. "Just too windy and difficult to fly. Even for me! I am sorry!"

"No worries, Kruk!" I yelled back. "We want to arrive safely. I don't think any of us are feeling up for lessons." About that time an especially hard gust of turbulence hit us. Toshek, out of his seat belt while coming back from the toilet, hit his head on the overhead bulkhead. He said he was OK, but I could see blood trickling down his forehead. Within minutes, he began to vomit, all while pressing a paper towel against his wounded scalp.

The headwinds eased up after a couple of very tiring hours. Thankfully, the last part of our flight was a fairly smooth air tour of the villages and towns surrounding Chelyabinsk. Kruk pointed out each of the closed cities we passed as the airport got closer. All around us were sites for weapons production, smelting special metals, refining, fabrication, and nuclear technology. Again, I thought of Richland and the nearby Hanford Reservation in Washington State as comparable instances of Cold War research once carefully hidden from enemy eyes. But now, none of these sites were hidden any more. Our satellites are always watching them, and their satellites are always watching us.

Kruk turned his radio down long enough to holler at us over his shoulder. "Fasten your seatbelts, please! We are cleared for landing in Chelyabinsk." He had been barking in English with the airport's control tower, but I could tell that he was having a hard time getting them to respond in English.

Kruk: "POLOT Flight 42, cargo plus passengers, requesting approach details. Over."

Chelyabinsk Tower: "*Pa ruski... pizhalsta...* POLOT 42 cargo! Chelyabinsk, Over."

Kruk: "International language of air traffic is English. Please. Thank you! POLOT 42 again requesting approach guidance. Over!"

Chelyabinsk Tower: "*Kurwa! Huj!*" That was one curse word each in Russian and Polish. "*Pa ruski!*" the controller demanded: say it in Russian!

Kruk: *"Da. Da. Daj spokoj!"* In Polish he asked the controller to give him a break.

Despite the international air traffic communication issues, (Read: local mafia bosses controlling institutions here, assuring a lack of safety and assistance for the common good) we landed smoothly. Yuri and Toshek took Kruk's conversation in his stride and were grinning as it occurred. Sofia? Not so much. I could tell this little glitch concerned her. Kruk brought the Gooney Bird up to the Corporate and Commercial Aviation hangar and terminal. Since our entire flight had been within Russia, no immigration or passport related formalities were required. Even so, there were more armed policemen and SWAT-team-looking characters carrying AK-47s than I had ever seen in one place. Because of them, we were asked to show our IDs, which caused a small sensation. To have an American arriving just as a serious SWAT action was about to take place. Kruk asked the ground crew officer helping us what was going on. The answer, though somewhat cryptic, sounded like a group of mafia types were expected to fly in at any time. Toshek, Sofia, and I looked at each other and, almost in unison, we all said, "I wonder if that is who we are meeting tonight!"

Whatever the answer to that question, Kruk had gotten us to Chelyabinsk before our deadline. He had even shown us a good time along the way. Before my tired, bloody, and slightly vomit-stained partners got too far away, I asked them if I could use three hundred dollars of our extra cash to tip Kruk for all he'd done. Neither Sofia nor Toshek objected. Toshek commented, "We have enough for the assholes ahead of us. Kruk deserves it."

Kruk was very grateful for the cash but, in true Kruk fashion, tried to put on a good face in refusing it. Albeit his protests were a little too short-lived to be believable. But good manners preserved, we gave the three-cheek kiss, I thanked him, and I told him he now had all my new contact numbers. We said goodbye and waved at each other three times. I had to jog to catch up with my colleagues, laden with my toolkit, my diplomatka, and a small suitcase.

About fifty meters ahead of Toshek and Sofia, I could see Yuri and Vlad standing behind a fence. It was being guarded by two machine-gun-bearing Russian gorillas larger even than Vlad. Even from that distance, aided by the light shining directly on our partners' lined faces, I could see they were as exhausted as we were. I was hoping they had matters well in hand and carried only good news about our coming week in the Siberian wilderness. But as we approached, their faces certainly weren't telling that story.

Chelyabinsk to the Lakes

It was nearly midnight, deep in the Siberian boondocks, and our little caravan had turned off the paved road a good thirty minutes ago. Following Yuri and me down this unpaved back route were Sofia, Toshek and Vlad, in an ex-Red Army truck.

After thirty minutes on this muddy trail, we came to the first fork. Yuri turned our Russian Jeep to the right. At this 'Y' the signs for Dubrovnoye pointed to the left. One referring to several *Ozero* indicated a right turn to reach the lakes. Oddly, out here in the middle of nowhere, I spotted a man with a walkie-talkie standing off to the side of the road, partly hidden by scrubby bushes. I turned to Yuri to see if he had noticed or intended to react to the man; he just nodded.

"Next intersection should be with welcoming committee," Yuri said calmly. Seven or eight minutes later his prediction came true. Lights flashing ahead of us turned out to be flashlights pointed in our direction; those resolved themselves to become six men. There may have been more, that we did not see. Those we did see wore paramilitary type clothes and were armed with short style AK-47 automatic rifles and small pistols in white holsters. These looked much like I remembered the Polish police carrying in the eighties, when I was a rookie spy trying to avoid their attention.

Here, though, Yuri wasn't trying to hide anything. His hand darted under his seat and pulled out a similarly styled automatic pistol with a large clip. He laid it on the seat between us. At that moment, I just about shit my pants, but managed to keep my cool as the unexpected firearm appeared. He rolled down his window and told me to do the same. As we came to a stop, I saw in the mirror that our big truck was still about a hundred meters behind us but slowly catching up. Several men were walking alongside it as it neared the roadblock where we were stopped. We were already outnumbered about two to one, not counting the others I was sure were lurking in the shadows around us. Through our open windows, I could hear the men near the truck laughing and making jokes about the bicycle strapped on top of the cab.

"American motorcycle, perhaps? Where is motor?"

"Toys for the childcare center, I think."

One of the men stepped to within a foot of Yuri's window, took off his hat and said, "Good evening! Here for some space parts?" At the same time, a man who look like his younger twin, about thirty years old and focused on the weapon on the seat between Yuri and me, walked up to about the same distance from my window. He had nothing to say, but stood silently.

Yuri answered crisply, "Yes. Gostonov and Gold."

The Mafia goon: "OK. Second vehicle?"

Yuri: "They will tell you. Maybe it's different for you than for me."

The men flanking our vehicle laughed.

The mafia goon then gave Yuri his instructions. "OK. Go straight ahead about one kilometer. Don't leave this road. No sightseeing. There will be big clearing with space for you and your camp at opposite end. You will see it. Bare dirt and some bushes for your latrine. Welcome to the Lakes."

As he spoke, I heard one of the sentries who had joked about the bicycle whistle and say, "There is woman with them! Americans are very kind to us!"

Instead of jumping out of our vehicle and telling them all to fuck themselves — I was indignant but not stupid — I sat quietly and reflected on what I had gotten myself into. I began to feel as if I was being dropped into a combat zone with only dollar bills to deflect bullets, or beatings. At exactly that instant, a feeling of dread like I had never experienced came over me. And, while the paralysis of that moment didn't last very long, the feeling remained constantly on the periphery of my thoughts. I noticed my breathing had gotten very shallow. I instinctively put my finger to my wrist. My heart was racing over two hundred beats per minute.

I wondered what Sofia was thinking now.

***

By the time I'd caught up to Vlad and Yuri at the Chelyabinsk airport, they were already helping Sofia and Toshek load their things into a pair of vehicles. Yuri was complaining loudly to Toshek about the space his ichthyol packages took up. He told him to load them last so they could quickly unload them wherever Toshek decided he was going to leave them in Chelyabinsk. I couldn't tell if this annoyed Toshek or if he had planned to store his valuable black treasure here while we disappeared into the wild.

"No room for Toshek's capitalism!" Yuri said, trying to make a joke of it.

Toshek wrote down an address where we would drop off the boxes on our way out of town.

Yuri asked him, "What is this place?"

"A doctor's office. He buys some of my product every month. He said he will help me." I could tell Toshek was reluctant to tell us too much about the extent of his ichthyol network. Still, this trip was making it all clearer. I once again saw why everyone called him the Ichthyol King.

Yuri barked out our seating arrangements for the long drive ahead of us. "OK. Fine. Andy! Give me your things here. We will throw them in the back." He pointed to a GAZ 69, a four-wheel-drive military vehicle slightly bigger than a Jeep. "You ride with me. We catch up on what's going on and some other news. More room in the 66 so Cindy goes with Vlad and Toshek." The GAZ 66 was a hulking off-road truck, originally meant for carrying troops.

"We are all going to choke to death from the fumes these Russian monsters are belching out!" Sofia cried out as she climbed into the 66 between Vlad, who was driving, and Toshek in the window shotgun seat. Vlad had avoided making eye contact with me since I joined the group. I hoped whatever had been eating him on the train two weeks ago was at least in remission. The last thing I wanted was for Vlad to abandon his security role, leaving me at the mercy of someone even scarier. Since he was part of the kidnapping and ransom deterrence program for my safety, I would have happily made amends with him — if I knew what the problem had been. I felt in the dark, though. Since he didn't seem to be on the warpath today, I decided to let it ride. As we got ready to roll, I pretended nothing had ever happened between us.

The 66 fired up without a problem, though it was loud and smoked a bit. The 69 sounded and looked a little like a World War II Jeep but it was all fine — as far as I could tell. I especially enjoyed seeing the old gray bicycle strapped on top of the big truck's cabin. The bike had balloon tires that looked like something from the fifties and a crude metal basket on the front. Altogether, it made for a strange sight as we lumbered off into the chilly Siberian night, smoke disappearing into the darkness. The poorly muffled diesel engines clattering loudly, echoing off a maze of socialist apartment blocks extending out into infinity.

Winding our way out of Chelyabinsk through miles of residential high-rises from the seventies and eighties, I wondered how Yuri could figure out where we were and how to get where we were going. Socialist urban planning, especially the Soviet version, had failed to anticipate the increase in popularity of automobiles, despite the U.S.S.R.'s decision in the late sixties to start mass-producing cars for workers. As central planners had neglected to plan for cars, or for the requisite parking spaces that came with them, the narrow streets were clogged with double-parked vehicles. That meant driving wasn't easy. And Yuri wasn't the most patient driver. The 66 was much wider than the 69 and Vlad was having difficulty threading the needle through these congested, poorly lit neighborhood streets. Also, having to drop off Toshek's ichthyol irritated Yuri. Even so, it was clear that he preferred to do that over having the tarry black shit occupying space in our vehicles.

As we finally emerged into the city's outskirts, Yuri complained once again about the ichthyol. "We're going to be cramped enough as it is when you find what you're looking for at the crash sites. I don't know how heavy it will be and I don't know how much room it will take. So damn Toshek can take care of his capitalism without it fucking us up or getting us killed somehow. Besides, these crazy mafia guys would probably steal it. That would send Toshek into a fit."

Yuri started to tell me a story about Toshek's ichthyol business getting in the way at a critical moment during a mission six months ago but was interrupted when Vlad began honking and waving us to pull over. His arm extended from the truck's driver-side window, pointing to a low building sandwiched between two twenty-story high rises. He turned the 66 off the road and we followed him, pulling up at an official-looking three-story building. The signs indicated it was a medical clinic; lights were on in the reception area. Toshek jumped out and knocked on the door. Thirty seconds later, a man in a white smock opened it and waved us in. We all jumped out to help Toshek get his boxes and bags unloaded.

This took less than five minutes. As we pulled away, I saw in the mirror that the man in the smock was waving to us. Whether to say goodbye or flip us off, I had no idea.

Whether because of that delivery or just the congested streets, we were behind schedule. Before we left the clinic, Yuri told Vlad we needed to make good time for the next few hours and urged him to push the 66 as fast as he could. We would be driving east on a relatively good highway, Number 30, so Yuri thought we would make up some time during the next 250 kilometers. After that, we would have to turn off the highway onto local roads. During this exchange, I heard for the first time the name of the village closest to where we would be camped out. It was Dubrovnoye. I also understood the area was dotted with lakes and forests and that all three sites were in a row within about fifty kilometers of that village. I heard the names of two lakes mentioned. First was *Ozero Bolshaya Kavyka*, which meant Big Fly Lake. The second was *Ozero Chasha*, which could be translated two ways: as Bowl Lake in Russian, or Skull Lake in Polish.

During the long ride, using my Polish and an overactive imagination, I mused about camping with big flies and skeletons everywhere.

Bouncing along in the 69, I remembered that I had almost bought a Russian GAZ Jeep two years back but had been warned off. Those in the know told me that searching for parts and constant breakdowns were the life of a Commie Jeep owner. And just as Sofia had said, the exhaust fumes coming into the passenger compartment were only occasionally overpowered by the cigarettes that Yuri had been chain smoking since we left Chelyabinsk. The 69 had a manual transmission. I could see that downshifting, then running through all the gears to speed up, was a hit-or-miss proposition if you cared about mis-shifts, grinding gears or a slipping clutch. Yuri had all the GAZ 69 moves down, expertly double-clutching, manipulating the choke when the carburetor would flood out without warning, and regulating the heat and air with twice as many levers as there were vents in the cabin. At times, the noise was deafening, depending on which gear we were in and whether we were passing such socialist tin-can cars as an East German Trabant, a Polish Syrena, or a Russian Lada.

Downshifting and punching the gas to pass a slower vehicle would make the 69 shake and then roar as the gas-guzzling four-wheel-drive monster picked up speed. The 66, always about a hundred meters behind us, while not as nimble, had the power to do whatever we were doing on the highway. I wondered if Sofia, squeezed into the cab between Vlad and Toshek, was suffering as badly as she had feared. I also wondered if her earlier air sickness might return with the combination of fumes and boat-like rocking I could see the big truck doing at every turn. However, she was doing, though, I couldn't do a thing about it as our little caravan roared through the Siberian countryside that night.

The whole time, Yuri drove like a madman. To take my attention away from the dangers that loomed on every curve, I pulled out my map. I tried to figure out where Katerina and Zhenia's estate was in relation to where we were going. It seemed like it was in the same general direction but I guessed we were heading quite a distance farther east than their place. I knew it was more than just a bad habit of mine. When things got a little tense, I'd often let myself get distracted by women, or at least thoughts of women. When I should have been worried about Polish military police, I'd been working through the Kama Sutra with that librarian. When Vlad had been gunning for me, I'd bedded down with Katerina. And now, despite the epiphany I'd had in Nowy Wies earlier today, and memories of how much I loved my role as husband and father, my attention now was veering between worries about Sofia in the truck behind me, and Katerina in her estate somewhere out there in the Siberian darkness.

After a jolting quarter of an hour, I gave up trying to find Dalmatovo. But then I decided to ask Yuri if he could find the two women's place on my map. I told him the name of the village. Not even slowing down, he took the map, nearly swerving off the road as he looked it over, but almost immediately stabbed the spot with his finger. He was showing me a place farther north but only about sixty miles away from our destination, Dubrovnoye. Handing me back the map, he added, "There are tourist buses going back and forth from that place you want to go. Is a small resort on the lake at Dubrovnoye." Yuri glanced at me a couple of times before asking, "Katerina is there?"

I nodded. "Da."

With two hours ahead of us before we left the highway, I studied the documents Joe had given me about the first, second, and third stages of the Soyuz. The pictures had been photocopied and weren't very clear, but it appeared that the most interest lay in the second and third stage debris. Joe had written, "If there is a choice between accessing second or third stage debris sites, go to the third stage site. That site will, of course, be further north and east of Baikonur. Securing technology within the attachment rings between the third stage and the payload or fourth stage is really our goal."

I had been surprised to learn that some of these rockets had a fourth stage.

Photos and some engineering drawings made it look like the prime target for our trip would be within a metal housing attached just inside the third stage's upper ring. The upper ring technology for the second stage was open and easier to get to, but not as hot a commodity for Joe. I asked Yuri if he understood why the three sites had been selected and if he knew anything about where the second and third stage debris was.

"We are only able to get to second stage debris this week. I asked our hosts about the site to the northeast," Yuri said, "and they had funny answer." He didn't elaborate.

After half a minute of silence, I asked, "What was their answer?"

"They said they have whole rocket on a trailer," he told me. "It will be delivered to where we are soon. But only if we are willing to negotiate more money, for anything we take from it."

It didn't take long for Yuri's revelation to sink in. Getting to the site tonight was all we had to do for the two most important targets: second and third stage attachment rings and whatever was just inside them that we could identify and remove. The logistical challenges of getting to two sites and dealing with the mafia-administered bureaucracy seemed to be cut in half — if what Yuri was saying was true. It sounded good to me. But the more I thought about it, I realized how unlikely it was that the 'whole rocket on a trailer' was really what we were looking for: debris from a spy satellite booster that we had been sent to find and perform surgery on.

I asked Yuri about this. "Do we have any way of confirming that their rocket on the trailer is, in fact, the third stage debris of the rocket we want?"

Yuri shook his head and looked at me as if I was an idiot. "Look at your papers more closely. There are all kinds of identifying numbers and letters for us to confirm it." His look, of course, was spot on. I was an idiot. After all the photos I'd made of just such markings on the Polish exiles' space-age monument at Nowy Wies, I should have understood this. My packet included five whole pages of detailed instructions about how to identify our target. After this exchange, Yuri spoke very little until we reached the intersection where Dubrovnoye Road left Highway 30.

It was getting close to 11 p.m. I knew that Yuri really wanted to arrive at our destination before midnight. At this crossroads was a small place that sold diesel and some food. Realizing we were not going into Dubrovnoye but taking a back road to the meeting spot, Yuri decided to stop for fuel. We all took a break and stretched our legs. As Yuri and Vlad were busy pumping fuel into their trucks, Sofia came up to me and said, "Let's walk a bit."

"Did you notice that you called me Sofia, once on the flight and once in the Polish village?" she scolded me as we walked. "Remember from now on to call me only Cindy. Yuri, Vlad and Toshek are trained for this. So you should be too." I nodded silently to acknowledge my mistake. Fully accustomed to being yelled at by a woman far and away my superior, I had no problem being scolded by Sofia — or Cindy, damn it! Then, as she did so often, she instantly shifted back to a more cheerful tone. "Did Yuri tell you we might have good situation? With the second site debris on a truck?" she asked.

"Yes! It sounds very good," I said, "if they haven't stripped it of the things we're looking for."

"Maybe they stripped it for us, and it is waiting for us to buy," she suggested.

"Maybe. We could be packed up and gone in two days, I think." Then a more personal thought struck me. "You seem less nervous about the situation and our safety than you did earlier today," I told her.

"Maybe I am. Yuri and Vlad got some respectable vehicles for this trip. I like the cage in the back of this 66. It is almost like a jail to lock someone up. Or a place to hide in and keep the bad guys out. Vlad is acting like civilized man, too. He is not so worried any more, like Joe was reporting." She continued, "Two things I wanted to tell you before we leave. First: I am Cindy because Sofia is a name our hosts might react to. That is because of something that happened earlier this year. During action at a factory near here. Joe said the name Sofia must disappear. Second: we stay together as much as possible. Getting us away from Vlad

265

and Toshek will be someone's goal. If that happens, we are at big risk. Understand?"

"I understand." I nodded.

Now she had a surprise for me. "Maybe you want news about Anatoly and Georg?"

My face must have lit up; I didn't have to say "Yes" for her to get the idea.

"Magic message machine in Novosibirsk was working this morning," she said. "Joe says congratulations for grabbing a big piece of weapons-grade uranium that was missing and making many people very nervous. Your American football tackle is already famous in Warsaw CIA office. Both Anatoly and Georg are sick from radiation poisoning. After this Soyuz debris project, Joe wants you to get back to Warsaw as quickly as possible. There is kind of pow-wow in Poland with other parts of the anti-terrorism team soon."

I listened silently to this 'magic message' from Joe, smiling and nodding to acknowledge each point. It was all good—except for one thing. It was clear to me that I should put my visit with Katerina and Zhenia on the back burner, something to do on my next visit. But I really had my doubts that I would ever come back to this place. My inability to be disciplined and follow my decisions through — wait; even to make a decision in the midst of my dilemma — was getting worse. I tried to take it one at a time: *I am now firmly committed to completing and maximizing the value from this mission, for the CIA and for myself. So fucking stay focused!* I repeated to myself. *That extra $1,000 will be put to proper use, not on some romantic side trip.* I patted myself on the back with that decision. And yet, right away, I couldn't help thinking. And my mind started wandering back again to my night with Katerina in her first-class berth, and then to how Sofia — Cindy! — and I had consoled each other. That had been less than twenty-four hours before but was already seeming like an eternity ago. *I am fucked up!* was all I could conclude.

"Let's go! Forty-five minutes to camping place," Vlad yelled in English, interrupting my little reverie. I was shocked. To my surprise, he had spoken. He hadn't grunted or growled. And had used my language! No wonder Cindy felt better now, quite aside from what I'd been able to do for her.

Instead of running to an outdoor toilet behind the fueling station, I quickly peed behind a tree before catching up to her. I had time to give her shoulders a squeeze before she climbed into the 66. I took my place in the 69 and Yuri immediately gave me a direct order. "No sex and no kissing from here on. It can be used to compromise you. I know these assholes very well."

His words woke me up to the fact that I was missing how close Sofia — Cindy — and I had gotten in Novosibirsk. It had turned out to be the perfect climax to our purloined-uranium job, just one more confirmation that this kind of work agreed with me. But I was wrestling with a tangle of mixed feelings. I also realized that my desire to see Katerina again was growing. I wondered if I should tell Cindy about Katerina and my crazy notion to go see her after we finished this operation. Knowing Cindy, I didn't think it would faze her. I also wondered if Yuri or Toshek had told Cindy about my strange meeting on the train with Katerina and Zhenia. And if I should reconnect with them, what if anything should I tell them about Cindy? And on top of all that, the most crucial dilemma of all: should I turn my back on all these temptations, be a responsible husband and father, get my silly ego under control, and go back home? Renata loved getting little gifts that are connected to her work. She'll light up, I was sure, when she saw and understood that I made an effort, that I thought of her.

Like an uncontrollable anxiety attack, my mind shifted again: Oh. My delight when Katerina and Zhenia shared that champagne breakfast in the first-class compartment. And again: No finer moment these past few days than Cindy under the bubbles. *Which of these?* was ringing in my head. I was increasingly overwhelmed. These clashing waves of sentimentality were coming at a time when I should have been more focused on the danger, everyone seemed convinced we were exposing ourselves to. Maybe my domestic, or romantic, or horny impulses were just my oddball reaction to the danger.

More than once in Moscow, Kiev and elsewhere I had felt myself cornered in situations I had gotten out of only by the skin of my teeth. But this felt different. Entering a place where the rules had been made up by someone else, where the law was whatever a mafia boss said it was, felt scary. Very scary. Walking — or running — away from a meeting gone bad in a downtown hotel is a lot different from driving thirty miles through three hostile check-points into the mafia-controlled boondocks.

There would be no escape routes except for returning on the road we came in on; no way out except the vehicles we were driving. It became obvious why Cindy was hypersensitive about us getting separated while in this vast 'mafia preserve.'

As we started down an unpaved side road, I ventured to ask Yuri about his intended approach with our hosts for the next couple of days. "Do you have any special strategy or technique for dealing with these guys? We'll be completely surrounded in their territory. How will you keep control of the situation?"

"Money," he answered without hesitation. "People need a little money to open their door. Then the promise of more money keeps that door open. Every request we make and every desire we—or they—have should involve the exchange of money. If not now, then the clear promise of money. Some people will not move one centimeter for us without a cash payment. That cash should be with us all the time." I took solace in the wads of dollars I had in my pockets and in the toolkit. Not quite as comforting as a gun might feel right now, but the thought bucked me up and made me feel better — for the moment. Yuri continued, "Other people are interested in making a business. We are here to 'purchase' some equipment that fell out of the sky. We need a price. We need terms and conditions. If we cannot pay cash, then we need to convince someone that we are good for a bank transfer." Yuri said all this as matter-of-factly as if he was lecturing in an NSU classroom. Yet we actually were winding our way down an increasingly narrow, muddy road, leaving the highway far behind us.

"And if we suggest a bank transfer, are we good for it?"

"We've done it before," Yuri answered. "I am hoping there is someone in this group we have already dealt with so there is some trust."

"What can I do to help guarantee we succeed?" I asked

"We want you to be the untouchable. Making them believe there is big money for them. Joe says you work for big American companies sometimes; you know philosophy of big money. You must act like there is money behind you; not in your pockets. If we get the Soyuz devices that we came for, then our ticket out of here will be cash, if we have enough. If cash isn't enough, then the answer is a transfer payment for them, and money in the future. All this must seem guaranteed."

I pondered his money strategy but had to ask, "Two questions: What does 'untouchable' mean? And why do we promise money in the future? Why can't we pay for the devices and get the hell out? It seems like making promises for the future puts us at risk."

"Harming you or kidnapping you needs to be understood as blocking money and not a way to getting money," he explained. "So you are untouchable. Answer to second question: Everyone wants to be part of big money. If we pay and try to leave, we'll never make it out, because someone, somewhere, was not paid. Gatekeepers will open the gate as we leave if they see us as a future flow of money for them, too." As he spoke, Yuri was fighting the stiff steering wheel to keep the 69 on the steadily narrowing, slippery track.

"And my last question: How does Vlad help you with this strategy?" I asked.

"Vlad takes care of paying the people that need cash immediately. These are the guys with the guns. But these guys are also always threatened and sometimes cheated by the big bosses." Yuri paused every few seconds; he was having a hard time keeping our Jeep on the wet road. "Vlad is scary," he continued, "but he also has big pockets filled with cash. Also, Vlad tries to watch for someone who might go crazy or loses control from alcohol. He is something like rich bodyguard."

***

After our encounter with the mafia squad, Yuri pulled up to the camp site, assessing how it was best to configure our vehicles in that muddy clearing. He left enough room for the 66 so the entry door to its cage was facing the bushes. My memories from that night are not so clear but I remember thinking that the bushes that formed our latrine were quite dense and afforded a great hiding place for someone. I think Yuri saw them more as excellent cover for us instead of effective hiding places for others. He stood in the lights of the 66 as Vlad pulled up and with hand signals directed him how he wanted to position the truck. Vlad hesitated, but did as Yuri showed him. As he was maneuvering the big truck, Toshek and Cindy jumped out of the cab and looked around to see if any of the welcoming committee had followed us here. We could hear voices in the distance but nothing that suggested we were being watched. At least not very closely.

Despite its low volume, Cindy's voice sounded almost frantic. To me and Toshek, she said, "Get as many lights lit as possible so I can see everything within one hundred meters of us!"

Toshek responded calmly, "Not a good idea. Our eyes will adjust soon. Let's keep light at low level. Set up your parabolic mics, let's have some tea, get this place organized, and you, Cindy, stay close. Maybe you go into the cage and hand things down to us."

Cindy agreed and climbed up into the cage, where most of our gear was. Between handing down cots and other supplies, I could see her putting on her earphones and testing her microphones. I noticed she was bringing down a heavier case that looked like it might hold optical equipment. On a hunch, I walked around and stepped up into the cage.

"Hey, Cindy, are those night vision goggles?"

In Russian she answered, "You're fucking right they are! And if I don't catch these assholes sneaking up on me, I'll shove them up one of those fuckers' ass!"

It's safe to say I was not the only one spooked on our first night at the Lakes.

Best Laid Plans

Even though Yuri had made sure his gun would be seen between us on the 69's seat as we arrived, he did not want us visibly carrying weapons, either in the camp or at the debris site. So that first night, when we all finally figured out where we were sleeping, some of us tucked pistols under our pillow or under the covers. Some did both. I, of course, had nothing until I grudgingly agreed to take a nine-millimeter automatic that Yuri nearly forced on me. He also confided to me that he felt he and his guys were already carrying too much responsibility for me.

Grabbing a handful of my jacket sleeve, Yuri pulled me out into the bushes behind the 66. He pressed the gun into my hand. In a low voice, thoughtfully keeping the rest of the team from hearing his lecture, he asked. "Can you shoot gun? I mean, did you do it before? Maybe you go hunting with your father sometime. Americans are famous for their guns. So, what about you?"

"Yuri, first of all, I feel like shit if you feel I am dead weight on the team."

"What is dead weight?"

"Useless," I responded.

"You are not useless. I am making you *more* useful. Be glad, OK? You are physical fit person. Toshek is grateful for it. Now we need you like you were back in Novosibirsk."

"OK. I am glad. What next?" Yuri made me feel better already. He was oozing an intensity I hadn't seen in him before.

He pulled two ammo clips from his pocket. "Load your weapon, *pizhalsta.*"

I surprised him by snapping the clip in and locking it in place in about half a second.

He smiled. "Your father liked guns?"

"No," I told him. "My crazy brother had an arsenal. I watched him playing with his guns. Cleaning them. Loading and unloading."

"So why you not wanted earlier to carry gun?" His expression suggested he thought something was out of whack.

"I just don't like them. I'd hoped I wouldn't have to carry one. But believe me, Yuri, I've changed my mind," I admitted.

"And what about shooting? You know to squeeze slowly and not jerk trigger?" He pointed to my safety and suggested I switch it to 'ON.'

"I am a good shot, Yuri," I said, feeling confident about that, at least.

"Good shot means you know how to point and hit target?" he sounded a little confused about my English.

"I know I can't show you now but you should trust me. I'm better with a twelve-gauge shotgun shooting ducks. We used to shoot out in the hills of eastern Washington and along the Columbia River."

"OK," Yuri said. "I am feeling better now, Andy. Sorry I said something about being too responsible for you. Maybe now you see how serious our situation is."

"Clearly we're deep in enemy territory," I said, "behind the enemy lines."

"Sounds like movie I saw with John Wayne, I think." Yuri laughed at his joke.

Looking at Yuri, I remembered that he had understood that line from the movie *Gallipoli* when we were on the train. I kept discovering things about him. Aside from doing contract work for the CIA, I bet he was a big movie fan. We returned to the 66 and 69 to continue setting up.

Cindy had her mics pointed in the general direction of where we thought the mafia camp and headquarters were located. While we couldn't see a lot, it was amazing what those mics could bring in. Cindy reported, "I don't know what they look like, but I can hear two guys talking about who will be doing whom later on."

Several hundred meters away, we could see, a large campfire was burning. With infrared scopes, we could see a small bacchanalia was under way there. Standing on top of the truck's cage, Cindy reported that primitive barracks and tents were set up around a larger structure, some kind of shop or possibly a trailer. And as she put it, "There is enough room for twenty or thirty normal people to sleep in those spaces. A hundred or so psychotic assholes could also be there. I feel like I am at a camp run by Jim Jones."

Cindy slept up in the cage. I was on a cot in our kitchen tent, which one would have had to walk through to get to Cindy. The last thing she needed tonight, after how the mafia assholes had reacted to her presence, was to feel responsible for anyone else's safety. I, on the other hand, was feeling great satisfaction that I was the one positioned to protect her, now armed and ready. Toshek slept in the spacious cab of the 66 and Yuri made a comfortable place for himself in the back of the 69. Vlad was nowhere to be seen but I had noticed him earlier folding blankets to make himself a bed. He was probably within earshot of all of us and we just didn't know it.

Before we turned out our lights, I had asked Cindy if the wild dogs I could hear howling were Eurasian coyotes or some other relative of wolves. She told me it was the European or golden jackal. They sounded amazingly like the coyotes I'd grown up hearing at night in eastern Washington. When I went hunting as a young man, I'd never allowed myself to be affected by the thought of killing an animal. This was the first time I had to think about different situations where I might have to pull the trigger — and possibly kill a human. I was sorry not to be able to talk to my partners about it.

By the time we were starting to doze off, the jackals had quieted down. It was only my imagination and fear of the human threat around us that made my sleep so fitful. I thought about Sofia — struggling to remember it had to be Cindy — and nearly gave in to the urge to go up and say good night to her. But I remembered my warning from Yuri. Anyway, I reminded myself, if I'd done so, I'd probably have been killed by friendly fire. Surrounded by two-legged jackals as we were, everyone was on edge and expecting uninvited visitors. Ever since having to get Toshek out of his bind with Anatoly, I could tell I was on the rise to be an equal with my partners. Carrying a weapon now made it pretty much official.

Twice during that eerily still night, I got up and peed. It crossed my mind that I needed to be careful that I didn't pee on Vlad. I didn't want to lose whatever good favor I had gained during the day by giving him the golden shower in a half-conscious state. I also had this weird moment of indecision thinking about carrying my gun when I crept out in the dark. If I dropped it while doing my business or if it slipped out of my pocket, that would be an embarrassment. A variation on that rhyme from *Full Metal Jacket* came to my head as I decided to carry it in the breast pocket of my jacket: "This is my pistol, this is my gun; one is for fighting, one is for fun." I wondered if Yuri the movie fan knew that one. I could hear the jackals howling again, almost like crazed laughter, as I crept back to my cot.

***

The light of day came none too early. We all wanted to see where we were and understand better where we were in relation to the other camp and the nearby debris site. Just as Cindy had gotten up on the cab of the 66 and pointed her night vision goggles toward the mafia camp, I jumped up in the same position and tried to get my bearings for where things were in relation to our camp. I couldn't see much, actually. It was a foggy morning and the mist was hugging the ground around us.

The gun fit snugly in my breast pocket when I buttoned it, confident that it couldn't fall out. That became its resting spot. I practiced several times reaching up with my right hand, unsnapping the button, and pulling out the gun. If Yuri had witnessed me practicing, it was my bet he would have joked about Robert DeNiro in *Taxi Driver*. "You talkin' to me?"

If anyone had indulged in anything alcoholic the night before, they had drunk alone. Vlad wandered in and out of camp, making tea and grabbing his own breakfast of canned fish. The only discussion with him was his brief reports of seeing a lot of activity over at the mafia headquarters.

Despite everyone's jittery nerves, the atmosphere in our camp that morning was surprisingly upbeat. Yuri even seemed optimistic, deciding to make some 'cowboy coffee' in hopes the aroma would entice the mafia scouts to report, as he put it, that "The American camp is drinking their cowboy coffee as we expected." Toshek and Yuri were surprisingly good cooks. They coordinated their tasks in whipping together a big sausage and scrambled egg breakfast. It included bread and butter and, if the eggs weren't enough, we had about a hundred cans of sardines and ten kilos of white farmer's cheese. All that could be used to make a tasty fish paste for open-face sandwiches.

Cindy, the last one to get up, was happy to have a good breakfast, but she was all business that morning. She was dressed in fatigues, a matching jacket that might have been a little large for her, and brown boots. June weather in this part of Siberia was usually a little warmer than what we were experiencing but it hadn't frozen during the night. The days, normally approaching sixty-five degrees during this time, hadn't gotten to sixty. I still had the climbing boots from my days hiking through the Cascades and considered myself well dressed for the wilds we were in. Except I didn't have a cowboy hat. That deficiency might have cast doubt in our hosts' minds that I was a real American businessman.

It seems impossible to us now, but at that time many Russians and Poles held the iconic image of the fictional oilman J.R. Ewing in *Dallas* as the consummate U.S. businessman. Because I had been in Europe almost ten years by this time, I had never even watched the damn show. That forced me to always lie and say, "Of course I'm a *Dallas* fan! J.R. and I are cut from the same cloth!"

While Toshek was cleaning the pots and pans from breakfast, we huddled in our makeshift kitchen tent for a quick meeting. We decided that anywhere we went this morning, Toshek would stay behind to watch our camp. We guessed that we'd soon be invited some place to discuss the next steps. Glaringly obvious this whole time, but a subject untouched till now, was how the money part of the deal would be handled. I knew I was the American 'investor' in the mix but I wanted to understand my role better. How did Yuri want me to behave? Were there details as yet unspoken?

I asked Yuri, "How much have these guys already received from us?"

"Almost three thousand dollars," he said.

I hesitated before asking, "How much cash do we have here?"

"Not including what you got from Joe, about a hundred thousand."

Surprised by the amount, I facetiously asked, "Is that going to be enough?" More seriously, I added, "It seems like a lot of fucking money for these guys sitting here in the mud." Too late, it occurred to me that the certain amount of disgust in my voice might have been taken badly by Toshek. He was, after all, one of those down-in-the-dirt traders.

"It might be," Yuri answered. "I don't know. These guys start their bidding at ten million and sometimes take ten thousand for worthless shit. I really can't tell you if it's enough." His voice revealed his frustration. He shrugged.

"You mentioned, Yuri, when we were driving that we can do wire transfers. Can we do a letter of credit based on receipt of goods or something that protects us?" I suggested trying to introduce standard business practices for risky deals. "Let's scare 'em and walk out of the negotiation, just to play the role they probably expect," I added, unsure if this fit Yuri's idea of doing business with bandits. "If they start making all sorts of claims about authenticity, we just say, 'Prove it!' and let them run with the ball."

Yuri was listening and taking notes. "We can suggest such things," he said, "but we shouldn't demand. Instead, if we are in a situation where we need to wire money, we take possession of whatever we can, and we signal to our bank to make the transfer. Having said that, it is possible that we won't be allowed out of the compound until someone confirms the funds have transferred and are in an account. That is one scenario." Yuri's scenario was exactly how I had done a deal on the Lithuanian border two years earlier. But in this case, away from any communication channels, we weren't sure how we would get in touch with our 'bank.' That was one of the most important things to find out as soon as we could. As we wrapped up the meeting, I asked Cindy if her Magic Message Machine worked out here. She shook her head and pouted. We were on our own. It felt strange to have no contact with Joe or Joe's people.

A few minutes later, Vlad stuck his head inside the tent. In Russian, he said, "Attention! We have the next welcoming committee coming. Two Lada Nivas with just drivers. No passengers. Probably coming to pick us up. I think."

Yuri thought about it for a couple of seconds, then told us to collect all of our bags that held documents and leave the most important mission-related items locked up in the cage on the 66. He had also suddenly decided that Toshek should *not* be left behind. Toshek's grin lit up at that news. I spoke louder than everyone as they were all talking, forcing resolution of the issue on my mind, "Are we taking our weapons or not?" I looked straight at Yuri.

"Only Vlad takes his weapons," Yuri answered without hesitation.

"Weapons?" I had to grin at this.

That got no response from Yuri but the emergence of the usual lop-sided shit-eating grin from Toshek, who was on the verge of a chuckle. We all hustled to gather our things, stowing our 'heat' in camp. I grabbed the key from the glove compartment in the 66, climbed up the side of the truck, and stashed my 9-millimeter in the cage along with most of our other gear.

We were ready by the time one of the two drivers stepped out of his car, speaking into a walkie-talkie. He was an impressive specimen, at least two meters tall, about six feet seven. His features reminded me of a cross between George H.W. Bush and the famous mountaineer Jim Whittaker, the first American to climb Mount Everest. He was almost jovial in the way he reported back to someone at his headquarters. "We have arrived to pick our guests up. They are busy preparing for their important day. The smell of American coffee and breakfast is still thick in the air! They all look to be in fine spirits, and we'll have them delivered to the office shortly. Over, Boss!"

His mid-length military khaki jacket with half a dozen pockets or more made it impossible to judge if our host and escort was carrying a weapon. His pleasant facial gestures and open-arm greetings were reminiscent of a politician receiving applause from a crowd. That's how this American reacted to his appearance, anyway. Vlad turned and gave Yuri a nasty scowl, hidden from our escort. I was interested to see how different his reaction was from my own; I interpreted it as, 'This guy is sleazy.'

I told Yuri, "Betcha they play a good guy, bad guy game. We just met the good guy."

"*Pravda!*" Yuri shook his head and a small grin appeared.

Our escort turned his attention to us as he switched off the walkie-talkie. "Good day, ladies and gentlemen!" He gave Cindy a small bow of the head. "Michael and the others are waiting for us. Our two little Russian Jeeps should be sufficient to take you over — unless you have something large you need to bring for our discussions. Your group is five people?"

Yuri and I began to step forward. I motioned to Yuri for him to wait. I mustered up my best accent. "*Dobryy dien! Mnya zovut* Andrew," I greeted him, introducing myself. All four of my teammates watched in silence as I concluded my remarks in Russian: "I am sorry, I don't speak Russian so well. It's true, there are five in our group." Expressionless until I finished, Sofia winked at me so everyone could see — except our host. I then turned things over to Yuri. "My associate will do most of the talking."

Yuri nodded his head and rubbed his chin. Under his breath, he told me, "Good move, friend." Then he addressed our host.

"Very good," Yuri said. "Michael is the one I have been talking to

277

for the past ten days, I hope."

"And you are also correct, Mr. Yuri," the tall man replied. "Michael is looking forward to meeting you all."

"Mr. Gold and I will go with you. Cindy, Vlad, and Toshek will ride with your colleague," Yuri instructed.

I joined them in Russian, "I agree with you, Yuri," reinforcing the fiction that I was in charge, Yuri merely our spokesman. I then reminded our host that he hadn't introduced himself.

"Very good! My name is Leo. More introductions when we get to the meeting. We gave you a little extra time this morning since you came in so late last night. We are behind schedule so hopefully we can get a lot done this morning and come to some agreements. I am sure you are hoping to see the crash site here as soon as possible. The security team at the site is expecting you sometime later this morning. They are there twenty-four hours a day, allowing no access for anyone without Michael's approval."

Out of Leo's earshot, Cindy joked to me, "Glad we know that now. Guess we won't be going there to walk our dogs."

I don't know why I said it, but I responded, "Or to steal a kiss."

Cindy's facial expression, to my eye anyway, meant, 'Oh, well.'

"What's up with all the English names? Michael and Leo, for example," I asked Yuri as we turned to gather our things.

"Being Russian doesn't always work in your favor when negotiating international deals," Yuri responded. "Committing bank fraud and carrying out other criminal acts. All the correspondence I have from Michael uses English spelling instead of Mikhail."

That made sense to me. It was just like Sofia wanting to be Cindy and me being Mr. Gold, the important American businessman whose part I was playing during this transaction. I had gotten my cue; the curtain was rising. *It's showtime!*

Negotiations

Splitting up as Yuri had ordered, we rode four hundred meters on a muddy gravel road to the trailer Cindy had seen through her night vision binoculars last night. Leonid — Leo — remarked that he had expected a larger group. Turning to me, he said, "I hope our American friend is enjoying the beauty of the Siberian steppes. It is this part of central Russia that I love the most, with the lakes and the small woods that dot the landscape. Farther south and the trees mostly end. It is here that we have a special kind of beauty. Someone told me that it is a little like West Texas here, but a lot colder in the winter."

I was tempted to comment that the lawlessness of West Texas in the 1880s also resembled this part of Siberia. But I kept my mouth shut and nodded in agreement.

The Nivas parked side by side, very close to the trailer, but we still had to wade through mud to the sloppily placed cinderblocks that formed a little porch. Apologizing for the "muddy mess," Leo led us into a room with a long table lined with decent looking brown office swivel chairs. At one end of the long room, a large but quite pretty woman about forty years old was making tea and placing packaged cookies onto a platter. I noticed she was nearly as muddy as we were, with a ring of dried mud around the bottom of her skirt.

At Leo's suggestion, we took seats facing the door. Yuri continued to show signs he was feeling good about elevating my status during the meeting. I whispered to him, "Your word is *gold* but I will do some talking, OK?" He laughed at my pun. I was positioning myself in the center of our group when we heard loud footsteps. Our hosts were to take the seats nearest the door. The unsettling thing about their approach was that their stomping was so loud but none of them spoke a word. Leo had been quite talkative, but now fell silent.

Four men in unremarkable suits entered the room and we all stood. My reflex to shake hands kicked in and I reached across the table. Only Michael reached back. I assumed it was Michael, since he had taken the seat at the head of the table. "Andy," I said.

"I am Michael," he confirmed. In that unexpected moment of being the first to introduce myself, I quickly pointed to my colleagues and said their first names. I enjoyed taking charge, even if just for the moment and just for appearances. If anyone owned this mission, I did. Amazingly, I congratulated myself, it had all begun from my insight and initiative way back in Antek's fax room. And now here we were!

Michael's response, pointing to his entourage, was simply, "These are my colleagues." He made no introductions.

For close to half a minute, Michael said nothing, looking at some papers and arranging them in front of him.

My assessment of that moment was that he did not know whether I would be the voice of our group or if Yuri would carry the conversation.

I resolved that by speaking up. "Michael, my Russian isn't what it should be, but I understand a lot. Yuri knows what I want and will speak for me. We'll break and translate when it's necessary."

A nod and a tight little smile suggested that Michael was relieved to have a Russian on our side of the table. Michael made eye contact with me on every point. He began with general questions about our arrival, asked if we had enough provisions to be self-sufficient, and how long we intended to stay. He suggested that his people might be able to provide us a few things but added, "Everyone is very busy so we can't really promise anything."

I reacted to his offers with a smile, thanked him, and said we understood: "*Spasibo. My ponimayem.*" I nodded to Yuri to speak. Our hand-offs and role-playing were going well.

"We will be fine in our little camp for the short time we plan to be here," Yuri said, "and with your good will and cooperation, we will all be happy businessmen."

Without further pleasantries, Michael dived right into the logistics of the third stage rocket on the trailer. "As I promised on the phone, we have your first choice Soyuz remains on a trailer. It is about forty kilometers from here at another guarded location. We are willing to release the entire trailer to you if you have a standard tractor that can pull it. We can also pull it someplace for you, but it must be covered and disguised. We want you to offer a reasonable sum for the whole trailer load."

Yuri gave me a quick glance as he responded. "Michael, it is interesting you decided to jump to the big prize first. Andy expected us to pay cash for items we retrieve here at this site and then start negotiations on the big prize." He looked at me again with the question, *"Ponimayesh'?"* Did I understand?

I nodded gravely, playing my part.

Michael's focus was indeed clearly on the topic of that 'big prize,' the third stage and trailer. "You can still pay cash for whatever you want from this site. That will make us very happy and it will pay our operating costs. But it is not worth our time for you to come here and bother us for a scrap or two of titanium. You can be sure that Mr. Andy did not come here for a bolt or a screw. Please accept our offer to travel to the priority site and examine it for yourself. If you like what you see, you will make an attractive offer, we will exchange goods for payment, and our deal is done. Very simple."

Yuri turned to me and whispered in my ear, "Act like you are giving me permission to say what I am going to say."

I gave him a solemn nod, hoping that would suffice for permission.

"Michael, it is definitely something for Mr. Gold to think about," Yuri said. "I suggest that you let me translate this more fully to him and we can reconvene in ten minutes." Yuri whispered, "I'm sure you understood. Show him that you do." I gave Michael and his henchmen another of the solemn nods I was getting so good at. Yuri spoke up, "Can we be alone for a short while?"

"Of course." Our hosts stood, bowed silently, and stomped out.

Yuri waited for them to close the door behind them. When we were alone, he started by hoping we could quickly agree on a strategy. "So, I think you understood most everything. He is pressuring us to make an offer on his trailer load — as a whole. This site was his cash cow but I think it is not so profitable now. Already he knows we want the third stage. This is what I propose. Vlad and I go to the trailer site with your instruction papers from Joe and confirm it is really what Joe wants. You stay here with Toshek and Cindy to see if the device below the second stage attachment ring is still there and can be removed. We should all be safe. Michael is going to be very surprised for such a quick deal and will likely accept a number less than one hundred thousand. We will make a follow-up deal on the rest of the material. And then we get our asses out of Dodge."

I liked it that Yuri knew the expression 'getting out of Dodge.' What movie had that come from? But I didn't love the idea of both Yuri and Vlad leaving us. It did seem fairly safe to remain with Toshek, to be with our things and close to our vehicles, but it wasn't what we had agreed upon earlier. And even though I knew that Cindy could take care of herself in most situations — probably better than I could — I was tempted to suggest that for her own safety Cindy go with Yuri and Vlad. I was almost ready to say it — but I didn't. Even in my refreshed role on the team, pretending to be the brains of the operation, I wasn't about to take charge of any tactical matters. This newly commissioned second lieutenant would still defer to my grizzled old sergeant when it came to making battlefield decisions.

***

After our central Siberian mafia hosts returned for another thirty minutes of relatively easy discussion, we came to an agreement. Yuri looked at me and said in English, "May I summarize our understanding of the agreement, so far?"

"Yes, of course, please do," I said — with my special nod.

Yuri began, "So, number one: It is agreed that three of us will stay and inspect the nearby site *and* if we identify what we want, you will price that part. And, if we agree to the price, you will remove it or help us remove it and take to our camp. Number two: At the same time, two of us will go with you to the trailer site and inspect it. You are expecting an offer for the whole trailer. Your price is five hundred thousand dollars. There is some room for reasonable negotiation. Is this what you understand from our discussions?"

Eye contact with Cindy told me she was not entirely happy with the agreement, but it was what we had come up with. We were going to live with it.

"Yes. We can start when you are ready," Michael said.

"Good." Yuri nodded, then changed the subject after nodding to me and raising his eyebrows, as if waiting for my permission to go on. "One last thing. One of your colleagues here is involved in a large military surplus supply business near Chelyabinsk."

A quiet man sitting directly across from me woke up when Yuri mentioned him.

"I helped a different American buy a lot of things there," Yuri continued. "We paid some cash and the rest by bank transfer. So, if we make an offer and pay some by wire transfer, you know you can trust us that we are good for it."

"It is not preferred," Michael said, "but I will talk to Oleg about his experience with you. Then we will discuss it. Possibly." As he spoke, Michael was staring at Oleg, who looked a little embarrassed by his unexpected rise to stardom at the table.

Michael turned back to logistical arrangements. "We will prepare a larger vehicle for our trip to the trailer site. I will call the security team at our local debris site and tell them to expect three potential buyers for inspection. In one hour. Do not give any money to the security teams. They are paid only by me.

"Another thing you must know, though. It is not healthy to be at the site here for too long. Ten minutes is maximum exposure. Then you should take a break," Michael warned us. "The security team will show you the safe zones and the danger zones."

"Fuel that came down with the rocket?" Yuri asked

"Yes."

Cindy rolled her eyes. Suddenly clapping her hand over her mouth, she whispered, "I knew I forgot something. The respirators."

***

Back at our camp, we had our final meeting, again in the kitchen tent. The agenda was our panic procedures. Yuri thought we were sitting in a good position with very little chance of things going south. It was what I wanted to hear. I felt good about his tight hold on these decisions. He told us that the presence of the other mafia bosses, especially Oleg, encouraged him. They represented a kind of conglomerate, he believed. The pressure for a *numer stulecia* with the rocket debris was a lot less since each of them had at least one business elsewhere that was doing quite well.

"You three stay within sight of each other," Yuri advised us. That seemed like good advice; I have two tough colleagues at my back, and we two men would be watching Cindy. "Who knows how Michael is treating his security team? You heard his instructions not to pay them anything. It means there may be a problem. If they are marginalized from the others, they could try to do something on their own. That's when it gets dangerous. We should be back by four or five in the afternoon. Tonight, we'll figure out where we are and what we do next." With that, the meeting broke up. While I'd initially thought it was best for Cindy to go with Yuri and Vlad, I was happy to personally be a part of assuring her safety. My sentiments and smitten state were still smoldering even as I felt my responsible family impulses firing.

The driver arrived in an UAZ, yet another type of ex-Soviet military Jeep, to pick up Yuri and Vlad. If all went well, they would be back from their trip to investigate and confirm the stage three debris in two or three hours. Then we would be ready to offer Michael a sum of cash sufficient to cover our retrieval of all the devices we could get our hands on and get us out of the 'mafia preserve.' For me, that safe departure alone would represent a very successful end to our mission.

Cindy, Toshek, and I viewed our stage two investigations today as insurance against the possibility that we were being scammed with debris that was not actually from the stage three site. If we found only the 'lower priority' housing and electronics today, we'd still be able to honestly say we had accomplished our mission.

Within half an hour after Yuri and Vlad's departure in the UAZ, Toshek, Cindy, and I were ready for our tour to inspect the local stage two debris. One of the Nivas we had ridden in returned. We had a simple plan for the visit. First, if we were allowed, we would spend as much time as possible carefully inspecting the debris. Next, we would discuss and decide as a group what might be our best retrieval strategy. And, as Yuri had emphasized so often, we had all agreed that we would not separate during the visit.

We piled into the car with my toolkit. Cindy carried her own tools in a small bag. If Toshek was carrying any weapon, it had to have been hidden in his coat. I had left my nine-millimeter in the cage of the 66, confident that the chance of anything happening was low. The meeting had gone off well. Yuri's assurances about the deal looking good made carrying a gun seem provocative. Among other goodies, my kit did hold the dagger-like knife I had been given at the embassy. My instructions on how to sever arteries or otherwise incapacitate an assailant were still fresh on my mind. Not-Q had issued the knife to me with explicit instructions to keep it with me. If I had really known how to use it, I might have thought of it as a weapon, as well.

Monitors

I was lying on my left side when I woke up. With the pain in my head, I didn't notice at first that my left hand wasn't moving out of the mud it was lying in when I tried to roll over and sit up. I attempted to make a fist and lift my hand again. That hurt like hell. I could tell there was something wrong, but my headache was hurting me even more. Then I understood why I couldn't move. I got a close-up look at a smooth, thin metal rod. I recognized it; I'd first seen it just a short time before. Just how long ago I couldn't really tell in the state I was in. It was now skewering my left palm, stuck deep into the mud, and keeping my hand pinned to the ground.

I stayed on my side for a moment. I was lying on a wooden pallet, out in the middle of an open field. I thought about what I was seeing. The hand wasn't hurting too badly but it looked gruesome. There was too much dark mud to notice the blood — which was good. I looked down and could see the strap of my toolkit was still on my shoulder. I hoped my only remaining weapon, the knife, was still inside. Tugging on the strap brought the toolkit up and over my shoulder blade. It seemed a little heavier than I remembered. Fortunately, it landed in the mud right in front of my face. I reached in with my right hand and, instead of grabbing the CIA dagger, I pulled out the old Army issue knife Toshek had received from the mayor at Nowy Wies. Staring at me was, "J.B. LONGAKER — U.S. ARMY". At first, I thought, "*I wanted the fucking scalpel for ripping out people's guts!*" but then realized the goddamn blade might break in the thick mud. The Army knife was clearly the tool of choice to try to un-impale myself from the rod, anchored deep in the ground. I also knew that eventually I was going to have to slide my hand off that long piece of metal but I wanted to do it standing up with some amount of control. And not until after wiping off the mud and shit.

My head was still hurting but the focus on my hand problem seemed to temper that pain. I began to feel very thirsty as I started digging around under my hand, hoping to loosen the rod from the mud. My mouth, I realized, was filled with dirt. I couldn't produce any saliva to spit it out. The gagging began again.

Under my hand, though, the mud was easily coming out. Soon I had cleared about six inches of space. At that point, I dropped the knife and tried gently flexing the rod back and forth to loosen it. I eased myself into a halfway seated position so I could pull with my good right hand. Finally, I felt it coming up. The rod slid out of the black mud more easily than I had hoped.

I sat on the edge of the pallet, breathing hard, steadying the rod with my right hand. My left hand was impaled exactly midway between the ends. I would have to pass two feet of metal through my wounded palm, and do it quickly. Even the slightest movement was starting to hurt like hell; I couldn't imagine what a long, slow removal process would feel like. Gripping the rod with my knees, I found a puddle and used my free hand to splash some relatively clear water onto the muddy metal. I wanted the surface to be as clean as possible as I slid it out of my hand.

Satisfied that the metal rod was shiny and almost clean, I got up on my knees. With my right hand, I grabbed the rod. I braced myself for the pain that was sure to come. The rod was horizontal. As best I could, I jerked it as hard as I could to the right while moving my impaled palm to the left. I cringed as I felt the metal sliding against the bones. In one movement I was free. 'I didn't even scream,' I silently congratulated myself. I was still on my knees, trembling from the ordeal, as fresh blood started to ooze out of the hole in my left hand. With the right, I flung the rod far away, back into the mud. I returned the knife to my bag and snapped it shut.

Adrenaline helped give me the energy to stand up. But as soon as I did, I would get sick and lose my vision. I reached up to feel my head and could tell that it was swelling along a line that ran up and back from my right temple. My left hand, thankfully, had gone numb so I had to rely more on my right. Sitting back down on the pallet, holding my aching head and hoping the nausea, vertigo and blackouts would go away, I tried to focus on my surroundings. First objective: see if I could spot Toshek anywhere. I couldn't hear anything over the buzzing in my ears. The one time I tried to yell, it nearly caused me to faint again from the pain in my head. At some point I was able to stand and remain upright. I set myself, to the best of my recollection, on a course back to our camp. Before staggering off, I checked to see I wasn't leaving anything behind that might have fallen from my toolkit and made sure it was safely clipped into my belt and around my shoulder.

***

After we'd left our camp early that afternoon, it had only taken us about five minutes to get to where we could see the main hulk of the debris. We had been going slower than one could walk, so I knew it was much closer to our camp than we had realized earlier. As far as appearances go, from where we were it just looked like a huge darkened pipe, as big as a bus, lying on the ground. Slow going on the muddy road, the driver swerving to avoid the deepest puddles, exaggerated the distance. At one point we skirted around a deep gully. The driver told us it was a crater from where twenty tons of Soyuz rocket first hit the Earth and bounced after a twenty-mile free-fall through the atmosphere. Pointing past the main body of the second stage, he said other pieces that had broken off or "came down with it" lay not far away. One thing we had all noticed as we got closer was the carcass of some large animal about a hundred meters from the main body of the debris. I wanted to ask our driver if the space junk had hit the animal, but before I was able to make my joke, I got my answer.

Toshek translated what the driver was advising us about. "Rocket fuel killed a lot of animals here. You'll see them as you walk around. We are suggesting that you do not spend too much time — maybe ten-minute intervals — at the debris site itself. We usually start to feel sick after that much time. It's probably still in the soil. Depending on the wind direction, get about fifty to seventy-five meters away for ten or fifteen minutes." Cindy and I nodded to each other, recalling that we had been informed about this, both in the docs from Joe and then directly from Michael.

The Soviets used extremely toxic Syntin, their name for 1-Methyl-1,2-dicyclopropylcyclopropane, as fuel for their Soyuz U2 class of rockets. I doubt that any Russian environmentalists were screaming about it during the Cold War.

"Well, that certainly will be a limiting factor on what we can get done today," I thought out loud. "Effectively, half our time will be spent detoxing."

Cindy was staring at the dead animals around the site.

The driver stopped about thirty meters away from the most visible debris. He said our "monitor" would be meeting us in a few minutes. "He is told to stay with you at all times to make sure you don't steal anything," he added, looking me straight in the eye.

I nearly stuck my tongue out at him but thought better. When Cindy heard him say this, she kicked me in disbelief. We needed to negotiate a protocol for this. That would've been a piece of cake after the way things had gone with Michael. Wasn't that the job I was best qualified for? We were laughing about it but, in fact, it was part and parcel of losing my label as 'dead weight.'

"If we find something we want," I asked, "what is the procedure for removing it?" Toshek translated my question to the driver.

The answer, also translated by Toshek, was, "Just tell the monitor and mark it on the diagram he has. You can negotiate a price with Michael."

It wasn't long before we observed three men come out of the nearest woods, walking directly towards the fallen fuselage. We were interested in the top or leading edge, where we hoped to find the attachment ring and the hypothesized target electronics package. If we were right, it would be just below the ring and attached to the inner wall, or maybe to the ring itself. We got out of the car and walked directly toward the rocket. I checked my watch: starting our first ten minutes. The three men followed us closely without speaking to us. They were, however, talking to each other about this or that "bastard" who had cheated them and about their schemes to "fuck him up" the next time they saw him. One of the men was carrying a thin metal rod, about four feet long. It looked like a car antenna but maybe twice as thick, and solid. Sometimes he would twirl it like a baton as he walked.

Cindy made no effort to hide the disgust on her face. In English, she whispered to me, "This is the asshole that noticed me in the 66 last night and said what he said about the Americans."

He was the youngest of the group and couldn't keep his eyes off Cindy as we examined the wrecked rocket.

All six of us, in two groups of three, huddled around the front of the second stage, a tube nine feet in diameter, big enough to walk into. I peered at its inside lip. There seemed to be several potential locations for small electronics to be tucked into the collar where the attachment ring for the third stage should fit. Standing inside, I tried to visualize the diagrams of the Soyuz U2-A stage that Joe had given me. I began to scrutinize the rivets, hoping to see an area where the fasteners looked more like screws. I did not have a torch but I knew Toshek and Yuri had a small one in the 66. We would get it if necessary, to cut out a piece. That was, of course, if our torch could cut the special high-performance alloys these rockets were made of.

It hadn't been obvious to me until now that our whirlwind tour of the Progress rocket factory in Samara had been useful. We'd seen these same components from our vantage point as Sergei had been leading us through production. While I was no rocket scientist, and the task at hand was minimally technical, I was the contractor who knew what to do at this moment. I was the one best prepared to do it. This was the 'come to Jesus' moment for this part of the mission, just as securing the uranium containers had successfully capped the Intourist action against Anatoly and Georg. Keeping Embassy Joe happy was my obsession and I realized this was the next critical moment for achieving that.

"I need a flashlight to check the line around the inside of the leading lip," I told Cindy.

She checked her watch. "We've already been here ten minutes. At most we've got five more minutes. How do you feel?"

"I feel fine." Everything was going according to plan. Better, even, than we'd expected. "The wind is blowing enough that I think the draft through the fuselage is giving us natural ventilation," I told her. "And you?"

"I feel nothing," she agreed. "Let's stay a while longer." With that, Cindy handed me a mini pocket flashlight. That let me see behind the inside lip of the opening where it was in shadow, about a foot off the ground. After about ten more minutes of going rivet by rivet, I saw no possible location for an electronics package. But in that time, I had covered only twenty percent of the whole ring. The part that loomed nine feet overhead represented a problem without a stepladder or something to stand on.

Cindy interrupted my discussion with myself as I was counting the rivets, giving each a negative grade. "Monitor Mike here is pointing to his watch, Andy, saying we need to leave."

Toshek heard this and nodded his agreement: time to begin moving away from the tainted soil. At about that time, the third monitor rejoined us and asked Toshek if he wanted to see the other parts of the debris site. Almost instinctively my head was shaking 'Hell, no' as the monitor suggested separating us. I was mildly shocked when Toshek agreed to this. He was probably thinking Cindy and I together would be fine. Or, because we had reached our ground contamination exposure limit, maybe he thought we'd all take a stroll outside the fuselage. In any case, I felt this was a decision requiring at least two votes in favor. I could have overruled his decision at this point. I didn't. I had a feeling he could take care of himself against the smallish monitor; he towered over the guy as they stood side by side. Toshek told Cindy, "I'm going to take a quick look at the other two debris sites very close to here. I'll be back in a few minutes." Cindy's only reaction was to nod. As Toshek headed off, I further rationalized my decision, observing Cindy absorbed in her work. Quite aside from how nicely she filled her military fatigues, they reminded me of how tough she was. *No one's going to mess with that bad ass*, I remember thinking.

While this is where my memory becomes very unclear, I'm sure I didn't understand the gravity of the situation and how exposed we were. I'm on my hands and knees scanning rivet by rivet of the metal ring in the forward fuselage with my back to my partner. She's not far away but being mirrored by a lecherous thug. Cindy and I were now alone inside the cavernous fuselage with just the two monitors. In the words of Not-Q, "Maintain the highest level of situational awareness in critical situations." Instead, I think I just kept looking at rivets. What I do have a clear memory of, though, was that the monitors' behavior changed immediately once Toshek left. Until now, their leader, who had been tracking Cindy's movements around the fuselage, inside and out, had kept his distance, at least two or three meters away. The next time I looked, he was within a few feet of her.

Alarm bells went off immediately. I sensed a problem. The man cleared his throat and began to address us both. He stuck uncomfortably close to Cindy. "If you find something you want to remove or take away today, paying me will be a lot less expensive than paying Michael. Depending on how big your souvenir is, we can make sure you leave the area safely. We will make sure Michael knows nothing about our little business."

Oh, shit! This wasn't the first fucker that Michael wasn't paying, I realized. *This guy's pissed he's being left out of the deal!* Yuri's 'Cash is our ticket out' mantra was coming true. And leaving the 9mm in the cage suddenly seemed a very unwise decision.

Cindy began to pull away from him, stepping around to my left where I could see her. I was on my fucking knees instead of my feet at the wrong time. I listened as the monitor elaborated on his offer, and watched as Cindy was doing her best to step away from him. A sour feeling of intense fear began to surface again. It should have been my signal to spring into action without delay. I waited too long.

"You won't be leaving this area without paying us, anyway," the monitor said, his tone decidedly more threatening now. "So wouldn't it be better if it was with your intended little treasure?"

I made two moves at the same time. I reached around for my toolkit, pulling it toward my side so I could get into it. The second move was to get onto my feet as quickly as possible. I was trying to push myself up when Cindy began defending herself against the asshole.

The monitor moved closer to Cindy again, lifting his hands as if expecting to go at it with her. Instead of yelling as a signal to Toshek, she surprised the fucker and shoved her open palm into the man's face. This started a fight. Nose already bleeding, he tried to grab her by the crotch. Then the brawl went full tilt. For me, that was the moment that the lights went out. The second monitor had seen me grab for my toolkit. He started yelling and kicked the left side of my head. Unbalanced by trying to stand up, I must have hit the fuselage along the ring. The skull fracture diagnosed later was on my right side, anyway. As I would learn later, Cindy put up quite a fight; it wasn't until the second monitor saw that I was out that they overpowered her. The number two guy stepped in to help monitor number one and together they manhandled Cindy to a guard shack some hundred meters away.

I don't know exactly how I got to where I woke up some minutes later. Most likely one or both of them had hauled me out of the fuselage. Whatever had happened, the front of me was covered in mud. My mouth was filled with it, too. I'd either been dragged face down to where I ended up — on that wooden pallet, which was about fifty meters from the shack

— or I had gotten up and made it to the pallet on my own, falling into the mud several times along the way. Maybe they had caught up and pinned my hand down to make sure I wouldn't get any farther. My head wasn't bleeding terribly but what had oozed out from my wounds on my scalp had dried in my eyes. Wiping the crusty blood from my eye socket with my right hand, I realized I couldn't see straight. I remember alternately gagging and vomiting, talking to myself and trying to figure out where I was and what had happened. In the distance I could see the second stage Soyuz booster rocket lying on its side in the mud. I remember being inside it when the stars came out.

Abort

Struggling to keep my balance as I staggered away from where I had been staked to the ground, I tentatively moved my head around, trying to find a position or angle that I could tolerate and would keep the world from spinning. As I stumbled on, memories flashed into my head of an accident I'd had in high school. I was upside down on a homemade gymnastics bar in my basement when it rolled out of its brackets. I fell upside down from about seven feet in the air, hitting the concrete with my head. The symptoms I was feeling at this moment were very similar to those I'd had fifteen years earlier. Unable to stand and terribly nauseated, I discovered that putting my head between my legs would bring back some semblance of balance. At a minimum, I would stop vomiting. That gymnastics mishap, so many years ago, was on my mind. I tried to remember what I had done during those first crisis moments as my father was trying to stand me up and get me into the car and off to the emergency room.

As I got moving across the middle of that muddy field, my plans were uncertain, but I *was* sure I didn't want to stay where I was. I saw absolutely no one as I zig-zagged down the sludgy black road, falling I don't know how many times. My feet kept slipping out from under me in water-filled ruts sometimes eight to ten inches deep. The worst of that walk back was when I slipped into the ravine the falling Soyuz booster had gouged. I slid four or five feet down its steep wall and landed submerged in muck. As I lost my footing, I drank some of the thick, muddy sludge and started to panic. I remember righting myself and standing in that gully, trying to figure out how I was going to climb out. All I remember is extending my arms out over the rim and digging my fingers into the muddy ruts, hoping I could haul myself out. Eventually, I'm not entirely sure how, I was out. My punctured hand only occasionally protested how badly I was abusing it.

Out of the ravine, I looked up every couple of seconds to see what was in front of me. Each time, the act of lifting my head brought on a fresh wave of nausea. That would start me dry heaving as I trudged along.

I remembered that somewhere ahead, I would soon come out into a large clearing. There I would be in distant sight of two critical landmarks. To my right would be the mafia headquarters. To the left, our camp. When I found that clearing, I kept to the left, hugging the scrub trees and bushes that rose ten to twelve feet high along its edge. I followed that perimeter, staying just a few steps inside the trees. The ground was drier there so walking was easier. Although I could use the skinny tree trunks to balance myself, their rough bark painfully scraped the gaping wound on my left hand, a constant reminder of my recent Russian piercing. Continuing my slow curve leftward, I was taken by surprise when the camp came into view. I was literally walking into our kitchen tent before I realized it.

Not being able to look up very well without causing the vertigo, I'd stumbled into the camp half blind. I was frantically trying to think what I should bring with me. Weeks ago, everyone at the embassy had been urging me to take as much money as possible. That would be useful in the event of a crisis that separated me from my protection. That moment had arrived, in a most disturbing way. Our mission's entire cache of cash was stored in a box that was nested in another box, wrapped in a bag, and stuffed under a seat in the cage on the 66 truck.

Getting into the cage was no small feat. Climbing up brought waves of nausea and the metal grab handles were made of iron rebar. The rough metal dug into my pierced hand. I unlocked the door with the key that had been hidden in the truck's cab and fell inside. I reached for the box under the seat and dug it out. My money was in a small bundle, separately wrapped, that I'd put my initials on. I tucked it into my toolkit. My five thousand dollars seemed like enough to take me to Bali and back. And, because I had casually tossed the gun into the box, I didn't see it. For whatever reason I can't explain other than my state of confusion and disarray, I didn't look for it. It was crossing the next few kilometers that seemed impossible now. Why it wasn't obvious that the gun might facilitate my escape had to be connected to my scrambled brains.

The events of the past hour had more than undone any sense of a plan or a goal. I was tempted to take the whole hundred grand that was earmarked for fallen rocket parts, but something told me to hold off. I decided that my own cash reserve should be enough — if somehow, I could get to Dubrovnoye. That name came from some memory I couldn't place.

Why Dubrovnoye? I struggled to remember why that place was important. *Fuck!* I remembered Yuri saying something about a shuttle bus. And a lake. *That's why!* I kept asking myself, *What then? Where does this fucking bus go? He told me. Yuri told me.* I sat with my head in my hands, struggling to bring back why Dubrovnoye was important. From the toolkit, I pulled out my map. My whole hand was shaking as I traced the roads out of Dubrovnoye to understand why it was important. Then it hit me in a flash. I saw the next town: Dalmatovo. *Katerina and Zhenia's place! Oh, motherfucker! Of course!* I recognized, of course, that my brains were fried. But they were able to focus on one thing: *That's where I'm going!* The place Yuri and I had talked about it on the road trip here. *Oh fuck, oh fuck, oh fuck.* I started crying. That made my head hurt even more. I stopped crying.

Rocking side to side, trying to get my mind off how much my head was hurting, I saw the Dubrovnoye to Dalmatovo shuttle finally crystallizing in my mind. *Of course. Yuri told me about it.* If, somehow, I could I get to Dubrovnoye. And if, somehow, I could catch the tourist shuttle to Dalmatovo. I have no idea how many times I tried to explain this to myself. *I am wasting time!* My muddled thoughts settled on Katerina. I had been a million miles from hope until I remembered that incredible coincidence: that her family estate was nearby. I remembered Jane's admonition: I should buy a pass good for all trains. Of course, I hadn't. I knew better; I'd decided that dollars were as good as a ticket. Memories began to come in a flood of emotion. Vlad's meltdown on the train. *Katerina! Dear sweet Katerina!* Rocking all night in her compartment. Her house, the refurbishment. *It will be safe. Go there!* I forced myself to focus on everything that gets me there. *Small steps. Out of the camp. Past the guards. Dubrovnoye. Shuttle bus. Dalmatovo. Katerina. And Zhenia. Niece.*

From the camp where I was now kneeling in the cage of a surplus military truck, Dalmatovo was a total of about 120 kilometers. In Siberian terms, that was practically next door. Not that I had any idea how I might cover that distance.

Considering all this, I was lying on my side in the cage but was high enough to see the low trees behind the truck through the back window.

Something had disturbed the tree nearest to the camp entrance; its branches were still shaking. Hoping it was Cindy or Toshek coming back to camp, I pulled myself up to get a better view. To my utter fear and horror, I could see the monitor who had invited Toshek away from us in the Soyuz fuselage. He was crouched very low, holding what appeared to be a nine-millimeter pistol. Very much like the one I had been given yesterday — and couldn't find now. I slowly lowered my head from his sight and pleaded with myself to stay calm — and be smart.

Realizing that the cage could be locked from the inside, I took a few deep breaths and turned a lever that was near my good hand. I prayed that it would lock silently. It did. Cindy's makeshift bed was unmade, which left four or five woolen blankets on the floor. As silently as I could, I pulled the blankets over me. Just then, I felt the 66 rocking. The monitor was climbing up to look inside the cage.

Knowing I had less than a second or two to get covered, I flipped the topmost blanket over my face and shoulders and pinned myself down as low as I could. I knew my feet were uncovered but they were below the window I assumed the armed asshole would be looking through. To see my feet, he'd have to climb up another step or move to the other side of the cage. I heard him try the latch. He swore loudly, ending his angry expletives with "Fucking American!"

The 66 shook again as he climbed down. It sounded like he was rooting through our camp. Afraid he would try the other side of the cage, I stayed down, taking the opportunity to cover my feet in case he took a look through the other window. It seemed like an eternity passed as I lay motionless on the floor. My thoughts drifted away to a different time and place. I saw the uneven walkway in Nowa Huta leading to my flat, lined with tricycles, ice cream wrappers strewn everywhere. Renata was inside with her girlfriends. Malgosia was sitting in the sandbox. Are these my final thoughts of my family? Should I have left Antek's faxes in his office and gone to Jane to sign up for that new English teaching job? Had I heard something encouraging in Renata's voice the last time we'd spoken?

How do I finish the sentence: *If I get myself out of this, I promise I'll...?*

Too many important faces, too much sex, too much disappointment, a lopsided accounting sheet, and a scale that was always calibrated differently — all of these made it hard to finish that sentence. I took another deep breath. Pots and pans were flying below me in the camp kitchen. I decided I'd finish that sentence only when I made it to Katerina's. If I made it.

Knowing it was risky but wanting to get the hell out of Russian mafia preserve, I waited a couple of minutes after hearing the last of the rummaging noises before I stood up in the cage. From the window, I could see the little trees moving, one after another, back toward the debris site. I hoped it was my unwelcome visitor returning to his colleagues. I unlatched the door and frantically went back to work on my escape plan. What had been 'what ifs' in a moment of introspection, lying flat on my back, unable to move, I cast aside. Now, finally, I could act. I didn't hesitate to do so.

In fact, though, I still had no fucking idea how to get out of our camp and past the guards, much less to Dubrovnoye, without being seen. But tucking the money into my toolkit, I remembered the map. Time for a closer look. Perusing the map on our way in, I had focused on the main roads. Now I began to look more closely for trails and undeveloped roads. The legend showed them, but I wasn't too sure of the vocabulary in Russian. It also didn't help that I still couldn't see clearly. The blood had mostly dried and crusted on both sides of my left hand. I realized I should clean the wound and make use of the well-supplied first aid kit from the cage of the 66. But instead of spending the time to do that, I opened a bottle and allowed cold water to flow over my wounded hand. It stung terribly and started to bleed again. Spotting a new pair of leather gloves on the truck's console, I grabbed them and put them on.

I have a faint recollection that, while gazing numbly at the map, trying to come up with a route, I thought of the bicycle strapped to the roof of the 66. It was awfully muddy for riding here. But maybe not, if I could get away from the camp. Maybe it could make me look like a local. *Yeah. It might.* Synapses firing in inefficient ways brought halfway associated images to mind. The basket on this bike was exactly like the one on Renata's. We must have ridden around the Green Zone, circling Krakow's city center, a million times. A different time. A different world. When the streets were decorated with propaganda posters. Socialist Realism. Images of heroic steel workers, far too healthy looking. Few cars on the street except for the *Milicja,* driving around watching us.

Who's watching me?

Krakow faded and the camp returned. *Goddamn it! How long did I zone out?* This was happening too often now. *Get the fucking bike!* It was all starting to make sense. Now to complete the effect: more props. *A disguise, maybe.*

I grabbed Toshek's smelly brown jacket and cap: very Russian, industrial style. The jacket and cap reminded me of the Heroes of the Revolution, as depicted on those old posters extolling the virtues of socialism.

My hope was that any guards or other mafia assholes I ran into would not yet have heard what had happened. With any luck, they would just think I was one of their comrades, bicycling out of camp. Complicating matters further, I had no idea what these three rogue security guards were really up to. Were Cindy and Toshek dead? Would all three monitors now be coming for me? Were there defectors closer to Michael who had staged this coup?

As much as I, myself, felt like a defector to my partners, the rules of an abort said I should be hightailing it now. I set my mind to that and drove my guilty demons as far away as I could. Not an easy task when they were all lined up for me. I urged myself to focus on my nobler goals than mere self-preservation. Foremost, I thought, was to follow my instructions from my handlers. *Be true* ranked right up there, too. Be true to family and marriage. *That feeds my drive to survive,* I convinced myself. Something easy to grasp. *Shit for brains.* I laughed out loud, still trying to focus on the map in front of me. *Dalmatovo… Katerina… Katerina… good for the cause… going there makes it all happen. Not love.* I forced memories of Katerina's body out of my mind. *Wrong motives. Stuff that in a box. Fuck that shit.*

The map showed a faint road — not labelled a trail, so maybe passable for vehicles — that cut through the woods, zig-zagged around a pond, then made what seemed to be a straight shot toward Dubrovnoye. A twenty-kilometer ride in the mud would be terrible but I was hoping the road or trail hadn't been used too much and that any ruts wouldn't be too deep. The bike's tires were fat, probably well suited for conditions around here. Shakily, I climbed the ladder to the roof. The bike was lashed to a railing with Russian-style bungee cords. Those are just rubber straps cut from an inner tube, without any hooks. I remember swearing under my breath for what seemed several minutes as I couldn't get the straps undone. I had left my toolkit with my two knives in the tent. Trying to grip anything with significant force made my damaged hand hurt like hell, but I didn't sense any bone damage. So I gritted my teeth, sweated through the pain, and tried not to worry that I was making the injury worse.

Eventually the rubber straps came loose, and I let the bike drop to the ground. The chain came off. But since it was loose anyway, it went back on without a problem. The tires were aired up and suddenly I realized I was in the middle of my first mission abort plan. If I had ever been scared on other missions, this was ten times worse than anything I had ever experienced. *Shit for brains... Renata cares. And the kids are waiting for you!*

My cowardly ass was shaking as I slung my toolkit more securely over both shoulders. Covered in mud, it was filled with a few of the spy toys I had come here with and an old US Army knife that had helped me escape my impalement. There was a lot of money in it and I had one clean, white Lacoste polo shirt. Renata's birthday present, which usually hung up in the closet between a million business shirts. She didn't like the way I folded my shirts. Don't ask me what I was thinking when I stuffed that into the bag. One other thing I thought to pack: Joe's folks had supplied me with procedures to use if I needed to make a phone call but code the conversation. I folded up the instruction sheets and tucked them in along with the money and the map. I'd thought about just getting to Dubrovnoye and trying to make the call, but I assumed everyone there would either be scared stiff to help me or simply working for these mafia bosses. In fact, I imagined that when I got to the town, I might see Michael or someone else from our earlier meeting. The map had showed me that Dubrovnoye was a tiny place. It had only a few streets that paralleled the lake front and the same number perpendicular to the shore. I just wanted to make it to the little resort and buy a ticket, or bribe whomever I had to, anything to get a ride to safety. Pushing the dilemma aside, Katerina's place was short term safety and shelter. Renata? She meant long-term happiness... I had to hope... especially now.

By the time I finally saddled up on the bike, nothing was left in my stomach to vomit. The continuing dry heaves scared me a little. I was alternately shaking and then burning up with fever. The 'lights' were still on, as well. I now understand what it means to see stars after getting hit hard. Since I had been kicked on one side and collided with a titanium-ridged wall on the other, I'd had constant tunnel vision. My peripheral view was just a shimmer and I could only see objects directly in front of me. But being able to sit on the bike and ride seemed a big improvement. My left hand couldn't really grip, but I could rest it on the handlebar, and my right hand was strong enough. With a last and not very fond look around our little camp, I ventured off, wearing my Socialist Hero cap and Toshek's jacket, to get me to the trail head or dirt road to Dubrovnoye that I believed was not far away.

Dubrovnoye

The bike bouncing on the uneven surface nearly did me in. I struggled to find a rut I could stay in without nearly shaking off my saddle. My head ached terribly and the shaking was making it worse. I was going very slowly, stopping occasionally to search for the entrance to the Dubrovnoye road. I got to within fifty meters from the mafia headquarters, way too close for comfort; fortunately, the people I saw milling about not more than thirty meters away didn't see me. Finally, I spotted a dry road heading into the woods to my left. As I pedaled toward that junction, I realized a couple of guys were standing a short distance away, looking directly at me. They waved at me; I could hear some laughter. If they were saying anything to me, I had no idea what. It may have been my imagination, but just as I turned down the side road, I thought I heard some yelling behind me. I didn't turn around. I began to pick up speed as the road wound through woods and thick brush, hiding me from whomever might have been behind me. My heart was racing as I began to think, perhaps I really could get away so easily. It bothered me that if this was a public road to the lakeside village, why wouldn't Michael have posted guards here? As I rode, my thoughts returned to my battered condition. The glove on my stylishly pierced hand seemed tighter now. It was probably swelling, I thought.

The farther along I got, the better the road's condition became. The ruts were not very deep, and my tires moved smoothly between them. After about two miles, I came upon a modern looking Russian Niva four-wheel drive. It was parked far enough to the side of the road that I could pass without a problem. The car was empty but I could see three men at the edge of the nearest forest. A chainsaw sat on the ground near where they were sitting around a fire, burned down enough that it was only smoldering. I could see several vodka bottles and something cooking or staying warm on the dying coals. Also visible were at least two military rifles leaning against a tree about ten feet from where they were sitting. Scared shitless and knowing I would be an easy target to pick off from that distance, I could again feel my stomach and chest tightening, trying to think how I should behave, as I pedaled as fast as I could past them. I lifted my hand to wave, turned toward them and shouted greetings to them, "*Zdravstvuy!*" as I passed. I could see that I had startled them.

They jumped up and made moves like they were reaching for their weapons. *Fuck.* Why hadn't I brought the 9mm? I knew I was a goner without it. I felt another wave of nausea come on, imagining being cut down in a hail of Kalashnikov bullets. One of them yelled loudly to stop: "*Stoy!*"

But instead of reaching for their guns, one of the men grabbed a bottle, took a swig and passed it around.

Relieved for an instant but knowing that I was either dead or captured if I stopped, I pedaled harder and laughed loudly figuring they would think I was just a drunken camp member they didn't recognize. NOT having the gun felt a good decision, for the moment. I imagined the consequences of getting caught with it or having a shoot-out: my little pistol versus assault rifles. I made it past, though, and added a couple of expletives, "*Jebane chuje!*" as I picked up speed and kept laughing. Maybe they didn't know the Polish phrase means 'fucking dicks.' As I turned back around, they had sat back down and were passing the bottle again.

Just after my encounter with the men having their vodka barbecue, I realized I didn't see any more vehicle tracks. As the road began to disappear, bushes were taking over the narrow opening I was pedaling through. A creeping fear began to overtake my exhilaration. Was this just a dead end? Is that why the tracks had disappeared? Excitement that I might have orchestrated a successful escape was curdling into dread. I had to slow down and finally stop as the path ended. It wasn't exactly a dead end but maybe worse. The road simply disappeared. Submerged in a black pool of water. Directly in front of me stretched a pond about a hundred fifty meters across. The map had showed a route veering off around a pond, but that way seemed completely impassable. Any attempt to go around would be stopped by what looked like jumbled heaps of boulders, logs, and scraps of old concrete pavement and building foundations. And there was no way I was going to turn around. The only way to continue my escape was to walk the bike through an area apparently flooded by that crudely bulldozed dam. I could see that the road reappeared on the other side. I dismounted and walked the bike into the opaque black water. It was icy cold and came up to my chest. The submerged road became very slippery and I could keep my balance only by using the bike to steady myself. I was worried that I would walk off the road since I could not see my feet nor tell if there were turns in the sunken hundred fifty meters I was attempting to cross. After what seemed an eternity, the water started to get shallower again, and finally I came out, high if not dry, on the other side. I saw that the bike was covered in a tarry algae or moss. Fearful of infection, I'd kept my left hand out of the black water. As fast as it was swelling up, I knew I would have to see a doctor about it, as well as my concussion. The mud, the moss, the blood on my head and face, and the smell of vomit that had gotten all over me probably made for a delightful scene. I was dreading having to appear in the open at the resort village, when I suddenly understood why I had packed the white Lacoste polo shirt in my toolkit. It would soften the blow of seeing me. Maybe.

Hopping on the bike after wading through the stagnant black water, I still had about ten miles of pedaling to get to Dubrovnoye. I was feeling a little better, beginning to pass farms and some small houses, as the road began to widen again. Its surface also became smoother, but I still had to steer my way around potholes. To make matters worse, my vision had not come back yet. But feeling safer for the moment, I decided I wanted to walk a bit. My butt was hurting; the bike's metal seat had lost whatever upholstery it originally had. I took the bike by the handlebars and walked alongside for several hundred meters, taking in the sights around me. Some cars passed and I just lowered my head without acknowledging anyone. Then one of the cars that passed turned around and came back. My mood dropped. That sick feeling spread again. Now, for sure, I knew I'd been recognized.

An older man with a cap like mine slammed on the brakes. Through his open window, his eyes confronted me and he started to open his mouth. Why was one of Michael's thugs stopping to talk, I found myself wondering, instead of leaping out to beat the shit out of me? And then I registered what he was actually yelling at me. "Thief! Drug addict!" He was accusing me of stealing the bicycle from his farm.

"Is that my bike, you young-ass punk? You just walked up to my barn and took it like a fucking gypsy! Stop right there. I'm going to get out and wrap that bike around your fucking head!"

That was a relief, but not a very big one. Realizing this situation could be just as bad as getting run over by one of the camp goons, I mustered up a mix of my bad Russian and good Polish. With a dose of anger equal to his, I told him, *"Konechno eto moj rower, kurwa chuj!"* Of course this is my bike, you fucking prick! *"Od dziecka, dazhe!"* I'd had it since I was a kid! In finishing, I cordially invited him to fuck off. *"Spierdalaj!"*

He looked at me strangely and then examined the bike more closely. Through the mud and moss, he must have gotten a glimpse of its real color, a kind of light blue. He shook his head disdainfully. "A woman's bike! It's not mine for sure!" As bullies so often do when challenged, he shifted his tone from anger to mockery and left me alone, laughing as he drove off. I jumped on the bike determined to make it to Dubrovnoye without any more delays.

The road straightened out. It was smoother. Missing the potholes required little effort. Less vibration on my hands and butt relieved the constant headache. Like on a spring break Oregon coast road trip, I began to ruminate on my predicament about a fucked-up, misspent life. No doubt I'd taken for granted the domestic comforts of home and family, despite the tedium and bickering in our cramped little flat in Nowa Huta. Occasional problems had interrupted years of joy. It hadn't been the other way around. Renata's happiness hit its peak during those times when she realized, I think it was one Christmas Eve with her family, that I'd given heart and soul to being her son's father. And it wasn't just the presents I'd bought him.

The road curved to the left and then the right for a kilometer and a half around a small village. Coming out on the other side of the village my mind swung back into more immediate hopes of finding my way to Dalmatovo. Once again, my imagination veered in a contrary direction. Now I envisioned Katerina at the door in the incredible yellow outfit she had been wearing when we said goodbye on the platform in Chelyabinsk. I wanted to take her into my arms again. I couldn't stay focused on that, either. Next, I began wiping my eyes on my sleeves worrying what had happened to Cindy, my extraordinary partner and one-time lover, since I'd aborted the mission. Atonement for all my sins was impossible. A decision to follow my heart was advisable. This heart, though, was experiencing complete arrhythmia.

My first glimpse of Dubrovnoye in the distance was a lovely sight. Not that it was particularly pretty or anything, but it represented the next step in my escape. At that moment, I thought it was the loveliest village I had ever seen. The trees and scrub along the road had mostly hidden the view, but now the farms and open country allowed me a vantage point from the roadway, slightly elevated over the surrounding land. I was back on the bike and pedaling steadily. My road went straight to the waterfront where it met the paved road that followed the shore. I had no idea which direction to turn. Right? Left? The sign for Dubrovnoye Center pointed left so I went left. I saw a grandmotherly woman in a scarf carrying groceries, including a lot of vegetables. I yelled to her in Polish, "Where is the sanatorium on the lake?"

She stood motionless and stared at me like she had seen Stalin himself.

"Hotel? Resort? *Noclegi*? *Wczasy na jezioro*?" I was trying any Slavic words I could think of related to hotel or resort.

She broke her temporary paralysis by pointing further left. Not a word from her mouth, though. I saddled up again, thanked her in Russian, and pedaled toward the village center. After two or three minutes riding quickly, shops and official-looking buildings started to appear along the waterfront. I knew I must be getting close.

Rounding a corner that led to a hidden cove, I saw a sign:

Dubrovnoye Hotel on the Lake
* Sauna-Restaurant-Cafe-Massage-
Salt Baths-Sport-Fishing-Hunting *

I had found my lake resort.

Before getting too close, I looked the place over. Not far from the hotel's main entrance were outdoor toilets and a place to change into swimsuits. I had been thinking about a shower but in this primitive village running water was just a dream. I had no interest in taking another dip in a lake, either. I could see some activity near the entrance and decided it was time to put on my Lacoste shirt and try to lessen the effect of mud, moss, blood, and vomit. Getting my other, saturated, shirt off and trying to keep the white Lacoste shirt clean was a fruitless task but I hoped I could look a little more presentable. As I was fumbling with my wardrobe upgrade, I noticed that my swollen hand had completely filled the glove I was wearing.

After all this, I remember, I was feeling very little fear. I was starting to let myself think I was going to get out of this alive after all. It was in that optimistic mood that I decided to approach one man with an official look about him to ask where the bus stop for Dalmatovo was.

Suddenly, though, the fear and caution came welling back up out of my empty gut. *Don't mention Dalmatovo, dumb-ass!* That would be my most obvious destination. And most likely a Russian mafia APB was out on me. I rethought my plan and decided to try acting more like a spy is supposed to. Before exposing myself, I would do some investigating from cover.

Hiding behind a large traffic sign, I caught myself holding my breath; I'd just barely avoided being spotted by the driver of a fairly new Volga sedan. I cursed myself for not noticing it until it pulled to a stop right next to the man I'd been planning to approach. The driver leaned his head out the window and had an agonizingly long conversation with the official-looking man. About me, I was sure. The car wasn't muddy enough to have come from the Soyuz preserve, but I had convinced myself that everyone was potentially a threat to my escape. I felt just a little relief when the Volga pulled away, but I waited for it to round the lake and disappear from view before I dared to come out. Maybe, I tried to convince myself, the guy in the car wasn't mafia after all. The other man didn't seem to show any sense of urgency, like he would if he'd been told to watch out for a fugitive. Maybe my judgment had been impaired by shock and blood loss. *What the hell.* I came out and walked up to the man.

I wasn't prepared for his reaction as I spoke in my mixed Russian-Polish dialect. "Excuse me, I want to go to Dalmatovo today. Can you help me?"

He turned with a sickening yelp of fear and scampered the full ten meters to the hotel's front porch.

I stood in the street, a little shocked, as he was now much farther away, hiding behind a pillar. Was it my appearance? Or the realization that I was that fugitive he'd very possibly just been warned to watch for? I decided to ask again. "Sorry, I've had a bad fall and hurt my head. I need to go to Dalmatovo. Can you help?"

Regaining his composure, the man cleared his throat. He said, "The bus is coming soon but all the seats have been reserved."

That was better. Maybe nobody here was looking for me — yet.

"If the driver allows you to sit with him in the front seat, you might offer him something extra."

"Where will it stop?" I asked

"Right here." He pointed to a couple of benches nearby.

"*Spasibo!*" I thanked him. I decided to go sit on the benches and wait. By now, other people had emerged from the hotel to stare at my multi-colored face and head, my muddy, mossy, dripping pants, and the snow-white shirt I was sporting. As I waited, I held my disguise under my arm, thinking I might need it again. The cap and jacket had done well to get me out of the mafia compound unnoticed but I had my doubts that it was my best outfit for successfully finishing my journey. I have a faint recollection of asking someone on the street for an aspirin — and getting the sort of answer I might have given someone who looked like I did. "Buddy, I think you need more than an aspirin."

By the time the bus arrived, a cool breeze had come up. I was back in my socialist hero garb with the coat buttoned up most of the way to my neck. Several times, I had nodded off. In a state somewhere between sleep and delirium, three women were standing in front of me. Someone was yelling at me to point out my wife. I kept saying, "She's not there!" In the next dream I could see my kids in the distance behind a glass wall. I was screaming for them to get their attention but they couldn't hear me. On my side of the wall were the seventh-floor prostitutes from the Intourist in Novosibirsk. They were playing cards, smoking and laughing at me. And each time I had woken up with people standing in front of me discussing and even arguing over the extent of my injuries. One lady had declared to another, "He was born that way! He's an idiot!" In the first few seconds after I awoke, I thought it was Renata saying I was an idiot.

Once I'd come to from my strange dreams, I could see that, all in all, the crowd waiting for the bus seemed to relax in my presence once I donned the cap and jacket. Who in Russia wouldn't feel better with Lenin's brother sitting right there — a little bloody and battered? But who hadn't occasionally gotten beaten up in this part of the world?

Even before the newly arriving hotel guests had stepped down from the bus, I was at the driver's window asking if I could offer him money for the empty passenger seat up front. He didn't look at me as I spoke.

He nodded but remained silent. I'm sure he recognized that I was a foreigner, but he was busy doing his passenger list and, I assumed, didn't want to be bothered too much.

"Here is fifty dollars. Is that enough to reserve the seat?" I said. As I handed the bill through the window, his blood-shot eyes opened widely and stared at me for just a few seconds. Without a word, he took the money, reached over, and opened the door for me. As I slid in, he moved his lunch, light-porno magazines, and thermos off the spare seat. We were separated by an engine cover that was quite hot. He put his things on a foam rubber pillow that I guessed he used to insulate his food, or his arm, from the heat coming up from the engine.

I looked at the tariff sheet for trips between Dalmatovo and Dubrovnoye that was pasted to the glove box in front of me. The normal price for an adult was about a dollar and a quarter at the current exchange rate. His $48.75 tip represented a decent week of wages in this poor part of Siberia. I had no smaller bills with me, and the way I was feeling, I could afford to be generous. All I wanted now was just a first-class ticket out of Dubrovnoye.

I fell asleep again as the ticketed passengers boarded the bus. We were halfway out of town when I woke up with a start and reached out. I braced my hands against the dashboard, desperate to stop the black Volga that I had dreamed was speeding toward us. My gloved hand left blood on the dashboard. The driver noticed but didn't say anything.

My head was still hurting. I was still terribly thirsty. Fairly quickly, the driver seemed at ease with me but we didn't talk for quite a while. It was a ninety-minute ride to Dalmatovo and about halfway there, I ventured to ask if he had something to drink. He pulled a bottle of vodka from behind the seat. I smiled but said I needed "*gasnica*"— fire extinguisher — first. He laughed and gave me a small bottle of *Oranzada*, an orange soda pop. I drank half the bottle and he acted happy to have helped. I refused his offer of a vodka chaser that came a few minutes later but decided it was safe to ask him for a much bigger favor. I rummaged in my kit and pulled out the photo and piece of paper Katerina had given me with the address of her estate. "Would it be possible to find someone to take me to this place after we arrive in Dalmatovo?"

Clearly surprised, he pulled himself up proudly and said, "I can take you to where the women live, and the men are working all the time. I know this place. I drive a truck during the weekend. I bring building materials here very often. Some rich women own it." His excitement overflowed from his smile to his hand; he patted me on the shoulder and nodded vigorously.

"You're shitting me!" I exclaimed, accidentally, in English.

He responded in English. "No! I really know her. Yekaterina I think is her name."

I couldn't believe my good fortune. Thoughts of Renata and Krakow were again driven from my thoughts. I told him I would pay him extra for this. He replied, "You already paid me for a first-class ticket and drinks for a week."

A little overwhelmed by the events of the day, I felt tears welling up in my eyes. Right here on his bus. I looked out at the passing countryside, trying to hide my tears from him.

***

Dubrovnoye Road ended at the Oblast Highway Number 354. We turned left for the last thirty kilometers to Dalmatovo. I learned that the driver's name was Nikolai and he wanted me to call him Nick. Nick had travelled to Brooklyn not that long ago and was amazed at New York City.

"I didn't have to speak a word of English the whole month I was there!" he exclaimed. "Brooklyn is filled with Russians and Poles and Ukrainians and Jews from everywhere! I loved that place! I gained ten kilos in four short weeks. I was eating and drinking everything since it all was good!" That reference to Poles in Brooklyn almost set me on course to imagine what might have been if Renata hadn't given up on San Francisco so quickly. I shut those thoughts down as quickly as I could in light of Dalmatovo and the final leg of my escape.

I was getting tired. My head was hurting again, too, from keeping turned to the left to listen to him. And, of course, my hand had never stopped throbbing. By now, wherever I tried to rest it, it left a bloody mark. At some point along the way, sleep overcame me. When I woke up, we were in Dalmatovo. Nick picked up his instructions for the next day at his dispatch office and then jumped back into the bus to run me out to Katerina's estate. He handed me a liverwurst and cheese sandwich with a small bottle of mineral water. Before we hit the road, he pulled out his own bottle. This time I accepted a shot of vodka. I noticed one reason Nick might have sympathized about my obviously injured hand. He had two fingers missing from his left hand and the other seemed crooked from arthritis — or just a hell of a lot of work. Nick was maybe fifty years old but looked like a rugged seventy. Sunburned and lined like an Austrian mountaineer, he was the first encouraging person I had met since we'd begun the journey from Chelyabinsk.

It was getting dark, but I could see the terrain was changing as we approached Katerina's farm. Larger trees and hills that appeared to be tended by farmers with proper equipment filled my view of the dusky countryside as we bounced down the road. After about twenty minutes, we turned onto a well-maintained dirt drive. It led through a long double row of trees to a large house. Pallets of lumber and other building materials were neatly lined up along the lane as we got closer. The old house was built of limestone and wood, with antique-looking windows and shutters. I was glad to see lights on, but I was prepared to be turned away if my friends were not there.

Knowing that the two were very busy with the complicated task of restoring such an estate, I was not surprised when the woman who answered the door told us Katerina and Zhenia were in Kamensk-Uralsky. They were trying to arrange something important with officials of the oblast, the Russian equivalent of a county. As Nick translated for me, the woman at the door suddenly blurted, "Are you Andy? Andy from the train ride from Samara to Chelyabinsk? I am Nadezhda! I have been helping Katerina and Zhenia for several years while they were gone to Moscow and Kiev."

"Yes. Yes, that Andy," I managed to reply. I think I was as surprised as Nadezhda was. "You know about me?"

"Katerina has been saying every day that she hopes you have time to come after your work in Chelyabinsk! You are early. She will be so happy! You seem a little tired. Ohhh... Is your hand hurt? You are holding it strangely. Please come in and I will make a room for you! Have you eaten? Is this your driver? Will he be staying, too? Oh, I've got to call Katerina right now! Excuse me for a minute. Please have a seat and take your shoes off and relax!"

Nick sat down beside me on a couch. Speaking softly, he explained very slowly in Russian that he thought Nadezhda should call a doctor for me. He said, "You probably just need some sleep, but I am a little worried about your head injury and your hand. The blood on your shirt and coat may have come from your ear. It is possible there is something more serious with your head. And that hand should come out of the glove. Can I tell Nadezhda this? Also, you have been twitching very strangely during your sleep in the van. I was worried it was a seizure."

I thought about what Nick was saying. I couldn't tell him not to say anything to Nadezhda, but I did suggest he not mention his diagnosis about seizures. Putting on my most serious face, I told him, "I always have seizures and anxiety attacks when I am in Russia. Isn't that normal?"

Nick seemed to take my joking seriously and gave it a moment's consideration. "Perhaps you are right!"

Nadezhda was back with us in a few minutes. She happily reported that Katerina would be here tomorrow afternoon after her meetings.

Nick immediately told her about his fears about my head. He suggested that we cut the glove off my wounded hand.

At this, she was looking me over very closely. Naturally, she immediately got around to asking how it had all happened. Diplomatically, Nick blurted out, "You know these American spies will never give you a straight answer. It was just a bad fall."

In Russian, I said, "Thank you, Nick! It is all true. What you said."

"I will call Dr. Sokolov before it gets too late. Maybe he will come before Katerina arrives tomorrow. If you get worse in the night, we can call him if it's an emergency," Nadezhda announced. "Will you be staying with us, Nikolai?" she asked.

"No. I am leaving now. Please let me know how things are going in a few days." He handed me a dog-eared piece of cardboard. "This is my card for my hauling business. I live less than ten minutes away and I have delivered bricks to this house several times. I hope I see you again." Nick kissed Nadezhda on both cheeks and then shook my hand. "Goodbye, Mr. Andy!"

Dalmatovo

Nadezhda beckoned me to follow her into a ground-floor bathroom where she cut the bloody glove off my hand. She turned my hand over several times, examining the swollen palm and the puncture wounds on both sides. With a little laugh, she said something about Jesus on the cross having such a wound. She washed the holes and examined them closely. Next thing I knew, she was brandishing a metallic tube from which a thick, black goo was starting to ooze. "Is good to fight infection," she told me, soothingly.

"Not necessary," I said, pushing away the ichthyol she was threatening to dab onto my wounds. I spared her the full story, but used my good hand to keep the vile stuff off me. My hand had already suffered enough. With a shrug, she screwed the cap back onto the tube. She finished by bandaging the hand, wrapping gauze around my palm four or five times.

"That's all I know how to do until Dr. Sokolov comes," she said. Then, hurriedly, she got to work taking care of everything else that could possibly make my visit more comfortable. Summoning a doctor sounded ominous to me. For all I knew, he was also making regular on-call visits at the mafia preserve and could telegraph them my whereabouts. Still, I resisted my impulse to refuse any medical help. I knew I needed it. For now, I focused my attention on Nadezhda as she took me on a short tour to make sure I knew my way around the house.

The kitchen was our first stop: "To make sure you don't go hungry. Please make yourself at home," Nadezhda urged me, then rattled on about her hospitality. "It will take me maybe ten or fifteen minutes to prepare the guest room for you. The bathroom is around the corner to your right. I've warmed up some blinis with cabbage and pork. It is on the counter in the middle of the kitchen. I hope you will like it. Zhenia always asks me to fix this when she comes home from wherever she has been. They are very good with some sour cream and spicy sauce. We have many spicy sauces to choose from; from every country that likes spicy food, I think! Zhenia is becoming the gourmet cook in this house with all the traveling she has done in the last three years."

"Thank you very much, Nadezhda. I am very happy I made the decision to come early." I meant it. "You are very kind. This home is fantastic."

"Please call me Nadya. It is easier for American pronunciation, I am told. But your accent is not so bad as most Americans. I think you have been in Europe for some time?" she asked.

"Longer than most Americans I know. But in Poland. Almost ten years now," I said. It took a conscious effort to refrain from saying too much to her about my life in Poland. In my state, a willing ear was far too easy to fall for.

"Congratulations!" Her grin suggested this had pleased her immensely.

I had to laugh. "Why 'congratulations'?"

"Because most Americans give up on foreign countries after a short time. They vacation for two weeks or maybe they try to live someplace else. But not many are able to adjust to life outside their own wonderful country."

There was a lot of truth to what Nadya said. I'd been terribly homesick in Poland until I got a handle on the language and had a life to go home to. That had taken three years. More than once during that time, I had nearly given up along the way. And now, sitting in Katerina's kitchen, I had to look back at my urgent impulse just hours ago to make everything better again back home. My life had been in real danger. I had been desperately scared. Those feelings were fading away now that I was feeling safe — and almost literally in the bosom of a new lover. I was once again tempted to admit to myself that I had pretty much given up on my old life again.

"You are probably right, Nadya," I said. "I sometimes miss my country, too. But I think I am sentenced to life in Europe now."

Now it was her turn to laugh. "I think I understand what you mean by 'sentenced.' Let me go get your room ready. I will invite you up later to inspect it. But now, if you want to take a bath or shower, I think you might feel better. And I will be able to see you better without so much dirt and..." She ended her sentence unfinished.

I finished it for her. ". . . and blood?"

"Well… yes." She cleared her throat with an embarrassed look on her face and hurried to tell me how to find towels and robes, adding a promise to wash my clothes after I was asleep. "Katerina also has clothes for men that are in closets all over the house."

That startled me. Thinking back yet again to my interlude with her in the first-class compartment…

But Nadya quickly did her best to put me at ease. "They belonged to cousins, uncles, and a lot of clothes we don't even know where they came from. But very nice ones." Nadya took me by my good hand and led me down a hallway lined with doors. She opened several closets that were, as she'd promised, filled with men's clothing. As I was considering which garments to try, she disappeared upstairs. Leaving me to imagine ex-lovers who had left suits to have something to come back for. I couldn't exclude that from my list of uncomfortable explanations for the used clothing boutique here at the Dalmatovo Estate.

After a long, hot soak, I had to choose from an array of robes hanging in the bathroom. I selected an off-white silk number with matching pants. The trousers fit perfectly once I hiked them up past my waist. The robe was long, and I loved the fit. Something between a Kimono and Indian-style lounge wear, I imagined. But before leaving the bathroom, I noticed how dirty I had left the tub. Coming down the stairs, Nadya laughed when she saw me bent over the tub, scrubbing away the filthy ring I had left. My first thought was that she was laughing at me for doing something Russian men rarely did: clean up after themselves. That made me ponder the real answer. Was this something I'd been trained to do in my marriage? By a wife who wasn't having lazy, entitled male ways? Or did it go back much earlier? To that same house in Oklahoma where my mother had taught me to take refuge in the tub — the same tub I was responsible for cleaning up after I'd used it. Did my ease in being a domestic partner come from my distant past? Or was it a product of the comfort I felt being a husband and father in Poland? It hadn't always been comfort and joy; sometimes it was kids vomiting and screaming matches in the kitchen at midnight and dirty bathrooms.

I was rinsing the last of the muck down the drain when Nadya said, "You chose an interesting thing to wear. It was Zhenia's mother's favorite house dress when she visited her parents here years ago. She was tall. I think you look wonderful in it."

"Oh, shit! I am sorry! I'll grab something else." I wasn't quite sure if I was apologetic for poaching on a family heirloom, or embarrassed at wearing women's clothing. In any case, I started looking for a better men's garment. I settled on a white terry-cloth robe, clearly a man's.

After showing me to my room on the top floor, Nadya said goodnight. I took some time to look carefully around. Family photos lined the walls, along with framed old diplomas and certificates hanging proudly over an ancient cherry-wood desk. On a large set of built-in bookcases, I saw a row of textbooks co-authored by Katerina's father. My Russian was just good enough to recognize that they were about metallurgy but that was all I could discern without looking up words in a dictionary. I was too tired for that, but well fed and clean — finally — and ready for bed. Of course, my hand was hurting furiously now, but I didn't have the courage to ask Nadya if she might have aspirin. Also, since arriving I had been conscious of what Nick had said about the blood from my ear. Although I hadn't seen anything on my towel after the bath, I laid a small, dry hand towel under my head just in case I was leaking. Katerina's bed linens were too nice for me to ruin on my first night's stay.

***

As peaceful and idyllic a nighttime setting as it was, I did not sleep well. My hand stopped hurting so badly when I propped it up with extra pillows but my headache raged most of the night.

When I did doze off, I had dreams that shook my demons back out of their cage. In one of these dreams, Cindy was chained to a wall and the rod that had been used to pierce my hand now impaled her through the sternum. The asshole who had attacked her was screwing her lifeless body from behind. I was watching from the cage of the 66, hiding from everyone, passive and helpless. Rolling from one dream to the next like a satanic disco DJ matching the evil beat from one record to another, in the next scene Renata and I were shopping for handicrafts in the Cloth Hall's market. That dream fast forwarded to a new flat where all her favorite things are laid out beautifully. The items we bought at the Cloth Hall adorn the new place. Renata's smiling face is outlined by the fire in the fireplace, and she is speaking sweetly to me. The scene shifts again and a sinister darkness descends over the fire's warm glow. Renata's voice begins to sound like it does over the phone when she's livid and the connection is bad. The static rises along with her volume. She's screaming and laughing at the same time. "You make no effort to speak properly! You only use your favorite stupid lines to communicate!" Her sociologist friend who always wanted to get into her pants cuts in and says, "You're married to a bourgeois American rube! He'll never fit into your life and your ways!" The dream ends as I'm handing Renata thousands of dollars earned from a dangerous mission. The DJ's record has started skipping. He's nowhere to be seen. All I can hear is Renata's voice. She is repeating in a manic tone, "Is that all? Is that all? Is that all!"

To make matters worse, around 4 a.m., an overpowering anxiety came on. This kept me awake as the sky grew light outside. I tossed off the blankets and stood looking out the window, rocking back and forth. I'd already been up three times, imagining I'd seen lights coming down the long driveway, but a closer look revealed no sign of any activity. Nevertheless, I imagined endless dangers lurking out there in the dark, beyond that stately avenue of trees. Thoughts crossed my mind of rounding up a makeshift posse with Nick's help, using the cash I still had. I knew it was an absurd idea, but real memories of Sofia fighting off that mafia prick in the fuselage were coming back to me. My equally real memory of running away from the scene, leaving her to an unknown fate, made me feel even worse. Until the first light, I kept seeing one face after another in my mind's eye. Renata. Katerina. Sofia. Even, for my own guilty good measure, Agata the librarian; the physicist on the train the night my wedding ring disappeared; the mother of the bratty kids on the train from Chelyabinsk to Novosibirsk; Natalya and her two colleagues. Even Alyona behind the bar in Moscow. Eventually the women's faces faded away and morning was heralded by the mafia monitors, Michael, and the rest of the Mafia Preserve Board, all leering at me.

That anxiety didn't fade until dawn had fully driven away the darkness, if not my dark thoughts. As the first sunlight came in the window, Nadya brought me a beautiful copper samovar of coffee with a matching cup. Recognizing that I did not feel well, she reminded me that Dr. Sokolov would be coming soon. He had called her to say he had rearranged his schedule to see me first.

As she was getting ready to close my door, I called out to her,

"Nadya!"

"Yes, Mr. Andy?"

"Are international phone connections possible from here?" I asked her. My horrible dreams and the realization that I hadn't gotten around to calling Renata from Novosibirsk as I had promised were driving a sense of urgency. I needed to let her know I was OK. I certainly had no intention of giving her any details of what I'd just been though but I wanted to check in. I would be nearly a week late in doing so; I fully expected her wrath. On the other hand, I wanted to hear her voice.

"It's not a problem anymore," Nadya said. "Katerina arranged for new lines coming here a year ago. We can make calls out to almost anywhere. You just dial '0,' wait for next tone, then '00' and then your country code and number."

"Thank you, Nadya. I may try to call Poland later." She left smiling, but her eyes made me think I was a difficult sight to see.

The strong coffee cleared my head. I took a moment to look more closely at the samovar. My translation of the Cyrillic engraving on the base of the exquisitely shaped vessel was, "Presented to Dr. Vasili Kuznetsov — in recognition of the important contributions made to the USSR in Science and Industry — 1975." I put the samovar down and was already going over what I might say to Renata if I got through and was able to talk to her.

Dr. Sokolov arrived before I had finished my coffee. He didn't seem to have any of the mannerisms I had recognized among the mafia types, but I still wasn't sure how much I should trust him — if at all. He scolded me for adding caffeine to my nerve-wracked state. "Definitely a skull fracture," he announced, fingering the swollen line on my head and examining the discoloration in my eyes and on my scalp. "The last thing you need now is a stimulant when you may be near a stroke! Or hemorrhaging! Any blood from your ears or nose?"

"The driver that brought me here thought he may have seen blood coming from my ear," I explained, "but I got so muddy and bloody after the incident that it could have come from my scalp."

"Whatever went through your hand doesn't appear to have broken any of your bones. Was it a nail?" Dr. Sokolov asked. "Or perhaps a bullet?" He looked over his glasses, gently flexed my hand and removed the bandages Nadya had applied.

"Something like a nail, doctor. Yes. Like a long nail."

"You have lacerations on both sides of your head. Can you describe to me how it happened and what kind of force or fall it was that you experienced?" the doctor asked.

"I hope that this story stays between you and me, Dr. Sokolov." Reluctant to tell him what had happened, I waited for him to acknowledge that he would be discreet. When he nodded to indicate "Yes," I told him, "I was kicked in the head by someone as I was bent over next to a metal wall. The scrapes on my left side are from his boot. The cuts and swelling on my right side are from where my head slammed into the wall. I was unconscious for some time. Then, when I awoke, I was immediately nauseous and had problems seeing. A metal stake had been driven through my hand to try to keep me from escaping. I vomited for hours while riding a bike twenty kilometers. I have only sketchy memories of the details about how I got here."

The doctor's eyes got steadily wider and his mouth hung open as he wrote my story down. "Oh, my God," were his first words. "You need to come with me — now — to go to my clinic."

That all-too-familiar jolt of fear hit me in the gut again. Where was this guy really planning to take me? But then I had a slightly more charitable thought. Maybe the doctor had put two and two together, guessing I was tangled up in some dangerous mafia business, and was trying to get me to someplace safer.

"Go now?" I asked. "What for?"

"To do an EEG. Be sure brain function is normal."

Remembering from my maps of the region, it seemed to me that Dr. Sokolov's clinic, being nearby in Dalmatovo, was very likely among the closest medical facilities to the mafia preserve. One of the first they would check with to find somebody who had gotten badly hurt, but had given them the slip. *No way*, I vowed to myself. I backed him off any thoughts of leaving the house.

"The last thing I want is to leave here," I said, "and be seen out and about by the people who did this."

Doctor Sokolov held my gaze, expressionless.

I added, "If this turns into an international incident, it will be unpleasant for all the people involved." After what I hoped was a stern, even threatening, look back at him, I added, "For everybody."

He put down his pen. "I don't mind working with Katerina to help keep you hidden — if that is necessary." He sighed. "The corruption in this region is crippling us. Your injuries sound serious enough to me to warrant some further exams. But I understand your hesitation." His finger tapped the table as he thought this over. "For now, though, I do need to give you a tetanus shot and some antibiotics for that hand; it is showing signs of an infection, too."

I began to feel better about the doc.

"Thank you, doctor. I don't expect to be here very long. But if I have any problems, I will have Katerina call you. She is supposed to arrive later today." I told him this without hesitation but regretting I had said as much as I had about my injury. I had to remind myself that, as wonderful a place as I had landed, and as lucky as I was, there was no certainty that Michael's people wouldn't still track me down.

"I suppose that is fine," Sokolov said. He pulled a vial and syringe out of a sealed package. Drawing the fluid from the vial with the syringe he told me, "I'll leave the prescriptions here later today. Please have Nadya or Katerina call me if there are changes or if your pain gets worse. And it should be obvious that you should not stress yourself at all." After giving me the tetanus shot, he looked at the floor before adding, "Even sexual intercourse might cause some complications, I am sorry to say."

I wasn't really prepared for that last recommendation. I wondered what had prompted it. What the remark might have meant about Katerina's reputation. Was he suggesting something I should have taken offense to? I shrugged it off, but with some consternation.

As the doctor was giving me some pain killers and sleeping aids, he pulled his glasses off and asked, "If you don't mind, I am curious how a young American businessman comes to this part of Russia — and gets beaten so terribly. Is there anything you can tell me?"

My danger alarm went off again. Why is he so curious about this? Who will he be reporting to? I fought to keep my paranoia under control. On reflection, I couldn't blame the doctor for being curious. But I preferred to satisfy his curiosity without giving any details whatsoever. "Business secrets, Dr. Sokolov. I *can* say that there are forces out there fighting that crippling corruption that you mentioned earlier."

He finished packing his things and shrugged. "Some kind of business to be in!"

Talking about business reminded me: "What can I pay you for this house call, Doctor?" I turned to a chest of drawers where I had stashed my toolkit with its wad of cash.

"Nothing now, Mr. Gold. Katerina will get my bill sometime soon."

I felt a little funny about that but didn't protest. What other bills might be coming due soon?

Who Can I Trust?

Dr. Sokolov was on his way down the stairs and I was getting dressed in my freshly laundered clothes when I heard a car drive up, its tires skidding in the gravel in front of the house. A glance out the window showed me Katerina getting out of the car and striding toward the door. Dr. Sokolov emerged into the courtyard to greet her. Through the glass, I could clearly hear their voices.

Suddenly I imagined a well-choreographed kidnapping, followed by a ransom deal. The skidding sound had touched off a nerve. Could I be surprised again as I had been before? What was I thinking, letting my guard down? None of these people had been in my life until two weeks ago! It was irrational thinking, I suppose, but in that moment the fear washed over my whole being.

But then the sight of Katerina, in the flesh, quickly calmed me down. No. I had to trust someone. Katerina gave me the only real hope I had. And finally, she was here.

A bit more relaxed now, I began to worry that, after what the doctor had learned, he might panic her. I opened the window and leaned out. "Dr. Sokolov! Please don't change your story. Remember? I am in perfect health, OK?"

Katerina looked up, beaming, as she heard my voice. She waved and said, "I will be up soon! But let me talk to the doctor first. He will tell me what is up with you, damn it!"

They talked for a lot longer than I had expected but this gave me a chance to take inventory of my toolkit and how much money I had left. When Katerina finally came into the room, I was decked out in my famous Lacoste polo shirt, once again as white as it had ever been. Probably whiter. Hanging the shirt to dry on the Nowa Huta apartment balcony would turn it gray in thirty minutes. That funny fact hit me in an unexpected way. I was a little uncomfortable to have to admit such a silly fact. My camouflage pants were, well, clean. Wearing camos in Russia made me feel like I was behind the lines in some secret war. Which maybe I was, in a way. In any case, wearing them in Katerina's presence made me even more uncomfortable, hurt my vanity even. After all, I had looked a lot more normal when she'd met me on the train.

I don't think it was my outfit, though, that Katerina reacted to. Almost immediately after she got a close look at the rest of me, she started crying.

I was shocked.

But of course, she must have been, too. "Your face and head are swollen and bruised," she exclaimed. "It is for sure that your skull is broken. You have serious trauma to your brain. And your hand. My God! It has been pierced like an ear!" She wrapped her arms around me and held me tight. After standing motionless like this for a minute, her first question was, "Did Vlad do this?"

"No," I said, as bravely as I could, trying to look surprised that she was so upset. I guess some part of me wanted to impress her by acting like my injuries were no big deal.

"Are you in trouble?" she asked. "I mean, is someone bad still looking for you?"

And with that, she'd punctured my mask of bravado. I wished I had an answer to that question.

"I don't know. Maybe. But I don't think anyone is sure where I am." *Until Dr. Sokolov makes his report*, I allowed myself to think, for just a moment. And then, ashamed of myself, I dropped the thought. "Probably my people from the embassy are trying to find out where I am now. That is, if anyone contacted them from my group." That, of course, depended on whether anyone else from my group had managed to get out like I had. I tried not to think about what might have happened to them, Cindy especially. Again, the demons were resurfacing, reminding me that I had run out on a team that was under attack. I had no idea if they were safe. And I still couldn't quite shake the worry that maybe, just maybe, I wasn't either.

These unwelcome thoughts ran through my battered brain as I stood, still holding on to Katerina, her body pressed tightly against mine, in the middle of her guest room.

I tried to explain a bit of what had happened. "I am having a hard time remembering things and exactly what happened," I told her. "The thing I'm most confused about is why everyone was gone when I woke up. I was lying on a wooden pallet in the middle of a muddy field, staked to the ground. We'd been working inside a Soyuz rocket fuselage with two guys watching us when I got kicked. The other guy had grabbed my partner; she was fighting back."

As I identified my partner as 'she,' Katerina loosened her grip on me and looked up.

"I was just starting to get up to help her," I concluded my story, "and that's when the lights went out."

I read growing alarm, mixed with tenderness, in Katerina's gaze. She took a hand and led me to the bed. I followed, very willingly. We sat down, side by side. I was glad to get off my feet again. I was even gladder to feel her next to me, despite a pang at the good doctor's warnings against strenuous activity.

I went on with my story. I didn't say much about my escape and journey to Dalmatovo but I did tell her I thought I was lucky. I also mentioned wearing a cap that made me look like a Komsomol — the Soviet equivalent of a Boy Scout.

"We should call to the embassy let them know you are safe," Katerina said. "I hope you will rest here at my house for a while. I have my own security person so I will tell him there is no one allowed without my permission. Nadya has lived through some interesting times with me, on 'high alert.'"

Even one level of security was enough to celebrate. I'd have felt better with a ten-foot electrified fence and an automatic silent alarm that rang in the U.S. embassy, but even a single motivated sentry with a dog helped me breathe easier.

I thought about her suggestion to begin making phone calls. I asked, "Would you mind if I make a couple of calls in a bit? Nadya says you have direct international connections from here."

Katerina was nodding her head. "International business woman needs good phone. Of course, you can call whenever you are ready."

Then Katerina changed the subject back to what had worried me when she first arrived. "Nadya says you have no clothes. She has been pulling out all the clothes that might fit you. They are laid out down on the big table. Let's go and see what we can find!" It took some effort to resist queasy thoughts of how this vast Macy's Men's Clothing department had been assembled in the remote wilderness of Siberia. This white Izod shirt had its own history beyond helping me in my current escape. It had once hung in a walk-in closet that built for Renata back when love was a part of that relationship. Katerina's house of clothes closets brought to mind three doors I had to choose from. Which would lead to my life ahead? I could see Monty Hall on *Let's Make a Deal* imploring me to make that choice. One door led to Poland; inside were plenty of suits and normal wear for a life with a family that needed me. The second door opened to a room filled with mysterious garb from around the world, each piece having a story of its own; each offered love and personal fulfillment. The final closet was filled with Not-Q's gadgets, secret outfits, and costumes to support endless adventures and dangerous liaisons, changing with every twist and turn.

It was impossible not to consider myself facing such a dilemma. But I couldn't afford to be pulled into that line of thought — at least for now. I tried to focus on the fact that the pieces of my escape plan were actually falling together. My glances into the rear-view mirror of fear were coming less and less often. And on that happy thought, Katerina and I rushed off to my private fitting.

Nadya had found six pairs of elegant European jeans, close enough to my size. I liked them. I suggested that we keep my shirts and jacket 'contemporary Russian' for now. Katerina understood. Since we had no idea if I would be hiding there for some time, I wanted to be able to go into the village without looking like I had just arrived from Monaco. Gray work shirts and some dressier knit shirts were hanging up by the dozens. It was easy to come up with a non-descript look that matched the local fashion.

With that taken care of and my new wardrobe assembled, I changed the bandage on my hand. Then it was time to start letting people know I was alive. Katerina was not asking too many questions about how I came to get attacked. She did know it was part of what she always called "Dirty business, since all business is dirty." As a result of her former professional experience, she just happened to have a list of phone numbers for the U.S. Embassy in Moscow. "Is there a certain number we should call to let your people know that you are OK? I have the general number and the Consular Division number."

She kept giving me new reasons to like her.

"Do you have the American Services number?" I asked.

"*Da*. I will dial it."

"One more question. How many government agencies are listening to every call from this phone?" My tone was facetious, but I had a serious reason for the question. I wanted her to know I was concerned.

"To be honest with you," she said, "I am sure that local ears are very sensitive. The only positive thing is that our oblast government is fighting corruption. And they are my friends. There is no other way, though, to make a call." It was worth the chance. Even if the call let the mafia know where I was, my handlers would know, too, at the same time.

"Do you mind if I try to get through to Krakow first? I should have called last week. It will have been almost three weeks now."

"Of course." Katerina said. She pointed to the phone, stepped out of the room, and gently pulled the door to as she left. I felt a funny twinge of concern that I was calling from a lover's house. It wasn't lost on me that Katerina was handling it all better than I would have in her position.

"Malgosia!" I cried as I heard her voice through the receiver.

She answered the phone, "*Hallo! Slucham.*" I'm listening. I was relieved she had picked up the phone but thought it a bit strange. She was only three years old. Where was Renata?

"*Kocham Cie, kochania! Gdzie jest Mama?*" I told her I loved her. And asked where her mother was.

"*Tato! Ja Cie kocham, tez!*" She loved her dad, too, she told me. That made me feel good — for an instant. And then came the rest. "Mom is with Mr. Marek. They went together to Warsaw. They'll be home in the evening. I am here with my brother. Call her later." I swallowed hard at hearing that. "Dobrze?" Yes. OK.

Not altogether feeling good about Renata and Marek traveling together to Warsaw but deciding not to quiz Malgosia about it, I told her, "Please tell Mama I called from Russia. Everything is OK. I will try to call again soon."

"OK. Bye-bye," she answered. I'd wanted to tell her to be sure not to forget to tell Renata I called but she hung up before I could say it.

Why Warsaw? Together? I wondered. A language conference? Talk to folks at a publisher's office? *Quit worrying. Gotta call the Embassy.*

I got through without a problem. "Hello, this is Andy Gold. Calling for Joe in American Services or in Consular Affairs. Please forward a message to him ASAP; he will know the Code AT Group. Tell him that I am OK." I left Katerina's phone number.

In less than ten minutes, the phone rang. It was Joe himself. He asked, with only slightly more concern in his voice than I'd ever heard, "Glad you called. Are you OK? Have you been to a hospital or seen a doctor?"

"Joe... please tell me, first. How is Cindy?"

"They beat her up but she's OK. I'll tell you more later. What about you? Someone taking care of you... and your head?"

"Yes. The doc says I have a fractured skull. My hand is sore but no bones are broken and the infection should go away soon. I'm feeling better." I wondered how much he knew. "Do you have the whole story?"

"I was told you got kicked," Joe said. But then he let me know there were pieces missing from his version of the story. "What's wrong with your hand? Cindy only told me about your head and being unconscious. They dragged you outside, I guess?"

"When I woke up, I had a four-foot steel rod shoved through my palm and two feet down into the muddy ground. Guess they wanted me to *stick around*. Getting my hand off that sonofabitch was fun."

Joe very rarely swore. But at this he exclaimed, "Jesus fuck, I am so sorry." He paused a moment before firing a question back at me. "Are you at your lady friend's house near Kamensk-Uralsky?"

"My God!" I was shocked to hear him ask. "How did you know?"

"Before you arrived at the debris site, you asked Yuri for help to locate her village on the map. He kind of thought that's where you'd head if you decided to abort. Do you remember asking him about the address?" Then he admitted that he'd already known the answer before he asked the question. "We've traced this number. We have your location on a map."

At that moment, I really drew a blank about whether I'd told Yuri about Katerina's place. My best reply was, "Maybe. Not really. I guess I must have said something to him — since you know I did."

"Yuri couldn't remember the address," Joe said. "He did remember that it was near where the shuttle from the lake drops people off in Dalmatovo." Joe added, "Oh, another thing to remember. This isn't a secure line. But we know who is listening in and have no serious concerns. Speak freely — within reason."

"So more about Cindy, please, and the rest of my, um, my

colleagues."

"Yuri and Vlad are fine." Joe went into his half-coded talk. It didn't seem necessary but he was using it. "They had a very successful fishing trip at the third stage site. They netted a whopper for us. Toshek is a little bruised from two hours of fighting the rubber straps those guys tied him up with."

"Joe! Come on! How is Cindy?" I was mad that he was leaving her to the end.

"She has a dislocated shoulder," he said. "But was wearing a seat belt."

"Seat belt!?" Oh. That was the code shit. I hated that amateurish coding we were using. As if anybody listening in — which was still entirely likely — would think we were really talking about a car accident.

Joe dropped the pretense and got right to the point. "She is doing fine in Chelyabinsk at a big hotel with nice restaurants, a bar, a swimming pool and sauna."

That was better. But relieved as I was at the news, I still had a million questions about what had happened after I got cold-cocked and everyone disappeared. Most important, though, it was sounding like Cindy had held her own against the two goons who made the mistake of going after her. At least that's what I understood from Joe.

"Joe, can I call Cindy? Do you have the number?" I asked him.

"It's the hotel where Yuri told you to meet him at when you were on the train," Joe said, discreetly.

"OK. Got it." I was relieved to hear this, since I still had that information in my toolkit.

Joe asked, "When should Yuri come to get you? Or will you arrange your own transportation and meet him in Chelyabinsk?"

"Give me two days to rest up," I said, "to see if my skull fracture kills me." I decided I had done enough travel planning for myself. "Yuri can come. And Joe, I need to arrange two express visas for Russian citizens to the United States. We will send details soon."

Katerina, it turned out, had been listening in the next room. When she heard that, she rushed in to say, "Andy, make it three visas! Please! Dr. Sokolov wants one, too!"

"Three it is!" said Joe. He had heard her urgent plea loud and clear.

"Unless you have something else, Joe, I should sign off." I began to feel huge relief that everyone I had left behind was OK.

Joe did have one more thing. "Why didn't you use your tracking device when things went bad and you left the site?"

I had completely forgotten about that silly little pen and the training on how to use it that I'd gotten from the embassy's tech expert. *If they'd had a shoe phone for me,* I thought, *I would have remembered.* I told Joe, "I forgot about it. Must have been the bump on the head. Probably a short-term memory problem, I guess."

"Fine. Don't linger there in Dalmatovo, though. Need to see you soon back in Warsaw."

"OK, Joe. Bye."

"Hey!" Joe caught me before I hung up. "Your wife was here in the American Services Section earlier today. I got a call from folks in the department and there's a meeting later on to brief me what it was about. You have any idea what's up?"

Joe waited a moment for me to answer. "You still there?"

"Uh, yeah. I was going to ask you if you knew why she was there." My voice must have gotten a lot quieter.

"Nope. I'll let you know when I know something," his voice full of assurance as always.

"Thanks, Joe!" I said, trying to echo his affirming tone.

Putting down the phone, I felt a shiver of cold dread shoot through me. *What the* hell *is she doing?*

Another Kick to the Head

I cleared my head of the tangled thoughts that had formed. I'd have to wait before pursuing Joe's revelation about Renata's mysterious visit to the embassy. I had to get ready for my next important call.

Sorting through my toolkit, I found the name of the hotel Yuri had told me to check into. I asked Katerina for help. "I need to make another call. This time to Chelyabinsk. I need to talk to Cindy — or Sofia — at the Hotel South Ural. Can you use your magic to try to find her, please?" Then it occurred to me that she was very likely to be using some other name. "She probably has an arm brace or sling from a bad accident," I added. "That should help to identify her."

Katerina quickly located the number and dialed it. During the wait, she asked, "Name like Cindy: is she American girl?"

"No," I said. "She likes to use the name Cindy, though. She is a business partner... who has skills I do not have. The same people hurt her, too, but I think she is OK."

When Sofia came on the line, she said in English, "Cindy here. Is this Andy?"

Katerina handed me the receiver. Again, with admirable discretion, she immediately went downstairs and out into the garden. Alone with Sofia on the line, my voice began to crack. I flooded her with questions about her health and with apologies for leaving her. I couldn't hide my emotions. I cried for the first five minutes as we caught up on our separate ordeals of the past three days.

"I probably wasn't thinking right, Sofia! I am so sorry I took off. You probably thought I was a fucking coward," I said between sobs.

"Jesus Christ, Andy! I saw how badly you were injured. Sticking around and risking more damage probably would have been worse. I am just so happy you were smart enough to find a safe place to go." She had taken on the role of consoler that I'd imagined I would be for her when I called. Just listening to her voice helped me to calm down. I realized just how incredible a woman she was and how lucky I had been to have her with me when it all hit the fan inside that fuselage.

Deciphering Joe's silly code talking and hearing Sofia's version of the story, I started to get a better understanding of what had happened after I got the shit kicked out of me inside the Soyuz rocket. By now I had stopped crying and was processing the sequence of events. Over the phone, Sofia helped me work them out.

As she had been busy slapping and punching the guy who'd grabbed her from behind, she clearly saw monitor #2 deliver the kick that sent my head into that six-inch metal bracket. I didn't immediately go down, so I got another kick. That's when I fell face forward into the mud.

Sofia's story filled in plenty of details that were sketchy for me. "Keeping that asshole away from me, shoving my palm into his nose, I worked my way around to where I could see if you were drowning in the mud. When your head hit the wall, the whole fuselage rang like a bell."

"That's what we say in English. I got my bell rung." My crying jag behind me, I was halfway able to find some humor in it.

"You weren't moving and your head was face down in that muck." Now it was Sofia's turn to get emotional. Her voice started to tremble. "I fucking freaked out but saw you moving finally."

"I can still taste the mud. And still feel like I'm belching rocket fuel."

"I fought the urge to kill him — which I could have done — but, instead, kept trying to get him to back off and let me take care of you." For a long moment, Sofia fell silent.

"Is that when the second prick got into the fight?" I asked.

"Your guy was a lot stronger and faster than the *skurwysyn* I was dealing with." I thought her epithet fit both of them. Bastards. "He just about ripped my head off even though I'd kicked him in the ribs." Sofia stopped again. "I could see blood on your head and face. It scared me." Another long pause. "He kept swearing at me. He got a handful of my hair and ripped it out as he was holding me. They managed to drag me into the guard shack. As they pulled me away, you were trying to get onto your knees but couldn't do much. That was the last I saw of you." I wasn't sure I heard right, but could have sworn I detected a sob in her voice. She quickly pulled herself together. "Finally, they locked me into a tiny bunk room in the back of their shack." I hit the mute button on Katerina's desk phone. I'd realized I was crying again, and didn't want Sofia to stop in the middle of her story.

"One prick stayed in the front part of the shack while the other left to make sure you weren't going anywhere. They were especially afraid that you might tell Michael what they did." What Sofia had no way of knowing was that this was when Bastard #1 had to have dragged my body out to the pallet and driven his rod through my hand.

"I knew that two bastards against me was not good in this small space," Sofia said. "I found the weapon I needed, though, behind the smelly cot. I almost laughed when I saw it."

"Weapon? What the hell was it?" I asked her. I almost laughed, too, hearing the way she was describing things.

"Shitty old Russian fake grapefruit drink. Bottle half full. Very rigid plastic. I knew exactly what to do: made it a razor-sharp weapon."

"Physical fitness training?" I joked.

"No, Joe's fight training for contractors. Which you should take."

I was already in awe of this woman; now more than ever. "You had enough time to make the weapon," I asked her, "before they came after you?"

"It took less than half a second. I slammed the bottle against a little table next to the bed. It became very sharp two-edge machete. While I waited for them to open the door, I practiced how I was going to slice their faces open." Her voice was utterly calm as she described this impending mayhem.

"How long did you wait?" I was curious about how long my bastard was busy outside, dragging me through the mud and skewering my hand with his cute metal staff.

Typical Sofia, she answered, "Long enough to plan how I was going to fuck them both up. And for them to make a fatal mistake."

"And that was?"

"They started drinking." She laughed. "By the time they opened the door, they were, as you say, 'three sheets to the wind.' They never saw it coming. I got them both in the face on the first two swings. The rest was easy."

Her description was gruesome. "Their fat from their face hung down from deep cuts on both their cheeks. Lips split wide open, gushing blood."

Glad as I was to hear that both bastards had been grievously harmed, this still made me a little sick to hear. "That surely must have discouraged them." I was hoping they hadn't had a chance to hurt her any more.

"It was mostly over. They stood and stared at each other — horrified — as I got ready to attack them again. They tried to grab me but I sliced their hands and arms." Sofia paused as if she was trying to remember. "They backed off. The stronger guy kicked the bunkroom door against my shoulder. That was all they could do. They took off into the woods, looking for the third guy."

I realized I'd been holding my breath. I let it out and expressed my admiration at her ingenuity

She pooh-poohed this. "I am strong for woman. But for anyone, good self-defense class can make you feel confident. Especially with drunk assholes."

I had to laugh, but also realized I was feeling a warm glow about how well Sofia had had my back. And so, as I was outside flopping around in the mud as if afflicted with mad cow disease, my partner had improvised a weapon to leave these men bleeding so badly, or just so terrified, that they abandoned their attack and disappeared. It wasn't entirely one-sided, though. The struggle had hurt her, too.

"Joe says you have some injuries."

"The strong guy dislocated my shoulder as I fought him to the guard shack. When I was looking for the weapon, I popped it back in." Sofia said this ever so matter-of-factly.

"Jesus, Sofia! That must have hurt!"

"It wasn't first time for dislocation. But I am a liar if I tell you it didn't hurt. The door that hit me when they left also hit my shoulder." Her story made me cringe. I couldn't help remembering wrestling match nightmares of teammates re-locating injured shoulders and the screams that followed.

After the bloodbath and beatings, she resumed her story, "You were nowhere to be found. We searched all around the rocket debris and back at camp."

"I had no sense of time," I told her. "No idea how long I was out."

"Not very long. Everything happened pretty quickly," she said quietly. "We put the puzzle together, though. The bicycle was missing from the cab of the 66. Michael's people said a funny looking man that looked a little bit like Lenin was bicycling past the mafia camp."

"Sounds like me." I laughed.

"Why you were screaming Polish swear words at guards on back road to Dubrovnoye?" Her tone sounded like she was telling the punch line of a funny Russian joke about alcoholics.

"It seemed appropriate." I was a little embarrassed.

"When we heard this, we knew you probably escaped with success." She added, "Toshek noticed at same time that his socialist uniform was gone, too. We both started understanding."

"Hopefully you didn't worry too much. I was sick with worry about you," I said, trying to admit to a little of my guilt in leaving her during the abort.

Sofia didn't comment about my worries. She answered, instead, "Yuri remembered a conversation in the 69 about the Dalmatovo address and suspected that was where you were headed."

I was impressed. My crew had pieced together a pretty accurate picture of what had become of me. I also wondered what they really thought of my decision to abort.

As our conversation made clear, Sofia had no idea about my being staked to the ground. So for now, I decided not to tell her. I knew Joe would eventually say something. I also kept quiet about hiding from Monitor #3 as he snooped around our camp brandishing his nine-millimeter.

The other half of our mission had gone somewhat better. While Sofia, Toshek, and I were having our fun at the second-stage site, Yuri and Vlad found and removed the exact third-stage devices Joe's partners were interested in. When they returned from the trailer site, they found Sofia and Toshek sitting in the locked cage of the 66. Over a bottle of vodka, they were fuming about the incident. Toshek was tending to his wounds from the rubber bands he had been tied up with. It seems the third monitor who had lured Toshek away to look at the other debris locations pulled a gun when he heard the screaming from our direction. He sat, keeping Toshek covered, until the second monitor showed up, excited to report that Cindy was caged and I had been "taken care of." Toshek was then wrapped up tightly with inner tube slices. They left him in the woods, wrapped to a tree, until he finally worked his way out of the giant rubber bands. When he returned to camp, he found Sofia there and me gone.

Immobilizing Sofia's arm and getting her pain killers — beyond the vodka shots she was already doing — was first on the to-do list at camp when Vlad and Yuri got back. First, that is, after Vlad took off in a rage looking for the guys who had attacked us. Vlad was unstoppable. He beat the living hell out of the first two — again. And by the time he was done with the guy who had pulled the gun on Toshek, he looked almost as bad as the ones who had tangled with Sofia. One very important piece of good news was that the three monitors were freelancing, not operating under Michael's instructions, nor acting out any kind of coup with Michael's underlings.

Not surprisingly, Michael was extremely angry about the incident. He personally walked over to our camp and tried to persuade Toshek and Cindy — as he knew her — to come out of the cage. They respectfully refused to do so, as Cindy screamed back at him, ". . . until Yuri and Vlad get back from whatever fucking surprises you've left for them."

All three of his rogue operatives got a third beating. Toshek and another, more trustworthy one of Michael's guards returned to the debris site the next day. Eventually, they found a retrievable device on the collar I had been looking at when I got kicked. Using a torch supplied by Michael's folks, they cut out the relevant section. In the end, Michael accepted just $80,000 for everything after Yuri casually mentioned that the U.S. Embassy would be alerted to my disappearance. That seemed to soften Michael up. He allowed our team to leave with all their prizes without any further delay.

Toshek had even had the presence of mind while packing up the booty to take soil samples from the debris sites. Joe must have been delighted to be able to report to Langley that his "contractor slouches" had completed all our mission assignments. I doubt that he mentioned to anyone that I was missing.

"So, does that mean the mission was a complete success?" I asked Sofia.

Just then, Katerina returned with coffees and pastries. She signaled that it was time for me to finish the call and join her in the garden. I'd been talking to Sofia for nearly 30 minutes.

"For sure it was," Sofia answered. "You must be proud! Uranium in the hotel, uncovering business contacts selling plutonium at Novosibirsk State University, a new contact to help with your rocket debris collection in Siberia, and more Soyuz rocket toys in Chelyabinsk. It is kind of an

335

American home run."

"You are a good partner, Sofia," I said. "Next time, we'll do a grand slam."

"What is a grand slam?"

"I'll show you when I see you. Which will be soon. I am sure."

***

Joe's call came much later that day. He wanted to let me know what he'd found out about Renata's visit to the Embassy. Before that, coffee with Katerina had been a pleasant but very quiet affair. Nadya had come and gone half a dozen times with treats and warm drinks, Russian headache remedies mostly. She'd finally sat with us. That quiet spring afternoon made quite an impression on me. I couldn't help but stare at these wonderful people who had taken me in and were so caring in my time of deepest distress. I couldn't imagine it getting worse.

I took the call in the bedroom. "Hi, Joe. What did you find out?"

"It's not good, Andy."

"Give it to me, Joe," I said. Somehow I knew Monty Hall was about to show me what was behind Door Number One. "That woman hates being in the American Embassy. Bad memories from the way the State Department treated her when she was getting her papers to emigrate and become a US citizen. Can't imagine what would motivate her to go there."

"She was with a lawyer. A guy named Marek something or other. There are official docs waiting for you here."

I could feel my throat tightening up. Now I realized the lawyer-philologist taking my daughter out for ice cream in Nowa Huta was somehow involved in real lawyering for Renata. My voice shook as I asked, "Divorce papers?"

"Sorry, Andy. Since they knew you were doing work for the US State Department in Russia, they got Polish Ministry of Interior to put cover letters on an official marriage annulment." Joe explained, "The Catholic Church wields a lot of power, so divorce isn't an option for a while."

"Is that good news for me?"

"What's funny here is that the annulment is effective as of yesterday. They somehow added up all your time away from the family and made it official without your knowledge. They are submitting it to file for a U.S. divorce."

I was starting to panic. "No fucking way, Joe!"

"Andy. It's here in front of me. We opened it to see what was up. My folks called the Interior people and got it confirmed. This Marek guy is a current Polish State Security officer. Former Polish SB. Polish KGB, if you will."

"I know what SB means!" I yelled back at him.

Joe was quiet for a long five seconds. "It was originally submitted for Polish State approval three months ago."

"Three months ago? She's been working on this for that long?" I couldn't believe what I was hearing. I started wondering how I could have been so stupid. "So, to fucking sum up: She's orchestrated an annulment, which is already effective, in order to get a U.S. divorce."

"That's not all, Andy. The annulment has language asserting that you are a threat to her children. There is a restraining order keeping you from returning to your flat in Krakow." Joe paused. I could tell there was more.

"What else?" I asked. My head was feeling a lot like it did while I pounded down the road to Dubrovnoye on that bicycle.

"Some bags and boxes of things were delivered here yesterday. I guess they are some of your things from Krakow." Joe tried to find a way to say all this so it would hurt less. I could tell he was very uncomfortable being the bearer of such bad news.

"Anything else, Joe?" I hoped I was asking for the last time.

"The only thing I have might be good news," He said, glumly.

"Wonderful."

"The letter from her attorney says that they will not seek any claims for money outside of Poland. Specifically, they mention your Deutsche Bank account in Berlin." Now Joe's voice sounded like he had no more surprises for me.

"Thanks, Joe." I hoped I could end the call as soon as possible. "Anything you need from me for now?"

"No. Get well. We'll have to talk soon about the future."

"What fucking future are you talking about, Joe?" I said. Joe had no response. I tried to change my tone a little. "Thanks. Chatatchya later, Joe" and hung up.

I went to the window overlooking the garden. Katerina was planting

337

tomato bushes along the patio's edge. For a second, I enjoyed the sight. Not just of her, bending over, but of this simple domestic moment. I yelled down to her. "I need to get some rest, Katerina. I'm going to lie down and try to nap."

She looked up and nodded. "Good idea."

New Horizons

The evening light was softening when I heard a soft knock. "Hello, Andy!" Nadya called through the door. "We are having dinner soon. Will you join us?" I'd been in my room alone several hours since my call with Joe.

"Thank you, Nadya! I am not hungry." I lied, saying I was making myself tea.

"OK. But you need to eat to get better."

"I understand. See you in the morning. Thank you. And please apologize to Katerina for me." I tried to say this as cheerfully as possible.

I sat in the room's gabled window, looking out onto the garden and driveway below. The sun had already set. Darkness was descending upon the wooded Estate at Dalmatovo. My circumstances felt strangely familiar but I couldn't quite place the memory. Then, I remembered a time years earlier, just before Renata. Ten years before, I had walled myself in my room in Warsaw during martial law, hiding from the terrors of that time. I'd had a view onto Pole Mokotowskie, Warsaw's Central Park. Decisions about my future, whether to throw in the towel on dreadfully depressing Poland or to stay, seemed as overwhelming then as my situation did now.

While I sat staring into the shadows, I hear another knock. Katerina asked to come in.

"*Mogu ya?*" May I? she asked. Without waiting for my reply, she came straight in and put a tray of food on the table. Without looking at me, she turned and said, "Have a few bites. I'll be back in a minute with something for your head."

I wondered what that would be. "Thank you, Katerina. I may not be able to eat everything but I'll try."

"Yes. Try," she said without emotion.

I heard water running in the bathroom as I ate half a boiled egg with a tad of fresh salmon lox and another egg with black caviar on it. I snuck two more mouthfuls before she returned.

Katerina came in carrying a large urn of steaming water, with two towels draped over her shoulder. She put the urn on the table next to the food and laid one of the towels on the desk chair. "Good. You are eating."

"Thank you. I didn't know I was hungry. This is delicious." I smiled slightly.

Pointing to the chair, she commanded, "Sit on the chair now unless you want more food."

I liked hearing her giving orders. I could see she wanted to take care of me. I already began to feel the lump in my throat growing; I wanted to hold her. I sat down and waited. I made sure she couldn't see my tears.

She fully immersed the towel in the hot water and then wrung it out as completely as she could. Folding it in half lengthwise, she wrapped it around my battered head, leaving my face uncovered. She pressed her hands against either side of my face, firmly holding the towel. I could feel each of her fingers against my head. After a minute or two, as the damp towel began to cool, she unwrapped my head, soaked and wrung out the towel again. This time, she took my head, pulled up her blouse and gently pressed my face into her firm, flat tummy. She wrapped her blouse around the wet towel and continued to hold me. I could feel the knots in my stomach and in my head beginning to loosen. Silently, she continued her tender caressing of my wounds.

She finally broke the silence. "Your face says you lost something very important."

"I think so. We talked about it, a little, on the train. Do you remember?" She still held my face in her hands under her blouse but had removed the towel. Her warm fingers were now slowly stroking my face and the back of my neck.

"You taught me a word, '*disown*'. Did your children disown you?" she asked.

"No. Not yet." I reached up and wrapped my arms around her waist. "That's next."

"Then just make sure that you stay in contact. Even if your wife or ex-wife doesn't allow it. Everything will be OK if you work for this." Katerina stepped back, took my face again and kissed me. It was exactly the way she had during our endless kisses on the train; when I had lain on top of her in a silent embrace.

She stepped back and took my hand.

I said, "Thank you, Katerina. I probably didn't lose as much as it seems."

"Probably not. I would stay with you tonight." She gave me a funny smile. "But doctor said 'No' for sex. Did he say it to you, too?"

I had to return her smile. "Yes. He warned me."

"Good night," she said. "Try to think about something that makes you happy."

"You make me happy, Katerina."

"See you in the morning, Andy."

***

Coffee in Katerina's garden in the middle of Siberia was like coffee in Tuscany — almost. I had been enjoying those morning interludes for several days now. For Zhenia, a new romantic interest had blossomed in Yekaterinburg, leaving Katerina and me alone together at the house, and with Nadya at a discreet distance keeping the place organized during the remodeling.

I sat with Katerina on a patio next to the house's trellised limestone wall. Roses climbed all the way up to the bedroom windows. An artesian well kept a constant flow of crystal-clear water flowing through the garden and into a man-made brook that wound around the estate before flowing down a hill toward the river below. A light, cool breeze was blowing that morning. The sun was brighter than I had seen it in weeks.

"Hey, Katerina! Joe says I shouldn't linger here too long with you. What do you think?" I asked.

"And what is this word 'linger'? To be lazy?" Katerina asked. She gave me a mischievous wink. "Or to have sex with someone?"

"Hmm. Neither, I'm afraid. But maybe there is a little of that on my mind, too."

Since the call from Joe informing me about the annulment, I'd twice attempted calls to Krakow. Both times: no answer. I'd decided that all I really needed was to hear Renata's angry voice confirming what Joe had said. That would help me cleanly turn myself away from what I had built up as the one door back into a relatively normal family life. Those other two doors that Monty Hall pointed to were still there — and looking more attractive every day.

We were sitting at a table in that garden, filling out the three United States Tourist Visa applications that had arrived by express mail. Joe had promised that all three would be given top priority, but I knew a consular officer still had the power to reject any one of them. For that reason, I sat and reviewed the forms to make sure they contained no obvious reasons for rejection. I worried that some hyper-conscientious paper-shuffler might decide to wield his power over a small problem that could have been avoided. As we had determined during our train ride from Samara to Chelyabinsk just a couple of weeks before, the only possible sticking point for Katerina and Zhenia was the absence of spouses for them to come back to Russia for. But with the amount of money they could show in their bank accounts and proof that they were employed, I doubted that there would be any problem. And, in the end, if there was a problem, the instructions on the applications said to call Joe about a final review.

"Once Zhenia gets in from Yekaterinburg, we'll send this off today," I said. "This guy from Minneapolis she's been hanging out with — the one studying art at the Institute in Yekaterinburg — is she serious about him? Does he know that she's leaving for his neck of the woods, soon?"

"Thanks for asking, Dad!" Katerina joked. "He finishes up his program in six weeks. They are expecting to meet up after that in Chicago."

A funny, maudlin feeling came over me, remembering that my own European and Russian adventure had begun nearly ten years ago with a similar study program. Mine was at the Academy of Economics in Poznan, Poland. That six-week study program had turned into the Ten-Year Plan. I hoped that the next stage of Zhenia's life adventure would be a long-term chapter with love as the theme. How she could take on a real relationship after three years of staged mating and dangerous liaisons was difficult to imagine.

"It should be a two-week turnaround time once we get them off. Joe's folks in Moscow will be hand-carrying the applications down to the consular office. Dr. Sokolov will have no problems, either. Is everyone ready for a trip to Chicago?" I asked.

"Not everyone is focused on Chicago. Dr. Sokolov will stay in New York, probably. He has Jewish family there. He wants to see relatives that left Russia many years ago." Katerina flashed me a smile. "But, yes, we are going to do all of the tourist things in America we can find out about."

***

Zhenia was a busy girl. Instead of returning from her visit with her beau in Yekaterinburg, she had gone to Moscow for a week to put together a wardrobe for her trip to the United States. I agreed to stick around and see if my headaches and other symptoms of my head injuries would begin to fade. My vision was not always right, and I would occasionally lose my balance in a way that was very unusual. On the plus side, my hand was healing nicely with hardly any swelling left.

Twice since I had arrived at the estate, I had experienced anxiety attacks. I couldn't control them, but could only sit and ride them out for several hours. Katerina realized things weren't right but let me deal with it in my own way. If it started in the night, my first reaction was to go outside and try to walk it off. The spell would begin with a general feeling of unease. It would start me hyperventilating. That would lead to heart arrythmia. The fear of my heart irregularity would increase my anxiety and I could feel my blood pressure going up. All this could last up to six or seven hours. I learned that letting the tears flow would almost always decrease the severity and shorten the length of the attack. That didn't fit into my preconceived ideas of how a spy should behave. But then again: how did I know what 007 — or Agent 99 — did to cope with their anxieties after a tough mission? And hadn't Sofia, the spy I knew best, confessed that her awful interlude with Georg would have left her crying all night if she hadn't invited me to share her bed?

Katerina, aware of my attacks, suggested that I "just have a good cry." I looked forward to the hot towel sessions with her. The doctor had finally approved "sexual activity" and thought it could help with the anxiety. Bringing the urn and the towel out usually meant that she was up for a "session" as well. I asked the doctor if he was a psychiatrist, too. "In Russia," he replied, "every doctor is a psychiatrist." Katerina made subtle attempts to advise me about divorce issues and about how to keep Malgosia and Staszek within my sphere. Losing contact with them still worried me.

Despite my handicaps, I tried to pitch in on the estate's many construction projects. In just a few days, I helped build a retaining wall for the garden and designed a pergola for the deck. Good food, lots of exercise, eating and drinking Russian home remedies, and walks through the woods to the small lakes around Katerina's estate slowly got me back into shape. Finally I decided I needed to start thinking about making arrangements to fly back to Poland. I would eventually have to deal with issues there, after all, though I had tried hard not to think about them too much.

Then, in a miracle of U.S. State Department efficiency helped along by well-bribed postal clerks in Dalmatovo, the three American visas came back, approved, within five days. We were all stunned.

That same afternoon, Dr. Sokolov showed up with presents for everyone. For Zhenia and Katerina, he brought out enough flower starts and tomato plants to fill a large garden. He also waived any charges for my treatment and delivered a case of vintage Soviet champagne for Nadya. Katerina offered him an afternoon at the house to go through her large collection of men's clothing. That was intended to help him improve on his neat but shabby wardrobe, a consequence of the chronic low pay for doctors in Russia. He immediately took her up on that, disappearing into her closets for the rest of the day. Meanwhile, I talked with Katerina and made plans to meet in America when she and Zhenia finally took advantage of their visas.

A second stunner occurred that same day. Joe called. He asked me to cancel any flight arrangements to Poland. Having made up my mind in the past weeks to face the music and support the Polish legal machinery now in motion against me, this was a devastating blow to my plans. I'd intended to take care of nagging personal baggage. Instead, he wanted me to go back to Novosibirsk in a week. Who knew how long this next stint would last? I tried to take it in stride when he told me but was admittedly thrown into confusion. While I had no intention of redirecting the locomotive that was hauling all my personal freight away in Poland, I wanted to have one eye on it if something should become derailed. As life in Poland had always taught me. Joe began to build an argument against this. He had a different vision for me.

"Dima's activities in Novosibirsk have rooted something out that needs our attention," as Joe explained it. "We see that the whole idea of planting ourselves in Novosibirsk through you has really started to bring some results — more than the cash that Dima has been making by getting into bed with the institutes around the TechnoPark."

"God, I hope he hasn't promised too much. At least not for guys I'll have to deliver on." I said this sheepishly, figuring Joe probably wasn't aware of Dima's modus operandi, including his always open palm and his bait and switch tactics. "Any details for me you can mention on the phone?" I asked, stalling for time, desperately trying to weigh the pros and cons of such a quick return to Russia."

"Aside from figuring out who are the likely compatriots to illegal sales, we also are seeing some good folks at these institutes coming forward with their own risk assessments about nuclear terrorism." Joe's tone was optimistic. "This was the sort of development we could only have dreamed of." Then he got into detail about what he was tasking me with. Joe wanted me massaging these organizations, setting them up for cooperation with our side. Specifically, that meant a U.S. Senate initiative to create an international monitoring body. "To reduce the risk of terrorists getting their hands on anything," as Joe summarized it.

My perplexity about my own delayed personal initiatives suddenly felt puny against this world-saving cause. The way Joe described my extended mission's goals actually inspired me.

With a chuckle, he added, "Toshek will be there hawking his Ichthyol Magic to the entire Russian Academy of Sciences and all of Dima's contacts. Yuri is already there. He will deliver a package of instructions and some cash to you. Cindy is working to get back into shape. She will show up eventually, after she's had physical therapy on her shoulder." Joe was doing his best to make the case: why I should accept. I could hear the expectation in his voice. "I hope after a few more weeks of getting yourself back into shape, you'll be feeling up to it again!

If instead of scheduling a trip to Cyprus, Katerina had allowed me to linger, however we chose to define the term, I probably would have refused the add-on work Joe was offering. It would have been easy to stay all summer in Dalmatovo. Coming up with an alibi for extending my trip was the next administrative thing to take care of. And whether I went back to Novosibirsk or stayed where I was, it was yet another problem for the mess in my personal life.

All in all, though, there was nothing else I could say except, "Please tell the team I'll be there soon."